Christmas in the Duke's Arms

Copyright – Christmas In The Duke's Arms

This book is a work of fiction. Names, characters, places, and incidents are the product of the authors' imagination or are used fictitiously. Any resemblance to actual events, locales, or persons, living or dead, is coincidental.

A Knight Before Christmas – Copyright © 2014 by Grace Burrowes
In The Duke's Arms – Copyright © 2014 by Carolyn Jewel
Licensed To Wed – Copyright © 2014 by Miranda Neville
The Spy Beneath The Mistletoe – Copyright © 2014 by Shana Galen

Cover Design by Seductive Designs
Image copyright © Novel Expressions, Inc
Image copyright © Shutterstock.com/Unholy Vault Designs
Image copyright © Depositphotos.com/Bezergheanu Mircea
Image copyright © Depositphotos.com/Lisa F. Young

ISBN: 978-1-937823-36-8
Print Edition

All rights reserved. Except as permitted under the U.S. Copyright Act of 1976, no part of this publication may be reproduced, distributed, or transmitted in any form or by any means, or stored in a database or retrieval system, without the prior written permission of the authors.

Table of Contents

A Knight Before Christmas
by Grace Burrowes 1

In The Duke's Arms
by Carolyn Jewel 67

Licensed to Wed
by Miranda Neville 153

The Spy Beneath the Mistletoe
by Shana Galen 219

Books by Grace

Ready for more holiday reading from Grace Burrowes? Please consider

What A Lady Needs for Christmas, a full-length Highland Victorian Christmas story

> *To escape a scandal, Lady Joan Flynn flees her family's estate in the Scottish Highlands. She needs a husband by Christmas, or the holidays will ring in nothing but ruin. Practical, ambitious mill owner Dante Hartwell offers to marry Joan, because a wellborn wife is his best chance of gaining access to aristocratic investors.*
>
> *As Christmas—and trouble—draw nearer, Dante and Joan's marriage of convenience blossoms into unexpected intimacy, for true love can hide beneath the most unassuming trappings, especially at the holidays.*

Grace also enthusiastically recommends:

> *The Rogue Spy* (November 4, 2014) by Joanna Bourne, fifth novel in the award-winning Spymaster Series.

Or treat yourself to Grace's upcoming Sweetest Kisses contemporary series, beginning with a pair of novellas...

> *Kiss and Tell* (November 2014), or A Kiss for Luck (December 2014)
>
> Or *A Single Kiss*, the first novel in the series, coming out in January 2015.

Books By Carolyn

The Sinclair Sisters Series
Lord Ruin, Book 1
A Notorious Ruin, Book 2

Reforming the Scoundrels Series
Not Wicked Enough, Book 1
Not Proper Enough, Book 2

Other Historical Romance
In The Duke's Arms, novella from Anthology Christmas In the Duke's Arms
Christmas In The Duke's Arms, Anthology
One Starlit Night, Novella From the Midnight Scandals Anthology
Midnight Scandals, Anthology
Scandal, RITA finalist, Best Regency Historical
Indiscreet, Winner, Bookseller's Best, Best Short Historical
Moonlight A short story
The Spare
Stolen Love
Passion's Song

PARANORMAL ROMANCE

My Immortals Series
My Wicked Enemy, Book 1
My Forbidden Desire, RITA finalist, Paranormal Romance, Book 2
My Immortal Assassin, Book 3
My Dangerous Pleasure, Book 4
Free Fall, Novella 1
My Darkest Passion, Book 5
Dead Drop, Novella 2

Other Paranormal Romance
Alphas Unleashed, Anthology
A Darker Crimson, Book 4 of the Crimson City series
DX (A Crimson City Novella)

FANTASY ROMANCE

The King's Dragon A short story

EROTIC ROMANCE

Whispers, Collection No. 1

Books By Miranda

The Burgundy Club Series
The Wild Marquis, Book 1
The Dangerous Viscount, Book 2
The Amorous Education of Celia Seaton, Book 3
Confessions From an Arranged Marriage, Book 4

The Wild Quartet Series
The Second Seduction of a Lady (prequel novella)
The Importance of Being Wicked, Book 1
The Ruin of a Rogue, Book 2
Lady Windermere's Lover, Book 3
The Duke of Dark Desires, Book 4

Other Historical Romance
Never Resist Temptation
P.S. I Love You, novella in anthology At the Duke's Wedding
Licensed to Wed, novella in anthology Christmas In the Duke's Arms

Coming Soon in Contemporary Romance
Novella in anthology At the Billionaire's Wedding

Books by Shana

Want more Moneypence and Q? Check out Shana's newest release, Love and Let Spy.

Pre-order the first in Shana's new Covent Garden Cubs series, Earls Just Want to Have Fun, coming in February 2015.

Check out Shana's other book series.

The Lord and Lady Spy series begins with Lord and Lady Spy.

The Jewels of the Ton series begins with When You Give a Duke a Diamond.

The Sons of the Revolution series begins with The Making of a Duchess.

The Misadventures in Matrimony series begins with No Man's Bride.

And check out the latest book in the Misadventures in Matrimony series, The Pirate Takes a Bride for only $2.99!

The Regency Spies series begins with When Dashing Met Danger.

A Knight Before Christmas

By
Grace Burrowes

Dedicated to one of my first friends, Jeanne McCarthy, with whom I shared ownership of a fine, enormous buck bunny named Fat Chance (we won him at a raffle at the church bazaar). That guy thumped so loudly, they could hear him in the next county.

Chapter One

A COMPETENT MAN of business could expect a comfortable life, but for the aggravations resulting from two kinds of people: former clients and current clients.

The former clients were usually deceased, deported, or demented, so Sir Leviticus Sparrow forgave them their crotchets. The current clients were an ongoing trial, albeit an entertaining one.

And then, in an entirely separate class of aggravation, was Mrs. Penelope Carrington.

"Won't you have a seat, madam?"

Levi gestured to one of two comfortable chairs by the fire. Amid a quiet rustle of black skirts, the lady passed close enough to him that he caught a whiff of roses.

"I do thank you for seeing me on short notice, Levi. Shall I pour?"

He was indifferent to the offerings on the tea tray, most at home sitting behind his desk, and not much given to socializing. The cozy fire, deep cushions on the chairs, and comforting familiarity of the tea ritual were intended to steer his clients more quickly to whatever point they intended to make.

With Penelope Carrington, however, Levi was in no hurry at all.

"Nothing for me," he said, taking the chair next to hers, "but you must help yourself to whatever appeals."

Levi watched her hands while she fixed herself a cup of tea. He'd chosen this service because the blue of the teapot exactly matched the blue of her eyes.

"I shouldn't take up much of your time."

"I have no other appointments today, Penelope. I am at your disposal."

She brushed a look over him, a trifle amused, as if she knew he'd cancel an appointment with the archangel Gabriel to spend half an hour with Penelope Carrington.

To spend five minutes with her.

"I have miscalculated," she said, setting her tea cup down after one sip.

She'd also lost weight since he'd seen her a month ago. He put several slices of fruitcake on a plate and passed it to her.

Rather than meet his gaze, she studied the fire, a lovely decision on her part, for it gave him a view of her profile. Penelope Carrington was not pretty as a girl was pretty, she was beautiful as a woman was beautiful. Her skin had the flawless delicacy common to the true redhead, her eyes tilted upward, like a cat's. Those eyes could laugh, they could praise, they could convey an intimate joke, and they could freeze social prospects for an entire season with one glance.

Her nose might have been daintier, though without that nose her face would have lacked the hint of character that held a man's interest so easily.

When Levi had taken a thorough inventory of her features, the sense of her words sank in. "My dear lady, you never miscalculate."

"With my late husband's investments, perhaps not, but in the more fraught waters of familial relations, I have blundered badly."

She wasn't capable of blundering. Levi had never had the pleasure or torment of admiring a more poised, dignified, decent woman.

"Eat something, and then you must tell me about this blundering. Whatever has gone amiss, I'm sure we can put it to rights."

She took a dutiful nibble of fruitcake, the gesture conveying forbearance.

Levi tried again. "What is the problem, Penelope?"

"I've changed my mind. I know what Sixtus's will said, and I've decided I need to marry after all. Need to rather badly and soon."

While she took a second sip of tea, Levi's world spun off its axis. She'd told him six months ago that she preferred the life of a comfortable widow to remarrying in haste simply to become the beneficiary of her late husband's entire fortune. Levi had begun to hope, to plan even.

He'd begun to scheme, though only in his head, of course. One didn't court a woman in mourning. Penelope was still in mourning—for another few weeks, she would observe half mourning.

"May I remind you, Penelope, if you want to remarry in an effort to secure the benefit of Sixtus's fortune, then you should find a husband before Christmas. That's not much time."

For old Sixtus had gone to his reward mere days before Christmas, and the will required that Penelope re-marry by the anniversary of the reading of the will, which had happened immediately before the New Year.

"That's why I've come to you, Levi. If I'm to find the right husband, I need your help."

Sir Leviticus Sparrow's mind operated at a rate inverse to the speed of his words or his actions. Pen had taken a year to understand this about him. Levi was brilliant, but his brilliance was no more evident on the surface than the teeming life in the sea was apparent from sunlight sparkling on placid waves.

Sixtus had called his man of business Sir Leviathan, saying his solicitor liked to dwell in the depths and had long tentacles of influence. The analogy hadn't seemed to fit the big, quiet, dark-haired man who'd shown up at Carrington Close once a month with voluminous files and little conversation.

Then Sixtus had fallen ill, and the visits had become more frequent.

"Is there any way to modify the terms of the will?" Penelope asked.

A slight pause—Levi Sparrow was a great one for pausing—and then, "No, my dear, not unless you find a crooked judge or effect a change of law. You have until the twenty-eighth of December to marry, or you will lose all but the jointure and life estate specified in the will. May I ask what has precipitated this change of position?"

So polite, while Penelope wanted to smash her tea cup against the hearthstones. "Must I tell you?"

His glance shifted to the desk, where he doubtless had more interesting business to transact than Penelope's marital campaign. The elegant manner in which he crossed his legs at the knee suggested he was irritated.

Well, so was she.

"You are under no obligation to tell me anything, madam, though if you are in trouble, if you have gambling debts, or if your grief has led you to intimate indiscretions which some fool thinks to turn to his financial advantage—"

"Indiscretions? You think I've been out merry-widowing, with Sixtus not yet gone a year? Dancing on his grave? You too, Levi?"

Levi Sparrow was not precisely her friend, but he'd been Sixtus's friend, also the solicitor entrusted with Sixtus's most delicate transactions and negotiations. For Levi to suggest she'd taken lovers during the limited mourning Sixtus had prescribed hurt.

Hurt badly, and did not bode well for her plans.

"My dear lady, calm yourself. I lost my Ann eight years ago." He took a bite of fruitcake, probably a strategic move to buy time to gather his thoughts. Levi gathered thoughts like old women knitted on familiar needles. Click, click, click, in rapid, sure succession, all of a piece.

"Eight years is a long time."

He fell silent. Levi liked his silences, just as he took liberties with pauses, and yet, Pen had forgotten this about him: He was a widower. He'd known loss, and maybe that explained why months after the condolence calls had ceased and all but the most determined bachelors had stopped sniffing about her skirts, Levi still came to see her.

He'd advised her against donating all of Sixtus's clothes to the staff or the poor, suggesting she keep at least a good suit of clothes, a dressing gown, and the old fellow's favorite riding boots.

She'd cried, clutching those boots. Cried for an old man who hadn't been able to sit a horse in years.

An astonishing thought intruded on that dolorous memory.

"Levi, are you telling me you took lovers during your mourning?" The question exceeded the bounds of any inquiry she'd made of him in the five years of their acquaintance. "Don't answer that. I'm left much to my own company, and sometimes I don't know if I've said something aloud, or merely thought it. I've doubtless taken my first step down the slippery slope of eccentricity."

Levi neither made light of her outburst nor ignored it. Instead, he picked up a piece of fruitcakes sporting a thick smear of butter and held it up to her mouth.

"You must eat. Cook takes her company baking seriously, and I offend her at my peril."

Penelope took a bite, smooth, fresh butter blending with candied fruit and spices. Another extraordinary thought popped into her mind, though this one she kept penned up behind her lips: He was teasing her somehow, perhaps even—dare she hope?—*flirting*.

"Excellent fruitcake, my thanks."

He set the remainder of the slice on her plate. "Do you think it impossible that I might have found companionship after my wife's passing?"

He must examine her lapse of manners, confounded man. "You're quite comely, Levi. You were probably swamped by ladies offering their company." She took another bite of fruitcake, because the words had come out all wrong. Levi was tall and well muscled, as if he spent long hours in the saddle or tramping his acres. He had startlingly blue eyes, disarmingly blue eyes, the only light feature in a face rendered dark by both sable hair and a paucity of smiles.

A jaded view of the human race was probably a solicitor's occupational hazard, like cow-pox befell dairy maids. Not fatal, and it had benefits.

And yet to Penelope, Levi was attractive. In his silences, in his rare dry wit, in his integrity, and in his devotion to a lonely old man, Levi was attractive.

He was also sporting the slightest approximation of a smile. "I was not swamped. My wealth is modest compared to what Sixtus amassed."

Plain speaking. She reached for a second piece of buttered fruitcake only to find Levi had put two more on her plate.

"It's a relief sometimes, when you say things like that, Levi. I do not flatter myself the bachelors condoling me so heartily are smitten with my charms. They want a wealthy widow to ease their difficulties. Mr. Amblewise's devotion beggars description."

He topped up her tea. "Vicars are as prone to pragmatic attachments as other men."

Was Levi? Could he be inspired to form such an attachment?

"You don't judge them, all the vultures trying to pluck wealth from Sixtus's estate?"

"From his widow?"

"Her." Pen wrinkled her nose at the young woman Sixtus Hargreaves Carrington had taken pity on six years ago. He'd married her and showered her with every comfort a devoted husband might bestow on a wife five decades his junior, despite the ridicule and snickering he'd endured as a result. None of his generosity—not the carriages, not the jewels, not the finery, not even the small thoughtful tokens—had been of any value to her at all compared to Sixtus's friendship.

"Sixtus's widow is very pretty," Levi said, the same way he might have remarked that the tea had grown cool. "Perhaps the bachelors are circling her because she brings repose and calm with her wherever she goes. Maybe they're drawn to the kindness in her eyes, or the willingness to laugh she keeps close at hand. Sixtus chose wisely. Do you doubt another man could show the same good judgment?"

The conversation had strayed far afield from its intended agenda, onto new and boggy ground—interesting, boggy ground.

"Are you scolding me, Levi, or complimenting me?"

"Perhaps I'm defending the bachelors. I call on you as well."

His penchant for logic was one of his less attractive features. "You and I discuss investments, projects, bills pending before Parliament. You warn me when your sisters are planning to call on me." And he never, ever made any improper overtures—drat the luck.

"I *warn* you?" He was the picture of the perplexed male, which might fool his sisters—they doted on him.

"Might we return to the matter at hand?"

He leaned back in his chair, making a sturdy piece of furniture creak. A log fell forward on the andirons, sparks shooting up the flue while Pen endured lawyerly scrutiny. If he'd been a barrister and he'd put her in the witness box, she'd have told him anything he asked. His silences bore that much gravity, the answers would have been sucked right up out of her soul.

"You have decided to marry. You may slap me for my impertinence, but I'll ask anyway: Are you carrying a child?"

Maybe this was also part of a solicitor's lot in life. They expected bad behavior from their clients.

"I will not slap you, and I am not carrying." If he'd known how absurd his inquiry was, Pen would have been even more embarrassed. "The problem is my sisters."

"Two, if I recall the number. Born within a year of each other. One shudders for your mother's constitution, if not her nerves."

He would know exactly how many sisters she had, and their ages. Levi was a baronet, after all, the sort of fellow invited to every house party in Nottinghamshire to make up numbers and add a dash of class among the gentry.

House parties at which he was apparently offered companionship of an intimate nature. Pen brushed a stray crumb from her lap.

"One shudders for my sisters' futures," she said. "On the strength of my expectations as Sixtus's devoted young wife, my dear papa has been living beyond his means. He has used my sisters' dowries to maintain appearances, but I gather from my mother that the situation has become difficult. One usually pays the trades in December, and Mama has applied to me to address even those bills."

Levi steepled his fingers and tapped them against his lips, as if considering a chessboard with only a half-dozen pieces left. He had a lovely mouth, which one tended not to notice because of all the lawyering that came out of it.

"Do you know the extent of your father's indebtedness?"

She did. Something else Sixtus had bequeathed to her: a keen understanding of figures, and of the power wielded by studying those figures. She named an appalling sum, a figure amassed over the past five years apparently, that included debts of honor, necessities, and all too many fripperies.

At the mention of the sum, Levi rose and took a stance with one elbow propped on the mantel—one of his many thinking poses, all of which were doubtless more attractive than he knew.

"Your sisters are not as pretty as you, neither are they as intelligent."

Penelope wanted to defend them—they'd had no devoted husband to take their education, their true education, in hand—but she remained silent. Levi was thinking, and she'd forced herself to come here and share her problem with him in part because he excelled at rational analysis.

While she was becoming eccentric and hatching peculiar schemes that did not involve Levi's legal expertise.

"Have you sought aid from Joseph Carrington?" Levi asked. "He's titled, wealthy, and your relation through Sixtus."

"Joseph is also again a new father, and if you think I'll bother Sixtus's distant cousin with troubles my family has caused, you mistake the matter."

"I will need to consider this."

The very outcome Penelope had been hoping for, though she was not comforted. Had she expected Levi to produce a fortune at her request? To dower her younger sisters?

To propose *himself* as her next husband? Acquisition of Levi Sparrow as a spouse should not be an easily granted objective, and yet, Penelope's foolish hopes would not listen to her common sense.

"My thanks then, Levi, and I'll leave you to it. You needn't see me out. I appreciate your time."

His expression turned severe. "Will you next offer to leave through the kitchen, Penelope?"

Oh, for the love of Christmas. Men were all alike in some regards, irrespective of age, station, education, anything.

"I did not mean to offend, Levi. I have called on short notice. You're a busy man. This matter is not exactly a legal—"

His rejoinder was to draw her to her feet and wing his elbow at her. She twined her arm around his and let him lead her through the house to the front hallway. No doubt to emphasize his point—whatever point he was making—he shooed the footman off and held her cloak up himself.

Black, of course. She looked hideous in black, but gray, mauve and lavender were flattering enough.

"Hold still." Not his reasoning, patient voice, but a voice that Penelope obeyed. While she tipped her chin up, he fastened the frogs beneath her chin then kissed her cheek.

The same friendly, perfunctory buss he'd given her dozens of times before, and it left her desolate. Desolation and widows got on very well after a time. She hadn't yet acquired the knack.

When she might have stepped back to pull on her gloves, she was instead enveloped in a pair of strong male arms.

"You are not to worry, Penelope."

The admonition was predictable, the embrace completely unexpected. She'd leaned on Levi in so many ways, that to have this too—a simple hug—seemed like an unpardonable imposition, particularly when she hoped he'd give her his very name. She mustered a small lecture of her own, though she delivered it from the comfort of his arms.

"I am not sleeping well and fatigue has made my dignity unreliable, Levi. If you indulge me in sentimental displays, I'll not answer for the—"

He gently pushed her head to his shoulder. This close, he was taller than she'd realized. He also bore the fragrance of lemons and cinnamon.

"You have borne up for a year since Sixtus's death. Before that, you spent five years as his wife and nurse companion, and before that you were the only sensible person in a family of featherbrains. You will allow yourself this moment of friendly comfort."

He spoke so easily in pragmatic imperatives. Tears welled, and Pen would have left his embrace except then he would have seen her face, looked into her eyes, and insisted on accompanying her home.

"I'm merely tired."

A gentle caress passed down her neck and to her shoulder. He gave her shoulder a slow, firm squeeze.

"You rest. I'll have a talk with Sixtus's trustees, and we will see what's to be done. Don't propose to anybody until you hear from me."

Humor, or the closest approximation thereto Levi Sparrow was capable of. Pen blinked her tears into submission, took one last bracing whiff of lemons and cinnamon, and turned out of his arms. She didn't bother to put on her bonnet, just snatched it off the gate-legged table, tossed a "Good day and thank you," over her shoulder, and retreated to the confines of her coach.

Where the tears came again, because if Levi Sparrow was attempting to make jests of her marital schemes, matters were dire indeed.

The lady had forgotten her scarf, an indication to Levi that Penelope's unshakable poise was suffering. He unwound a generous length of lavender wool from the coat rack in his front hallway and brought a soft bunch to his nose.

Roses, but not the heavy scent of damasks. A hint of nutmeg underlay the floral fragrance, just as hints of blue and green had been woven through the lavender. The yarn was a blend of lamb's wool and angora, very plush, very pleasurable to touch.

"Excuse me, sir, but you have a guest in the small parlor."

"Bannon, you're supposed to clear your throat, scuff your shoe, and otherwise avoid the near occasion of sneaking up on your employer."

Bannon's expression didn't alter, suggesting he'd both coughed and scuffed his shoe while Levi parsed the scents of roses and hope.

"My mistake, sir. Mr. Stoneleigh is enjoying the tea tray. I explained to him you were with a client. And sir?"

Now for the bad news. Levi hadn't taken two steps in the direction of the informal parlor. "Out with it."

"Stirring-up Sunday is soon upon us. The staff will decorate the house."

A warning, not a request for permission. Levi's staff had opinions, most of which they were well paid to keep to themselves. Their opinions about the Christmas holidays, and the need to decorate the house within an inch of its life, they made known every year.

"Understood, Bannon. Make up the green guest room, if you please, and warn Mrs. Helmstead that Stoneleigh will likely want a bath."

Bannon bowed, showing the patch on the top of his head no longer covered with hair. Bannon hadn't sported a bald spot when he'd come into Levi's employ—though that had been ten years ago.

The small parlor was cozy and commodious rather than a temple to tidiness, a room where a man who'd completed a winter journey north from London might make himself comfortable.

"Stoneleigh." Levi closed the door to keep in the heat and keep out the servants. "I see the various malefactors loose on the highways didn't bestir themselves to interrupt your journey."

Stoneleigh rose, dusting crumbs from his hands. "I came by post—faster and safer and less likely to be used by former clients. You're gaunt. Have you taken to wearing mufflers? I can't say lavender flatters you."

This was Gervaise Stoneleigh's version of a warm greeting. Levi folded the scarf into quarters and put it on the mantel.

"A client's forgotten accessory. I've ordered you a bath."

"Good of you," Stoneleigh said. "The Duke's Arms is full up, and everybody in the common was gabbling about highwaymen with no Christmas spirit."

Stoneleigh was a Byronically handsome devil, never in want of female companionship or proper invitations, but not much given to socializing. When Levi's path had crossed with Stoneleigh's as young fellows starting out, they'd enjoyed an instant mutual regard.

"You may remove to The Duke's Arms when they have a vacancy," Levi said, "though the talk of highwaymen is grounded in unfortunate reality. Cook, will, of course, be heartbroken that you'd rather have the fare of a coaching inn than what she'll prepare for you."

Levi would also be disappointed not to have his friend's company as winter closed in.

Stoneleigh ran pale fingers over the folded scarf on the mantel. "You have lady clients?"

"A few. Widows sensible enough to seek professional assistance with their business affairs rather than relying on sons, brothers, or cousins. May I offer you something to take off the chill?"

"You may." Stoneleigh resumed his place in the middle of a blue brocade sofa. "While I will offer you all the gossip I know in exchange for the use of that hot bath before dinner is served."

Levi crossed to the hearth and set the fire screen aside. The Midlands in December was no place to find oneself at a coaching inn, though The Duke's Arms was comfortable, friendly and clean. When the fire was making a better effort to toast the room's inhabitants, he poured two servings of one of the finest Armagnacs in the realm.

"This is why I impose on your hospitality," Stoneleigh said, sitting back with his drink. "You must have saved the man a bloody fortune for him to keep you in libation like this."

Levi took the chair that had long since learned the exact contours of his fundament. "I saved his reputation, which was worth several bloody fortunes. How's business in old London Towne?"

They talked about who was being considered for a judgeship, what former associates had got up to mischief, and which MP was introducing the most daft legislation—a topic that might have occupied them until spring.

Levi fished in his pocket and held up a shiny gold sovereign. "Take this."

Stoneleigh made no move to take the coin. "Why?"

Bloody barristers. "So I might require you to hold the next topic in confidence."

Slowly, slowly, Stoneleigh reached for the coin, as if he expected the money to hiss at him. "Are you in trouble, Leviticus?"

A careful question—open-ended, but not flippant. One of the premier barristers in the land probably found all of his friends turning to him for advice sooner or later—the friends who'd committed crimes, that is.

"Not in the sense you allude to. I haven't broken any laws that I know of, though I find myself in a situation."

Was this how Levi's clients felt when they brought their problems to him? Confused, self-conscious, ashamed of their confusion? Ashamed of themselves?

"You want to break laws," Stoneleigh suggested. "Or you want to break heads, which amounts to the same thing."

"Perhaps I shall break your head, Stoneleigh. What I want to do is remarry."

Stoneleigh took another sip of his drink, clearly expecting all conversation to pause while he savored his potation and let the finish come to full bloom.

"This is not a legal question, Levi. You don't retain a barrister to explain the fine points of courting. Who's the lucky girl?"

He had to ask that, in case the lady in question was a client of his, or a client's wife, daughter, niece, cousin, granddaughter, god-daughter. The practice of law endlessly cramped a man's facility for gossip.

"You don't know her, and she's not a girl. She's a lady, and a widow."

This provoked a frown. "Please tell me you're not considering some weedy old besom who'll read psalms at every meal and look down her nose at those of us who waltz? Christmas is coming, and you'll not want to spoil the holiday for your staff by marrying an antidote. I suppose a lengthy engagement would allow them to find other positions."

A weedy old besom?

"I am the same age as you, Gervaise. Why would I take to wife a weedy old besom?"

The next perusal held a guarded hint of pity. "When Ann died, you became a weedy old besom yourself, all ponderous silences and grim determination." And then, more softly. "One worried for you."

Thank God men drank when they socialized, lest little admissions like that require them to *look* at one another while they flayed each other's dignity.

Levi stared at his glass, then at the fire. "Enduring grief takes a certain amount of grim determination, something I hope you never learn first hand."

Stoneleigh set his drink on the table, such that the leaping flames in the hearth created a small answering fire in the glass.

"You have been widowed longer than you were married, my friend. You've served your sentence, paid the restitution. Marry some bouncy little baggage half your age who'll give you babies and turn your life upside down. One of these days, I intend to."

Levi's gaze drifted over Penelope's soft, luxurious scarf. Did she want children? Would she want *his* children?

"That is an extraordinary admission."

"My housekeeper had opinions on the matter, says no proper lady would want to marry a fellow who consorts mostly with criminals."

"You never consort with a criminal you believe to be guilty as charged. That's half the reason people want so badly to retain you."

Stoneleigh shrugged, as he always shrugged, shot his cuffs, or remarked upon the Corn Laws when somebody mentioned his legendary legal scruples.

"Most of us are guilty of something at some point," he said, "and now you're preparing to commit holy matrimony for the second time. Recidivist offenders seldom earn lenience, you know."

"Neither Ann nor Penelope would consider marriage to me a jest. Penelope is Sixtus Carrington's widow. She grieves his passing sincerely."

"Midas Carrington saw his three score and ten some time before his death. If you're considering marrying the woman, she's not more than half that age. In some small, honest corner of her soul, she was relieved to see Carrington shuffle off this mortal coil, if only relieved for him. Death is seldom a dignified proposition."

Stoneleigh ambled over to the decanter, poured himself another tot, and did the same for Levi. His movements were relaxed, confident, almost careless, and yet, without a word being said, Levi had the conviction Stoneleigh had buried somebody he'd loved, and loved dearly.

Levi would not dare to probe such a well guarded wound. "Regardless of her feelings for her late spouse, Penelope Carrington is a lovely woman. She's kind and restful without being dull. She sits in judgment of none and enjoys a lively interest in things commercial. She can beat me at chess."

Stoneleigh sniffed his drink consideringly, as if this last detail were the most interesting.

"*I* don't often beat you at chess."

"Your concentration is usually wanting halfway through the game." Though the first half of the game was always a well fought skirmish.

"You seek to become engaged to the fair Penelope." Stoneleigh resumed his seat, but this time toed off his boots and crossed his stockinged feet on the low table. The familiarity of such a presumption—left over from student days—was endearing and precious.

"So you go down on bended knee," Stoneleigh said. "Mouth a few smarmy sentiments, slobber on her hand, and have the banns cried. You're a bright fellow. What's the problem?"

"God help the woman you decide to court, Stoneleigh, and God help you if that's your idea of how to go about it. Have we discussed Sixtus's will?"

"Wills." Stoneleigh spat the word. "Give me the assizes any day over chancery. Wills were devised by Old Scratch to torment those he hasn't got his hands on yet. Carrington was wallowing in filthy lucre, so I expect his will was complicated."

"Not particularly, which means it would be that much harder to overturn. He left a respectable portion to his only surviving family, Joseph Carrington, a distant cousin. As for the rest, it goes to Penelope in trust if she remarries by December 28. If she fails to remarry, or remarries after that date, she gets only a comfortable jointure and use of a dower property that will produce some income."

"The old fellow wanted her to remarry promptly. Generous of him."

Levi considered discarding his own boots and decided against it. "Diabolical of him, more like. He ensured Penelope would view all suitors importuning her during her year of mourning as fortune hunters, which they likely are."

"You're not?"

"I am quite comfortably situated, thank you kindly, though much of my wealth is tied up in investments." He'd considered dowering Penelope's sisters—he was still considering it—though his wealth was not easily accessible, and dowering her sisters would not address the debts her father had amassed.

Stoneleigh wiggled his toes. "You're not that hard to look upon, though a bit short on animal magnetism and ready charm. Won't she have you?"

Whatever animal magnetism was. "I haven't asked her. I haven't felt I had the latitude to take her as my fiancée."

"Why not? You're not getting any younger, and somebody has to inherit that baronetcy. Civilization is threatened every time a title lapses—you were an English schoolboy. You know your Holy Writ."

"I cannot approach Penelope Carrington about the possibility of becoming my fiancée, because shortly after Ann's death, I may have acquired a prospective wife. My understanding of these matters suggests that having more than one fiancée at a time can become problematic."

Chapter Two

"**F**ETCH ME A gun, and I'll rid your house of vermin!"

Squire Hungerford was on his feet, his expression as choleric as if a rat had crossed the carpet rather than a rabbit.

"He's a pet, Mr. Hungerford." Penelope bent to pick up the bunny, which was a somewhat cumbersome undertaking when Franklin weighed a solid stone and went limp as an old rag at the prospect of impending affection. "A gift from my late husband."

"A bloody"—Hungerford took out a handkerchief and mopped his brow—"I mean, a blasted rabbit, given free rein in the house? A sign the late Mr. Carrington was several hounds shy of a pack, madam. A man of sense would not allow such a creature in his household."

Penelope buried her nose in the fur at Franklin's nape. "Thank goodness I was not married to a man of sense, then. I much prefer this little fellow to a half-dozen stinking, muddy dogs, don't you?"

She had blasphemed on purpose, of course. Squire Hungerford was a man in his prime, and he never missed a hunt meet.

He stuffed his handkerchief in his pocket. "Hounds, madam. One never refers to them as dogs."

Penelope indulged in a momentary cuddle with her rabbit. Whatever else was true, the blond, bluff Hungerford was not husband material. Not for her.

"My sister Diana would know the difference, I'm sure. You've met her?"

Hungerford's head came up, like one of his dogs—hounds, canines, whatever—catching a scent. Perhaps he'd start baying next.

"Capital girl, Miss Diana. Absolutely first flight. Has an excellent seat and isn't missish at the kill."

What finer endorsement might a young lady have than that? Penelope walked toward the door, leaving her guest no choice but to fall in beside her.

"My mother is having a small dinner in two weeks to start the holiday celebrations, Mr. Hungerford. Shall I see that you get an invitation?"

He blinked, and in the nature of that blink, Penelope saw him changing course, from considering Sixtus's fortune as the marital prize, to considering a wife who was horse mad and knew the difference between dogs and hounds.

To Hungerford's credit, the deliberation was brief. "Always pleasant to get together with the neighbors over the holidays. Assemblies are fine, but too much hopping about goes on to truly enjoy the conversation."

They'd reached the main hallway, where Hungerford's hat, gloves and riding crop sat on the sideboard and his great coat hung from a peg. The footmen had been pressed into service making ropes of greenery, and yet, Penelope did not want to put Franklin down so she could assist her guest.

Hungerford was a widower—he at least knew how to put on his own coat. He tapped his hat onto his head and cast a stern glance at Franklin, then an equally stern glance at Penelope.

"If there's anything you need, madam, you must not hesitate to apply to me. I realize your mourning has not yet run its entire course and the holidays can be lonely for those of us who've known the loss of a mate. I am ever your servant."

He bowed smartly, a bodily salute, though Pen was glad her arms were full of Franklin, lest she suffer the tickle of Hungerford's blond mustache against her knuckles.

"My thanks, Mr. Hungerford, and I'm sure Diana will be very pleased to know you'll join the family gathering."

Then he was gone, thumping down the front steps, riding crop thwacking against his boots.

"Thank you," Penelope said, cradling Franklin close. "I thought I'd be trapped in the parlor until spring, listening to 'by Firebrand out of Windylegs.' I don't suppose you care if it's a dog or a hound when it's trying to put you on the dinner menu, do you?"

If Franklin had one shortcoming, it was that he didn't purr. He was a very good judge of character, though, and a sumptuous pleasure to pet.

"We have a note to write to Mama," Penelope said, "and then we'll see how matters are progressing below stairs."

She'd barely begun the note when Bella, her under-housekeeper, tapped on the door.

"Morning, mum. Sir Leviticus Sparrow has come to call."

Bella hadn't finished her recitation before Levi wedged himself through the door past the servant. He set his hands on Bella's shoulders and moved her a step to the left as easily as he'd move a coat rack.

"One hardly needs to announce me, I hope. Penelope." He bowed gracefully, no hurry to his civilities. "And Franklin. Good morning." He didn't quite bow to the rabbit, but he acknowledged the beast with a sort of half nod between the fellows. "I hope I'm not intruding?"

"Of course not. A tray, please, Bella."

He held up a hand, and Bella stopped mid-turn. "No tray for me, Bella. Shall we instead inspect the troops, Penelope?"

The day was cold, sunny, and breezy. Nobody in her right mind would consider it weather for strolling the barns when she could instead spend yet another interminable hour talking to her rabbit in a nice, boring parlor.

"Brilliant notion. We'll have chocolate when we come in, Bella, and tell somebody to man the front door, please."

Levi was still peering at her. "You look like you could use some fresh air, and as if Hungerford overstayed his welcome."

"Franklin put him to rout."

"Good man, Franklin. Now go stop the draft coming in through the French doors. There's a lad." He scooped the rabbit from Pen's grasp, petted the beast briskly, and set him on the floor. As if Franklin understood his orders, he lippity-loped over to the terrace doors and did indeed stretch himself against the base.

"The house is hot for him," Penelope said.

"The floors are plenty cold. Now let's be about our errand, shall we?"

Five minutes later they'd traversed the frozen yard to the small barn that housed the rabbit hutches.

"These have to be the happiest rabbits in the known world," Levi remarked. "Also the furriest."

The barn was chilly—angora rabbits were well protected against the cold—but it was sheltered and bore the good scents of straw and clean livestock.

"They make me happy," Penelope said. "I wonder why that should be."

Arms linked, Levi took her up and down each aisle, his steps matched to hers.

"They make you happy because this is your enterprise, your project, and it has turned out quite profitably. When clients ask me how they can help their tenants generate cottage income, I always suggest your rabbit scheme."

"It's old-fashioned," Penelope said, bending down to touch the inquisitive nose of a dun-colored doe named Bathsheba. "The women and children can manage it, the manure is useful, the fur is quite valuable, the spinning can be done at home, or the wool can be shipped north for blending." She caressed the rabbit's velvety ears. "How fare you, my lady?"

"That's the doe who has the big litters, isn't it?"

He would recall such a thing. Penelope straightened. "Sheba's a good mother, but lately she's been getting out. We haven't figured out how, and she always comes hopping home. I have a list of bachelors, Levi."

His expression didn't change, but the feel of him beside her changed, became less the family friend and more the reserved man of business.

Drat. Why couldn't he offer her an alternative?

"A list? Was Hungerford on that list?"

"He was. He is not. He threatened to shoot Franklin. Now I ask you, what woman needs to be defended against a bunny?"

A hint of humor threatened in Levi's eyes, then faded. "Franklin ought to chew the blighter's boots to ribbons for such an insult. Who is on your list?"

Who wasn't? She'd considered every unmarried male over the age of eighteen, because Levi had had months to intimate that his friendship had marital potential, and he'd never so much as twitched his nose inappropriately. A woman had to be practical—and ruthless. Sixtus had insisted this was so.

Pen rattled off the top ten names. As she continued her tour of the barns, Levi's arm was no longer twined with hers. That was better, more businesslike, less of a strain on her composure.

"So render your opinion, Levi." Of the bachelors, please, not of her.

"These are boys, Penelope. Young fellows of good name who won't know a thing about managing your business, nor about"—he waved a black-gloved hand in spirals—"how to go on with a lady wife. Are you seeking a manageable spouse?"

She didn't answer immediately, but rather, paced down the aisle with him, past the bachelor bucks. Their lot was largely to grow fur and look handsome. Could she tolerate such a husband?

Did she have a choice?

"Penelope?"

"There's a method to my list." This was part of what she'd wanted to tell him three days ago, but hadn't found the words. She still hadn't any words. "How does a man kiss his wife, Levi?"

Levi sauntered past a row of empty cages. He was tall, unhurried, exquisitely turned out in his riding attire, and to appearances not the least taken aback by her question.

"I had only the one wife, and I can't say managing business affairs has equipped me to answer your question. Could you explain yourself?"

No, she could not. "How did you kiss Ann?"

"With my lips?" He glanced over at her and probably saw that his jest was not appreciated. "Very well. I kissed her differently depending on the occasion. I often kissed her precisely as I kiss you." He brushed his lips over Pen's cheek, a fleeting, friendly warmth, nothing more.

"That's not what I mean. I mean, how did you kiss her *as a husband*?"

His gaze made a circuit of the barn, past piles of clean straw to fluffy rabbits hopping about in spacious, comfy pens.

"We're quite alone, Penelope. Profuse discourse on such a topic is not in my gift. Shall I show you how I kissed my wife?"

Penelope managed a nod while Levi removed his gloves. If a man kissed with his lips, then he should have no need to take off his gloves—

Warm male fingers slid along Penelope's cheek until they cradled her jaw.

"After a long day of listening to my clients whinge and whine about every conceivable topic—their investments, their gout, their intimate associations, their lack of same—I would find my lady at her account books or her correspondence. Perhaps she was in deep discussion with the housekeeper over the menus, or planning some entertainment. Ann worried that I did not get out enough socially, and she had ambitions for me."

A second hand cupped Penelope's jaw. "I'd see her, the woman I loved, and thank God that I had a means of providing for her and keeping her safe. She'd look up, her expression would lighten at the simple sight of me—*me*—and she'd drop what she was doing and offer me her embrace. I would kiss her, thus."

His hold on Pen became firmer, but no less gentle. He tipped her face up and settled his lips over hers like a benediction, like a prayer of gratitude and gladness. He took his time, acquainting their mouths, lingering, greeting with touch what gave him joy.

God in heaven, he had loved his wife dearly.

Levi's hands drifted down, over Pen's shoulders and back, making her wish she wore naught but a chemise—not even a chemise—the better to absorb the warmth in his caresses.

"Put your arms around me, Penelope. A man greeting a woman he's cared for, worried over, and missed wants to feel her embrace. He needs to know he's welcome, even in his own home."

Levi was welcome. Pen slid her arms around his waist, let herself lean against the muscular bulwark of his chest. Ann Sparrow had known years of such embraces, such kisses. Years of Levi caring for her, missing her, and worrying over her.

"You would hold each other, simply hold each other, like this?"

"Not often. Holding Ann was like holding sunlight. She had great energy and much enthusiasm for her tasks. Fleeting hugs, always heartfelt but never prolonged, were more the norm. I was the one—"

He paused. Not his usual pause, either.

Penelope rested her cheek against the wool of Levi's coat, wondering how any woman could have danced out of such an embrace.

"Do I take it, Penelope, that Sixtus was a reserved husband?"

She eased away, and he let her go. "You raise a difficult topic." Particularly when a woman's wits had gone haring off. She crossed to the bachelor bucks, took off her gloves and lifted a fine young fellow with luxurious gray fur. "This is Casper. I've considered him for the breeding pens because of his excessively agreeable temperament."

Casper was a slug in rabbit fur. He got along with everybody, like a tame buck ought to.

"Sixtus never discussed the private side of his marriage with me," Levi said. He spoke from where they'd kissed, several yards away. Wise of him. "I concluded there wasn't much of a private side, particularly once you became settled in the marriage."

His inquiry was quiet, as if considering a point of history, which in fact, he was.

"Not much of one in the sense you allude to," Penelope said. "I asked Sixtus about it several months after the wedding night. He assured me that were he fifteen, even ten years younger, he'd make a regular nuisance of himself—those were his words—but time had taken a toll on his manly humors. I was free to entertain myself however I saw fit, provided I did not get with child or cause scandal."

Levi took out his gloves, refolded them, and stuffed them back in his pocket. "This has to do with that old barony, doesn't it?"

To the point, that was Levi. That he could kiss her like *that* one moment and discuss business the next had to go under the heading of Unendearing Traits.

"The barony and simple marital decency. If either Sixtus or his cousin had a male child, that child would likely win a petition to bring the baron's title out of abeyance. Sixtus thought Cousin Joseph was the more deserving resource. Joseph did not agree, and thus—"

Thus, she had hundreds of rabbits, the most fecund species on the planet, to comfort her in her widowhood, but not one child. She set Casper back where he belonged, among pens where all was domestic harmony and security, provided one was a buuny.

"So why the kiss, Penelope?" Levi spoke from very near her. She turned and leaned forward, resting her forehead against his chest.

The kiss had been because she was desperate, and Levi wasn't making overtures, and contingencies could all too easily become reality.

"They'll know, Levi. Any widower who weds me will know I'm a complete tyro as a wife. I was married for six years, and Sixtus hardly ever—" She couldn't finish that thought out loud. "I don't want to embarrass Sixtus's memory, I don't want to embarrass myself, and I do want to make a wise choice, but I'm choosing blind."

"Close your eyes."

What was he about? She closed her eyes, and Levi shifted so their bodies were quite proximate, to the point that he'd insinuated a leg forward, pressing himself against her even below her waist.

When his mouth touched hers this time, the kiss was a different beast entirely. No tame bunny of a kiss, this was a ravening predator intent on investigating every corner of her soul. She tasted him—lemon drops and cinnamon sticks—as his hand wrapped around the back of her head, preventing her from dodging or ducking.

As if she could have, or would have. His tongue seamed her lips, teasing, tasting.

"Open, Penelope. Open your mouth for me."

Not a man of business making a suggestion; but rather, a freelance knight come to storm her defenses. She complied, enough for him to convey to her the role a tongue might play in a kiss.

Or two tongues. Penelope's wits scattered like March hares, until she was clinging to Levi and learning the shape of his teeth with her tongue.

"That," he said, taking her hands in his and stepping back, "is how you might expect your husband to kiss you when his intention is to take you upstairs."

Levi's voice had changed, gone from the clipped, topiary accents of the well educated solicitor, to the soaring, tangled mysteries of the forest primeval. Levi knew much more than he'd just shown her.

Much, much more, and he'd never even hinted that Penelope tempted him to share that knowledge.

She dropped his hands. "You see my dilemma."

"I see that you're making the simple complicated, my dear. May we sit?"

Penelope didn't want to sit, she wanted to dash up to her room and cry—and not particularly for Sixtus.

"Are you about to lecture me, Levi?"

He waited while she took a seat on a bench near the feed room. "I'm about to talk with you and to provide reassurances on a matter I hope we need not discuss again."

He softened his words by taking her hand when they sat. She wished he'd do only that—hold her hand—rather than provide a legal sermon on some other topic.

"What is this dilemma you think you face, Penelope?"

Calm, maddeningly calm, but he was trying to be helpful, too, and for that she loved him—that, too.

"If I marry one of the younger fellows, the boys, as you call them, they'll want children and expect me to have knowledge of matters of which I am ignorant."

"Not an outlandish surmise. And the widowers?"

"They want a mother for their children, which is quite understandable, but they'll expect me to have even more familiarity with marital matters, having already had wives themselves."

"I see."

"No, you do not. I'm a widow, Levi. I can't go around sampling the kisses of every prospect to ensure his intimate attentions will be bearable. I have no time, my reputation will be in shreds, I know next to nothing of the wedding night, I have no—"

A husband apparently learned an entire arsenal of kisses. When Levi took her mouth this time, he was telling her quite clearly to cease and desist, and offering a strong incentive to do so. His kiss took the wind from Penelope's sails and the thoughts from her mind.

When he withdrew, and they were again sitting side by side on the bench, hands joined, Penelope slumped against the sturdy boards behind her.

"You do understand the mechanics of copulation, Penelope?"

He would explain compound interest to her in the same inflections. "I breed *rabbits*, Levi."

"Just so. Then you comprehend enough. No man with any sense will expect that Sixtus was in a position to teach you the habits of a houri, so to speak. As for the rest—" His hold on her hand became more thoughtful. More personal. "Ann was very unimpressed on our wedding night."

What? "With you?"

"I was young, hardly more experienced than she, and she was not raised to place much value on passion in a marriage. Few ladies are." He sounded wistful, but did he miss Ann, or miss the years during which he might have encouraged her marital passions?

"I'm sorry, Levi. You've been so understanding of my situation all these months, and it never occurred to me your own grief is what makes you such a good friend."

He eased his fingers from hers and put on his gloves. "Do you kiss all your friends like that, Penelope? I can't say I'd advise it."

She had learned to know him a little better, maybe as a result of having kissed him. He was teasing her, mostly.

"I've never kissed anybody like that. Do husband and wives really kiss so enthusiastically?" So passionately.

"Some husbands, some wives. Not all the Puritans emigrated, certainly."

When Penelope and Levi emerged from the rabbit barn, the day seemed more temperate, the sunshine brilliant on the remaining patches of snow. Penelope shaded her eyes and regarded her escort.

The man who'd kissed her as if he cared for her, worried over her, and missed her.

"Will you stay for chocolate, Levi?"

"Chocolate would be agreeable. If there are more names on any lists, Penelope, I'd like to hear those too."

Of course. She'd hoped to review her lists with him for two reasons. First, he'd know the gamblers, rogues and heavy drinkers in the local surrounds; second, she needed to find a way to ask him if he'd represent her in any settlement negotiations.

Though what she really wanted to ask him was to kiss her again, because she absolutely lacked the fortitude to ask him to marry her.

"She wants me to advise her in the damned settlement negotiations. Wants me to suggest terms so some spotty boy can waltz off with her fortune and more spotty boys can waltz off with her sisters."

When a man was professionally bound to hold close the confidences of all and sundry, he learned to choose his confidantes wisely. Levi's horse, a stout bay gelding by the name of Thomas, had never violated the trust his owner reposed in him.

"It's a good thing those rabbits like the cold, and a better thing a man's winter attire hides the more vulgar evidence of his interest in a woman."

The carnality of that interest had come as a shock, and Levi Sparrow did not enjoy being shocked.

"I did not know I *could* be shocked."

Thomas took exception to the reflection of sunlight on a puddle, mostly for form's sake. Geldings were much concerned with form.

"Ann always said I romanticized my attachments. She was practical."

She'd been a touch condescending when she'd offered such observations, amused by her callow swain. She'd also been right. Levi had grown up at a distance from his sisters, and after the age of eight, without a mother. He tended to regard women as not simply another gender, but an altogether different and more worthy species.

On at least one occasion his bias in this regard had yielded disastrous results. He thrust that thought aside and ran a steadying hand down Thomas's neck.

"When Penelope Carrington kisses a man, she does it as if he's sunlight, air, water and every other necessary element delivered for her personal delectation." That was before she'd gained much experience beyond kissing. "She knocks a man off his pins. This man, anyway."

He'd thought of Penelope as a muse, a lady not entirely of the earthly realm, a woman to be cherished and protected, as he'd cherished and protected Ann. He had not thought of Penelope as a woman whose kiss could part him from his reason and make him adore her for it.

Worship her in an entirely different and more passionate manner.

The idea that some other fellow might plunder those riches in Levi's place was untenable.

And yet, finding himself embroiled in the kind of scandal that would cost him his livelihood and standing in the community was equally untenable.

What was needed—what was always needed before any problem could be properly analyzed—was more information. When Levi had turned Thomas over to the groom, taken off his spurs, and passed hat, gloves, and coat to a footman, he made a straight line for the study.

Gervaise Stoneleigh sat at Levi's desk, boots propped on one corner, sleeves turned back at the wrists, a journal open on his lap. Odd, how one of the most brilliant legal minds in the realm looked exactly like any other fellow making himself comfortable at his labors.

"Have you had a chance to read the letters?"

Stoneleigh glanced up—he did not thunk his boots to the floor and scramble into a different chair, or stand and put his attire to rights. Levi was pleased that the informality they'd known as younger men was yet available to them.

"You missed luncheon."

Levi ambled over to the fire, added coal, and pokered in some air. "I joined Mrs. Carrington for a meal, the better to listen to her evaluate the various candidates for her hand. I'm to have a special license at the ready, send a pigeon before nightfall. All must be prepared for a quiet holiday wedding."

"I like a woman with a sense of organization." The chair scraped as Stoneleigh set the journal aside and rose, bracing his hands on the small of his back and arching. "It's cold in here."

"These things will happen when a man scares the staff away with his imperious demeanor, then forgets that fires do not feed themselves."

Stoneleigh blinked at the now roaring blaze. "You were quite a poet as a younger man."

"I was an ass."

"One can be a poet and an ass, witness Byron."

Lawyers and their penchant for evidence and counterexamples. Bother the lot of them.

Levi took the chair closest to the fire and realized he was hungry. He hadn't eaten much at lunch, he'd been too busy offering evidence to Penelope, to wit:

Mr. Fletcher went through a prodigious number of young, pretty maids.

Mr. Deal went through a prodigious amount of gin—not a genteel wine drunk, or even the more gentlemanly brandy. The man swilled *gin*.

Mr. Hammersmith had had seven children in six years with his first wife, there being a set of twins in the litter somewhere.

Mr. Farrington was regularly seen coming out of a certain establishment in a questionable neighborhood, where it was rumored he took opium.

They'd been down to the gamblers before Penelope had given up and asked Levi to come by tomorrow to resume the same exercise. Her list had been curiously devoid of the more reasonable prospects Levi could have mentioned.

But had kept to himself.

"You're brooding, Sir Levi." Stoneleigh lowered himself into the other chair on a sigh. "Or perhaps you're cogitating. I favor the brooding myself."

"Because you're better looking than Byron, you can call it brooding. For your information, I am considering whether to order a tray. Sorting bachelors leaves one peckish."

Kissing Penelope Carrington left one starved for sustenance other than food.

"I meant what I said about your poetry. Puts one in mind of Wordsworth on a gloomy day."

"You've read a great deal of Wordsworth, have you? I had lost my wife not three months earlier. All my days were gloomy." His nights had been worse, and then along had come the ever-so-sympathetic and friendly Miss Amanda Houston, with whom he'd occasionally crossed paths socially.

A small legal matter, she'd said.

"You weren't too gloomy to lose your sense over a woman."

"The poems were written to Ann. I sent them to Miss Houston as a sort of confidence, a way to not be alone with my sentiments, to share them with a friend. I was an absolute, utter, unconditional fool. The question is, am I an engaged fool?"

Chapter Three

AN INTERROGATION FOLLOWED Levi's question, like a thousand interrogations he'd put his clients through without once considering how the questions felt on the receiving end. He had blithely hammered away, "just to get a sense of where matters stand." The questioning struck him now as a form of brutality, like surgery without laudanum.

When did you first correspond with her?
Did you copy every letter you sent? Why did you copy them?
Did you keep her letters? Why not?
What gifts have you given her? How often did you call upon her?
Then, when Stoneleigh had thoroughly demoralized the witness with the inexactitude of his recollections and the lack of sensible motivations for his actions, the more difficult questions began.

"Did you advise her to seek another man of business?"
"Did you correspond with other women?"
"Why didn't you break it off?"
And the one question Levi could answer easily: "Were you ever intimate with the woman?"

"I was not, not in the sense of copulating with her. I never even kissed her."
"Not ever?" The two words whipped out with the metallic ring of a sword drawn from its scabbard.

"Stoneleigh, do not browbeat me. I am not a client who seeks to send counsel to the assizes with a pack of lies and prevarication. My pride is not that great when the issue affects the rest of my life. I tell you plainly: I bungled egregiously but not entirely."

The admission brought no relief, no sense of being unburdened by confession, and yet, more needed to be said.

"I came undone when Ann died, but a man cannot *be* undone. In his mourning, he is expected to attend to his business, to run his household, to appear for services, to see his clients. The ladies have a year to recover their balance. A man's balance is not to falter, except perhaps briefly at the graveside. His coats acquire a black armband, his mirrors are draped in black, little more.

"I did not cope well," Levi went on, "and Amanda Houston took shameless advantage. I thought she was a friend. She was a predator. The one bit of sense I exercised was to remain true to my wife's memory in intimate terms for two years following her death."

"And thereafter?"

"A couple of discreet liaisons while in London. Nothing more." And thank God those women had been after nothing more than a little comfort and a fond farewell.

"No passing encounters in York? A casual afternoon at a midsummer picnic? A tickle-and-kiss on the way to the hunt meets? An accommodating maid with a generous heart and a wandering eye?"

"Do you ever practice law, Stoneleigh, or is your life an incessant effort to elude desperate women?"

Stoneleigh crossed his arms and his ankles. "It would go better for you if you'd been fornicating your way all over the Midlands, comporting yourself like a tom-cat under a full spring moon. As it is..."

Stoneleigh was frowning now, not a good sign.

"As it is," Levi said, "I wrote a few pages of mourning poetry and shared some of it with a woman who has used my correspondence to imply that she considers us engaged. She alleges that a poem entitled 'When We Two Can Remain Together,' and others of its ilk, entangled me in an offer of marriage—to her. This is why single gentlemen are taught to never, ever correspond with single women, regardless that those women present themselves as confirmed spinsters and friends."

He had been such a fool. The very same kind of fool who retained his services regularly.

A human fool. His Christmas token would be a portion of humility packaged with regret sporting a sprig of self-disgust and a droopy bow fashioned of remorse.

"You also told Miss Houston that her kindness and charity led you to esteem her over all living women, and you could not foresee a time when her friendship would not be necessary for your wellbeing. Et cetera, et cetera."

Levi was still hungry, he did not feel in the least like eating, and damn Stoneleigh for having a near-perfect memory anyway.

"Had you read her letters to me, you might understand the extent to which she was eliciting my responses. She fretted that I found her company tedious. She worried that a woman of such limited intellectual accomplishment could not be any sort of friend to a man of my worldly education. She appeared good-hearted, self-effacing, and so very, very understanding of my loss."

Stoneleigh snorted. "She understood your loss. Understood it better than you did. So why didn't she lead your meek and unresisting self off to bed?"

"I hope because I would not have allowed it, and she sensed this—she's canny as hell—but I've come to suspect Miss Houston has lapsed from time to time in her spinsterhood, and she did not want me to become aware of her lack of chastity."

Stoneleigh sat up, his attention coiling as Franklin's did at the sound of rabbit food hitting a porcelain dish in the parlor across the corridor.

"Lapsed?" Stoneleigh repeated. "As in, suffered the intimate attentions of a man not her lawfully wedded husband? That sort of lapsed?"

Levi didn't want to tell this bit, the part that revealed how completely he'd been taken advantage of.

"I'm invited to any number of social gatherings—hostesses overlook my lack of ready wit because I am single and solvent. Then too, their husbands like to ask me for business advice over the port."

"And you"—Stoneleigh waved a hand—"tell them to come 'round the office where there's greater privacy, and if they're serious, they will, and if they're merely trolling for free advice, you're spared the indignity."

Ann had been the one to explain to Levi how that should be handled. Men all over the shire were likely in better financial health because they'd dined with Levi Sparrow.

"The military sorts are the worst," Levi said. "Because I trotted around on the Peninsula for a few years, I've acquired a literal army of long lost brothers who think it my duty to turn them all into nabobs over a glass of mediocre wine."

"One has pitied you, Levi."

The last of Levi's interest in food died. What he wanted was a drink, and for this interview to be over.

"I observed Miss Houston enter her bedroom at a house party this autumn. Twenty minutes later, Mr. Jefferson Vanderburg entered that same room and closed the door. He remained private with my supposed fiancée for more than an hour, whereupon he left her boudoir, cravat undone, boots in hand, looking in much greater charity with the world. At another house party this past summer, Cheevers Dauntry had the pleasure. Miss Houston is not chaste, but she's discreet, choosing fellows whose wives would fillet them, not necessarily for straying, but for causing scandal. She's shrewd."

Ann had also been shrewd, though the quality had been a virtue in her.

Mostly.

In the considering silence that followed, a seed of despair germinated in Levi's heart. A lady could misstep, and a gentleman's offer of marriage still stood. Nothing but the lady's own demurral relieved the gentleman of his obligation to keep his promise. This was not a fine point of the law. Every bachelor from John O'Groats to Land's End learned this precept before he'd stolen his first kiss.

"You could approach her paramours, threaten to bring suit for prostitution."

"Legally, I could, and then I would be a man who takes advantage of a woman alone in the world but for some doughty aunt, a woman with only modest financial security, a woman who—it will be said—turned to me for business advice. Six men would also have to admit to paying her for her favors, which in addition to being untrue, would embarrass their families. It's too sordid. I won't do it."

To put that position into words made the seed of despair grow roots and twine those roots around hopes regarding a wonderful, shockingly passionate woman whom Levi would die to protect.

"Life can be sordid, my friend. You're a solicitor. You know that. You knew that a week after you'd hung up your shingle."

Stoneleigh was commiserating; his words only *felt* like a scold.

"We're at a stalemate, Miss Houston and I. She says we're engaged, I say we're not. She occasionally commandeers my escort to some social function, and I go rather than start a war. I need to not only start a war with her, I need to win one, and do it in less than thirty days."

"I could threaten suit," Stoneleigh mused. "Rattle the sabers, do my impersonation of the Scourge of Temple Bar."

"You are the Scourge of Temple Bar. Also a damned decent fellow. There's nothing to sue her for."

Devilment came into Stoneleigh's expression at those observations, though they were the simple truth. He never represented a client whom he believed to be guilty. The result of retaining Gervaise Stoneleigh to represent one was an advantage in the courtroom before opening statements were even begun.

"I could propose to the lady, get her to accept my suit." Stoneleigh lowered his lashes, the resemblance to Bryon uncanny. "I can be very persuasive."

"Save it for the jury. I won't ask it of you—you'd be the one left with the breach-of-promise problem."

At that, Stoneleigh shot to his feet. "You're arguably engaged to a woman who lies, cheats, tricks, and takes advantage of a man's grief. She's a damned confidence artist. Unless you're willing to compromise your gentlemanly scruples, as long as she has your letters, she is in a fair way to become your next lawfully wedded wife. The only solution I can see is for you to decamp for parts unknown."

Stoneleigh rarely lost his temper, and when he did, it was usually a display of frosty verbiage designed to flay somebody's dignity into thin, bloody strips. This outburst was the exasperation of a man who cared for his friend and didn't see any good options for that friend.

Despair branched upward to nearly choke Levi's dream of a future with Penelope. Who knew a man's soul was fertile ground for such a fast-growing weed?

Stoneleigh plucked his coat from the back of Levi's chair. "You could burn her house down, get rid of the letters that way."

"She keeps them in her reticule, bound with green ribbon. She's waved them at me on occasion."

"You can't buy her off?"

"I've tried. A pension, a lump sum, a combination of the two, a profitable estate in Kent, and her reply is to ask me why she should settle for crumbs when she can have a baronet and his entire estate?"

"You were a lamb to slaughter, Sparrow. I am sorry. If I'd kept a better eye on you, this would not have happened." He slipped sleeve buttons into his cuffs and shrugged into his jacket, so casual, but the words were not what a barrister or solicitor offered a client, and that was an oversight.

"This is my fault, and I will deal with the consequences."

Levi should order a tray. Dinner was hours away, and a man needed sustenance whether he wanted it or not. He rose and considered his now properly attired guest. "Where are you off to?"

Stoneleigh wrinkled his nose. "My visit to the wilds of Nottinghamshire on this occasion is because the archbishop's great-niece finds herself in a spot of trouble. Great-Uncle wants to retain my services. I'm making up my mind. Clergy are the very devil as clients. Before the Uncle Right Reverend sends for me, I should look in on Oxthorpe. Our paths have crossed from time to time."

"You keep company with dukes now. Oxthorpe isn't exactly sociable." But then neither was Levi, if he could help it.

"Oxthorpe is a fine host, which fact I charge you to hold in confidence. Don't brood. We'll talk further. Don't wait up for me, either."

Levi used two fingers to loosen a fold of Stoneleigh's cravat from between coat and waistcoat. At one point, they'd had a single decent suit between them and had shared it back and forth depending on need.

"Further talk won't change the facts."

"No, but it might admit of a solution to those facts. I know a number of competent arsonists who are discreet, reliable and work for reasonable rates." Stoneleigh headed for the door, a man of the law turning his thoughts to his next case.

"Oh, the advantages resulting from regular association with criminals."

Stoneleigh winked and departed, leaving a resounding quiet in his wake. A man of the law learned to make these exits, to slip away before the client's self-pity became hysteria or resentment turned into violence.

Though how interesting, that an arsonist was recommended by the very traits that described a successful man of business: competence, discretion, and reasonable rates.

"I HAVE BEEN haunted by a kiss."

Franklin regarded his mistress with an unblinking bunny-eyed stare. He'd been a breeding buck and was a worthy repository of concerns relating to matters of the heart.

"I never knew. I simply and completely never knew. And now—" Now Penelope wanted to know a great deal more than Levi had shown her with a few kisses. He'd become a different man, a different animal too, in the course of that kiss. One whose greatest strength lay not in his legal mind, but in the sheer power and appeal of his male body.

"He was aroused, ready for the breeding pen. I marvel that a single kiss—a kiss with *me*—could affect him so." Penelope glanced out the library window, a location she'd chosen because it afforded a view of the drive. Franklin was keeping watch too, having sprawled along the cold panes of glass at the window's base.

"I am hatching a plot, Franklin."

Himself thumped a back leg, which had Socrates, the marmalade library cat, squinting sagaciously from a reading chair. They had a thoroughly negotiated truce, and posturing, like that thump from Franklin or the occasional hiss and growl from Socrates, were required protocol.

"My plan is flawed by a lack of adequate intelligence with which to execute it. Sixtus was forever gathering intelligence on his investments."

A sizable bay riding horse turned up the drive at a businesslike trot. That would be Thomas, a fellow of sober mien and reliable work ethic—like his rider. As Penelope slipped on her cape and made her way to the stables, she wondered if long ago, before becoming uninterested in breeding matters, Thomas had dreamed of passionate horsy-kisses, and if the fillies had speculated about offering him more than kisses for their own pleasure.

Levi was handing the reins off to a groom when Penelope gained the stable yard.

"Madam, good day. You need not have braved the cold to greet me." He took her hands in his—drat their gloves. Levi's perusal was no different from every other perusal he'd given her, though he did not kiss her cheek. "You're looking well."

She was looking tired, from having spent the entire night in the unaccustomed endeavor of scheming.

"The weather is moderate today, Levi, and I haven't ventured out since yesterday. I hope I'm not keeping you from other clients?"

For the first time, she wondered how many of those other clients were also widows. Spinsters, distant female relations, lonely women...

He brushed his lips over her cheek, bringing her a whiff of lemons and cinnamon. "You are not a client, Penelope. Sixtus was my client, you are...not a client."

And not a friend? Maybe that was a good thing. She took his proffered arm and steered him toward the foaling barn.

"We're not to pay a call on the leporines?"

"We checked on them yesterday, and Franklin sends his regards. He's taking tea in the library with Socrates." Where Penelope ought to be with her guest—and where the ghost of Sixtus lingered a little too closely for what Penelope had planned.

"One wonders what a buck rabbit and a tom-cat have to discuss," Levi mused, "beside the obvious."

Whatever he alluded to, it wasn't obvious to—*oh*.

"Do men often discuss that sort of thing when private with each other?"

"Young men discuss almost no other topic, except their wagers, their horses, or their bodily miseries. Why are we wandering about the stable yard, Penelope? We ought by rights to be having a cup with Socrates and Franklin while we assassinate the character of any bachelors or widowers who escaped scrutiny yesterday."

"Odette foaled out last week, a fine filly."

He gave her a look, not a man-of-business look, perhaps a man-who-means-business look.

"My congratulations to the new mother."

Drat and blast. How was a woman to advance her scheme upon a fellow when he could detect her intentions in less than a moment?

"We brought Agnes in to keep them company. Agnes isn't due until March, though Mr. Davey suspects twins because she's carrying so low."

Penelope was babbling. Fortunately, they'd arrived at the foaling stalls, where Odette—nigh a ton of equine motherhood if she weighed an ounce—was standing over the foal who slept on the thick bed of straw. Agnes, a mare of equally imposing dimensions, dozed against the near side of her own oversize loose box providing the horsy equivalent of moral support.

"Are they sisters?" Levi asked. "They'd make a nice matched team if one's tastes ran to chestnuts."

Pen took off her glove and offered Odette a scratch under the mare's hairy chin. "Cousins. Squire Hungerford would know their genealogies back to the Flood, did he own them."

"Hungerford, whom you will not marry."

Levi's voice had come from directly behind her, and Penelope could feel him, a solid wall of Levi Sparrow in riding attire, his coat open, his hair windblown. She wanted to run her fingers through that hair, but would have to face him to do it. Instead, she stroked her hand over Odette's great, velvety roman nose.

"I certainly hope I'm not destined to become Mrs. Hungerford. I've set the squire on Diana's trail. They'd suit admirably. Do you ever consider remarrying, Levi?"

He reached around her, offering the mare a sniff of his fingers, which were bare now. "Not often. Marriage, particularly remarriage, is a complicated undertaking."

While kissing was the simplest thing in the world. Penelope turned, seized the lapels of Levi's jacket, and went up on her toes to mash her mouth against his. She missed, hitting his jaw instead of his lips.

"Penelope Carring—"

She found his mouth, and he sighed against her kiss. He went still, not resisting, exactly. The blasted man was *thinking* about whether to kiss her, which would not do at all. Taking a leaf from his album, Penelope wedged her leg between his, snugly, unapologetically.

Let him think about that.

Except—Penelope's initiative did not go as planned. Levi's arms came around her just as snugly, and his fingers threaded through her hair. His tongue dallied with the corners of her lips, and Penelope could no longer manage her own balance.

"I've got you," Levi growled. In contrast to his voice, his kiss gentled, becoming lazy and s*eductive.*

Great balls of bunny fur, what the man could do with his mouth. He wheedled, he flirted, he dared, and offered worlds of sensation and emotion on a lemon- and cinnamon-flavored platter. Pen treated herself to the cool, silky pleasure of his hair beneath her fingers, heard the mare whuffling softly—encouragingly?—behind them.

"No thinking, Penelope. Only kissing."

Only kissing? She was bent back, completely dependent on him to keep her on her feet, and against her thigh, even through her cape and his breeches, a solid tumescence arose. When Levi shifted to use his mouth at the spot where her shoulder joined her neck, Penelope understood why a lady's knees might go weak.

"I could take you here, Penelope. Right up against this stall. Is that what you want?"

His voice flayed her remaining wits, until the sense of his words sank in. "It might be."

Gone in a blink. The heat, the strength, the passion of him, all whisked away to leave a dark-haired, considering stranger two feet away.

"I suppose that wasn't the right thing to say?" she asked.

Irritation flicked over his features, and beneath that, something else—bewilderment? Men of business likely developed a fine sense of how to mask their emotions.

"What are you about, Penelope? And no stalling while you organize your testimony. We'll sort this out here and now."

"We'll sort it out in the feed room." She took him by the hand, which even given their two shared kisses was a bold gesture. He came along, though. That was heartening.

They reached the small room in the center of the barn where grain, spare headstalls, lead ropes, and grooming supplies were kept. Foaling supplies were here too, though when a mare had decided it was time to give birth, one mostly watched and prayed.

Levi towed her over to a bench and sat her down. When he'd closed the door behind them and flicked the lock closed, he turned to her, hands on hips.

"What are you about, madam, kissing me without warning where anybody might come along?"

"Do you interrogate witnesses like this, Levi? Behind closed doors, hands on hips, glowering like Headmaster with a naughty first former? Will I get a birching if you don't like my answers?"

That reply startled him. His reaction was limited to a momentary lift of his eyebrow and an instant of speculation in his blue eyes.

"We will not discuss birchings if you expect me to remain coherent. I kissed you yesterday to make a point, and did so more or less at your invitation. Today you're the one kissing me, and I don't recall issuing any invitations."

He wasn't as composed as he'd like her to believe. He kept glancing around, head up, like a horse in a new pasture. The air was thick with the scents of grain, hay and livestock, though Levi looked as if he expected the footman to intrude with the tea service at any moment.

"I am a widow, Levi. Why shouldn't I engage in a dalliance?" She heard the hounds of the shire baying in the distant reaches of her imagination and prayed her insouciant tone was convincing.

"You may engage in any dalliance you please, Penelope, but why me? Why now?"

Because with you it could be more than a dalliance. Much, much more.

In defense of her wits, she studied his boots. "My marriage did not leave me with a great deal of experience. I would address that ignorance before I choose another mate."

Her marriage had left her with no experience whatsoever. No need to share that detail when Levi was regarding her as if she'd sprouted bunny ears.

"All you seek is a dalliance?"

Like any good solicitor, he was trying to pen her in with yes or no answers. Like anybody who'd raised rabbits, Penelope knew to dodge off to the side.

"I enjoy kissing you, Levi. I have little practice with such matters, though, and there's so much more—"

He was beside her in two long strides, settling on the narrow bench uninvited. He also took Penelope's hand in his, his grip warm and not the least tentative.

"You must be careful, dear lady. You can't accost anybody who catches your fancy. You're a wealthy widow, as far as they know. Men will try to take advantage."

"You will not take advantage of me." Not if she delivered herself to him naked and wrapped in a Turkey carpet.

"A husband who esteemed you would not take advantage. You're hell-bent on marriage, and this, this flight of fancy, is some form of bridal nerves. I'm sure of it."

A low shot, considering he wasn't entirely wrong. "You've been a bride, Levi, that such an experience is within your ken?"

"Two of my sisters were brides." He kissed her knuckles. "I was a groom."

Not only did Penelope raise angora rabbits, she was also the mistress of a large working estate. Taking a hint from the mares who had refined hard-to-get to a rare art, she rose and headed for the door. She would have swished her tail if she'd had one, and tossed her mane.

"If you cannot accommodate me, Levi, then I'll simply invite Hungerford around on a weekday afternoon—"

Levi's hand slammed flat against the door directly in her line of vision, his breath fanned across the back of her neck. A buck bunny headed for the breeding pen would not have moved more quickly than Sir Leviticus Sparrow had crossed the feed room.

"You will do no such thing. If you must have your infernal holiday dalliance, Penelope Carrington, you will have it with me."

Chapter Four

Any man who'd served on the Peninsula, any young man who'd completed his education in old London Towne, learned that some women gloried in the pleasures of the flesh. Such dear creatures gave up any pretense of propriety—Levi needed to believe this had been a choice on their parts—in exchange for a trade they found to their liking, or at least coin they found to their liking.

In a separate species entirely were proper women, ladies who guarded their virtue unto death, ladies sheltered from all that was sordid and earthly. One courted and married such women.

The theory of the two different types of women, with their mutually exclusive spheres of operation, had held up well throughout Levi's marriage. Restrained passion, even thinly veiled tolerance for procreative activities, was to be expected in a wife.

A loving husband did not complain about such restraint. He respected it, kissed his wife's cheek, and repaired to his own bedroom after easing his needs. He engaged in frequent bouts of self-gratification, and he pursued his work with an intensity that made sleep a necessity at the end of each day.

Alas, the theory that separated women into naughty and nice took a sound beating when, two years after Ann's death, Levi had been called to London on a case, and he'd found himself keeping discreet company with the widowed cousin of a former neighbor.

She'd yodeled her passion to the rafters and clutched Levi to her breast like a female sailor on shore leave after two years at sea. She'd expected him to stay the entire night in her bed, availing herself of his charms as much as three times between midnight and dawn. She had, in short, opened his eyes.

When her immediate successor—a vicar's widow, no less—had behaved similarly, Levi's theory of differing varieties of women had been bludgeoned into oblivion.

He had accepted the intriguing notion that decent women could be passionate.

The corollary under consideration now was that Penelope Carrington was such a decent woman, and she wanted to be passionate with *him*.

"Levi, where are we going?"

Sweet Saints. He was holding hands with her before horses, rabbits, and any other curious onlookers. He untangled their fingers, wrapped her hand over his forearm, and continued their progress toward the house.

"We are going to bed, Penelope, because that seems to be what you want. A gentleman doesn't argue with a lady."

Not when she was Penelope Carrington offering a dalliance to Leviticus Sparrow. He would deal with the rest of it—the courting, the threat of litigation from *that woman*, the sorting and cataloguing and pondering, later.

Beside him, Penelope kept pace. Her staff would be discreet, of course. Levi would be discreet. A man trained in the law might wonder if one could be discreetly passionate. Levi, however, didn't give a flying, fur-lined damn.

He held the door for her. "Say something, Penelope. Make polite protestations, pretend to misunderstand, or indicate your consent."

As she walked past him, her hand brushed delicately over his falls. An accident, to all appearances, the sort of touch that happened and was assiduously ignored.

"My cloak, if you please?" She turned her back to him, the gesture both imperious and submissive—or maybe Levi was simply that ready for the breeding pen. He peeled the garment away from her and hung it on a hook. Before he could shrug out of his coat, Penelope had come around behind him to ease it from his shoulders.

She let his riding coat slide down his arms, then folded it, and while he watched, took a whiff of the sleeve.

"Cinnamon and lemons."

His corollary underwent a refinement: Certain decent women used propriety like an incendiary device, such that a man became so bloody aroused he was at risk for taking her in the foyer of her own domicile.

Levi slapped his gloves onto the sideboard. "Upstairs, Penelope."

He'd lecture her later about a staff that left the front door unattended, and lecture himself about ordering a woman into bed.

Though she was already on the presentation staircase, five steps ahead of him, and probably swaying her backside about like that purposely. He followed her, eyes on the prize, and wondered if this was what the buck rabbits felt—stupid, happy, aroused, and determined.

Ambling the barns with old Sixtus, Levi had seen a few of those occasions. Seen the frantic gleam in dark rabbit eyes, seen the young fellows spend before they even reached their lady's side. The memory gave him some purchase against his disintegrating composure.

Penelope paused outside her private sitting room. "Shall I ring for a tray, Levi?" Her voice held a gratifying hint of a tremor. "Perhaps later." He reached past her and opened the door. "After you?"

She squared her shoulders and sashayed past him, leaving a hint of roses in her wake. He followed her into the cheery haven of femininity, where he'd taken a hundred cups of tea, and locked the door behind them.

Penelope kept walking, marching toward her private apartments.

"Penelope?"

She stopped, turned, and gave him a look more impatient than seductive. "The bedroom is this way, Levi."

"I'm aware of that, but you seem to have lost track of one pertinent detail regarding the present situation." *His* voice had no tremor. His self-restraint, however, was quivering at the breaking point. "Come here, Penelope."

Being female, she held her ground, looking him over again. Levi stayed where he was and kept quiet until she stepped closer, then closer still.

"What am I forgetting, Levi?"

Without touching her anywhere else, he grazed his lips across hers, gently, slowly. A great sigh went out of her. He repeated the caress of his mouth over hers as her arms settled about his waist.

"I forget everything when you do that, Levi. Your kisses—"

On the third pass, he did not retreat. He sipped at her mouth, tasting peppermint and eagerness—also a little uncertainty. "You forget, my dear, that—"

She groaned and went up on her toes, which meant Levi had to steady her in his embrace. Penelope Carrington was the perfect armful of female, soft, curvy, and warm. While she kissed him and nuzzled at him and made delightful yearning sounds, she got softer, curvier, and warmer.

"I forget...?"

"You forget—" Levi traced his hand down the side of her ribs, slowly, slowly, coming within inches of her breasts. She was corseted, and he would delight in relieving her of her stays. "You forget that *I am not a rabbit.*"

In the face of that eternal verity, she rested her forehead against his chest, which meant Levi couldn't see her face. He could feel her, though, pliant and lovely against him. How long had it been since he'd delighted in the simple feel of a willing female wrapped in his arms?

"I do not know how these affairs are conducted, Levi, how one prosecutes a dalliance, other than to expect copulation is involved." She sounded like a barrister addressing opposing counsel. All big words and careful admissions.

"I am glad you don't know. I have little experience with it myself."

She looked up, her gaze suggesting she needed to verify that he wasn't jesting. He let her see that he was in earnest, and she gifted him with such a smile—shy, intimate, pleased.

Pleased, *with him.*

"We go on as we prefer, Penelope. I prefer to savor the gift of intimacy with you rather than devour it in a headlong fit of gluttony."

She was clearly torn. She wanted to *be* savored, but wanted an agenda as well, a map to guide her around the worst heartaches and embarrassments a dalliance might entail. That much, Levi could give her.

"Here's how this works, my dear. We disport for our mutual pleasure, as friends and as intimates, and when you say the disporting is at an end, it ends."

Hopefully, it ended with a ring on her finger.

"You can prevent a child?"

"The only way to entirely prevent conception is to abstain. We can share pleasures short of joining or be cautious in our intimacies." He would not use the careful, Latinate word she'd chosen: copulation. Let the rabbits copulate. With Penelope Carrington, Levi intended to make love. He kissed her temple. "If we create a child, we will marry. You can have no doubt of that, or our dalliance stops before it's begun."

She nodded against his chest. He hoped she was blushing. He also hoped that marrying Penelope—should God grant him that blessing—didn't precipitate litigation for breach of promise that would mean professional and social ruin. Hope had never been his strongest suit. He vowed to improve on that.

"Levi?"

"My dear?" *My love.*

"Will you help me take off my dress?"

Such courage. "If you will assist me out of my clothes as well."

He let her take the initiative, let her be the one to lead him into her bedroom, an inviting, airy space featuring an enormous bed embowered by green velvet hangings. The quilt sported red roses on white, the whole of it welcoming in a way that was both domestic and feminine.

"You like soft textures," he said, running his hand over the quilt, which was, of all things, flannel. "Is that why you raise those rabbits?"

She untied his cravat, took his sleeve buttons and cravat pin. "Anybody would love stroking my bunnies. Angora wool soothes the soul. You like fine clothing."

He did, which was an insight. Part of the pleasure of being a man of business was looking the part: competent, well put together, tastefully prosperous.

"I'd like for you to get me out of my fine clothing, Penelope."

She smiled that secret, pleased smile, folded his shirt and set it on the clothes press. He was left standing in only his breeches, wonderfully aroused, while she was fully clothed.

"When does your monthly befall you, Penelope?"

Her smile disappeared like a rabbit popped into a hedge.

Levi wanted to kick himself. Penelope wasn't like those other widows, and certainly wasn't a soiled dove. Regarding this topic, she might be more like Ann, who would have had a tart lecture about a woman's bodily privacy had he asked her such a question.

"In about two weeks. Why?"

Bloody hell. "You are fertile now, in all likelihood. We will limit our pleasures."

She looked at the bed, not at him. "You will explain this to me?"

"Later. Now I will be your lady's maid."

Discordant, uncomfortable thoughts hopped around the edges of his lust as he undid the dozens of hooks down the back of Penelope's dress.

This was how he'd pictured his nights with Ann. A contented domestic intimacy, such that he'd have no need of a valet, and she'd become comfortable with his tending to her at the end of the day. He would brush her hair at night, she'd watch him shave in the morning.

Marriage to Ann hadn't been like that. She'd kissed his cheek after dinner and wished him pleasant dreams.

If he'd wanted to visit her later, he'd tell her, "I'll be up in a bit, if that suits."

She'd had two answers: "Perhaps another time," which was for when her female organs kept a calendar different from the one in Levi's head, or, "In a bit, then."

Just once, might Ann have smiled at him and suggested he make haste to her side?

Penelope kept her back to him, her nape begging to be kissed in the broad light of day.

"Will you undo my stays, Levi?"

"Soon." Levi slid his arm around her waist and set his lips to her shoulder. "You carry the scent of roses even here, and your skin is softer than that wool you spin."

She drew in a breath as he brushed his fingers over her back. "This is how you savor me?"

She said nothing more for long, long moments while Levi used his mouth to learn the contours of the bones at the top of her spine and his fingers to take every God's blessed pin from her hair. He was pleased to see she didn't lace too tightly, nor did she tense when he had her standing in only her chemise, still facing away from him.

"Don't turn around, Penelope. Give me one minute."

"One minute only, Levi. Whatever you're about, standing here in my shift in the middle of a room with little fire is not how I'd intended—"

He turned her by the shoulders. "I folded your clothes most carefully. We'll warm up the bed in no time."

Oh, the look on her face. The wondering, awestruck, pleased look on her face. "Levi, you are *naked*."

He'd gambled, stripping off all his finery for her, and he'd apparently won. "This savoring business goes both ways, Penelope."

"You are completely, utterly, nakedly lovely."

While he stood before her, cock at full salute against his belly, Penelope went on an inspection of his person. She walked 'round him one way, then the other. She ran her hands over his chest and back—*and* his derriere—and took a nibble of his shoulder. Her touch was soft, warm, and lovely. He could have spent merely from the sensations of her hands on his belly and thighs.

"This part of you," she said, frowning down at his cock, "looks quite in readiness for breeding."

I am not a rabbit. Levi developed instant sympathy for those young bucks unable to hold their fire when faced with impending delights.

"That part of me is possessed of as much patience as you need, Penelope. Though I'd rather exercise my patience on the bed."

"Shall I take off my chemise?"

If she did, he'd lose all dignity. "You'd rather leave it on, wouldn't you?"

She blushed, a hot pink testament to inexperience that rose from her chest up her neck to her hairline. "I'll leave it on for now, Levi."

Thank God. "Into bed, Penelope. We'll cuddle, and you can decide what to do about that chemise." Assuming he didn't tear it to shreds first.

She climbed onto the bed, taunting him with a flash of delectable, well rounded derriere, and then flopped back the covers to welcome him onto the mattress. When he settled in beside her, she slipped an arm beneath his neck and tucked her body right next to his.

He had said they'd cuddle. It would not occur to a woman who cuddled rabbits and cats that she was to be the cuddlee rather than the cuddler.

"I understand better why Franklin is such a sanguine fellow," Levi said. "You excel at cuddling and you smell divine, Penelope."

To his surprise, he was rather accomplished at cuddling himself. While she played with his hair and he with hers, they talked of the years he'd spent studying the law, of Gervaise Stoneleigh, whom Penelope decided had been made lonely by brilliance. Between Penelope's explorations of Levi's chest and ears, they described favorite desserts and books and music. As Levi talked about campaigning across Spain, Penelope stroked her fingers over him, lazily campaigning her way past his reason.

And yet, when she leaned up and kissed him, Levi was nearly surprised. Penelope's hand sliding down, down, to trace the length of his engorged cock nigh unmanned him.

He retaliated by cupping her breast, an exquisite handful of female softness, topped by a ruched nipple that fit delightfully against his palm.

"Enough savoring, my lady."

She didn't turn loose of him. "What comes after savoring?"

He applied a touch of pressure to her nipple. "Pleasuring."

"Levi, I don't know—"

Kissing was part of pleasuring. In the course of kissing her, Levi shifted them so Penelope was on her back, and the Chemise of Perpetual Modesty went sailing across the room.

"You first," he said. "The lady's pleasure always comes first."

Not all ladies were capable of experiencing pleasure, but Penelope was. Levi knew that like he knew the elements of a valid contract.

To his immense satisfaction, the lady's pleasure also came quickly. She liked the attention he paid her breasts, arching into his hand, clutching him to her when he settled his mouth over her nipple.

He liked that when Penelope began to move restlessly against the sheets, it was all he could do not to mount her and thrust home. Instead, he trailed a hand down to tease at her curls.

She went still, opened her eyes and lay panting on her back. "There's more isn't there, Levi? You won't leave me in this condition and call it pleasuring, will you?"

He brushed her hair back from her forehead. "Tell me about your condition."

"I am expiring with want, fevered and desperate, for you, Levi, for more of your touches and kisses. Why are you looking at me like that?"

Such words. Words freely given, *to him.*

"We'll make you want harder, Penelope, then harder still." He urged her over onto her side so he could arrange himself along her back and insinuate a hand between her legs. A few minutes of exploring damp heat, and he knew she liked his third finger applied just *there* in a steady rhythm with a sure pressure. When she came, he felt how her body clutched at the pleasure he gave her, tightly and then more tightly still, until she was silently consumed with it, shaking against him, then sighing with the aftermath.

"Levi."

To hear his name whispered like that, rosy with affection, laced with a touch of awe, made his heart thump oddly against his ribs. Penelope took his hand from between her legs, shifted so she was lying as much on her belly as her side, and used his arm to drape his larger frame over her, a blanket of male heat and desire over her prone form.

"May I conclude my lady is pleasured?"

Her pleasure mattered to him. Ann hadn't sought that sort of satisfaction, and had Levi forced it upon her, she would have been vastly discommoded. Penelope's pleasure was a different matter altogether.

"I am thoroughly pleasured." She kissed his fingers, which had to bear the fragrance of her arousal. The notion was intoxicating. "You are not."

"Hold still." He fitted himself to her closely, so his cock was wrapped in her heat, angled to rub along her sex without risking penetration. "Hold very still."

She braced herself back against him, letting him thrust into the slick, sweet torment that wasn't quite coupling. He wanted this to last, wanted to savor this too, but it had been too long since he'd indulged himself, and his reserves of restraint were sorely depleted.

He came in one endless cataclysm of satisfaction. He didn't worry that he was imposing, that he was taking too long, that he was making a mess, that he was too heavy. For a succession of moments, wrapped around Penelope Carrington, Levi simply and completely gave himself over to pleasure.

And then, when he'd kissed her nape and tucked the covers up around them, gave himself over to sleep.

He awoke with a profound sense of relaxation permeating his body, mind, and spirit. Penelope slept on though he was half-lying on her, his nose buried in her hair.

Soft hair for a redhead, fragrant, silky—

Before his cock could add a few more adjectives to the litany, Levi untangled himself from Penelope. He eased from the bed, made sure she was completely covered, put the wash water to use, and got into his clothes.

A remarkable encounter, all around. That Penelope should choose him to break the fast that had started after her wedding night was extraordinary in itself. The pleasure had been profound, the conversation...

The cuddling.

Levi let Thomas walk the entire distance home, the better to wallow in memories that would take their place among his most cherished recollections. The proprietary manner in which Penelope had wrapped him in her arms, the way she had moved against his hand, the shy passion that had blossomed into roaring female lust.

As Levi handed the reins to his groom, unbuckled his spurs, and turned for the house, a pang of grief hit him.

Outside the stables, all was brisk sunshine, freedom, and the lingering scent of Penelope on his skin. Inside his house were coal fires, responsibilities, client files, and the whole sticky, stinking mess of *that woman*'s designs on him.

He took a deep breath of pure December air, summoned the feel of Penelope in a boneless sprawl against his naked body, and forced himself to walk into the house.

Where he found, sitting right on top of his stack of correspondence, a note from Miss Amanda Houston, informing him she would adore the honor of his escort to the Christmas assembly in two weeks' time.

"I HAD A specific purpose for my call this afternoon, Mrs. Carrington."

Mr. Amblewise was such a serious fellow, though kind. Very kind. When Penelope's sister Doreen pestered him with theological questions, he was the soul of patience.

"I'm always pleased to see my friends," Penelope lied smoothly. She would have been much more pleased to continue dreaming of the unbelievable intimacies Levi had shared with her. "More tea?"

Amblewise's blond brows twitched, as much a facial tic as an expression. "Please, and perhaps some of those excellent sandwiches?"

Vicaring was hungry work when undertaken with such sincerity. Penelope refilled her caller's plate and wondered what Mr. Amblewise would think of a visit to the rabbits. He'd probably have a sermon all ready on the virtues of meekness.

Franklin gave one mighty thump with a back leg from his place under the piano, causing Mr. Amblewise to startle with a sandwich halfway to his mouth.

"That is a very disagreeable noise. Do they make it for any reason?"

"They make it as a warning, I suppose. The back legs that propel a rabbit across the heath at such speed can also lay open a man's arm. Then too, rabbits are well supplied with teeth. One doesn't want to cross a rabbit, particularly not a breeding buck, unnecessarily."

I am not a rabbit. Though hadn't Levi been an endless treat to pet and cuddle and enjoy? Pen's mind fairly boggled with what had befallen her less than two hours earlier. No wonder rabbits were such happy creatures.

Amblewise cleared his throat and kept his unfinished sandwich in his hand. "As I was saying, my call today has a specific purpose, Mrs. Carrington."

If he started quoting Ecclesiastes, Penelope would stomp her foot—loudly.

"I'm sure you'll enlighten me directly, Mr. Amblewise." Though not like Levi had enlightened her.

"Indeed. As your spiritual counselor, and as pastor to our little flock at St. Melangell's, I have watched with great attention and admiration the manner in which you have borne your grief this past year. I have kept you ever in my prayers, prayed that the burden on your spirit might be no heavier than is meet for a lady whose spouse went to his reward in the fullness of his years."

He had a lovely voice, a voice more substantial than his slight, pale frame, and yet his words said nothing, not until he got to the part about, "... and there comes a time when, though it requires courage and fortitude, one must walk again in the proper society of one's devoted friends. I believe that time has come for you, my dear Mrs. Carrington, and thus extend to you my sincere hope that you will regard me as your escort at the Christmas assembly."

Should she offer a murmured "amen" in lieu of "more cakes?" A rumored leak in the parish hall could mean the holiday gathering would default to her own ballroom, and thus, of all women, she might well require no escort.

She certainly did not want the vicar hanging about her all evening, for in observance of the waning days of her mourning, she would not dance a single set.

"You raise an interesting point, Mr. Amblewise, and remind me that winter is advancing. I will quite possibly host the assembly—Sixtus always enjoyed the holiday gatherings—but am concerned that my sisters will feel self-conscious should they not have escorts for the occasion."

Though her sisters would be dancing the night away, while Pen kept an eye on the dessert table, the punch bowls, and the young men alternating between the two. Sixtus had more or less sponsored the living, and thus Penelope had taken a generous interest in the assemblies in St. Melangell's parish hall.

"Your sisters, Mrs. Carrington? Both of your sisters?"

"They do tend to go about as a pair." Then the implication of his question struck her: All those earnest questions from Doreen, Amblewise bowing lingeringly over

Doreen's pretty hand, Doreen's penchant for sketching knights errant of ascetic mien with prominent crosses on their banners and shields.

I am not a rabbit, either. Pen got to her feet and rang for a servant to take the tray away.

"You know, Mr. Amblewise, I'm sponsoring this assembly—my first since Sixtus's death—whether we hold it at Carrington Close or the parish hall. Sixtus would want me to see to the festivities, but having to play hostess will leave me very concerned for Doreen."

He was on his feet, eyebrows nearly vibrating. "For Miss Doreen? She seems the veriest angel to me. Knows her Book of Common Prayer by heart."

Doreen had probably memorized the thing in a fit of the ruthless determination for which any girl with two older sisters might become well known. Penelope laced her arm through Amblewise's and escorted him from the formal parlor.

"Doreen's older sister is as yet unmarried, Mr. Amblewise. For any young lady, that presents the prospect of lonely, lonely years while she waits for her turn with the dashing swains, and Doreen does so love to dance."

Dancing was a touchy subject. Dissenters weren't the only ones to frown on it, nor on spirits, nor on gambling for farthing points. If Amblewise was to be coaxed into Doreen's gun sights, he'd need a goodly helping of tolerance.

"High spirits early in life require an outlet," Amblewise declared. He was perhaps five years Doreen's senior.

Penelope beamed up at him as they approached the front door. "Then I'm sure you'll enjoy standing up with her." She stuffed a box of sweets into his hands—the kitchen was nothing if not attentive—wished him a very good day, and thanked him kindly for calling on her.

Then went back up to her bedroom, stripped off every stitch, and closed her eyes, the better to catch even a hint of lemons and cinnamon wafting from the pillows.

Chapter Five

"WHAT DO YOU advise?" Levi asked. "You're a veteran of many encounters with the fairer sex, and one of the cleverest barristers in the realm had no words of wisdom for me. Then too, you'll know something of animal magnetism, whatever that is."

Franklin wiggled his nose slowly. He reclined on a parlor windowsill, the cold glass doubtless appealing to his well insulated sense of comfort.

"I cannot bear the thought of our Penelope marrying some buffoon who won't appreciate her," Levi went on, "but my own situation is complicated."

Franklin was the largest exponent of his species Levi had ever beheld, and yet, the rabbit hopped from the window to the back of the sofa, to sofa seat, to the floor, as delicately as a bird. His destination was a basket of correspondence sitting beside the rocking chair Penelope had angled near the fire.

"I'll not avail myself of a lady's correspondence," Levi said. "Not when she might join me at any—Penelope. Good day."

The object of Levi's delight and worry quietly closed the parlor door and stood two yards away, looking delectable in a dark green velvet dress and lavender shawl.

"I'm not exactly wearing second mourning," she said, "but this dress is warm."

"Sixtus would never have judged you for elevating practicality over convention, and neither should you judge yourself."

Franklin thumped a back foot at that sentiment and resumed his place by the cool of the window.

"Franklin agrees," Penelope said.

"Has a single intimate encounter made strangers of us, Penelope?" For she remained where she was, right by the door. Levi crossed the room and brushed a kiss to her cheek. "I would not for anything jeopardize my friendship with you. If my attentions were not to your liking—"

He'd get drunk for a week then likely drown himself in a rain barrel. Penelope spared him that admission by placing two rose-scented fingers over his lips.

"Your attentions were very much to my liking. Very much, Levi."

"Do I hear a 'but' appended to those assurances?" He heard something, and considering he was a man encumbered by a self-appointed fiancée, he should not even have been listening.

Penelope went up on her toes and kissed him on the mouth. She was a fast learner, having already acquired the knack of twining herself around him as she tasted him, of pressing herself against him in a most agreeable and distracting manner. Had Franklin not delivered a hearty thump to the windowsill, Levi might have let the kiss rage unchecked right over to the velvet sofa—or the floor.

"Penelope, we must talk."

She withdrew from his embrace. "About the bachelors? I cannot consider them, Levi, not after what transpired upstairs yesterday. There's a further impediment to my plan to marry by Christmas, one I have yet to discuss with you."

A fiancée qualified as a substantial impediment.

"Then let us visit the barns and talk." Cold air being an aid to a man's focus in certain circumstances.

"You always listen to me, Levi. That's one of the things I lov—I esteem most about you."

She'd nearly admitted to loving something about him. A blast of weather straight from the arctic would not have cooled the pleasure Levi took in her partial admission. Fortunately for his composure, Penelope consented to walk the aisles between pens of furry rabbits, arm linked with Levi's as she had a hundred times before.

"Bathsheba is not her usual self," Levi said when they paused beside her pen. "Has she been truant again?"

The rabbit was a fine dun-colored doe, on the large side, and possessed of a luxurious coat. Something in her eyes was dull, though, or turned inward.

"She hasn't caught," Penelope said. "Not for lack of trying, either. She's disappointed in herself because she'll have no babies this spring."

The rabbit looked bored rather than disappointed. "Penelope, talk to me."

Her reply was to bundle against Levi while all the bunnies looked on. "I'm disappointed in myself, Levi."

He stroked a hand over her hair. "For taking me to your bed yesterday?" That would be no less than he deserved, a scheming hoyden insisting he marry her and the woman he longed for no longer interested.

"Never for that. Levi, I was not honest with you."

Levi had grown so inured to the vicissitudes of his trade that he nearly expected otherwise decent people to lie to him.

"You didn't dissemble about anything of significance, Penelope. I've an instinct for falsehoods."

"I said I lacked experience, Levi, but what I ought to have said was that my marriage to Sixtus was in name only."

Levi at once resented his winter clothing—because it interfered with the intimacy of their embrace—and was grateful for it, because simply holding Penelope stirred his desire.

"Your marriage to Sixtus was as loving and devoted as any I've seen." On his worst widowed nights, he'd wondered if old Sixtus had not enjoyed greater devotion from his wife than Levi had ever enjoyed from Ann.

"Sixtus was all that was dear," Penelope said, "but our marriage was not consummated."

Levi could tell by the tension suffusing her that the disclosure was upsetting. "Non-consummation isn't grounds for an annulment, Penelope, and under English law, vows cannot be dissolved posthumously in any case."

She stepped back and ran a hand over Bathsheba's plush coat. "Levi, I am yet chaste, though I'm a widow. This will not do."

He sorted possibilities when he'd rather have kissed her.

"You do not want your next husband to know of Sixtus's inability?"

"Of course not, but my next husband will also expect me to know what I'm about. I grasp almost nothing of a wife's conjugal duties, and yesterday only proved that."

"Yesterday proved a number of things. Let's visit the new foal, shall we?"

Levi tossed out that gambit, because he suspected Penelope was working up her courage to proposition him into relieving her of her virginity. He'd like nothing better, but not because Penelope needed an expedited course in wife-craft before she wed some other man.

Penelope gave Bathsheba a final pat, then took Levi's arm as they crossed to the foaling barn. Save for the horses, the place was deserted, exactly as Levi had hoped. He led a silent Penelope into the feed room, and this time he both locked the door and propped a bag of oats against it.

"That sack has to weigh nearly half what I do," Penelope said. "You toss it about as if it holds feathers."

"You are diminutive, and I'm highly motivated to ensure we have privacy." He dared not take the place beside her when she settled on the narrow bench, though, because his breeding organs had plans for their privacy other than conversation.

"Please sit, Levi. When you loom over me, I can't think straight."

He piled a second bag of oats against the door and *then* sat. "You labor under a misconception, Penelope."

"I labor under the prospect of ruin for my sisters," she said, taking his hand. "I've added some names to my list."

"You think women married for more than few weeks must all be sirens, wise in the ways of passion, skilled at pleasing their husbands and enjoying the intimate varieties of marital bliss. You are mistaken."

She tucked her chin lower, into a scarf of soft blue that matched her eyes. "I know not all unions are blissful. My own parents barely speak, and yet, somehow, they managed three daughters."

What Levi had to share with her now would have felt disloyal when he'd been newly bereaved. Eight years after the loss of his wife, the words were merely sad and honest.

"Ann never troubled to acquaint herself with the intimate pleasures I might have afforded her. I gather from what's said at The Duke's Arms around a late-night hand of cards, many men aren't even permitted to visit their wives' beds once a few children have come along. No decent fellow will expect you to bring anything other than marital goodwill to the conjugal bed."

Levi intended to relieve Penelope's fears with his admission, to assure her that sexual skill mattered little compared to her many endearing traits.

"You are not relieved," he observed when Penelope got up and began to pace the small, shadowed space.

She kicked the sacks of oats, then kicked them again. "I wish I knew how to curse, Leviticus Sparrow."

Definitely not relief. "Curse at me?"

"Blast and drat, not at you. At the situation."

Levi wasn't relieved, either. "What aspect of the situation?" And which situation? His? Hers? A situation involving some daft old squire who'd gone down on creaking knee while Levi had been pouring out his troubles to Gervaise Stoneleigh?

"I'm trying to trick you back into my bed, Levi, and you won't be tricked. I must rid myself of an inconvenient store of chastity, and I cannot abide the notion of enduring that process with anybody but you, and you refuse to oblige me!"

"Penelope, you'll worry the horses if you continue to shout." She'd already worried him, for Penelope Carrington never shouted.

"Then let them be worried, for I am worried. I had hoped that if I could entice you to my bed—as if a virgin widow knows anything of enticing—then you might enjoy the encounter sufficiently to"—she kicked the oats again—"offer for me."

Levi took her by the arm and drew her into his lap. "You seek an offer of marriage from me?"

She heaved a sigh and wrapped an arm around his shoulders. "Yes. Only from you."

PEN HAD ALWAYS treasured the sense of calm Levi wore like a well tailored great coat. Calm voice, calm eyes, calm hands, that was Levi.

She wanted to shriek at him now.

"You see me as a known quantity," he said, linking his arms around her. "A man already broken to the marital bridle, a connection with Sixtus."

"You're an idiot." Penelope kissed him, because a fellow's lap was an excellent vantage point from which to share kisses with him. "I see you as my friend, Levi, in whom I can repose all my confidence and trust." More kisses, as if she'd kiss sense into his handsome head. "I see you as my lover, the only man with whom I crave marital intimacy."

He did not kiss her back, but instead, pressed his cheek to hers. "I have not been honest, either, Penelope, though you do me great honor."

You do me great honor was the polite prelude to a firm rejection. Penelope scrambled off Levi's lap and settled on the stacked sacks of oats, the only seat available out of kissing range from Levi.

"I have made a fool of myself," she said, arranging her skirts in an effort to muster some dignity.

"Not that, my dear, but my situation is complicated. You said you wanted a dalliance, Penelope, and I had hoped that I might build on your interest, until an offer from me would meet with your approval."

"It would," Penelope replied, though the look in Levi's eyes was not that of a man on the verge of a proposal.

He stood, and he was quite tall. Penelope was ready to scramble to her feet when Levi lowered himself beside her, sitting right on the dusty floorboards.

"I have a problem, Penelope, in that at present, I am not precisely in a position to make an offer."

Not precisely in a position... Solicitors used words as deftly as a reaper wielded a scythe or a swordsman his foil. Dread collided with uncertainty in Pen's belly.

"Are you married, Levi?"

"No, I am not, nor do I expect to be in the near future, but I might well be engaged."

Marriage was a contractual business, though increasingly, a sentimental one as well.

"Either you are engaged or you're not, Levi."

"She says I am, I say I am not. I haven't yet found a means to resolve the matter that won't result in scandal for my sisters, and Daphne is not yet married."

Daphne resembled Levi most closely, though she was nearly fifteen years his junior. Tall, shy, serious, and dark-haired rather than fashionably pale. Levi would never jeopardize her chances at a happy union.

"You've been waiting until Daphne has a husband to resolve this, haven't you?"

"I have, but then, I don't see a resolution even then. The lady is most adamant that poems I wrote to her constituted an offer of marriage, while I know they did not. I missed my wife, and the verses from a certain perspective are ambiguously worded. By the time I understood that this woman had designs on me, I'd already escorted her to a number of social functions."

Penelope cast back to formal dinners, assemblies, hunt balls, and came up with a name.

"Amanda Houston." The greatest bitch ever to make up numbers at an otherwise enjoyable house party.

"How did you guess?"

Pen wished he'd protested or tossed any other lady's name into the discussion, for Amanda Houston was shrewd, pretty, and determined.

"Every time I saw you with her, Levi, I worried a little. You made a handsome couple, but her expression when she beheld you wasn't…wasn't…"

Levi sat cross-legged on the floor, not a much-respected man of business, not a decorated veteran of Wellington's staff, but a man engaged—ironic word!—by an enemy he could not comprehend.

"She regards you as a prize, Levi, like a stud bull led home from the auction, helpless to deny her bidding."

More than Penelope fretted for her family, more than she fretted for herself, she now worried for Levi. He'd be quietly miserable married to Amanda Houston, and Amanda would delight in that.

"I am not a rabbit, Penelope, and I am also not a breeding bull. The lady has stated her claim, but I have not accepted it, nor will I."

"Levi, listen to me. Sixtus had house parties, and you were often invited to them. Amanda also attended two of them as a last-minute companion to some other guest, and she did not comport herself. That is to say—"

Levi took her hand, his grip somehow different than it had been previously. He wasn't being gallant or even flirting, he was instead *connecting* himself to Penelope, anchoring himself.

"Amanda behaves one way in the churchyard and another behind closed doors. I know that, Penelope, and I'm hoping she's caught in a misstep sooner or later."

Women like Amanda weren't caught in missteps unless they wanted to be. Sixtus could have made that point more effectively than Penelope, but she tried anyway.

"Levi, when Amanda finds herself with child, she'll claim you're the father. You'll marry her then and have a cuckoo to inherit your baronetcy, too."

His dark brows drew down nearly into a single line, suggesting he hadn't considered this scheme.

"Diabolical, but it makes sense. Why else would she keep me in her pocket all these years?"

Because he was handsome, honorable, a baronet, comfortably fixed, and would make an excellent father to any child in his keeping. Penelope considered Amblewise's cool hands and the dog hair on Squire Hungerford's breeches and wanted to weep.

"I longed for you to make love with me today," she said, kissing Levi's knuckles. His hands bore a whiff of leather and lavender, good, sturdy scents that Pen would always associate with the sadness of his revelations.

Levi rose in a single graceful surge, then tugged Pen to her feet. "I long for the same thing, Penelope, and I shall not admit defeat. I have a plan for extricating myself from Miss Houston's claims. When that plan is executed, you will have an offer from me so quickly, you might indeed mistake me for a rabbit."

His tone was solemn, but his grasp was warm.

Penelope leaned against him. "Is this a very devious plan, Levi? Only a devious plan will do for this situation."

"Devious and deceptive," he said, sounding wonderfully confident.

"Then I have two conditions. First, you must acquaint me with the details of this plan, allowing me to refine your scheme and participate in it to the extent practical."

He kissed her nose. "Of course. The second condition?"

"We will have this discussion in my bed, *right now*."

TRULY, PENELOPE CARRINGTON was meant to be Levi's wife. She hadn't judged him for his misbegotten entanglement with *that woman*, and Penelope was sufficiently confident of Levi's plans to anticipate marital vows with him.

"Penelope, you must be very sure. If my scheme goes awry, I will still offer you marriage, and you will have Sixtus's funds to see to your family, but there will be unkind talk." Also, quite possibly, a civil lawsuit for breach of promise, and Levi had no confidence Stoneleigh would be free to represent him in a messy civil case.

"Your scheme will work, Levi, and there will be no talk." She led him from the feed room, her hand on his arm as if they'd been discussing nothing more scandalous than the recipe for the ladies' punch at the assembly.

Levi had the sense that by taking him to bed, Penelope was assuring herself of their eventual marriage, a leap of faith he could not entirely share.

Though neither would he disappoint his lady. They were adults, both of them had lost a spouse, and strict adherence to propriety did little to make an otherwise lonely life worth living.

"I will marry you, Levi," Penelope said when they'd reached her sitting room door. "You or no one."

"And I will marry you," Levi said, the words a vow. "You or no one." Regardless of lawsuits, scandal, ruin, or scheming spinsters.

Penelope slipped through the door, then locked it behind Levi, and wrapped her arms around him.

"I want to decorate this house," she said against his mouth. "I want to hang mistletoe from every rafter and tie golden bows on all the candles."

Marriage to Sixtus had been lonely for her, at least in this physical regard. Levi knew what that felt like and kissed her back.

"Your year of mourning ends next week. Decorate to your heart's content. Sixtus would have wanted—"

Her hands went to his cravat. "*I* want, but I do believe Sixtus meant for me to marry you, Levi Sparrow."

Sixtus had been that crafty and that loyal a friend. Levi wished Sixtus was still about, to aid them in their scheme—a daft sentiment.

"Perhaps he did want us to marry. He asked me to take special care of you, to maintain my friendship with the household after the condolence calls had ceased."

Had insisted—more than once—that Penelope would have no one else she could trust, and Sixtus had apparently been right.

Marrying Penelope might cause all manner of difficulties for their families. Levi let her undress him anyway, as a husband accepted that mundane intimacy from his wife, and returned the courtesy to her.

"You have regained some of the flesh you lost with Sixtus's last illness," he said, untying the bow of her stays, something he'd not done for Ann even on their wedding night.

"When he was ill, Sixtus kept trying to shoo me away, kept telling me to tend my rabbits. Franklin bore him company when I couldn't. What are you—are you *kissing* me?"

Kissing her, sniffing her, nibbling her. Levi was on his knees behind her, acquainting his nose with the exact contour of the dimples at the base of her spine.

"I'm getting to know you. Were you aware that here"—he grazed his nose straight up her spine as he rose—"you bear the scent of carnations?"

"Perhaps roses and carnations are related. I love your scent—lemons and cinnamon. It's bracing and soothing, masculine and different."

She *loved* his scent. Levi started a list, as if he were taking notes in preparation for joining suit.

"I love your softness," he said, sinking his fingers into her hair and searching out the pins. "I love that you're both sweet and fierce. You didn't allow Sixtus to send you away very often, did you?"

"Two hours a day," she said, as her braid slipped down over her shoulder. "I cried for some of those two hours, though I visited the rabbits as well."

A cheering thought befell Levi, despite that his schemes had yet to bear fruit. They'd bring their babies to meet the rabbits, and use the angora wool to blend the softest, warmest weaves for the baby blankets.

"Will you undo my falls, Penelope?"

She turned, wearing only her chemise. "You're allowed to miss Ann, Levi. Allowed to save a corner of your heart to mourn her to your last day."

"I will keep Ann ever in my prayers, but right now, her memory is not foremost in my thoughts." His voice was steady as Penelope undid two sets of buttons with delightful dispatch.

She wrapped her fingers around his shaft. "Gracious, Levi. What *is* foremost in your thoughts?"

He was hard, eager, and still wearing too many clothes. "You are. Shall we finish undressing me?"

She had his waistcoat and shirt off, then stood back so he could shove out of his breeches and linen. With Ann, he'd kept a nightshirt on, and she'd remained tucked cozily beneath her covers and nightgown, not a single candle lit. With Penelope, only naked skin to naked skin would do.

"The chemise goes, my dear."

"How will I stay warm?"

"I'll keep you warm."

Her chemise went sailing to the foot of the bed at an impressive speed, and then she was plastered against him, her nose mashed to his throat.

"You are hot as a toasted brick, Levi. Shall we get under the covers?"

"Soon." Penelope was nervous—*Levi* was nervous—but the moment wanted savoring. He would be her first. She would be his forever and finally. He cupped her jaw and kissed her with all the respect, hope, and passion in him, all the dreams and wishes one heart could contain.

When she let him up for air several minutes later, Levi scooped her into his arms and carried her to the bed.

"Leviticus Sparrow, those sheets will be freez—!"

He tossed her onto the bed then came down over her. "If you yell, the servants will hear."

She looked intrigued with the notion. "What if *you* yell?"

"The entire shire will hear me. The assembly will soon be upon us. Get your staff busy decorating the house, Penelope. The roof of the parish hall is said to leak."

Levi had made certain of if, in fact.

Penelope kissed his nose. "Decorate with lots of mistletoe?"

"Bales of it." Mistletoe was part of Levi's plan. Kissing was apparently part of Penelope's. She kissed him as if to make up for all the years her late husband had been friend, mentor, companion, and frustration to her. Kissed Levi as if she believed his desperate plan would work without having heard it.

Kissed him until he was poised over her on all fours, suspended between exuberant lust, gratitude for her faith in him, and determination that she have him for her husband and knight before Christmas.

"Levi, I love kissing you."

I love you. "The sentiment is mutual. I love being naked in bed with you, love making love with you during business hours, love that you're all over with the fragrances of meadows and gardens in the middle of winter, love—"

She squeezed his backside. "You can write poems about all that, but for now, might we please get on with things?"

"No more poems," he said, dropping his forehead to hers and threading a forearm under her neck. "This next part might get a tad uncomfortable, Penelope."

"I wouldn't want you to suffer for anything, Levi. What can I do to make it less uncomfortable?" Her next squeeze was gentler, followed by a fortifying pat.

God help him. "You have to be patient with me, let me take my time, not rush me."

She wrapped a leg around his waist. "Very well. If that's what you need from me, then I'll be the soul of patience, and if it's too difficult, you can stop. I know you've been alone for a long time, Levi, and I refuse to distress you."

"I love you," he whispered, easing forward into her heat. "I purely, simply, hopelessly love you." He paused, having gained the first increment of penetration and knowing another inch would cost him his powers of speech.

"I love your kindness and pragmatism," he went on, pushing forward again, gently, gently. "I love your hair, your kisses, your conversations with Franklin. I love"—he withdrew half the distance, all he could manage—"the determination in your eyes when the lads forget to change the straw in one of the pens. I love—ah, God, Penelope, I love all of you."

She was wet and willing, and the only person in the bed showing signs of distress was Levi, for desire rode him mercilessly as he slowly, slowly joined with his intended.

"This feels..." Penelope's second leg vised around his flank. "I like this. You're inside me."

The words were simple and obvious, the wonder in Penelope's voice was profound.

"You're all around me," Levi said, hitching her closer. "You're in my arms. In my heart."

"You're in my bed. Don't stop, Levi. I'll die if you stop."

So would he. He created a rhythm slower than desire clamored for, but gratifying in the response it wrung from Penelope. She moved beneath him, held him to her desperately tight, and kissed him with an open-mouthed ferocity that nearly cost him his control.

What saved Levi was the last, smallest fraction of his rational mind, the part that always observed, always analyzed. He used that stubborn bit of sanity to catalogue the novel ways Penelope's passion delighted him.

She sank her nails into his fundament.

She twisted her fingers through his hair.

She moaned into his shoulder as passion overcame her in a shuddering, panting, litany of "Oh, Levi, Levi, Levi..."

While he endured, held on, and held *her.*

"This is marvelous," she whispered long moments later. "We must be married, Levi, and soon. Say a prayer that we're snowed in *a lot* this winter."

He kissed her ear. "You're all right, then?"

"I'm glowing inside like the Christmas star itself. Will you get us a special license?"

"Of course. Shall you glow again, Penelope?"

He didn't want to make her sore—not until they were married and could share a soaking bath the next morning.

She glowed twice more as evening descended, and Levi's faith in their eventual marriage—or his passion—was such that the last time, he lit up the sky with her, until Penelope slept tucked against his side, and Levi wondered when they'd have a chance to discuss his great, lofty—hare-brained—scheme for foiling Amanda Houston.

Chapter Six

Mr. Stoneleigh was certainly handsome, and Levi claimed he was a dear friend, but he made Penelope a trifle uncomfortable.

"She doesn't think I can be charming," Mr. Stoneleigh complained, as if Penelope weren't sitting in the same parlor.

"Neither do I," Levi said, jabbing at the logs on the andirons. "I think you can impersonate a charming man, though, much as you impersonate aggrieved innocence and thundering outrage. Please avoid the mistletoe."

A difficult undertaking when Penelope's entire house fairly dripped with mistletoe thanks to the ladies on the decorating committee.

"You've involved an innocent rabbit in this scheme?" Stoneleigh asked, sipping his punch. "Levi, perhaps you've been working too hard."

Penelope smiled sweetly at Levi's friend and accomplice. "At last count, Mr. Stoneleigh, Franklin had more than three thousand descendants. He's not an innocent rabbit, and Levi and I consider him a friend."

Levi rose and put the poker back on the hearth stand. "Franklin also has no speaking parts in this farce, while you do, Stoneleigh," he said. "Shall we take our places?"

"The courtroom is a theater," Stoneleigh muttered, rising and tugging down his waistcoat. "I will be such a warm-hearted, charming fellow, the snow will melt from here to the West Riding. Two decades from now, grandmothers will still remark the year that handsome Mr. Stoneleigh graced the Christmas assembly and broke every heart—"

Franklin, who'd been keeping his own counsel against the French doors, thumped the floor as loudly as a pistol shot.

"Couldn't have said it better myself," Penelope murmured. She took Mr. Stoneleigh's arm, while Levi fetched Franklin.

"Give me about fifteen minutes," Levi said, leaning over to kiss Penelope. "From both of you, I want quantities of charm, wide-eyed disbelief, and convincing dismay. Come along, Franklin. Time for you to be least in sight."

Levi and Franklin left, the larger of the two confiding something masculine and none too delicate to the smaller fellow.

Mr. Stoneleigh's expression was more puzzled than charming. "I've never seen Levi like this. He used to be the soul of reason, the epitome of logic, and a font of precedent. Is this *your* doing?"

"I certainly hope so, though Levi took a direct hand in flavoring the punch, too. If I'm to play the part of the bereaved widow reluctantly entertaining my neighbors for a holiday assembly, then you'd best start looking supportive and smitten, Mr. Stoneleigh."

Levi had taken the Carrington household staff in hand, and the decorating committee had turned Penelope's ballroom into a fairyland of blue, white, and gold—and mistletoe. Her neighbors were in there, twirling about more merrily by the moment.

Stoneleigh peered down at her—he was as tall as Levi, but his height was imposing rather than comforting.

"Sir Levi is smitten," he said. "I never thought I'd see the day. Well, 'tis the season of miracles, is it not? Witness, I'm about to be mistaken for charming."

He patted her hand, then escorted her through the door, giving every appearance of a man doting on his companion.

Truly, barristers were an amazing lot. As half the shire hopped and stomped about on the dance floor, Penelope introduced Mr. Stoneleigh as an acquaintance of her late husband's—Sixtus had known everybody—and a *dear* friend of Penelope's, which he might eventually be.

When they'd made the rounds of the locals, including no less a personage than the famously reserved—and fashionably late—Duke of Oxthorpe, Penelope brought Mr. Stoneleigh to meet her sisters.

Precisely fifteen minutes after parting company with Levi, Mr. Stoneleigh was seized by a violent, loud sneeze.

"Excuse me," he said, producing a silk handkerchief and whisking it about under his formidable nose. "Perhaps the greenery affects me."

In a corner of the ballroom, the sight of Levi passing Miss Houston a second cup of punch *affected* Penelope.

"Isn't mistletoe poisonous?" she asked.

Miss Houston took the cup, patted Levi's lapel in an exasperatingly presumptuous manner, and said something Penelope was glad she couldn't hear.

"Smile, madam," Mr. Stoneleigh warned pleasantly as the musicians brought the set to a close. "Levi did, indeed, take a personal interest in that Greek fire you're calling your punch."

Which was being served in quantity to the simpering, smiling, sleeve-clutching, lapel-patting, fiancé-stealing Miss Houston.

"I hope she spills it on her bodice and every bachelor in the shire is on hand to lend his handkerchief."

"Creative, though her kind sometimes enjoys that sort of thing. Where is your guardian rabbit?"

"Where no one will find him. Your eyes look a bit red, Mr. Stoneleigh. Or shall I call you Gervaise?"

She'd surprised him. Penelope hid her glee by lowering her lashes and introducing Mr. Stoneleigh to Mr. Amblewise's mama, up from Town to join her son for the holidays. Mrs. Amblewise was a merry, substantial lady who doted on her darling boy.

Mr. Stoneleigh sneezed again, and Penelope didn't think it a theatrical gesture.

"Are you well, Mr. Stoneleigh?"

Out came the showy handkerchief again, waved in all directions. "Quite well. I'm merely affected by the decorations."

"You are a very convincing actor. Would you like some punch?"

"Dear lady, if I value my health, that punch is the last libation I would allow to pass my lips." He leaned closer as they approached a sprig of mistletoe dangling from a Roman statue's spear. "They're leaving the ballroom. Try to look smitten, Mrs. Carrington. With *me*."

She went up on her toes and kissed his cheek. "Happy Christmas, Mr. Stoneleigh."

"It's your damned perfume," he said quietly. "I cannot abide roses, though my step-mother favors them." He moved away, as if to admire the mistletoe.

"Not much longer, Mr. Stoneleigh, and you will look very convincing."

"I *am* very convincing," he snapped, sneezing yet again. "I can't wait, or I'll be wheezing like an asthmatic princess."

"Not yet," Penelope hissed, pulling him over by a window that had been cracked to let in fresh air. The dancing would soon begin again, and then the ballroom would grow very warm indeed.

"Better," he said, stuffing his handkerchief in a pocket. He went still, standing very straight, like a hound on the scent. "Good God, I thought you said the rabbit wasn't to be a part of this."

"He's not," Penelope said. "Not in truth. Why?"

"Because I'm certain I saw a rabbit's fluffy little bunny-arse disappearing through the door. We haven't any more time, madam."

"But Levi and Miss Houston have only just left. Franklin is above stairs, I tell you." Though Franklin had a way of wiggling open doors that were closed but not latched, of disappearing into the wainscoting and reappearing in interesting locations.

"Two minutes," Mr. Stoneleigh said, dragging the window open another three inches.

They were the longest two minutes of Penelope's existence, while all around her, her neighbors milled about, swilling the punch, nibbling cakes, joking, and waiting for her to signal the orchestra to resume. In the small parlor down the hall, Levi was closeted with Miss Houston, while somewhere in the house, Franklin was apparently on the loose and about to ruin Levi's carefully wrought scheme.

"Mrs. Carrington," Mr. Stoneleigh declaimed in tones that would wake the sleepiest of judges, "are you telling me there's a *rabbit* on the premises? A *live* rabbit? I cannot abide rabbits. They give me the most hideous sneezing fits."

Squire Hungerford came striding through the crowd, his gold waistcoat a lovely complement to the ballroom's blue and gold velvet curtains.

"Damned thing is loose again? He's enormous, I tell you. Would feed my steward's entire brood a fine Christmas meal. Shall I get my—"

Diana, bless her, put a hand on the good squire's arm. "No shooting in the house, sir. Penelope is very attached to Franklin."

"Franklin was quite dear to Sixtus," Penelope said, which was true enough, though Sixtus had also considered his decanters quite dear and his naughty drawings by Mr. Hogarth dearer still. "I should hate for harm to befall him."

Which it would not, if Franklin remained where Levi has deposited him.

"We must find Mrs. Carrington's rabbit, then," Mr. Stoneleigh said.

"Capital notion!" Hungerford thundered.

"But quietly," Mr. Stoneleigh added. "One doesn't catch a rabbit by marching up to it singing *God Save the King*."

That was probably the entirety of what Mr. Stoneleigh knew about catching a rabbit, but the neighbors apparently understood his wisdom. The murmuring and muttering ceased immediately.

"Franklin is very partial to the small parlor," Penelope said. "The French doors mean the floors in that room remain cool, and rabbits like Franklin cannot abide heat."

"Let's split up," Mr. Stoneleigh suggested. "Some start at the top of the house and come down, some try the family wing, and some to the servants' wing. You lot"—he gestured in the direction of Amblewise and Hungerford—"come with me."

The duke was apparently disinclined to go rabbit hunting, but several small groups left the ballroom, whispering and smiling, though not to the destinations suggested by Mr. Stoneleigh. As best Penelope could figure, most of her guests had disappeared in the direction of various conspicuously displayed bundles of mistletoe, which was, thank goodness, all part of Levi's plan.

MISS AMANDA HOUSTON closed the door to the small parlor, then swilled her punch like a drover downing his first ale at the end of a 20-mile day. Rather like a drover's doxy, the seams of her gown were straining, and her brunette hair looked more disheveled than artfully styled.

"We'll announce our engagement tonight," she said, setting the empty mug aside—her third, for Levi had given her his, then switched glasses lest the lady suffer unnecessary thirst.

"Happy Christmas to you, too, Miss Houston."

She marched over to the sofa and flopped down, while Levi opened the door to the corridor a few inches.

"Propriety now, Sir Levi? Isn't it a bit late when we've been engaged all these years?" She grinned, as if she'd made an exceedingly clever joke.

"Mrs. Carrington has a house rabbit and a cat, and they find this room among their favorites. We are not engaged, Miss Houston."

"Call me Amanda. Mr. Vanderburg calls me Mandy. I like that. I would like to be Mandy Sparrow."

Either the lady was very confident of herself, or she was tipsy—or both.

"Perhaps Mr. Vanderburg called you that at the Newmans' house party?"

A narrow foot clad in a dancing slipper thunked onto the low table before Penelope's sofa, then a second foot joined it.

"Either the Newmans' or the Hunder—Hungerfords'. It's time you married me, Sir Levi. You have a soft spot for the Carrington widow, I know it."

"Penelope is a dear friend, and you and I are not engaged."

Did he hear footsteps in the hallway? Was that a giggle?

"We're engaged if I say we are," Miss Houston said, sitting up straight. "I assuredly do say we are."

Levi raised his voice to courtroom-declamation level. "I never proposed to you, Amanda Houston."

"What difference does that make?" She rocked herself, one-two-three, onto her feet, then caught the arm of the sofa for balance. "You wrote those beautiful poems to your departed wife, though you forgot to mention that good lady by name, and you sent those poems to me. You ought not to sign your correspondence, Sir Levi. Ann said you were too innocent for your own good."

"Innocent I might be"—or might have been—"but I have never offered for you, and I shall never marry you."

Miss Mandy Houston blinked at him owlishly. "Ann said you were a terror in bed. I am too, you know. All the fellows say so, especially the married ones. This time next month, I'll be a terror in *your* bed."

"You'd blackmail me into marriage, and then expect intimacies with me?"

In the corridor, somebody sneezed.

"What was that?"

"Probably Mrs. Carrington's rabbit. He makes a deal of racket. Answer the question, Miss Houston. Are you saying you'd not only keep a grieving widower's poetry about his departed wife when he'd asked for his letters back repeatedly, but you'd also use that correspondence to force him to marry you?"

She ran a gloved finger along the mantel, then examined her fingertip. "Not a speck of dust."

"Miss Houston?"

"Yes," she said, sashaying closer to Levi—and to the door. "Yes, Levi Sparrow, I would cheerfully blackmail you, and though it might take you a while, sooner or later, you'd find your way to my bed. You're the sort who wants children, and there is that baronetcy."

An honor earned in battle, appropriately enough. "If I refuse to be blackmailed?"

She made a farcical pout. "What is she called? Dabny? Daphne? You have a sister who's so quiet I can't recall her name. The dear creature tipples, I suppose, or has gambling debts. I might decide she has a fondness for her laudanum, or—oh, this would do nicely—for other women. I haven't decided yet. You'll marry me, Levi. I'm tired of those other fellows and, quite honestly, running out of money. Twelfth Night will do, don't you think?"

Another noise came from the direction of the corridor.

"That wasn't a rabbit," Miss Houston said, her hand going to her middle. "We'll need a special license if we're to be married that soon. Be off with you. Send me a maid and have my carriage brought around. For some reason, I feel poorly."

A third sneeze confirmed that Levi, by contrast, had grounds to feel exceedingly fine. He was about to tell the woman so, when the door swung open and an ample older lady came barreling into the parlor, a crowd of Levi's neighbors behind her.

"Amblewise, is this the sort of holiday nonsense your parishioners get up to?" Whoever she was, she had excellent timing and knew how to project her voice.

The vicar appeared at her side. "Certainly not, Mama. Miss Houston, what have you to say for yourself?"

Yes, what could Miss Houston possibly say, when half the shire had overheard her confess her schemes, past, present, and future?

A gaunt fellow with thinning sandy hair and a drooping mustache cleared his throat—Vanderburg, if memory served. Looked as if the punch hadn't agreed with him, either.

Miss Houston's gaze slewed around the growing crowd in the parlor. "I think I'm about to be sick."

"You can be sick once we lock you in the storeroom at The Duke's Arms," Squire Hungerford said. "I'd be a poor excuse for a magistrate if I ignored brazen announcements of blackmail."

Levi let the squire's bluster hang in the air, for this threat wiped the smiles from the faces of those enjoying Miss Houston's predicament. Hungerford would do it too—would lock her in for a few nights among hanging hams, sacks of flour, and boxes of eggs.

Then dismiss the charges when the case came before him in Monday's parlor assizes, though Miss Houston couldn't know that.

"All I want is my letters back," Levi said. "I want them back now."

"I'll want to see Miss Houston at the manse tomorrow morning," Amblewise snapped.

"Get her things," Levi said, "and somebody look in her reticule for my letters."

Amblewise's mother did those honors, fishing out a largish flask before she extracted the packet of letters from Miss Houston's purse.

"These are your letters?" Mrs. Amblewise asked, holding out a stack tied with a green ribbon.

Levi took them, feeling as if Ann could finally rest in complete peace. "If somebody would see Miss Houston home, the rest of you are likely ready to resume the dancing. Has anybody seen Mrs. Carrington?"

"Gone to look for that damned rabbit," Hungerford groused. "She'll never find it in a house this size. Miss Diana, shall I lead you out?"

Diana obligingly led the good squire from the room, while Amblewise departed with Doreen on his arm.

Levi was soon once again alone with Amanda Houston, who leaned on the mantel, crying like a child.

"Stop it," he said. "I would never have married you. This way nobody has to suffer for my scruples—except you, and you deserve to suffer."

She dabbed at her eyes with a gold handkerchief. "I can't stay here now."

"Very likely the point of Vicar's meeting with you tomorrow. Vanderburg at least isn't married. Had you mentioned the names of any of the married ones, they'd likely stuff you on the coach to London by force." Abetted by their wives and sharp pitchforks.

Though Miss Houston wasn't to blame for men who chose to break their vows, was she? A fraught moment stretched, with pity pulling Levi one way and anger pulling him the other.

"Sir Leviticus? I was told I'd find you in here." Penelope stood in the doorway, looking lovely in her dark green velvet dress. "We never did find my rabbit. Miss Houston, are you well?"

Miss Houston stuffed her handkerchief into her reticule, then snatched the flask and stashed that among her effects too. "I am quite unwell, Mrs. Carrington. If you'll excuse me, I'll be going."

"What a pity that you must leave. Happy Christmas," Penelope said, with every evidence of sincerity.

Miss Houston swept out, Penelope closed the door, and Levi nearly collapsed with relief.

"Send a footman to follow her," he said. "We cannot trust that woman."

"Yes, we can," Penelope replied, wrapping her arms around Levi's waist. "You were about to give her money, weren't you, Levi? You felt that sorry for her, and after all the misery she's caused."

"She's pathetic, and God knows what will become of her. A man disporting as she did would be said to enjoy healthy manly humors, but she's female, and so—"

"So she's judged differently. You are too fair-minded, Levi." Penelope kissed him, and his nerves settled, just like that. "You were magnificent, and you need not trouble yourself over Miss Houston."

Penelope left Levi's arms only long enough to lock the door.

"She will find a note," Penelope went on, returning to Levi's embrace, "in the pocket of her cape informing her that a sum certain awaits her in the City offices of Mr. Gervaise Stoneleigh, and further, that various gentlemen of the shire would appreciate if she'd collect that sum in person. I expect she'll be waiting for the stage at The Duke's Arms tomorrow morning, assuming no highwaymen interfere with the coach's schedule."

Levi rested his chin on Penelope's crown. "Unless she can catch a southbound stage tonight. Did Stoneleigh suggest that note?"

"Franklin did. Won't you ask me to dance, Sir Levi?"

Down the corridor, fiddles in close harmony lilted along in triple meter. "I'd like nothing more."

For now.

He led the lady to the dance floor by way of several batches of mistletoe and waltzed her down the room under a smiling portrait of Sixtus as a younger fellow. The mood of the crowd was happy—a half-dozen men were doubtless very pleased to be dancing with their own wives, and even His Grace was on the dance floor—while the punch flowed freely.

When Penelope pled fatigue, Levi quietly offered to light her up to her room, and if anybody remarked his gallantry, well, what were holiday revels for?

"We should let Franklin out," Penelope said. "We have him to thank for tonight's happy ending."

"He merely sat wiggling his nose in Sixtus's chambers," Levi said, though the rabbit did deserve thanks. Were he not a fixture in Penelope's house, the entire plan would not have worked.

"I am confused about something," Penelope said, as they made their way down the shadowed corridor. "Mr. Stoneleigh claimed to have seen a rabbit leaving the ballroom, though I know you would have fastened the door securely after you left Franklin up here."

"Perhaps Stoneleigh had been at the punch?"

"Surely, you jest, Sir Levi. Did you hear him sneezing in the corridor?"

"All three times." The door to Sixtus's room was still latched, just as Levi had left it. When they had the privacy of the room, Levi set his carrying candle on the desk by the windows and drew Penelope into his arms.

"I ought to wait until morning," he said. "I had planned to make you a lovely speech with all the rabbits looking on. Spring is coming. You'll soon have a deal of baby bunnies."

"Franklin is somewhere here in Sixtus's chambers. Might you make your speech before him?"

Levi released his lady and went down on one knee. "I'll make my speech before you. Will you marry me, Penelope? Will you become my wife, and if God is generous, the mother of our children?"

A muffled thump came from the direction of the bed.

"You too, Franklin, of course," Levi added. "A lady's household accompanies her when she takes a husband, and Penelope wouldn't think of leaving you."

A second thump followed, more softly.

"Penelope?"

"We say yes, Levi. We say a delighted, exuberant yes, and Happy Christmas too!"

She drew him to his feet, and though the room lacked mistletoe, kissed him soundly. Her kisses were more potent than punch as far as Levi was concerned, and the true holiday celebration was overdue to begin.

"May I escort you to your bed?" Levi asked.

"Or you may carry me, though I'll take the candle, if you must impress me with your manly—Levi, there are *two* rabbits on that bed!"

Penelope had raised the candle so more of the room was illuminated, and indeed two furry bunnies reclined on Sixtus's bed, only one of whom was Franklin.

"We're not the only couple to become engaged," Levi said. "I do believe that's Bathsheba."

"Sheba, you minx!" Penelope crossed to the bed and cuddled the doe in her arms while Franklin wiggled his nose patiently. Bathsheba had lost her listless, disappointed expression and had become, in Levi's opinion, the most smug-looking bunny on God's earth.

"They make a lovely couple. We'd better start picking out names, Penelope."

She returned the doe to Franklin's side, picked up the candle, and led Levi from the room, leaving the door slightly ajar. Levi accompanied his lady to her own bedchamber, where they did, indeed, spend much of the night choosing names.

Or something very like it.

In The Duke's Arms

By
Carolyn Jewel

Dedication

To my co-conspirators in this project: Grace Burrowes, Miranda Neville, and Shana Galen. I am so glad to have been asked to contribute to this project. What wonderful writers to work with.

Chapter One

The Duke's Arms, Hopewell-on-Lyft, Nottinghamshire, England, 1817

AWARENESS SHIVERED DOWN Oxthorpe's spine. He had no notion why but took the reaction as a sign he ought to pay attention. He braced one booted foot on the edge of the plank table and tipped back his chair until it rested on the wall behind him. He had no company at this table by the fire. It was a place reserved for him alone. A carved swan and griffin adorned the top of his chair.

That no one dared join him suited him. He preferred solitude even when in public. Especially in public. He sipped the dark ale the innkeeper brewed in his basement. As good or better than any produced by the larger brewer two towns over. Wattles, the proprietor of the coaching inn, supplied Killhope with a regular measure of this ale.

The common room of The Duke's Arms was crowded with a mix of locals and travelers. The locals were closing out their day with dinner before heading home. Others awaited their connections to parts north or south. From his seat, he could see the inn's wooden sign with its painted swan and griffin echoing, rather loosely, those carved into his chair.

When he was not looking out the windows, his inelegant position gave him a view of his boot. The left of a decent pair of boots. Suitable for the country. He'd liked them well enough three years ago; the leather was supple even still. But these excellent boots did not have the folded top cuff of his new boots. Nor did they have a maroon tint to the leather, which he thought would set a fashion—if it was possible for a man like him to set a fashion for anything but striking fear into hearts.

He ought to be wearing his maroon top-boots and was not. Because he could not. The left of his new boots, never worn but for assuring the fit, had gone missing from Killhope. Servants had searched the house and grounds top to bottom and found nothing.

Just as he was about to conclude that nothing untoward was going to happen after all, the front door opened.

Winter air blasted through the room. Several of the patrons near the door shivered. A woman of about thirty came in. Oxthorpe straightened his chair and set his beer on the table. For the last month, he'd been telling himself he was prepared for this moment. He was not. This was inevitable, that they would at some point be in the same place. His heart banged away at his ribs.

She was dressed against the chill in a black woolen cloak, hood up so that one did not see the color of her hair and little of her face other than that she was pale complected. She was of medium height. Her eyes were brown, not that he could see that from here, but they were.

The maid closed the door behind them and stood to one side, hands clasped and head down. Of this he approved, both that her maid held her employer in the proper respect and that she'd brought a servant with her.

With one hand, because she held a paper-wrapped parcel in the other, the woman pushed back the hood of her cloak. A spray of tiny blue flowers adorned her brown hair. She had hair combs, too. Ebony, if he was not mistaken. This was an embellishment he had never seen from her in Town. "Good afternoon, Mr. Wattles."

Miss Edith Clay brightened the room with her presence. Just from walking through the door, she'd made the room a happier place. This was true despite his having spent the last several months assuring himself his recollection of her had to be incorrect.

His recollection was not incorrect. It was appallingly accurate.

Wattles grinned from behind the bar where he stood to pull beer or ale from the tap and tell stories or, often, listen to them. "Delightful to see you, miss."

Mrs. Wattles, who had emerged from the kitchen for a word with her husband, saw Miss Clay and headed toward her. She wiped her hands on her apron and folded them beneath the fabric. "Always a pleasure to see you, Miss Clay."

"Thank you, Mrs. Wattles." Her smile hollowed out his chest. She'd changed since last he saw her. She was brighter. More vibrant. Happiness suited her. "You are so kind."

The Wattleses' daughter, Peg, came into the common room from the back carrying an empty tray, heading, he presumed, to the kitchen.

"You're early to pick up your dinner, miss," Mrs. Wattles said.

Peg stopped to curtsy. "Good day, miss."

"Peg. I hope you're well." She tugged at the wrist of one of her gloves. Blue kid.

Her focus returned to Mrs. Wattles, and while she was so engaged, Oxthorpe took the opportunity to study her and tightly wrap up his response to her. He had a clear view of her from where he sat. To see him, however, she would have had to look in the shadows at the rear of the room, and she had not done so. Why would she? She'd not come to see him. For one thing, his visit this afternoon had not been scheduled.

Waning afternoon light shone through the windows to the courtyard, with its glimpse of the Great Northern Road. A groom hurried toward the stables at the rear, his arms wrapped around his middle. Her maid was not a Hopewell-on-Lyft local. He supposed she must be from London.

"Yes, I am a little early picking up my dinner," Edith said. "But that's not why I've come. Not the only reason, that is."

Strange, seeing her without her younger and prettier cousin. In London last year, and later in Tunbridge Wells, he'd got used to seeing them together. Inseparable those two, even though Miss Clay was the elder by a decade. Two years younger than he. Unlike him, she was cheerful. Always pleasant. So bloody, horribly happy even though she had no particular looks, and at the time he met her, no fortune whatever. She had been, in fact, entirely dependent on her relations.

Mrs. Wattles waved to her daughter. "Tell them Miss Clay is here to pick up her supper."

"Yes, Mum."

"Thank you, Mrs. Wattles." She glanced around the room, but her gaze slid over him. Even in London, always happy. "How is your father, ma'am? Better, I hope."

Mrs. Wattles's father was ninety years old and, lately, in failing health. "As well as can be expected, I think. He says thank you for the bread and broth you sent."

"I shall send more, if it would be welcome."

"He would enjoy that, miss." Mrs Wattles bent a knee. "We'd be grateful if you did."

She adjusted the parcel in her arms. The light through the windows turned her hair shades of walnut. "I hope you'll let me know if there is anything else you need."

"Thank you, miss."

By no stretch of imagination was Edith Clay anything but a pleasant-looking woman. Not unattractive. But nothing to make a man's head turn. She wasn't young. At twenty-seven, nearly twenty-eight now, thirty was not far off for her. A woman, not a girl. Her cloak separated to reveal a portion of a blue frock. Robin's-egg blue. That was unusual, her wearing colors. She never had before.

"I am here on account of a mystery most deep, Mrs. Wattles."

One of the laborers in the far corner of the main room came forward with a chair. The man set it down near where Miss Clay stood near the bow windows with her parcel in her arms, then backed away. Another of them pushed forward a chair for her maid. Her maid sent a grateful glance in the direction of the men.

"Thank you," Edith said.

He did not understand this fey power of hers to make people like her. He wondered if she'd walked here. If she had, she'd have a mile and a half through the cold when she left, and uphill, too. There might be snow, this time of year. Likely so with the way the sky looked.

Edith perched on the edge of her chair, knees pressed together, feet aligned. She'd sat just so before, a woman of no importance, whom no one noticed when she was quiet. "I hope you can assist me."

Mrs. Wattles clasped her hands underneath her apron. "Whatever we can do."

She settled her parcel on her lap. "Did you know, Mrs. Wattles, that when I moved into Hope Springs, I found a note pinned to the wall in the entryway? Just above a crate. I thought it odd."

These were now more words than ever he'd heard her say at one time. In London, she had guarded every word against her elder cousin's disapproval. There were more differences between the woman she'd been then and what she was now. Besides the fashionable clothes, her face was more animated, and though she was not a beauty, there was something there. She seemed freer now than she had been. Who would not be who had made a similar escape?

"What did the note say?"

"It was left, I presume, by the previous inhabitant, by way of instruction. It said, 'For Items Found.' Is that not peculiar? I thought it peculiar." She had a good, strong voice. She smiled with her voice, too. This, he thought, was the magic that had drawn him to her.

"What did you find?"

"Ah." She held up her gloved index finger. "I suspected as much. There have been things found at my home before."

"There might have been." Mrs. Wattles laughed.

She unwrapped the parcel she held. Several of the laborers and many of the travelers in the front room craned their necks to see. "When I returned from my morning perambulations to the vale and back, I found this in my driveway." She held up a boot. A gentleman's gleaming boot of maroon leather with a folded-down cuff. "Is this not most mysterious? I have not been in Hopewell-on-Lyft very long, so perhaps it is common, but it seems uncommon to me."

True. She'd been here a month, no longer.

"Perhaps one frequently finds a boot in one's drive." She was laughing at herself, delighted with the absurdity. So were the others. He, too, was smiling. Even though it was his boot.

Peg had returned from the kitchen, and she eagerly explained. "It's Mr. Paling's collie, miss. From Killhope." Paling being his groundskeeper. The man had a three-legged collie who followed him everywhere.

Edith tilted her head. Wide-eyed innocence played to perfection. "Are you certain? For this seems so very much like a boot, to me. It's not at all collie-shaped."

Mrs. Wattles laughed. Edith hadn't a mean bone in her body. Not one. She meant to amuse, and she did. He was amused, though he did not want to be.

"Mr. Paling's collie is excitable," Mr. Wattles said. He'd refilled someone's beer and now held it in one hand. "When she's in such a state, why she'll snatch up something near and dash away with it. She leaves it wherever she is when the passion wears off."

"Ah."

"When he comes here with the dog, we are careful to put away anything she might carry away with her." Wattles pushed the beer to the man waiting for it. "You're not so far from Killhope, miss. It's bound to happen."

"This is the duke's boot?"

Mrs. Wattles glanced over her shoulder at him. So did her husband. And Peg. And several of the locals. "I can't say if it is or it isn't."

Edith did not notice the stares in his direction because she was examining his boot. "Well. Not a princely boot, then, but a noble one. Yes, I see that now." With a sigh, she re-wrapped his boot and retied the string. "I do wish I'd guessed that before I walked in the opposite direction from Killhope Castle."

Oxthorpe stood. He could do nothing else.

Her hands stilled, and her smile faded away. She stood and dropped into a curtsy. What did one say in such situations, when one knew a lady disapproved? "Miss Clay," he said.

"Duke." She'd given the field laborer a happier smile than she gave him. Most everyone else had stopped smiling, too. This was the effect he had on others. He was the Duke of Oxthorpe, and though he did his duty by his title and his estate, he was not beloved. He did not know how to be beloved the way Miss Clay was.

"You have my boot."

She turned her head to one side. To avoid meeting his gaze. "Do I? Your Grace."

"I'll try it on and let you judge the fit."

"That will not be necessary."

"It is when you doubt that it is mine." He walked to her, and she handed over his boot. He examined it when he'd sat on a chair Wattles brought for him. He would not have gone through with his ridiculous challenge to her except she thought he would not.

At last, she looked at him. Without warmth. "It isn't the collie's fault."

He drew off his boot with less effort than he'd expected and put on the other. A perfect fit. "There are tooth marks." Too late he understood he'd spoken gruffly. Possibly, she thought he accused her of damaging his boot.

Her expression smoothed out, and then she did what she would never have done before. She smiled brightly and said, "I assure you, Duke, they are not mine."

This was amusing. He recognized that. Several people guffawed, and he heard others trying not to laugh. Without allowing his annoyance and dismay to show, he changed boots again. "You relieve me, Miss Clay."

Once again, he had offended her. He should not care. He did not care. Why ought he to care about a woman like her? Except he did. He bowed, jaw clenched against the possibility that he would say more to offend. He strode out of The Duke's Arms with his bloody damned boot.

Chapter Two

Edith flicked up her hood against the cross-wind. The air smelled like snow and felt like ice, and she hoped she made it home before either made her walk exceedingly unpleasant. She now regretted her decision to walk to The Duke's Arms with the no-longer-mysterious boot. She and her maid would be thoroughly frozen by the time they arrived home.

She walked faster, her maid keeping pace. Behind them came the thud of hooves on cold dirt and the creak and rumble of a carriage. Not the mail traveling south. She'd have heard the commotion of that.

She moved to the edge of the road. Her maid did the same. The carriage slowed, passed her, then stopped a few yards ahead. Her heart sank. Even without a coat of arms, this could only be the duke's carriage. No one else in Hopewell-on-Lyft could possibly drive so fine a vehicle and besides, the groom clinging to the back wore the duke's livery.

The groom jumped down and ran to hold the head of the lead horse. The animals, four matched chestnuts, were fine enough that even she took a breath at their quality. Horses like that must cost hundreds of pounds.

The carriage window lowered and Ryals Fletcher, Duke of Oxthorpe, stuck his head out.

Wind blew his hair into disarray. Even so, he was grand and somber and terrifying. Not yet thirty. As if age mattered at all. Despite his relative youth, he frightened everyone with his stern face and eyes that looked at one with a thousand years of wealth and privilege. "Miss Clay."

She walked to the door so she would not have to shout a reply to his summons. She curtsied and said, "Your Grace."

"It is cold."

"It is winter." She reminded herself he was a duke, a man of significant wealth and responsibilities. She reminded herself that he had courted Louisa and stood poised to break her cousin's heart or make Louisa the happiest woman in England. There was yet hope for the match. Her cousin Clay had invited him to Holmrook for Christmas and, as yet, he had not declined.

He pushed open the door, and his groom jumped forward to hold the door and put down the step. "I will see you home."

She might have refused, except that her maid shivered, and indeed, she, too, felt the bite of the wind despite her thick cloak. Fifteen minutes with the man would not kill her. "Thank you."

The duke stepped down. Impeccable clothing. Beautifully cut and worn on a frame that hinted, no, shouted, at physical strength. This had surprised her when she'd first seen him in London, that he looked like a man who controlled his body as harshly as everything else. She did not care for tall men.

"Your maid, too," he said. A laugh rasped along his throat, a growl from a man who appeared to have never laughed in all his days until now. From the side of her eye, she saw the groom look away. "No one will say I ravished two women."

My God. Was there anyone less gracious? Of course, if one was the Duke of Oxthorpe, who owned the better part of the land here and around Hopewell-on-Lyft and, indeed, the parish, one need not be gracious. He knew his place, and it was above everyone else. Far above.

He signaled to the groom with a motion that included her maid. "Keep that safe for Miss Clay."

With a grim expression, the groom took the dinner Mrs. Wattles had wrapped up for her. This being the cook's night off, Edith had fallen into the habit of taking away dinner from The Duke's Arms. The Wattleses were excellent innkeepers, and the kitchen at The Duke's Arms did a brisk trade for locals as well as travelers.

The duke extended his hand to her, and only then did it occur to her that he might be distinguishing her because of Louisa. He was not a man to make decisions in haste, that much she knew. She put her hand on Oxthorpe's and got in. His fingers closed around hers, and she felt the strength in him. She found it unpleasant, this awareness that he was so much stronger and larger than she. Her maid came in after.

The duke took the rear-facing seat. Could such a joyless man really be not even thirty? He ought to be a century old at least. And yet, he had succeeded in winning Louisa's heart.

"Thank you," she said when he'd settled himself. He'd left his hat on their side, and she handed it to him. Beaver, with grosgrain ribbon around the base.

He set the hat beside him. The carriage started up. Edith smiled, got no reaction for her trouble and settled on a study of the interior. As good an excuse as any not to look at him. Lacquered wood, black leather seats, gilt lanterns, and everywhere some echo of his coat of arms; a swan or a griffin carved or painted or worked in metal.

In these quarters, alas, it was impossible to behave as if she did not know he was there. Besides, it was rude, and like him or not, she did not wish to be rude to anyone, particularly not a man who oozed rank from every particle of his being, from his clothes, to his carriage, to the sapphire in his neckcloth.

He was handsome, and this was a circumstance that had surprised her in London, and again in Tunbridge Wells, and yet again in The Duke's Arms. Now, too.

Handsome, yes, in an austere and condescending way, with a narrow face and sharp cheeks, and his shockingly intense eyes. Even with his thick, dark hair mussed by the wind, he was frightening to behold.

She tried another smile and again—nothing in return. No doubt he thought of her as little more than a servant, for her cousin Clay had treated her as if she were nothing more than that—without the need to pay her wages. Her parents had been in such financial straits when she was a child that they had been obliged, and grateful, to send her to live with her father's cousin.

Having done her best to be polite to the man, she contented herself with staring at her lap or at his hat on the seat beside him. She imagined him wandering the corridors of Killhope with no friends to keep him company, no callers not there on business, no one but his staff in the lonely, empty, dreary rooms. Killhope Castle was aptly named, for she saw no hope of anyone there ever smiling.

She stared out the window for some minutes then made the mistake of glancing out the other side. Her gaze collided with the duke's. His eyes were a clear, pale green. Why was he staring so intently when there was hardly another woman less interesting than she?

She smiled again.

He did not.

How awkward this was. Never had she met a man less careful of his impact on others. She frowned. Not that, not uncaring; oblivious. This puzzle distracted her from the dreadful silence. During her time in London, she had observed many a gentleman, more than a few of noble descent, and they had all been pleasant to her cousin, some more so than others, depending on their hopes for Louisa.

The duke, while never directly offensive to her, had not been an easy man to be around. Even in company his silence soon went from unpleasant to oppressive. She knew she was not the only one to feel that way. She knew Louisa had overcome the man's silence. With her own eyes, she had seen him be charming to Louisa.

Once again, she caught his gaze without intending to. Thank goodness she had no reason to feel Louisa's despair of him. "I expect there will be snow tonight."

"Yes."

During those interminable years in her cousin's household, she had perfected a cheerful smile, and she gave him one now.

The duke leaned forward, a palm propped on his knee. "What fool walks out on a day like this?"

She'd spent so many years being agreeable because she must that she instinctively bent her head. But why, she thought as she did, ought she say nothing to such a statement? Why, when she was beholden to no one, ought she be silent? She lifted her chin. "It is a mile and a half from my home to The Duke's Arms. A walk of thirty minutes if I dawdle."

"Uphill."

"On my return, yes."

"You should have driven into town."

She folded her hands on her lap and kept to herself the fact that she did not yet possess a carriage. A wagon, yes, but not a carriage. Any moment they would be at her home, and she would be quit of this unpleasant man. She did not say another word until they arrived at Hope Springs. Her good mood returned in force. This was her home. Hers alone. The deed had her name on it, and when she went inside, everything would be hers and arranged to her taste.

The groom came around and opened the door. As she brought up the hood of her cloak again, the duke stepped out and stood beside the door, his hand extended to her. She let her maid out first and then descended herself, fingertips on his gloved hand.

As she curtsied to him, a snowflake drifted between them. She hated that he was right about the weather, not that it would have killed her to walk home with a few snowflakes in her hair. "Thank you, Duke. You were kind to convey me home in this weather."

He nodded.

Why wasn't he getting back in his carriage? She curtsied to him again. "Good day, Your Grace."

His eyes were as cold as the snowflakes in his hair, for he'd left his hat in the carriage. "I will escort you to your door."

Every word he uttered was a command. Gruff, with no kind intent at all, and she, even with her new circumstances, had no choice but to endure. "Thank you."

Halfway to her door, the duke put out his elbow, and there was no remedy for this new awkwardness except for her to loop her hand through his arm. She was warmer at all the places where their bodies were close. Her front door was a mile away. Ten miles. A thousand. Could he not walk faster?

"You put in slate."

"I beg your pardon?"

He nodded at the paving stones. "Slate."

Her maid had already gone around to the back with their supper. "I did not wish to walk in the mud when the weather is damp."

"I approve." What haughty words. Good heavens. What if he'd not approved? What if he believed slate was the very worst material for her to have installed? Would he have expected her to remove it and replace it with something more to his liking? Likely he would have. Likely, some of his neighbors would comply with such an expectation. Cousin Clay would have.

"Thank you."

"You are welcome."

Now he sounded as if he thought she'd hurry to her desk to write letters in which she informed her friends and acquaintances that the Duke of Oxthorpe had approved of her slate. She sneaked a look at him. He probably did think that.

At last, they reached the top stair where she put a hand on the door and bent a knee to him. "Thank you, Your Grace."

He gazed at her with his disconcerting eyes, and just as she was about to go inside without any resolution to their awkwardness, he said, "I never saw you wear that color before."

She glanced down at her blue dress. What a singular thing for him to notice. "It is a new frock."

Snowflakes melted in his hair. "Do you miss your cousin?"

Well, then. This was a development. Was all this awkwardness between them because of Louisa? "Do you mean Louisa?"

"I doubt you miss Mr. Clay."

"I do not." For Louisa's sake, she smiled. "I'd begun to wonder if you'd forgotten Louisa."

"No."

This was a most excellent development. He *did* feel something for Louisa. He did. "Louisa and my cousin Clay are memorable, I'm sure you'll agree."

"What of you?"

She cocked her head, wondering what he meant by the odd inflection of his question. "Me?" She waved a hand. "I am the least memorable woman you'll ever meet."

"I disagree." His eyes bored into her. "I have never forgotten you."

Chapter Three

At twenty past two, Edith knocked on the door of the Thomases' home on the eastern side of Hopewell-on-Lyft. She'd not meant to be late for this meeting, for this was not a social call, but the walk to the other side of the town had taken longer than she'd anticipated.

A wagon and two strong drays had been a necessary purchase for her move to Nottinghamshire. She had known at the time of her preparations for removal to Hope Springs that she would need a vehicle for her personal use. She'd continued to put off the purchase, because every time she reviewed her budget and expenses, the cost of a carriage and suitable horse paralyzed her. Her father had spent unwisely, and that had ended with her sent to live with her cousin Clay.

The example of her father had taught her that while a single unwise purchase might cause no significant damage, a series of them would. Spendthrift choices multiplied. Her move to Hope Springs had come with unanticipated expenses. More furniture needed than she'd thought. Rooms that needed more than new paint. Fabric for curtains that she would not come to despise. A chimney to repair, a new hearth for the kitchen, half the buttery to be rebuilt once she'd bought cows and a bull. Chickens, too, and geese. There were gardens and lawns to manage. A flagstone path from the drive to the house. Servants to pay.

A carriage and associated expenses seemed intolerable when she could walk. No decision meant no change in her present finances. Every penny spent outside her allotted budget brought the specter of ruin closer. And so, despite the inconvenience, despite knowing she ought to have a carriage of some sort, she did not decide what to buy and continued to walk. Next quarter, she would make the purchase. Or the one after.

"Good day, miss." The Thomases' butler took her mantle, her muff, and her hat.

"Good day to you, too." She felt the difference between her being Miss Clay, dependent relative of Mr. Clay, and being Miss Edith Clay, a lady in possession of a fortune. She'd been invited for herself, and here she was, in pale pink muslin and silk, with a cashmere shawl around her shoulders.

"This way, miss. They are waiting for you."

In the parlor, she was not received as the least significant of the Clays, nor expected to behave as if she were. These women were waiting for her, not her relations. She'd been invited to join the committee that organized and raised funds for the quarterly assemblies. She had been flattered and thrilled to accept. The Christmas assembly was the largest such affair of the year, with residents from all ranks included in the celebration. The women here would, she hoped, become lifelong friends. Already, she knew she liked Mrs. Thomas exceedingly.

Mrs. Thomas met Edith halfway across the room. The older woman kissed her cheek. "Welcome, welcome. You know the others. Mrs. Anders, Mrs. Pembleton, Mrs. Herbert, and Mrs. Quinn. Mrs. Carrington was unable to attend today, but sends her regards."

"Good morning, ladies." She curtsied. "I could not be more delighted to be here."

"My dear Miss Clay, do sit. We have an excellent tea." Mrs. Thomas escorted her to the table where the others were gathered. Edith made a mental note of the food and drink and the setting. One day, their meeting would be hosted at Hope Springs. She intended to make a good impression when her turn came.

"Thank you. So many delightful treats, Mrs. Thomas." Cheese, bread, meats, an array of pastries, cakes, and biscuits. Mrs. Quinn, a woman of Edith's age, poured her tea. "Thank you, ma'am."

"You're quite welcome."

Edith found herself presented with full privileges to choose whatever she preferred. Neither her cousin Clay nor his wife would later take her aside and tell her how impolite it was for a lady of her station to take anything but the smallest, least interesting selections.

While Edith was busy serving herself, Mrs. Pembleton produced a slim notebook which she opened. "This last public assembly of the year is, as you know, to be held Monday, December the twenty-second at the parish hall in Hopewell-on-Lyft." She looked around the table. "It is agreed we shall relocate to Carrington Close should there be a recurrence of last year's incident with the roof."

"Have we written to Mrs. Carrington to express our gratitude?"

"Yes. Done last week. Now, due to generous donations from His Grace and from Miss Clay—"

Polite clapping followed that announcement, which Edith acknowledged with a nod. Her donation to the committee had been a good use of a portion of the monies she allotted for charity.

"—our budget for the Christmas assembly is flush with funds. Extra decorations have been ordered and a wider selection of refreshments added to the menu." She glanced around the table. "We do need additional servants. If each of you would lend two healthy footmen for the day before, the day of, and the day after, I daresay we shall be competently staffed." She frowned. "Two footmen and two maids if we are at Carrington Close."

"Yes, yes," Mrs. Thomas said.

"His Grace has once again offered the use of his kitchen staff. I have written to thank him for that generosity."

Edith added to the clapping. When Mrs. Pembleton completed her report on the committee's efforts so far, she lifted a hand.

"You have the floor, Miss Clay."

"Hope Springs contains several acres of oak forest. May I offer to collect mistletoe from these trees? If there is a supply of ribbon, lace, or other notions from the decorations obtained for our purpose, I can provide all the bouquets of mistletoe we might wish to have at the assembly. After sending round a suitable sample for approval, of course."

"An excellent suggestion. Thank you, Miss Clay." Mrs. Pembleton made a note. "I will send you such samples as might be useful for your exemplar."

Mrs. Pembleton folded her arms on the table and put her weight on them. "I am determined that *this* year we shall persuade His Grace to attend the Christmas assembly. All our hopes for a Christmas miracle rest upon you, Mrs. Thomas."

"I make no guarantees of a miracle."

Edith took in the various reactions to that. No one seemed astonished by the request. "Does he never make an appearance?"

"Not since 1810," said Mrs. Anders. "Before your time, Mrs. Quinn. And yours, Mrs. Thomas."

"Has he stayed away every year?" Edith kept her opinion of the duke's deliberate absence to herself, but truly, this was not well done of him.

"He prefers to stay locked away upon that hill," Mrs. Anders replied.

Edith's admittedly unfounded notion that His Grace the duke lived in dungeon-like conditions cemented itself in her head. She imagined him treading lonely passageways, a candle barely able to penetrate the dark, and all about him a dank and dampish smell. "He is a man driven by duty," Edith said. "Perhaps we might see success if we remind him of his responsibility to let the people of Hopewell-on-Lyft see him at our assembly."

"An excellent strategy, Miss Clay," Mrs. Thomas said.

She hid a pleased smile behind a sip of tea.

"It's never worked in the past." Mrs. Herbert added more sugar to her tea. "Even my poor dear Ernest, who would have been heir to the Earl of Hillforth were it not for Carbury, could never persuade him. I do think he should emulate the condescension of his neighbors of the better sort."

Edith decided then and there that Mrs. Herbert, a recent widow, was not destined to be a friend.

Mrs. Thomas let out a long sigh. "He ought to make an appearance, I agree. And Miss Clay is correct that one's best hope of convincing him to do anything is an appeal to duty. However, Tuesday last, Mr. Thomas and I dined with the duke, and when I asked if he would attend this year, he replied that he would not be at Killhope."

"Such a pity," Mrs. Anders said, "that he did not return here with a bride when he was in London last season. We had such high hopes for him." She turned to Edith. "You do not know Oxthorpe—"

"Oh, but—"

"We were all of us convinced he would be married by now," said Mrs. Quinn.

"If only he'd found his duchess while he was away," Mrs. Thomas said. "*She* would surely convince him that to appear at our Christmas assembly must take precedence over most any other duty."

Mrs. Pembleton made additional notes while she spoke. "At least there is yet hope for those of you with daughters."

Mrs. Thomas shook her head. "As delightful and beautiful as are the young ladies of Hopewell-on-Lyft, I think it doubtful Oxthorpe will marry locally. If he meant to, he would have done so by now."

"A duke," said Mrs. Herbert with a delicate sniff, "must marry from the highest ranks of society. To marry for love would be a serious dereliction of duty, and as Miss Clay has been kind enough to remind us, our duke puts duty above all else. No, Oxthorpe must make a marriage of politics, or one that cements his fortune. There can be no other criteria. Do not imagine that he would marry for love."

"If we but knew what happened in London," Mrs. Quinn said after a moment's silence. "Did he meet any suitable young lady when he was there? Might he have fallen in love with a woman who spurned him?"

"Good heavens," said Mrs. Anders. "What young woman in her right mind would refuse a duke?"

"It happens," Edith said, "that I was introduced to him when he was in London." She found she rather liked the astonishment this produced. She answered questions as they came at her. Where had they met? Who had introduced them? Had they spoken often? Had the duke singled out any young lady? "My cousin, Mr. Clay, is an acquaintance of a gentleman who is a relation of an uncle of the present Viscount deVere. The duke attended a fete given by Lord deVere, which we also attended." She waved a hand. "Our introduction to him was made there." She looked around the table. "The duke was quite taken with my young cousin, Miss Louisa Clay."

Mrs. Herbert reached for a cake and placed it daintily on her plate. "Did he frighten all the other suitable young ladies?"

Edith glanced around the table. These were women she hoped would become friends, but she would not speak ill of the duke. "It's true he is a man of few words, but when he was in London, he was as charming as any other gentleman of like reserve might be. I mean to say, more charming than one might expect of him. There were times, I vow, when I was glad he was silent, for some gentlemen are never quiet."

"Quite true," Mrs. Thomas said. "For all his solitary ways, our duke is a man of parts."

"He is." She laid a hand on the table. How odd. She felt protective of him. He *had* driven her home. Regardless of how awkward that had been, he'd not left her to walk home in the cold. "It was thought by many that he would offer for my cousin Louisa. She is accomplished and attractive, and as gracious as one can imagine. You never in your life met a more agreeable young lady than she."

"Did he distinguish her?" Mrs. Quinn asked.

"He did."

"How often did he call on her? If he did." Mrs. Quinn leaned toward her, eyes wide. "Did he?"

"Three or four times at least in London. That many times in Tunbridge Wells and again when we were back in Town." On every one of his calls, Edith had sat in the parlor with Louisa and the duke, or walked with them in the garden, doing her best to keep the conversation going when Louisa flagged in the face of his silence.

"Tunbridge Wells, you say?"

"Yes, Mrs. Quinn. This past March, we went to Tunbridge Wells, and who should appear at the same hotel? His Grace."

The ladies of the committee exchanged significant looks.

"He danced with Louisa three evenings in succession."

"One wonders," said Mrs. Pembleton, "why he did not make her a proposal."

Edith would never forget Louisa's despair of the duke, nor that her cousin Clay had pressured his daughter to bring the match around. As if she could have done so by being constantly reminded of it. "An offer was expected, and not just by my cousin Mr. Clay." She lifted her hands. "The duke, as you have all observed, is a singularly reticent man."

"Dour," said Mrs. Anders. "A dour man."

"No. No, not dour." But in that she must relent. Mrs. Anders was correct. "Perhaps a little, but His Grace is a man who does nothing without great and long reflection. He went to Tunbridge Wells, after all, and he did greatly distinguish her there."

"If he loves her," said Mrs. Quinn, "he will see her again. He must."

"Love." Mrs. Herbert raised her delicate brows. "I tell you, love will have nothing to do with his marriage when he makes it."

"Nothing else will do but for him to put everything in motion for his bringing home a bride," Mrs. Quinn said.

"Where did you say your cousin lives?" Mrs. Thomas asked.

"Northumberland. Near Holmrook."

"If it is true," said Mrs. Herbert, "and I doubt very much that it is, he ought not have delayed in bringing the matter to a conclusion. He risks a great deal by waiting to declare himself."

Mrs. Quinn set her chin on her palm and sighed. "A young lady might wait some time for the sake of a handsome duke."

"Does anyone know if he's called on the vicar recently?" Mrs. Anders asked. "That would tell us if we are on the right path, here."

"Oh," said Mrs. Pembleton. "Oh, my. I hadn't realized."

"What is it?"

Mrs. Pembleton looked at each of the women in turn. "Yesterday I called on Mr. Amblewise, and he mentioned the duke had just left."

"This is wonderful news. Wonderful. So encouraging." Mrs. Thomas clasped her hands. "He told us, Mr. Thomas and I, that he expected to be at a property of his at the time of our assembly." She gave them all a significant look. "A property of his in Northumberland."

"Your cousin lives in Holmrook, did you say, Miss Clay?"

"Yes."

Mrs. Pemberton lifted a hand. "In Northumberland."

"That means nothing," said Mrs. Herbert.

"I do know," Edith said, "that my cousin has invited the duke to visit them."

"He's called on the vicar. He will not be at Killhope for the holidays. What else could it be except that our duke is in love?" Mrs. Quinn rested a hand over her heart. "Ladies, here is our Christmas miracle."

Chapter Four

WHEN EDITH LEFT the Thomases after the meeting, the weather was clear, and her spirits were considerably buoyed by such strong evidence that the duke was more serious about Louisa than she'd thought. He'd been invited to Holmrook for Christmas. He had told Mrs. Thomas he would not be at Killhope at the time of the assembly. He'd called on the vicar, Mr. Amblewise, only a few days in advance of when he would need to leave for Northumberland to make Louisa an offer of marriage.

By the time she reached the eastern outskirts of town, though she remained delighted about the duke and Louisa, the cold was now foremost in her thoughts. The wind had come up, and clouds obliterated any sign of blue skies. With the weather deteriorating like this, she would be a block of ice by the time she was home. She pushed her hands deep into her ermine muff and increased her pace. If she walked quickly, she could be home in under an hour.

She crossed the bridge over the Lyft and headed into the heart of town. She left her hood up, which kept her face and shoulders warmer, but also blocked her view of the road through town. Shop signs creaked ominously in the wind. At times the noise muffled the sounds of carriages and wagons in the street.

"Miss Clay."

She turned, knowing whom she would see. The duke sat in a very smart curricle stopped at the nearest side of the street to her. His crest decorated doors of gleaming green lacquer. He'd put up the top to protect against the weather and turned up the collar of his greatcoat. He seated his whip and touched the brim of his hat. He managed to look dashing and forbidding at the same time.

She curtsied. "Your Grace."

"You are walking to Hope Springs?"

"Yes, Your Grace."

"In this weather?"

She glanced around and gave him a smile. "I haven't any other weather to walk in."

"I shall drive you home."

There was no dissuading him, she knew that. He had made his pronouncement, and no one defied him. There was, as well, the simple fact that she would much appreciate a ride, for it had turned colder than she liked. "Thank you."

He set the brake and dismounted. He was wearing his maroon boots, and they did look well on him. "No parcels, Miss Clay?"

She put her hand on his in preparation for stepping up. "I was at Mrs. Thomas's. For a meeting to finalize plans for the Christmas assembly."

"The Thomases?" He did not hide his astonishment.

"Yes." She smiled at him. "Is it true you never attend the assembly?"

"In previous years, I have had prior engagements."

Two steps up to enter, a quick grip atop the back of the seat, and she was on the bench. She imagined herself driving a curricle like this and thought the image rather fine. He swung up beside her. She gave him as much room as she could, but he was a man solidly built and wearing a thick coat. They would have a cozy drive to Hope Springs. "All the ladies think it a great pity that our leading citizen will not be in attendance. You will not reconsider?"

"It is not a matter to be reconsidered. A previous engagement is just that." The duke reached underneath the seat and took out a blanket. He shook it out and laid it over her legs, leaving it to her to cover her lap more fully.

"Thank you. You would attend, then, if you found you had no such engagements?"

"I cannot say. Perhaps." He settled onto the seat and took up his whip. In such close quarters, there was no help for the fact that his shoulder and thigh pressed against hers. "Why did you walk there?"

She considered an untruth, but could not bring herself to lie to him. "I do not yet own a carriage."

He flicked the whip, and the horses started. Two bay geldings, matched in all particulars, including, she realized now, gait. His other hand tightened on the reins. "Why not?"

"It is an expense I had rather avoid just now."

"A necessary one for a woman who is sole head of her household."

She bowed her head and looked at him sideways. She did not expect him to be looking at her, but he was. "You are correct," she said. In all likelihood, this man would soon be her relative. "No one could be more correct."

"Which begs the question, why do you not have a carriage?"

"The expense. Taxes. I'd need another groom. I should want something smart, too. I know I would, and so I would spend too much. Then there are horses. They, too, are an expense."

He sent her a skeptical look, and she deserved every bit of that scorn. She did. "Have you spent all your money, then?"

"Of course not."

"I repeat my query."

"I confess it, Your Grace. I am over my head in this matter. Drowning." He would soon be in the place of head of her family. Its ranking member, once Louisa was his duchess. "My cousin Clay never let me drive, and I wouldn't know how to choose the right horses, the best for my money, and I don't wish to be taken advantage of. Suppose I buy a young horse when in truth it is not? I might buy a horse with a bad gait or a roarer or one not suited to a carriage, or that's bad-tempered or doesn't like women."

"Miss Clay—"

"One hears such terrible stories about old horses sold as young ones, or that have infirmities or other disorders foisted off on unsuspecting buyers. My own father famously paid over four hundred pounds for a stallion he meant to put to stud. The horse died of old age a week after the purchase."

"If you feel you would fall prey to such schemes, seek expert assistance."

"Who am I to ask? I have been in Hopewell-on-Lyft a month. I do not know anyone well enough to ask for such help." She leaned her head back. "It isn't only horses, but everything. Everything. With every potential expense set before me, I fear I'll make the wrong choice."

"I doubt that."

"No?" She sat straight. "I do. I doubt passionately that I will choose correctly."

He shook his head. Was that pity? Disgust? She could not tell.

"I ask you, what's to prevent me from losing my head and spending every penny I have on foolishness and fripperies?"

That earned her another scornful look.

"Cousin Clay was forever reminding me that my father had a fortune once and lost it with one terrible decision after another. He overspent, his investments went bad, he did not save, and then he married my mother, and that was unwise as well. I cannot tell you how unwise that was, according to him. Now I cannot shake the conviction that I, too, will find myself destitute and dependent. Again."

"Have you invested any of your money?"

"No." She wished she could melt into the fabric of the chair.

That answer earned her another astonished glance. "None at all?"

"Some in the five percents."

"There's that, then."

"Not enough. Not enough. What if I invest badly? Or not wisely enough?"

"I see no evidence you spend beyond your means."

"You don't know that." Where their bodies touched at shoulder and thigh, she was warm. Her feet were no longer as cold as they had been, and the blanket over her lap kept her legs warmer, too.

"No," he said after a short time had passed, "I do not."

"I bought insurance. Fire insurance."

"On Hope Springs?"

"Yes." Her stomach clenched. She did not wish to have a conversation that exposed her as baldly as this. All her faults for him to see.

"Fire insurance is not a reckless purchase."

"It might have been."

"Allow me to observe that your difficulty is not the decisions you make, but the ones you do not. You have not made purchases you ought to."

"I'm hopeless. Hopeless, I tell you."

He continued, unperturbed. "Delaying necessary purchases when you have the funds to make them is a false economy. If you fail to repair a leak, you will have a greater expense in future."

"I've already repaired the roof. And a chimney. And rebuilt the dairy."

"Do not despair. You are able to take decisions."

"I had not expected all those expenses at once."

He did not speak again until they were past The Duke's Arms, and Edith, having concluded the subject was dropped, turned her thoughts to happier ones of fashioning bouquets of mistletoe.

At the base of the hill, he gave his whip the lightest touch, and the horses moved in identical strides. A curricle like this, with horses as perfectly matched as these, would be a dream to own. How could she not look smart in such a curricle?

"I will assist you."

"Gathering mistletoe, do you mean?" But, no. He could not mean that. She'd not told him of her need to gather mistletoe.

He gave her a puzzled look.

"Pay no attention. I've let my thoughts run away with me. I offered to gather mistletoe from Hope Springs as decorations for the assembly. But you could not have meant that, for I hadn't told you of my plans. What do you mean, you will assist me?"

"I will assist you in the purchase of a suitable vehicle, the appropriate cattle, and in the hiring of an additional groom."

Yet more evidence of his intent to marry Louisa. If she were to find herself his relation, why, of course he would assist her. A man like him would consider it his duty. "I don't want to put you to any trouble."

"I will present you with several choices and give you my reasoning for them. Once you've decided, I shall procure you the horses."

"That's generous of you."

His sideways glance told her he knew the reason for her hesitation. "Tell me what expense you cannot bear to exceed."

"Twenty pounds."

He laughed. "Will you drive a cart? Or a wagon? Pulled by an ass?"

"No." Her stomach clenched again, but then, if she could trust anyone's good sense and advice, it was the duke's.

"Well, then."

"I considered a curricle, you know. I think I should like one exceedingly." She ran a hand along the top of the door on her side. "Yours is so dashing."

"A curricle, Miss Clay, and suitable cattle will set you back more than twenty pounds."

"I do not need a coat of arms on mine. Nor gilt paint."

He turned down the drive to Hope Springs. "If you spend less than two hundred pounds, you will have nothing but regrets."

"Two hundred pounds?"

"For an amount nearer to what you wish to spend, I recommend a gig and a single horse."

"That will do, then."

He stopped his curricle before the house. "Very well, then."

Chapter Five

Oxthorpe finished with Goodman two hours earlier than usual. They'd got through all his legal correspondence. Replies to letters requiring a response had been drafted and were ready to prepare for his signature. He'd reviewed ledgers and several investment proposals, all of which he had rejected. Goodman cleared his throat.

"Yes?" Why the devil did the man look as if he stood poised to drink hemlock?

"About your attendance at the upcoming festivities?"

"What festivities?"

His brow furrowed. "At St. Melangell's, sir."

Oxthorpe examined the point of his pen and, not to his credit, dissembled. "One's attendance at church is hardly festive."

"The Christmas assembly, Your Grace. At the parish hall."

"What about the assembly?" He no longer attended the assemblies. Not any of them. He donated generously. That was enough.

Goodman tugged on the bottom of his waistcoat and cleared his throat again. "But, Your Grace."

"Yes?"

"I have heard from several sources that your attendance is considered a positive fact."

"Your sources are incorrect." He dipped his pen in the inkwell as if he intended to write out one last letter. Goodman did not move. "I am otherwise engaged on the evening in question."

"Your Grace..."

He did not so much as glance at the man. "Good day to you, Goodman."

His solicitor bowed and took his leave. The door closed softly after him, and Oxthorpe found himself alone. Just as he preferred.

He put down his pen then picked it up again. Deuce take the Christmas assembly. He'd gone once and had been expected to enjoy himself. He had not.

He stared at the sheet of paper before him, his pen poised as if he were about to put ink to paper. He did have correspondence that ought to be written in his own hand. Letters he owed to friends and his few surviving relations, all elderly women.

The invitation from Mr. Clay required his personal response. Or, he could make his too-long delayed call at Hope Springs.

He had, in one of the drawers of his desk, the details of two suitable choices of conveyance for Miss Clay. These must be acted upon quickly if she was to secure her choice. Therefore, he was doing his duty by calling on her ahead of other tasks that were before him.

He cleaned and put away his pen and capped the ink, then assembled the documents he'd compiled and gathered for her. He gave Mycroft instructions to have his horse brought around and went upstairs to change. If, while he was changing, he was more particular than usual about which breeches and coat, which gloves and whether his hair had been sufficiently tamed, his valet had no complaint of him for it. He wore his new boots.

With the documents tucked away in his coat, he went to the stable block. One of his grooms waited with his mare at the ready. Five minutes later, he was riding toward the border with Hope Springs.

There was no reason to believe he'd find Edith at any of the oaks on her property. It would be foolish to check, since such a detour would take him a quarter of an hour out of his way. His mare, however, divined that his intentions and his desires were not the same, for she took the path toward the oaks, and he did not dissuade her.

He did not believe in fate, but good fortune? Yes.

She *had* told him she would be gathering mistletoe, after all. It would be his misfortune should he arrive at Hope Springs and find her out. If she was not at home, he must either wait or return to Killhope and delay his business with her, to her detriment. In light of that possibility, a thirty-minute delay in reaching Hope Springs was an excellent hedge.

He came over the rise and saw first the dark green shadows of the wood, then, among that dusky green, a flash of gold. His breath caught. If this was Edith, he hoped to God she was not in those dense oaks with no one to see to her safety. Not with the self-styled New Sheriff of Nottingham harassing and robbing both travelers on their way north or south as well as the good citizens of Hopewell-on-Lyft. A man desperate enough to train a gun on innocents would think nothing of trespassing on privately held, enclosed lands.

As he drew nearer, he made out a ladder leaning against the thick branch of an oak. The top of the ladder disappeared into the tree. To the right of the ladder was Edith's maid, looking up at the trees and whomever was on the ladder. Whether he'd seen the maid's gown when he saw that flash of gold, he could not say.

His fear that Edith herself was on the ladder was assuaged when she emerged from the trees. She held her bonnet in one hand and stood, eyes shaded with a hand, when he came close enough to speak. A breeze caught at her mantle and revealed a stripe of a yellow-gold gown.

He dismounted. From the look of things, she had been in the trees herself. Oak leaves and bits of moss clung to her hair and shoulders. He found the enthusiasm behind her untidiness quite charming. "Miss Clay."

"Good afternoon, Your Grace." Her eyes lit up, though there was no reason to believe she was pleased to see him, as opposed to pleased to see anyone at all. She curtsied. Her maid did the same and retreated several steps back. "What brings you here?"

Her naturalness around him was a consequence of her having no personal expectations of him; this he had understood from the start. She did not see herself as the sort of woman in whom he would take a personal interest. Nevertheless, he did not think it was his imagination that she was less formal with him than previously.

"I have information to put before you."

Leaves and smaller branches rustled, and Edith glanced into the tree. "Have a care."

"Below left!" came a masculine voice from the tree.

Her maid dashed to the other side of the ladder, a basket in hand. Something green dropped from the tree. The servant placed the basket to catch the mistletoe.

"Well done, Jim Dandy." Edith looked into the tree again. "Well done."

The man called down, "One more, and we've all we can take here, mistress."

"Good, good."

Oxthorpe walked toward the ladder and Edith. Beneath the branches, the ground was covered with oak leaves. There was no frost here. The maid stood on the other side of the ladder. Her basket was full of mistletoe, with the occasional twig or oak leaf among the leaves and berries. Nearby were three large bundles of mistletoe, tied up in squares of white cloth. "A good afternoon's work."

"Yes." Edith was cheerfulness itself. "Our assembly will have mistletoe everywhere you look."

That damned assembly. It wasn't enough that he donated the bulk of the funds or that he gave up his kitchen staff and cook for the duration. Not that he begrudged the expense or the inconvenience of a cold dinner, but every year he was bombarded with all manner of sly and not-so-sly hints that he attend. He had no wish to attend. He had, in fact, arranged to be away from Killhope at the time. "Ah, yes. You are on the committee."

"I am."

She would be there. At the assembly.

And he would not be.

"I have promised them mistletoe, and I mean for us to have more than you can imagine."

He glanced at the basket and the other bundles. "Success is within your grasp."

She laughed, and he was pleased to have amused her. "We've done a fine job here."

He brushed an oak leaf from her shoulder. "You have."

"We'll be the next week tying ribbons and lace."

"Why?"

"On the mistletoe. This year's decorative theme is blue and white grosgrain ribbon with blond lace."

"How festive."

"Yes, won't it be? I am so sorry you won't be there." She put her hands on her hips. "Never fear. I will raise a glass of Mr. Wattles's famous cider and toast to your good health."

"Thank you."

She beamed at him. "Then I shall wish all present and future residents of Hopewell-on-Lyft and Killhope Castle a very merry Christmas and happy New Year. What do you say to that, sir?"

"Will you stand under the mistletoe and wait for a gentleman to kiss you?"

Her cheeks pinked up, and, good God. No. No. God, no. She thought he meant she would be waiting all night for such a thing. "That is not—"

"If Louisa were to come, there would be a line of gentlemen." She spoke too quickly, and her smile was gone.

"I daresay. Miss Clay—"

She took one of the leaves from the basket and held it up for inspection. "Did you ever see more perfect berries?"

Jim Dandy began his descent of the ladder. Instinctively, Oxthorpe steadied it. "Never," he replied to Edith, desperate to repair the damage he'd done. "Except at Killhope."

As the servant came down the last rungs, she laughed. "I say we repair to Killhope this instant and compare, for I'll warrant *my* mistletoe is the most perfect this side of the Vale of West."

He managed a smile. A small one. He took the mistletoe from her and examined it in the sun. He ought to go to the bloody assembly and kiss her beneath the mistletoe. *That* would cause a stir. "You will lose that wager, Miss Clay."

She stepped forward and squinted. "I would not. That mistletoe is perfect."

There was a moment when she stood underneath the mistletoe he held. The world swooped around him like a drunken lark. He ought to kiss her. One kissed a lady who stood beneath the mistletoe, though she hadn't done so on purpose.

Impossible. He could not do something so outrageous. In front of her servants. She would be offended. Or worse, she would endure the contact and ever after hold him in even greater dislike.

She might kiss him back. God, what if she did?

He lowered the mistletoe and tossed it in the basket. Behind this tableau of his hopes and her utter blindness to them, Jim Dandy put away the sickle he'd used to cut the plants from the tree and walked off with the ladder and two of the bundles of mistletoe, and that ended everything.

Her outing was done. Her maid covered the basket with a white cloth she tied to the handles to keep the mistletoe secure, picked up one of the other bundles, and followed in the steps of Jim Dandy. Offended, no doubt, on behalf of her mistress. Oxthorpe led his horse and walked beside Edith for the ten-minute return to Hope Springs. When they came near the stables, he handed off his horse to Jim, along with a coin for the servant's troubles on his behalf. "I shan't be longer than an hour. Give her water and hay, thank you."

"Your Grace."

He accompanied Edith into the house. She left him in the parlor, and he found he could not sit still. He paced the room, stared out the windows. Examined the walls and the repairs made to the chimney. He'd not seen the interior of the house since he and Goodman had made an inspection prior to its sale. She'd repainted and put up new curtains. The house had not come furnished, so that had been an expense that must have set off her spendthrift worries.

The furnishings she'd chosen reminded him of the woman who lived here. Nothing to admire, and yet he wished to be here. To stay here and be surrounded by rooms that settled him. He was at ease, and the longer he stayed, the more he found to like.

While he waited, taking in what she had done to make this her home, another maid brought in tea and a tray of biscuits, cold meats and bread. He recognized her from Hopewell-on-Lyft. Edith came in shortly afterward. On his feet, he swept a hand toward the desk at one side of the room.

"I have drawings to show you." Without saying more, he walked to the desk and set his papers on the surface. "And a proposal for you."

Chapter Six

GOOD HEAVENS. EDITH gazed with some amazement at the scene in her parlor. The duke himself. In her house. She must remember every detail so that she could relay them to Louisa in her next letter. The Duke of Oxthorpe was seated at her desk as if he discussed business with her every day. Because he loved Louisa and wanted to be kind to his future relations.

Predictably, he took up all her attention. She wished Mrs. Quinn had not swooned over the man and thus made her so aware of his looks. Before, she had acknowledged that he was handsome. But now? Several times when he'd found her in the oaks, with leaves in her hair—could she have appeared any more undignified?—she'd lost her train of thought because she was struck by how green his eyes were. Or wondering if his hair was as soft as it looked.

Or whether he was a competent lover. Her mind went blank while her body flushed hot.

He looked over his shoulder at her, and his look of dry curiosity jolted her.

Confounded by that inappropriate reaction, she lifted the teapot and prayed God she did not look as stupefied as she felt. "Something to drink, Duke?"

He went back to his documents. "Thank you."

She poured his tea, which she knew he took plain. This fact she had observed during one of those interminable hours when he'd called on Louisa, and it had been her role to keep the conversation from dying.

Their fingers touched when she brought him a cup and saucer, entirely accidental, but her stomach lurched with recognition of him as a man. Behind the clothes, behind the title, he was a man who must have had lovers, who likely kept a mistress. Raven's-wing black his hair was, thick and glossy, and with a tendency to stand up after he'd run his hands through it. Which he had done twice.

He set his tea atop the desk and stood to hold a chair for her. She sat, and he fetched another chair for himself. She was no innocent. Once, just once, when she believed she would be forever bound to a dry and empty existence with her cousin Clay, she had taken a lover. They had neither of them thought their attachment would last beyond a few days. Then a few weeks. Two months. She had discovered the beauty of a man's body, the fit, the differences, astonishing uses for one's mouth. All that she'd put away when, at last, they'd parted ways.

Oxthorpe brought that roaring back, and it did not make sense. He loved Louisa. If he was here now, it was because of Louisa.

His attention flicked to her bosom. But no, that must be her imagination. She smoothed the lay of her skirts. Her gown was pink satin and gray silk with slippers to match and all in colors she loved because they suited her, because she had not been allowed to wear them before. As yet, she had little jewelry, but one of her first, early purchases had been a string of pearls that went well with this gown and her skin.

"Here are two choices for you." He laid out the papers he'd brought. The top two sheets were advertisements from a carriage maker in Nottingham. "Both these"—he pointed at the first—"are within your budget." He went through the respective costs, the taxes, the maintenance of each, the cost of the horse that best suited the purpose.

The information he'd run through threatened to slip away, and that was disconcerting. It was not her usual experience to find herself so flustered. He was not here for any reason but to do her a good turn. A man like him had no personal interest in a woman like her. She tapped the papers he'd put before her. "May I?"

"Yours to do with as you wish."

"Thank you." She studied the drawings and imagined herself in either of the gigs depicted on the sheets he'd provided. Both were small vehicles, but there would be room for her maid. He was right. Either would be an excellent choice. She went through the expenses he'd listed, written in a precise hand on a sheet of smooth, creamy paper.

Her stomach clenched again. The repairs to the house had just been settled, and here she was about to take on the expense of a gig, a horse, and another servant. She knew she ought to. She knew it. But she resented the need. She could buy something less expensive. She did not need to look smart or have a dainty mare. She could use one of the drays.

He put a hand on the papers. "Miss Clay, may I speak bluntly?"

"Please."

He shifted on his chair, and she was again pulled, unwilling yet enthralled, into recognition of him as a man. "You have been put to some expense, outfitting your house."

"I have." This was true, and his understanding of that settled her.

"You wish to economize." This, she realized, was his element, the managing of details. Choosing among facts and taking a decision.

"I do." She leaned an elbow on the desk. Her difficulties by the oaks were vanquished, the awkwardness she'd felt earlier now gone in the face of his competence here. "But I do not wish to be poor again."

"Economy is not always a savings."

She nodded. Again true. Nothing she did not know, yet, to her shame, knowledge she had been unable to put to use.

"A paradox it would seem, but true," he said. She was so accustomed to his brusque manner of speaking that she was taken aback by the lack of disdain in his reply. Taken aback and then grateful.

"Yes." She swallowed. "You are correct."

"If you do not buy the vehicle you need, then you will find yourself out the expense of what you buy now, in addition to what you must purchase later when you understand you do not have what you need. What is proper for a lady of means."

She met his eyes and did not see the usual chill there. "I could sell what I buy now."

"Not for the price you pay today."

She folded her arms on the desk and buried her head there. She squeezed her eyes closed, then opened them and turned her head to the side of the desk where the duke sat. At least he wasn't mocking her. "Yes. Yes, yes, yes. You are right. I know you are right."

"Of course I am."

She sat straight, and then he smiled, and she drowned in her visceral reaction to that.

"Either of these would be suitable." He set a finger to the drawings. "I will, if you permit me, arrange the purchase and find you a horse."

One could admire a man's looks without thinking oneself his equal. She could. She had done so for all her adult life. "You are too generous."

"Not in the least." He drew a breath. "I have another suggestion."

"I am all ears."

"I have a curricle."

"The one I rode in, do you mean?" Yes. There. She had set aside the fact that his body was shaped by muscle. There was no denying him that, but she need not do anything but say to herself, *this is a fact about the Duke of Oxthorpe*, in the same way she would note that his coat was blue and his boots were maroon. "Is it awful of me if I tell you how much I enjoyed that?"

"No." His mouth twitched. "I mean another, however, which I have intended to take to a property I own in Northumberland."

Louisa. He meant his impending visit to offer for Louisa. What else could he mean? "The reason you will not be at the Christmas assembly."

"One of them, yes. I will sell it to you, if you are interested."

"What is the other reason?"

"Affairs of business."

He'd answered her too quickly, and that got her thoughts stuck on his admission of more than one reason for going to Northumberland for the Christmas holidays. He quirked his eyebrows. She tipped her head to one side. The curricle was the excuse for his trip to Northumberland. If he did not wish to tell her yet about Louisa, she understood that. He was a private man. She understood that, too.

"How much?"

"Not what does it look like?" he asked, smiling again. "Not what is its condition?"

"I presume you are not scheming to sell me a wreck."

"No." He smiled again, distractedly, and tapped the larger of the gigs in the advertisements. "I will sell it to you for near what you would pay for this. I would, naturally, have it refinished to remove my coat of arms at no expense to you."

She gazed at the paper and felt her chest tighten. Every expenditure was a debit to her income, and they added up at an alarming rate. "Higher taxes. A greater cost."

"That is so." He sounded resigned.

"Two horses to keep rather than one."

"The curricle was custom-made. To exacting specifications."

She raised her head from the papers he'd set before her. She wanted to. She did. But there was no need for a curricle, however dashing it would be. "Thank you for your generous offer."

His reply was a brusque nod.

"I sincerely mean that. I am flattered by your condescension and kindness. I need a carriage of some sort. But not a curricle when a gig will be more than sufficient for my needs."

"Miss Clay." He slouched on his chair, stretching out one leg. She swooned a little every time he smiled at her this afternoon, and now? With that slouch that spoke of a man at peace with his magnificent body? She was nearly insensate. "May I speak frankly yet again?"

"You may, but I must tell you it is not necessary to ask permission again. I hope and expect you will always speak frankly to me."

He tapped a finger on his thigh. She refused to look. She could not allow him to see her look. "You did not, until recently, have a fortune of your own. Nor any expectation of one."

"True."

"You do now."

"I do." Three times dead.

"You bought Hope Springs."

"I did, Your Grace."

He waved a hand to indicate their general surroundings. "This property suited your budget and your new future. Its purchase was an excellent decision."

"That was my opinion as well." She laughed and leaned toward him. Praise from the Duke of Oxthorpe. This was a day that must live forever in her memory. "I hope to live into my dotage, you see."

"So hope we all." He propped his elbow on the desk. "I presume your cousin was worse than useless after you came into your money."

She did not answer immediately, for the politics of her possible answer robbed her, momentarily, of her honesty. Then again, if he meant to marry Louisa, he must already know what her cousin Clay was like. He was not the sort of man who would be fooled. "The change in my fortunes was, for him, a setback."

"No doubt." He met her gaze, smiling a little, and that sent her thoughts racing to what a man might do with his mouth. "You've no husband to manage your remaining funds."

That shocked her, that he would broach such a subject with her. "I have not."

"You would do better to marry than live here alone."

"I will soon be twenty-eight. Not decrepit, but I haven't the youth gentlemen look for in a bride."

"A false statement."

"Well. Yes. Again, you are correct. After my good fortune became known, I refused the offers of six or seven gentlemen at least."

"Not one of them tempted you?"

"One or two, perhaps." She fell serious. "To marry in haste did not seem wise. My life was in such upheaval, and in all honesty, those who approached me or my cousin with offers were not gentlemen I knew well."

"That is a commendable caution." He lifted his gaze to hers. "No one you know well came forward?"

Her heart skipped. He could not know about her past or that she'd hoped, for a time, that the man who'd taken her to bed would call on her and lay his heart at her feet. He hadn't, and she'd been a fool to think he might. She had never been a suitable wife. They had not suited in that manner, and they'd both known it.

"If I were to marry, and I think that unlikely, sir, I had rather marry a gentleman whom I admire and respect."

"Someone who admires and respects you, one hopes."

"Yes. Precisely." She glanced down, then back at him. He remained slouched on his chair, but everything else about him was alert.

"I will write to my banker and my solicitor. Mr. Madison will reply because I will have instructed him to do so. Consult with him and decide if you wish to put yourself in his hands. Mr. Goodman, my solicitor, will call on you. He is at Killhope nearly every day."

Outside, the light changed as clouds moved across the winter sun. The shadows of his face changed with the light, and she thought of him lying in bed as the morning sun changed the light. "That is beyond generous. Thank you."

His response was immediate, and not what she expected from him. "I do not like your cousin, nor the way he behaved toward you."

Slowly, she frowned, and he met her gaze head-on. "That is not Louisa's fault, you must know that."

He sat straight. "If you mean, did my dislike of him prevent me from making an offer I would have regretted, the answer is no."

Thank God. Thank God. Louisa's heart was safe. "You won't regret your decision. You won't."

"I assure you, I do not."

"I promise you, you will carry away the woman you love. What is a father-in-law you do not care for when you have all that your heart and soul require?"

His body stilled, and she had the awful premonition that she had said something he found objectionable. "Thank you for your advice."

She put a hand on his arm, desperate to repair the damage of her misstep, whatever it had been. "I'll write to my cousin Clay. I have nothing to lose by telling him he has made himself disagreeable to you. He will take measures. He will. Don't allow one man's unpleasantness destroy your future happiness."

"I have no plans to do so." He retreated behind the cool green of his eyes, and her heart constricted. She'd said something wrong to make him so distant, and she'd give anything to know what. A clock somewhere near chimed the hour. "I'll take my leave. I will arrange the purchase of the gig and a horse. Do not be astonished if I send a man round for you to interview. He will have a character from me."

"I'm sorry. I'm sorry if I've offended you."

"You haven't."

She searched his face, and he was impenetrable. Impassive. "Liar," she whispered, her chest tight.

They locked gazes, and she felt the connection to her toes. He reached for his tea, forgotten there on the top of the desk, and again she lost herself in the intensity of his eyes. "What a remarkable coincidence."

"Miss Clay?"

"The green of my china is an almost exact match for your eyes."

He held up his tea cup and examined the color, and she did likewise, in that she studied the cup and then his eyes, and he obliged her by looking at her without blinking, and that made them both laugh. "Now you have taken your china into dislike."

"I haven't at all." Relief that he wasn't annoyed any longer made her giddy. "You have pretty eyes, Duke. I like my china even better now that I know the color is Killhope green."

"Am I to rest easy knowing that every night you'll take a knife in hand and think of my eyes?"

"Yes." She burst out laughing. "Yes, Your Grace. Every night an attack." Elbows on the desktop, she propped her chin atop her interlaced fingers. "I wish you would speak like this more often."

"I wish to stay on good terms with all my neighbors. And their knives." He put down his tea and straightened the papers he'd brought.

"I think I may be the only person alive who knows you are amusing."

"And I hope, Miss Clay, that you keep my secret."

Chapter Seven

OXTHORPE GAVE HIS horse its head, and his mare left the path and flew across the field. He'd had stallions with less strength and grace than his mare. She gathered herself to take the hedge, and they were airborne. Flying. They took the ditch between two fields, the stone fence after another. She knew the route for this morning's ride and kept her gallop another two hundred yards before she slowed and trotted to the path that would take them downhill to the Lyft.

The air was crisp, though last night's snow hadn't stayed on the ground. Another day of unusually mild weather for the time of year, then. Undoubtedly to be soon followed by a storm that would make them long for a day such as this one. As yet, the sky was gray with no threat of rain or snow.

Ahead of him, a hare darted from beneath the bramble on his left. His mount danced a bit, but she was not a horse that startled easily. The hare more slowly zig-zagged across the grass in the direction of yet more bramble. Not a hare, after all. From the looks of the creature, an Angora rabbit; someone's escaped livestock. He did not keep Angoras, though for all he knew, Miss Clay did.

The pond that marked a portion of the boundary between his property and Miss Clay's came into sight. If he were to look behind him, he would see the distant towers of Killhope. Were he to continue downhill and past the pond, he'd end up at Hope Springs where only a faint curl of smoke revealed its location.

Legally, the pond was his, but previous occupants had for years been permitted to fish here. Edith, however, was unlikely to lay claim to that right. He would have to mention he did not mind if she sent her gamekeeper to fish there. She'd hired a local man into the position vacated by the previous gamekeeper who'd retired when the property changed hands. A word with him might be in order on that subject, as well as an inquiry about wayward Angoras.

He dismounted on the Killhope side of the water, away from the stream that fed into the Lyft. When he returned to Killhope Castle, it would be to ten years of work to be done in a day. Letters to sort, documents to read. Accounts, reports, and bills to review. Letters to write; a mile of them. Even here in the country, so far from London, there would be callers to meet and appointments to keep.

If it were any season but winter, he'd go for a swim and delay his return to duty. He examined the water. Barely a ripple across the surface. Any ice there might have been earlier in the morning had long melted. The day was cold, but not freezing. There was no reason not to brave one last swim of the year.

He stripped off and laid his clothes on shrubs near where his horse examined the vegetation for edible shoots. Which his mare found. Naked, he waded into the water. Cold. Damned cold, but not freezing. He'd taken colder baths in his life. Either he was man enough to face the cold or not. He struck out and stroked as fast as he could, pushing himself.

Faster than his usual pace, for he wanted the heat of exertion, the burn of muscles used. Faster. Faster yet. He reached the other side, gasping, used up and glad for every thud of his pulse. He stood in hip-deep water, wishing he had someone here to time him. He had not swum so fast in all his life. The snap of cold air cut through him, invigorated him, reminded him he could feel. He stood, eyes closed, face turned to the sky. He did feel.

"Duke."

He knew her voice without looking. A calming timbre, and so often with a hint of amusement. In London, and later in Tunbridge Wells, he had often fancied no one but him heard that sliver of wit. How could any man hear that and not be fascinated? He did not move. One did not display one's nude body to a woman whom one was not about to take to bed. It was unlikely that would happen. But, well. The damage was done, wasn't it? Most of his privity was under water.

"You are on my side of the pond."

Hands on his hips, he looked at her. The world went from gray to colors—the backdrop of green fields and woods behind her. Ebony cloak with a flash of ermine lining, a dress of bronze and green, gloves to match the green.

He said, "Killhope lands include the pond."

He did not want to go to his grave knowing he had risked nothing for the woman he wanted. He wasn't an ass, though. Or if he was, he did not wish to give her incontrovertible evidence of the fact. What to say to her, then, when he knew he was likely to speak too gruffly?

She cocked her head, cheeks pink from the cold he did not yet feel. "Does that mean I have less property when the water is high and more when it's low? That hardly seems fair."

"I'll have the survey copied for you." A safe reply. As dull as that stack of correspondence in his office.

She pursed her lips and then smiled like it was spring. "It's not as if I shall raise an army and battle you for possession."

He returned her gaze. "If this were Edward's time," he said, "or Elizabeth's, or any of the Henrys, I'd marry you, and the property would be mine."

She broke into a grin. "You'd come to my house in the dead of night and carry me off?"

He willed her to understand how little this was in jest. "I would appeal to my sovereign and come away with a royal decree that we wed immediately."

"A better solution than armies poised to battle." She stood several feet from the edge of the pond. Gaze averted. He'd seen that absent look from her dozens of times in London. She thought herself invisible, and was not. Not to him. This was the second time he'd mentioned marriage to her. The second time she heard nothing but his words.

"At any rate," she went on, "I shan't dispute that you are currently in the water, whichever of us it belongs to. But you'll catch your death if you stay there."

"I won't."

"It is winter, Your Grace. And as you once sagely advised me, only a fool goes out in the cold."

He had a mad urge to wade out of the pond and—What sort of monster would impose his naked self on a woman? She would not appreciate a display of male nudity she had not asked to encounter. She hadn't asked and wasn't about to, for pity's sake. He stayed in the water. "It is not cold."

Steadfastly, she smiled at the vista to her right. "How odd, do you not agree, that we two are within ten feet of each other and have entirely different experiences of the temperature?"

"No."

"It cannot be significantly colder where I stand."

The wind picked up, and the cold bit hard enough to prickle the surface of his skin. He willed himself not to rub his arms.

She peeked at him, and her eyes widened. "Shall I fetch your clothes?"

"No." He ought to say something more. Do something. But what? Swim away? That seemed abrupt.

No one had expected him, of all men, to pay attention to a woman who wasn't young anymore, who had no fortune, and who was not particularly handsome. He hadn't. Not at first. She had been nothing. A companion to her cousin, the young lady whom others thought he ought to marry. He'd thought so himself, until he'd spent more time in conversation with her than Miss Louisa Clay.

What to say? He had no experience with situations like this. He had no difficulty with women. In the main, he didn't. He had a mistress he liked well enough, currently in London. She entertained him in bed because he made it convenient for her to be there exclusively. They understood their relationship and its boundaries.

He imagined himself saying, *May I ask a favor of you?*

And she, not knowing what he intended, would likely reply, *Shall I fetch your clothes?*

He could point to the other side of the pond and say, *Would you go there, take my watch, and time how long it takes me to swim back?*

She'd hurry to his clothes and find his watch. She'd raise her hand as a signal to prepare himself, and he would wave back and prepare himself for the return swim.

He'd swim the way he had before, fast and faster yet, and when he reached the other side, he'd stand, water sluicing off him.

She'd clutch his watch, all smiles, and God save his soul, he wouldn't care in the least that her smile came at the cost of his dignity. His dignity could go to the devil if it meant she smiled because of him. *A record*, he'd say. *My fastest swim yet.*

None of that happened.

None.

Because it was unthinkable that he could ask her that. If he did, he'd not manage the right words nor speak in the right voice. He'd imply she would steal his watch while she did him this ridiculous, absurd, undignified favor that presumed a familiarity between them that did not exist.

She would feel, as he did, that such a question was inappropriate and unbecoming of him. Insulting. He shivered, once.

Before him, she sent a rueful look to the skies. "Forgive me for keeping you." She curtsied. "Good day to you, Your Grace."

"Miss Clay." He watched her stride away, and only when she was out of sight did he make the return swim to the Killhope side. He was bloody cold and never so glad in all his life that he not been a fool.

He could not have borne her thinking him a fool.

Chapter Eight

A GENTLEMAN'S BOOT stood directly in Edith's way. She was on the path that led from the rear of Hope Springs and wound upward to the ridge above the Vale of West. The boot was upright, as if the owner had carefully placed it there to fend for itself, the devil may care for its fate. Precisely and exactly there. It was maroon leather and an exact match for the one-half of a pair of boots that had been deposited in her driveway the day she'd walked to The Duke's Arms and met Oxthorpe himself. How odd to encounter it again. Here. A walk of many minutes from her house or Killhope, for that matter.

She was halfway through a favorite ramble of hers that took her past the pond, though not to it, and up the hill with a view of the vale that took her breath every time she saw it. A thin layer of snow covered the ground, already more melted than not. The grass remained crunchy with frost.

She had no expectation she would again encounter the duke here, naked or otherwise. This was now in doubt. Here was his boot. Might not more of his clothing be nearby?

She picked up the boot and detoured to a point where she could see enough of the pond to determine whether the duke was there and might merely have dropped his boot. However, she saw no sign of Oxthorpe or his clothing.

Killhope was half a mile distant. Hope Springs was a mile and a half away. She set off for the castle with his boot tucked under her arm. Though the castle sat atop a hill that made the towers visible from most everywhere in Hopewell-on-Lyft, much of the structure was hidden by dense growths of oaks and pines. At the border between the two properties, the footpath she'd been following turned to a groomed path that led downhill and then, abruptly, uphill to the castle.

She emerged from the tree-shaded path into a meadow that would have been pretty but for the forbidding stone walls of Killhope at the other side. A driveway of finely crushed and raked gravel swooped around from the front and led to the stable block to her right.

The rear gates, tall, black ironwork with a griffin on the left side and a swan on the right, were open. Massive wooden doors were locked in place against the stone walls. As she walked through the gate, she felt very small indeed and unduly aware of the holes above through which Oxthorpe soldiers would have poured boiling water or oil onto enemies.

Killhope's inner courtyard, bisected with a raked gravel path that led to the front doors, also open, could have held an army. Not so long ago, it surely must have. The Fletcher family had begun their history of nobility as original Earls of the Marches. Groomed lawns filled the spaces between the drive and cobbled walkways that led to various wings of the castle, or to the well, or to the cannons chained to the walls and still trained on the countryside below. Perhaps in expectation of another Cromwell?

To her right, across the courtyard, the front gates were taller yet, and not two wooden doors, but one of wood painted black. A massive iron chain held up the portcullis. The duke's banner flew from the wall above, flapping in the breeze. Everything she saw here was tidy and clean. Even the cannons were immaculate.

She did not, however, see a servant to whom she could entrust the duke's boot. Smoke curled from the chimneys and curtains had been drawn, so it wasn't as if no one was home. She considered leaving the boot in the middle of the courtyard, perhaps atop the cover to the well. There would have been a lovely irony in that. She did not.

She walked toward the front gates and found the wooden steps to the entry door. At one time those steps would have been portable, to be put away in the case of a siege or attack. She stood on the top stair facing a brass door knocker in the shape of a swan. She was forced to admit that Killhope, so far, was not the dreary, ancient heap of stone she'd imagined.

The duke's butler, one Mycroft, opened the door at her knock. From time to time, she saw him in Hopewell-on-Lyft on the duke's business, and she'd seen him in The Duke's Arms lifting a pint with her butler when they happened to share the half day her cook was off, too.

Mycroft gave a smile that did not suit the reputation of his most cold and forbidding of employers. "Good morning, Miss Clay."

She extended the boot with one hand and pointed in the general direction of Hope Springs with the other. "I found this."

He took the boot from her and examined it for new dents in the leather. "Thank you, miss. It was kind of you to bring it here."

"Has anyone considered buying the dog its own boot?"

"Ah, miss, what haven't we tried? Several times already we've relocated where the footmen polish His Grace's boots. It seems she's a particular fondness now for these boots." He leaned in. "No others will do now. I fear she believes the boots are hers."

"Dear me." Behind Mycroft was an enormous arrangement of roses—white and red and pink—each bloom or bud perfectly formed. Fern leaves had been added to the arrangement, too. You'd think it was the middle of spring here instead of winter. "Oh," she said. "Oh, those are the most beautiful roses I have ever seen in my life."

Mycroft stood aside, and she walked straight to the table and breathed in. "They smell wonderful." She breathed in again. "How thoughtful to put them here where guests may be delighted by them." Privately, she wondered how many guests a man like the duke might have to be delighted, with or without roses. Social callers, not business callers.

"His Grace insists, miss."

"Is that so?" The duke did not seem the sort of man to care about flowers. What an unexpected discovery, that he should insist on such a thing. From duty, no doubt, not for reasons of aesthetics, surely. Then again, he possessed a sense of humor that perhaps no one but she had witnessed. Was it not possible that there was more to him than she thought? "How is anyone growing roses in winter? My garden is completely fallow. Everything cut back to the root. I haven't a single leaf or flower."

"A conservatory."

She froze, for that was not Mycroft's voice. She turned her back to the flowers, and there he stood. Not naked. Heavens, she could not erase that image from her mind. He wore tan breeches, a gold waistcoat worked with tiny red dots, and a carelessly tied neckcloth. His buff coat made his eyes colder than morning frost. He wore a perfectly good pair of boots. Entirely serviceable. Because, as she knew, he did not have both his top boots.

"A conservatory." She had seen him nude. Nearly nude. Standing in the water. A naked duke. "Yes, what else could it be but that?" For the second time, she was flustered by her reaction to him. "I ought to have guessed."

That flicker of something in his eyes surely meant he agreed she should have. A handsome man, yes, but so cold, so haughty, she could never entirely dismiss the uneasiness she felt around him. In London, she'd been as uninteresting to him as she was to any other gentleman who called on Louisa. She'd been impressed by his rank, of course, but all she need do in those days was give him his due respect, and that was that.

Good day, Miss Clay, he'd say in his somber way, and she would smile and say, *Good day, Duke*, and he'd turn to Louisa, who was too often struck dumb, and bow to her. *How lovely you and your cousin are today.*

Of all the gentlemen who called on Louisa, the duke had been both the most terrifying and fascinating. When it became clear his interest in Louisa was more than incidental and that there would surely be a match between them, it had been Edith's duty to chaperone. With Louisa unable at first to be herself when the duke was present, Edith had found much of the conversational efforts had fallen to her. She had been happy to do so, happy to watch her cousin slowly relax into her natural, gracious habits around the duke.

"I wish you good morning." She bent a knee. "I have returned your missing boot."

His gaze flicked to his butler, holding the boot. He was an overweening presence here, too, just as he had been in London and Tunbridge Wells. And her drawing room. No one else mattered now that he stood here with his chill eyes. A little of Louisa's trepidation crept up on her.

"I must be on my way. Good day to you, Duke." She nodded at Mycroft. "Good day."

The duke tipped his head backward. "You will see the conservatory."

The authority of the words caught at her, wrapped her up in his imperative. She did not wish to. Not in the least. She opened her mouth to make an excuse, but Mycroft cleared his throat. "You will much enjoy such a tour, Miss Clay."

She dismissed as absurd the notion that the butler meant to smooth over his employer's gruffness, and that it was done from fondness for the man. She could not imagine an unhappier place to work than Killhope Castle. Nor a more cheerless employer—except, he was not dour all the time. He wasn't.

"May I take your cloak, Miss Clay?" Mycroft gave her such a desperate, plaintive look that she could not bring herself to beg off.

She handed over her cloak. For Louisa's sake, anything. "I should be delighted."

Mycroft folded her cloak over his arm and accepted her hat as well. She shook out her walking dress and reached up to secure a few hairpins that had come loose during her walk.

"This way." The duke strode off, and she hurried after him. She caught up, but had to lengthen her stride to keep pace with him.

The interior of the castle was nothing like her imagination. The dank walls and darkened rooms of her imagination did not exist here. The tapestries hung on the walls had not been drizzled and thus retained the glitter of gold and silver thread and did their part in keeping the cold at bay. Sconces and candelabras contained beeswax tapers, and there was mirrored glass to reflect light. As they walked, they passed a niche with a suit of armor, and it occurred to her that one of his ancestors must have worn that gleaming steel.

She knew his history, or at least the history most often repeated about him. His father had died before Oxthorpe's birth. His mother had left him in the care of tutors and advisors and passed away the day after he reached his majority. Though he had not been an orphan, the fact was he had lived his life here, without either parent. "You grew up here, Duke?"

He gave her a cold look. "Yes."

"At Killhope, I mean to say."

"I did."

She imagined a young boy with dark hair and pale green eyes wandering the corridors and passageways, alone, with no one but tutors and servants to keep him company and entertain him. No wonder he was so solitary a man, if he'd grown up here with no friends or boys his age.

He stopped at a set of double doors carved with a swan on one side and a griffin on the other. He opened the door with the griffin and held it for her. "You ought to have sent a servant."

She kept her smile. She must. One did not insult a duke. She had no wish to insult anyone, least of all a neighbor, and even less one who owned most of the land for miles. "In future I shall know better."

He set off down a short, wide corridor hung with paintings she would have loved to study. "I hope so."

That was too much. Edith glared at his retreating back. "I have done you a service as well, Your Grace."

He stopped walking and faced her. "What service is that?"

"I have twice found and returned your footwear."

"I have acknowledged that."

"I ought to have left your boot where I found it."

"As I said." He spoke with infuriating calmness.

"And you say I ought to be married." She shook her head. "You, sir, are sadly and badly in need of a woman's gentle influence."

"I do not deny that."

She gave him a sideways look. "You understand your shortcomings in this respect and take no measures to remedy them?"

"There we must disagree."

She could not help smiling. "Then you *do* intend to go to Holmrook for Christmas."

"I have made no such decision. Is that the reason for your sharp tone, Miss Clay?"

"No, Duke, it is not." There was no more maddening man on this earth.

"May I inquire what I have done to offend you?"

"You are a duke, yes. I acknowledge that I am nothing and no one compared to you."

His dark eyebrows drew together. "I hope I have not given you cause to believe such a thing."

"It's true. There's no point pretending it isn't. You were kind to offer your assistance in the matter of my crisis of transportation."

"Thank you." But his words dripped ice.

"Neither of those things mean I welcome you sharing your low opinion of my decisions."

"I feel," he said, "that you do not refer to my criticism of your lack of decision about a carriage."

"Don't be willful."

"Never."

Hands on her hips, she said, "I felt it was more expedient and convenient to you, sir, to return your boot myself rather than walk all the way home and ask one of my servants to bring it here."

"My apologies, Miss Clay, for giving offense. I did not intend that."

Her stomach dropped to her toes. His eyes, such a cold and pale green, were really quite remarkable. When he looked at her, it was like being taken apart from the inside out.

"But it is very much the case that you could have left it there."

"No, Duke," she said softly. She could not—would not—tolerate his treating her in this dismissive fashion, as if she were as cold as the blood that ran in his veins. As if she cared for nothing but rational decision. "I could not have."

He let out a long breath. "I suppose not."

What was she to make of that flicker of resignation in his reaction? "I would not have left anyone's boot in the field. Not even yours."

"One of the servants would have gone in search of it."

"I found it first."

"So you did." He turned away. At the end of the corridor, he opened one of a pair of doors that were twins to the ones at the other end, with the same beautiful carving of his coat of arms. Again, he held the door for her.

Even before she passed him, she smelled roses, and then she forgot the petty irritations of her exchange with the duke.

"Oh. Oh." She stood inside, entranced.

The door he'd held for her opened onto a lengthwise oval of paradise, a more recent addition to the castle, for nothing like this would have been attached to a structure meant to instill dismay and despair in attacking armies.

A passion vine wound around a marble arch to her left. Opposite that was an orange tree. Roses grew along the entire long side of the oval. White gave way to pink gave way to red. A climbing rose with white blossoms streamed along a column and over a limestone arch.

To her right, a servant knelt in one of the beds, and not far from him a black-and-white collie lay on her side. He saw them, put away his shears and the rest of his implements and edged toward the bare outline of a door meant to blend into the wall. The collie followed, hopping on three legs.

Edith walked farther in. Delighted. Astonished. "How do you get them to bloom this time of year?"

"Paling."

This proved to be the servant's name, for the man turned and bowed to the duke. Like Mycroft, he did not seem fearful or terrified of his employer. "Your Grace."

"See to it that Miss Clay has roses to take home with her."

"Sir."

"Hardly necessary, Duke." That earned her another icy look. "But—that would be lovely. Thank you."

Paling had already retrieved a bucket from some hidden cavity, and now he pulled his shears from a pocket and headed for the roses.

"Have you a favorite color, Miss Clay?"

"They're all so lovely, I could not possibly choose."

"That is not an answer."

No man could have more thorns than he. Either he was silent as a block of ice or on the verge, she was certain, of telling her how deeply he disliked her and wished she would stay away. "Pink."

"Plenty of the *Duchesse de Montebello*, Paling."

That he knew the names of the roses disconcerted her. The duke of her slowly crumbling imagination was not a man who knew such things. Not a man whose servants would smile. Yet. And yet. He had offered to help her buy a gig. And a horse. She had seen him naked, near naked, all pale skin and muscled body. Adonis rising from the water. He had made her laugh. More than once.

These were not feelings she ought to have where he was concerned. She did not wish to think of him as a man. She couldn't.

To put some distance between them, she walked toward the marble stairs that led to an interior terrace. Here, there were two upholstered benches, several chairs, and a table. To her left, a wide and tall glass door with a pointed top was closed against the winter air, but here, he'd cleared the trees to unblock the view of the Vale of West. At the far left edge of the window glass, she could see one of the castle walls. That marble terrace meant that in summer and spring one might sit outside and admire the prospect.

Was it possible he sat here in awe of the view? Surely not. Surely. How could he not, in the face of such beauty? The view swept her away, took her breath and her words. Heedless of her audience, uncaring, she stood in the center of this terraced view and spread her arms wide. Head back as she breathed in, she turned in a circle.

She ended up facing the duke. He remained on the landing above the stairs. She lowered her arms, and he flushed. If she hadn't known better, she would have thought him embarrassed. What could possibly make a duke uncertain of himself? She smiled at him and forgave him every cross look and word they'd ever exchanged. "Mycroft was right. I have enjoyed this. Thank you for showing me this. I am glad, so glad, you insisted."

He nodded. A curt movement of his head, and she was, for no reason at all, convinced that the man before her was not in dislike of her but simply a man who did not have words come easily to him because he'd grown up alone.

She thought of him as a boy. Lonely here, with no father and no mother to hold him, only the servants for company, and Killhope as an unceasing reminder of the centuries of duty and responsibility that were his. Her heart twisted up.

Chapter Nine

I F HE SPOKE, there was no possible outcome but another disastrous exchange of words at cross-purposes. The chances of him finding both the right words and the right inflection were, in his experience with her thus far, vanishingly small. He would either growl at her, or tell her what was in his heart. She wasn't some young girl who would accept a proposal of marriage from him merely because a duke bent a knee to her. God in heaven, he would not want her to be such a woman.

He floundered in the waters of his admiration for Edith. Men like him married for the suitability of the match. They married young, to secure the line of inheritance. They married nobility, or else for reasons of money, property, and politics. He'd done none of that. None. The thought of doing so now turned him dead inside.

There was merit in a marriage made for reasons of duty. Until Edith, he'd intended to make just such a marriage. Had his life not taken such an odd turn, he might this moment be married to a woman—likely Miss Louisa Clay—who would have accepted him for reasons of his rank rather than her heart. He would have had no quarrel with that result. They would have made the pattern from which others might make similar marriages of suitability.

Then, Jesus, weeks after his hopes for Edith lay in tatters, after days and days of rumors and gossip about the men who had offered for her once her circumstances were so changed, she'd inquired about Hope Springs. This he'd learned solely because of his insistence on reviewing with Goodman the details of his estate.

For ill or good, he'd picked up the letter from her solicitor to his and said, "This offer."

Now he feared what the future might bring. That leaden weight in place of his heart was dread that she'd moved here because she believed he would marry her cousin and hoped to be close to Miss Clay without making a nuisance of herself. Dread that she would meet some other man and see in him all the joy of life that he lacked.

"I will see you home." The words came out all wrong, with gruff emphasis on the word *will*. One look at her, and he lost all chance at serenity. Because he had never in his life cared whether anyone liked him. He'd never thought about it. Until her.

She intended to tell him no. Because that was her way. Because she was worried he might throw over her cousin on some whim or other. She was not wrong in that, since, in fact, he did mean to. Just the other day, when he'd felt the delay in a response to Clay's invitation was yet another message, he'd replied to the man's letter, which included a breezy, amusing paragraph from Louisa. In his single-paragraph reply, he wished Clay and his daughter all the happiness of the coming holidays and ended with the dry fact that he intended to remain at Killhope until February or March and then remove to Wales until June.

He presumed Clay would understand his letter for what the rejection it was. He took a breath. "It is cold."

She touched a near blossom. "You admit that, do you?"

"There have been six robberies between here and Hope Springs."

"Not in daylight."

"Two."

She glanced at him. "Not recently."

"Tuesday last. Friday."

"I never heard that."

"The road goes through the woods not once but twice." He held back a fierce smile when he saw the moment she acknowledged he was correct. "Nor will I send you home with flowers to manage on your own."

"In that case, thank you, Duke." She curtsied, and it was well done, in that way that never yet failed to make his heart clench.

It was her grace that had first caught his eye. That and the fact that three weeks into the Season, everyone he knew, lady or gentleman, had eventually remarked in passing that they very much liked Miss Edith Clay, and wasn't Miss Louisa Clay a pretty young thing? Men wrote poems in praise of Miss Clay's beauty, but they all wanted Edith to sit beside them at dinner.

On their return journey through the house, he stopped a servant and asked to have his carriage brought around. In this he was fully competent. He could instruct his staff without losing himself. He gave instructions. They were carried out.

They resumed their walk with him infernally aware of her keeping pace. Her gaze moved from place to place, to open doors, to statues occupying niches, to the chandeliers and sconces. Doubtless, she had imagined he lived in a dungeon, a moldering heap where the blood of ancient enemies yet stained the floors. He'd heard the talk. The local stories, most too fanciful by far, about how his home had come to be called Killhope.

He stopped at the next door. "The saloon." He refused to look at her. "The second level I added three years ago." He pointed to the open second level with a walkway and walls lined with shelves of books. He could propose to her. She might accept because of his rank. Because he was Oxthorpe. She might. He thought, hoped, desired, that if she did, she would eventually come to love him. If she didn't? If she never loved him? No fate could be worse than life without her regard. He'd rather live without hope of her love if her marriage to another man brought her happiness.

"Do you entertain here often?"

He wanted to put her back to the wall and take her mouth. He wanted to hold her tight and see where that led them. He knew how to kiss a woman. A lady. Even with the raw edge of lust there, he could kiss her. Wanted to, at any rate. "No."

They continued in silence. He stopped at the drawing room and stood by the door while she wandered a few feet inside. She turned in a slow circle, head up, for it was the frescoed ceiling that made this room a delight. "I am transported."

She spoke softly, in awe, and when she focused on him, he gave a brusque nod in return.

"If I had such a ceiling as this, I would lie on the floor hours of every day."

"I might have done so."

She tipped her head to one side, plainly working out if he'd spoken in jest or was serious.

"In my youth."

Somehow he had not bungled his response, for she appeared genuinely delighted with their exchange. "A well-spent youth."

"Yes."

Their last stop was a smaller drawing room, his favorite room to sit with the morning *Times* and a sporting paper or two. He'd placed his favorite chair where there was a glimpse of the Lyft wending its eventual way to the pond between their respective properties. The rest was obscured by the woods where some damned fool was playing at highway robbery and calling himself the New Sheriff of Nottingham.

"How pleasant it must be to sit here with such a prospect to admire." She looked over her shoulder at him, as ever, not in the least affected by him or his consequence. Not one whit. She was a lady, yes, but she would never believe herself the sort of woman who might marry a duke. "You aren't the sentimental sort, are you?"

"I'm told not."

She considered him, and he felt the curiosity behind her scrutiny of him. He had no idea what to make of that and so pushed off the wall he'd leaned against and headed for the door. She followed.

By the time they reached the entry, Mycroft waited with her cloak and hat in hand. A footman held the roses, securely wrapped in paper and tied with string. A suitably large arrangement, he was pleased to see. The roses wouldn't last much longer this time of year. Paling had worked a bloody miracle getting so many blooms out of season.

Having assisted her in donning her cloak, Mycroft produced Oxthorpe's greatcoat. While he shrugged into it, he heard his carriage arrive in the courtyard. He accepted his hat and pulled his gloves from his pocket. Mycroft glided forward and opened the door.

The air was crisp and clear, though a breeze carried a few wisps of smoke into view. He handed Edith into the carriage, then entered himself and accepted the roses from the footman. He handed them to her.

She laid them on her lap and put a hand on the strap to brace herself when the coachman snapped the reins. The interior now smelled of roses. They were half the distance to the road before either of them spoke.

"We shall have more snow soon," she said.

"Yes."

"This is my first winter in Nottinghamshire." She smiled. "Is this weather unusual for the time of year?"

"No."

She bent her head over the flowers. He knew she was not beautiful. He knew she did not see herself as the object of a man's lust. He knew if he told her he found her desirable, she'd not understand his meaning. She'd think he meant something other than marriage. In that, she would be right, but a man could want both things from the same woman. "They're lovely."

Silence descended. Her cloak was good wool. Thick and inky black. It would do for a Nottinghamshire winter. Her boots were sensible, too. Solid construction for walking. He approved of how she'd spent her money to outfit her wardrobe.

"What did you feel when you understood you held the winning ticket?"

Slowly, she lifted her head, and their gazes connected. This time he did not look away from her. He wanted this atom of truth from her. "I was shaking." She held out a hand. "Trembling. Cold and hot all at the same time. I must have read the numbers a hundred times. I was lightheaded."

"You did not swoon."

"No, though I wonder I didn't. I ought to have." She pressed the back of her hand to her forehead and fluttered her eyes. "If ever there was a time a woman should swoon, it's when she's won seventy-five thousand pounds in the lottery."

"Not you."

"No." That was agreement with him. She held up a hand, palm down. Her fingers shook. "Look." Her words were soft, so soft and, yes, that was a quiver. "I'm a-tremble at the recollection."

Reckless abandon washed over him, and he wrapped his fingers around hers. "As would anyone be."

"Not you."

He waited too long to reply, for she tugged on her fingers. But he did not release her hand. "Once," he said, aware he was taking the conversation into dangerous waters, "I won ninety-seven thousand at Faro."

Her eyebrows drew together. "Faro?"

He released her hand. And there went any improvement in her opinion of him. Of all the fool things to confess, why that?

"Recently?" She let go the strap.

"I was seventeen, and it was the first time ever I set foot in a"—he almost said *bawdy house*—"gaming establishment."

"Oh." Her cheeks pinked up. She understood the sort of place he'd been.

"And the last."

"You were seventeen. Oh, reckless youth."

"I was perfectly sober."

"Ninety-seven thousand pounds."

He nodded. The blacklegs and Mollies had done their utmost to keep him in the house—spirits, food, women, men, and promises of perversions involving all of those things. The women had got him in the door, but they could not prevent his leaving. "I collected my winnings." Vowels, banknotes, and two deeds. "And I went home. Every day I send my thanks to the heavens that I made it home without being robbed."

Her eyes widened, and then the grin she'd been fighting broke out. "From a youth who gazed hours at such a marvelous ceiling to one who stood at a Faro table."

"An indiscretion of youth never to be repeated."

"Ninety-seven thousand pounds." She whispered the numbers as she settled a hand around her throat. "Goodness. What if you'd lost?"

"You may believe that I did not speak of it to anyone."

She bit her lower lip and looked at him from beneath her lashes. His stomach swooped to his toes. "I did not tell a soul. No one, until my winnings had been deposited in the bank. And even then, I visited my banker to be sure I would be allowed to withdraw funds."

"As you were."

"I was, and it was the most"—she closed her eyes, but opened them again immediately—"the most wonderful freedom. I stood in the Bank of England, five one-pound notes in my pocket. More money than I'd ever had in all my life, and it was mine."

Five pounds lost from his pocket would be nothing to him, though by nature he would both know and resent the misplaced funds. He could imagine, but never understand, a life where five pounds represented a vast fortune. The fact was, his last quarter's income had approached thirty thousand pounds sterling. One of those damned deeds he'd won as a feckless seventeen-year-old had been to a lead mine that added a tidy sum to his balance sheets.

Edith leaned toward him. There was a connection between them, true and real. "I will confess something to you, but only if you promise never to breathe a word to another soul."

"Unless you confess a crime." The rich blue of her bodice looked well on her. Very well. She'd a wardrobe of color now, instead of those plain and sober hues.

"A failing of character that breaks no laws, though perhaps that's worse."

He nodded. The carriage began the descent that would take them through the first of the woods before the bridge into Hopewell-on-Lyft.

"My cousin Mr. Clay was cross with me when I came home that day. He felt I'd taken an unwarranted liberty being gone so long, and he took me to task. I'd taken one of the upstairs maids with me, you see, and she was wanted while we were out." She touched her upper chest. "But I listened to him tell me how ungrateful I was for all that he'd done for me those many years, and I thought to myself, I have five pounds in my pocket that did not come from him. I am wealthy now. Wealthier than he. I said too pertly, I confess it, 'Mr. Clay, cousin, I am removing from your house this day.'"

"And?" What a moment that must have been for her. If he'd been there in witness, he'd have cheered her on.

"And—" She sat back, quite satisfied with herself. "Well, sir, I hired away the maid and one of the footmen, and we three removed to the Pulteney Hotel where we stayed until I purchased Hope Springs. Mr. Clay called on me once to tell me again how ungrateful I was. In a pique, I sent him a hundred pounds in repayment for the cost of my upkeep."

Plainly, she expected disapproval from him, but he could not disapprove. Not ever. He'd disliked Clay from the moment he saw how little the man cared for Edith, and could not bear to think of her wondering why the man who stood in place of her father had no shred of kindness for her. "You did not deduct the cost of your labor?"

"I ought to have." She laughed, a sound of delight. His heart soared at the triumph of amusing her. "Louisa sent me a lovely note, though. She wished me all the best and hoped we would meet again one day. She is a well-bred young lady."

"Agreed."

"I love her for her generosity and friendship. Anyone would."

"I am glad you were not alone." There went his heart and his hopes again. Killed dead. Did she think she could persuade him to offer for Miss Louisa Clay?

She put a hand on his knee then snatched it away. "I'm sorry you were."

He said nothing to that because there was nothing for him to say that was not dangerous. The carriage crossed the bridge into Hopewell-on-Lyft. The Duke's Arms would soon be on their left, then another wood and the hill to her home. The mail coach had just stopped at The Duke's Arms and there was a deal of accompanying noise. When they were past, he lowered the glass.

"Why Hope Springs?" he asked. They were in the woods now, and he could not help watching the road as much as he could given the trees and the coming turn. "Besides the legend of Robin Hood, that is."

"Who would not wish to live so near where Robin Hood and Maid Marian were lovers?"

"Who indeed."

She lifted a hand and, with a shrug, let it fall to the seat. "I asked my solicitor to find me properties in Nottinghamshire and, behold, Hope Springs was on the list and well within my budget. And I thought—"

The carriage shuddered to a stop. The coachman shouted, an inarticulate sound abruptly cut off.

They were not yet at Hope Springs.

"Stand and deliver."

Oxthorpe reached under the seat for his pistol.

Chapter Ten

Edith put a hand to her mouth and told herself not to panic. Nothing would be gained by that. The fact that Oxthorpe was sanguine helped. His mouth thinned, and there was something dreadful about his focus. From nowhere, he'd produced a pistol. Now that she saw it in his hands, it was as if the weapon were the only living thing in the carriage.

His coachman shouted, "Oi there, you poxy devil, do you know who you've stopped? The bloody duke himself."

Hope and denial both washed over her. A man must be desperate indeed to rob a duke.

Oxthorpe checked his pistol and murmured, "Don't be a fool, John Coachman."

Another voice replied, "A gentleman with a right deep pocket, I'll warrant."

The duke slid closer to the left-side door. "Remove what jewelry you cannot bear to lose, Edith. Leave the rest, or they'll know something is amiss and search the carriage." She removed a bracelet and the ebony hair combs that had belonged to her mother as quickly as she could. Her necklace and earrings must be sacrificed.

He tapped a panel at the far side of the carriage and exposed a hidey-hole. She handed him what she'd removed. He traded the wallet in his pocket for the much-thinner one he took from inside, then deposited her items and closed up the panel.

The carriage door opened on the side nearest her, and her heart slammed against her chest. Had the robbers seen what the duke had done?

Cold air rushed in. "My liege," the robber called out in a sing-song voice. "Come stretch your legs and take the air."

Oxthorpe surged forward, blocking the doorway. From behind him, she caught a glimpse of a lanky figure dressed in ill-fitting black clothes. The highwayman trained a pistol on the doorway. The duke was out of the carriage now, his own pistol held behind his back.

"Who have you got with you?" He waved the gun. "Let's have him out. Non-compliance means a shot through the heart. Come on, lad. Out with you."

Edith descended, frightened, yet reassured by the duke's calm demeanor. Still with his pistol concealed, Oxthorpe assisted her from the carriage.

Two men had stopped them. One trained a pistol on the coachman, who'd been made to dismount from the top seat of the carriage. The second highwayman had a youth's gangly, loose-limbed body, a boy primed to murder. An ill-fitting mask obscured his face. Early in his criminal apprenticeship, she thought.

The other robber was a more solid man. "Madam Duchess," this robber said. He did not waver in pointing his gun at the duke. "Your purse and your jewels. Empty your pockets, if you please."

One hard look from the duke stopped her from denying she was the Duchess of Oxthorpe. She did as she was told and divested herself of the jewelry she had retained. She also made a show of going through her pockets. "I haven't a purse, sir."

"What? No pin money of your own?"

She shook her head. How could the duke be calm at a time like this? Oxthorpe rested a hand on her shoulder. "My love," he said. "My dearest." She moved closer to the duke. "My wife is with child, sir. I beg you, allow her to return to the carriage."

She put her free hand on her stomach and willed herself to look as if that were so.

"We'll have your cloak and your slippers, too, ma'am."

"In this weather? This is an outrage." Oxthorpe took a step forward.

She did not have to pretend to be afraid. "No." She clutched his coat, though she knew enough not to interfere with whatever might come to pass with his weapon. "No, you mustn't."

"Duchess." His gaze lanced through her. He ordered—commanded—with that look. "Return to the carriage this moment."

The older robber was implacable. "Leave the cloak, if you please."

She divested herself of the garment and dropped it to the ground beside the other items. The younger one scooped up the smaller items and shoved them into his pockets.

"The carriage, my dear." Nothing betrayed Oxthorpe as anything but serene.

She complied, but her heart beat too fast, her hands shook, and her legs felt disconnected from her body. These ruffians had weapons, and even after they'd emptied their pockets, the duke had not been allowed to return to the carriage.

Once she was inside, Oxthorpe slammed the door shut. Through the glass, she saw him move forward, a lunge toward the gangly young highwayman. She hadn't expected him to be so fast. At the end of that motion, somehow, Oxthorpe had two pistols. He pointed one at the youth and the other at the older man.

Oxthorpe addressed the younger man. "Return my wife's possessions if you please. Do not move, sir." He adjusted his aim when the other highwayman shifted. "Do you think I don't recognize your voices? The way you stand? You were brought before me at the quarter sessions eighteen months ago and plainly learned nothing from the experience."

The older man kept his hands lifted. "I'm the New Sheriff of Nottingham."

"The devil you are. Go home to your family and pray God you are never again so stupid as to try your hand at highway robbery, for I promise, I will have no mercy on you another time." He shifted the positions of both guns. "I'll see your backs or see you dead."

The gangly robber took off running.

"You." Oxthorpe sneered. He turned his full attention on the remaining man. "I don't want to see you before me again. You and your brother will hang if you continue in this fashion."

The other highwayman dashed into the trees, too, and it seemed an eternity to her that Oxthorpe sighted along the barrel of the pistol, tracking the man's progress through the trees. Any moment she expected him to fire.

He didn't. He lowered his hand and stood for some moments, staring into the woods. In this new silence, the coachman gathered the remaining items on the ground, but he staggered when he straightened, and everything scattered once again. The duke looked at him. "John?"

"A mean knock on the head, Your Grace."

He nodded to the top of the carriage and handed one of the pistols to him. "Up then. I'll drive." He held up a hand and in clipped words said, "No argument."

Before Oxthorpe came to the door of the carriage, he retrieved all the items on the ground. He handed her their things and deposited his in a pile on the seat. He dropped the pistols into the pockets of his coat. "He's in no condition to drive, Edith."

"I understand."

"I'll have you home in no time." He secured the door, and a moment later, the carriage was headed uphill again. She could not afterward decide if it had taken a lifetime to reach Hope Springs or, as he'd promised, no time at all.

She was, she thought, perfectly fine. Entirely in control of herself while she walked to the door with the duke at her side. She had her bracelet and hair combs safely in her pocket. As he had the last time he walked with her to her door, he said nothing. This time, though, he stepped inside with her.

"Your Grace, I—" She put a hand over her mouth to stop the sob that rose in her chest. Her tidy, happy world had been severely shaken.

He was a duke. If she'd won a hundred and fifty thousand pounds she'd not be his social equal. That he was standing here in her house was a miracle of condescension. That he had called her his duchess and said she was with child—the invention of desperation, but my God. My God. He'd called her *my love* and *dearest*.

He put a hand on her shoulder. A light touch. "Shall I call your maid?"

Her heart was lead. So small and heavy. "You might have been killed."

A faint crease appeared between his eyes. "Your point?"

"That you might have been killed."

"So might you have."

"*I* did not confront two desperate highwaymen. Blackguards who could have murdered you."

"Neither one of them was The New Sheriff of Nottingham. In that respect, those two are imposters who ought to know better than to play at such games."

"That was no game. Or do you intend to argue no one's pistol was loaded?"

His expression turned fierce. "No."

"How do you know they aren't the ones robbing everyone left and right?"

"Allow me to represent to you that I recognized them instantly and that, further, I saw them at The Duke's Arms at the same time the actual New Sheriff robbed some other poor soul."

"Does it matter?" She could scarcely speak. "You could be dead now, and it would have been my fault. You were right. You've been right about everything. I ought to have left your boot in the field."

"I—"

"I ought to have refused to let you drive me home."

"Edith—"

The sound of her given name shocked her. He'd called her that before, when they were in the carriage and he was preparing to face death. He'd said her name the way a lover would. He could not possibly think that. *Edith.*

"Come here." He took her hands in his, and she walked forward as if he were anyone, an everyday person, anyone one might simply meet. He folded his arms around her, and she leaned against him.

There was a moment of awkwardness. In the back of her whirling thoughts, a voice warned her not to presume like this, but he drew her close, so close. His arms around her broke a barrier, demolished her defenses. His body was solid, and his heart beat steadily. She was racked. Shaken by what had happened, but far more by what could have happened.

"We might both be dead." She sniffed and breathed in his scent. "Lying there at the side of the road, bleeding. Gone."

"Darling." His low, soft whisper wound around her. "Where are your servants?"

Chapter Eleven

EDITH WALKED INTO the stationers accompanied by her maid. While Edith headed for the counter, her maid found a seat on a bench along one side of the shop. The proprietor leaned his forearms on the counter top. "Good day to you, miss."

"A good day to you, sir. Come now. You know why I am here. I have your note in my pocket."

"That I do, miss. That I do." He reached under the counter and brought out several sheets of paper.

"Oh. Lovely." She spread the paper out on the blotter that covered a portion of the counter. She had already purchased stationery printed with her name and direction at the top: Miss Edith Clay, Hope Springs, Hopewell-on-Lyft, Nottinghamshire. She'd even commissioned the design of a rose to be printed in red on every sheet. An extravagance that had been a fair trouble to have done to her satisfaction. This custom paper of hers was one of the expenses that leaped to the front of her mind whenever she fretted over having spent too much money.

And yet, here she was because the stationer had sent her a note to the effect that he had just received shipments from Paris and Florence and would she be interested in seeing them first? The sheets before her were samples for her examination.

"This is the Italian?" she asked.

"Yes, miss."

"Lovely." There was a blue cast to the paper she quite liked. She held up the other. Smooth grained, a fine, tight weave. "The French, I take it."

"Indeed." He set pen and ink on the counter. "Go ahead, miss. You'll not know if this is paper you want until you've written on it."

"Right you are. Thank you." She examined the pen. "You have one of the steel-nibbed pens."

"Newly arrived from London."

"Do you like it? It's not too rough on the paper?"

"I've not found it so. I have a quill, if you prefer."

"Oh, no. I should like to try this." From the corner of her eye, she saw there was another customer. He'd been on the opposite side of the shop. She dipped the pen in the ink but froze when she realized it was the Duke of Oxthorpe and that he was making his way to her.

She held the pen suspended over the bottle. Somehow, this man who had never been anything to her but a title—words, a crest, a man whose existence was embodied in the word Oxthorpe—had become someone she knew well enough to expect they would greet each other. Remarkable. She, Miss Edith Clay, a woman of no consequence, was personally acquainted with a duke. "Your Grace."

She owed him her life.

The duke nodded in his curt way. "How do you do, Miss Clay?"

She tapped the nib of her pen against the rim of the inkwell and curtsied. "Well, thank you. May I hope the same for you?"

"Yes." He wore a green coat, buckskins, and the maroon boots. In one hand he held his hat, in the other, a notebook. His hair, medium length but thick and black, was cut short at the sides. She had an inappropriate urge to discover what it would be like to run her fingers through it.

He fell quiet, but she understood this was his way. He was not a talkative man. Once, she'd imagined him sitting alone in his house, a monster ready to devour anyone who came near. What she imagined now was a man who had both his rank and his natural reticence working against him.

She smiled at him. If he continued in his gruff ways the rest of his life, she would defend him to anyone. Anyone. "I very much like the notebooks sold here."

"Daykin & Towle make excellent paper." Daykin & Towle being the local papermaker.

"They do. I have laid in my supplies." She turned to the sheet of Italian paper and wrote her name across the top. "From time to time, however, I wish to write upon paper that speaks to me in a foreign language. I see myself now, sitting at my desk, dashing off the most amusing note on the finest Italian paper." She mimed writing. "My dearest Louisa, I had broiled smelt for breakfast. They were most excellent."

"*Affascinante.*"

She laughed, and the duke might actually have smiled, though one could never be certain. He was no troll beneath the bridge, not if he could laugh. She dipped her pen again and wrote quickly at the bottom of the sheet before her nerve abandoned her. "I am having a small party tomorrow evening. You ought to come. At six. Mr. Amblewise will be there. Mr. Jacobs is an astronomer from Bunney. I do not know if you have met him, but he has engaged to show us the stars if the night is clear."

"I know of him."

She wrote:

Miss Edith Clay requests the honor of your presence at Hope Springs for dinner and stargazing, weather permitting.
Thursday at 6:00 pm

Respondez, s'il vous plait

Underneath the last line, she drew a flourish and blotted the paper. She carefully folded and tore the sheet and handed the bottom portion to the duke. "There. I am sure you have obligations every hour of the day and night, but should you discover you are not otherwise engaged, I would be delighted to have you join my party."

He unfolded the sheet and examined the page gravely before he tucked it into an inside pocket of his coat. "I will consult my schedule."

"*Grazie, Duc.*" He would never accept, of course, but she was glad to have made the effort. If he did not wish to make friends, that was his choice. But if he were to attend, he might find he had made one or two. They parted and went their separate ways, and Edith could not help feeling they might themselves one day be friends.

Later that afternoon, she was sitting down to tea when her butler brought her an envelope on a salver. But this was not the post. The letter, with its distinctive seal, was from Oxthorpe. She took the letter. "Thank you."

"There is a boy waiting outside, miss." He bowed and extended a second letter, this one intriguingly thick and also from Oxthorpe. "He's brought a gig and a horse he says are for you."

"A boy?" She opened the thicker of the letters, beyond curious at receiving not one but two letters from him. Inside this one were three folded sheets. The topmost was an invoice for the gig and necessary accoutrements, the second for the horse. The combined amount was enough to make her heart beat faster. She had the funds, she told herself. This purchase would not bankrupt her.

On the third sheet, he'd written two paragraphs, on paper with his crest embossed at the top. They informed her he was attaching the invoices and sending along one William Benedict, who, he had reason to believe, would make her an excellent groom, if she were of a mind to hire him.

She looked up. "Tell Mr. Benedict I will be with him shortly."

"Yes, miss."

She slipped the other letter into her pocket, for this development required her time and attention. In far less precise letters at the bottom of the paragraphs, though it was plain the entire document was in the same hand, was the word *Oxthorpe*. Once, that word had conjured up a cold and forbidding feeling.

Outside, William Benedict stood beside the gig. A young man of seventeen or eighteen, tall and gangly, he snatched off his hat when she came down the stairs. He bowed. "Miss Clay."

He struck her as familiar, but she could not think where she'd seen him before. She walked around the gig. Gleaming black-lacquer body with a black leather seat and folded-down cover. The inside rims of the wheels were painted yellow, the spokes green. The duke's colors, which she supposed must be a coincidence. Perhaps the carriage maker did so for every vehicle the duke ordered. She ran a hand along the leather seat and the side of the gig.

"Are you from Hopewell-on-Lyft, Mr. Benedict?"

"No, miss." He watched her walk around to the horse. "From Bunney."

"I like his looks. Do you?" She patted the gelding's shoulder. It was dark gray with a black mane.

"I do, miss." He shifted his weight between his feet. "You'll have no trouble with him."

She considered the young man, and his familiarity to her was as coincidental as the colors of the gig's wheels. If Oxthorpe believed in this boy enough to send him to her, then she would not disagree. "His Grace recommends you highly. Do you know why?"

Benedict swallowed hard. "I'm grateful for the chance, miss. I work hard. I'm honest."

"So long as you want to earn an honest wage."

He swallowed again. "Yes, miss."

"Would you like to work for me?"

"I would, miss." His hands crushed the brim of his hat. In short order they settled the details of what she would pay, his days off, that she expected to see him at church, and that she would pay for two suits for him to wear.

"You will have no desire to supplement your income by any other means, I hope."

"No, miss. Thank you, miss." He met her gaze for only an instant before his focus skittered away, but his cheeks turned bright red.

"Go around to the back after you've seen to the gig and the horse, then. You'll be looked after."

"Thank you." He bobbed his head.

"You'll let me know if there's anything you need."

"I will, miss."

She had a gig. A very smart gig among gigs. There would be no reason for her not to hold her head high when she attended the next meeting of the assembly committee. For that, she had the duke to thank.

It wasn't until two or three hours later that she remembered Oxthorpe's other letter. She left off writing to Louisa about her gig and the beauty of the horse that was new to her stables, and drew the letter from her pocket. She bent the paper enough to lift the seal without badly breaking it. This must be instructions for remitting the monies she owed him. But it wasn't. It was his reply to her impromptu invitation to dinner, signed with his title. *Oxthorpe*.

Not his regrets.

An acceptance.

Chapter Twelve

What if no one came? Edith jumped up from her seat in the drawing room and began pacing again. This was her first official dinner party at Hope Springs, and she was nervous about her guests and all that might go wrong. Dinner might be burned. She might spill something on her gown—she wore her best silk tonight, and her ebony hair combs, too, because she now considered them doubly lucky; because of her mother and, now, the duke.

She smoothed her skirt and told herself she would not consult the time again. She did, though. She'd had acceptances from them all but Mrs. Quinn and her husband who had an engagement that night. The members of the assembly committee, naturally. Mr. Jacobs, the astronomer, and others.

What if her guests had been robbed on their way here? Whoever this New Sheriff of Nottingham was had robbed a gentleman on his way to Scotland just three days ago.

Outside, she heard a carriage arrive. Until her butler announced Mr. Thomas and his wife, she was convinced the arrival must be either a servant carrying regrets or the constable with terrible news of the fate of one of her guests.

Mrs. Thomas came in first and Edith was beyond relieved for their safe arrival. Mr. Thomas met her with a hearty "Good evening," and a bow over her hand. His wife was all smiles and a quick kiss on the cheek.

"You had an uneventful drive, I hope?" Her encounter with the highwaymen had made her anxious about the safety of all her friends. Word of the duke's bravery had got out, not because he'd said anything, but because she'd told everyone who would listen.

"We did, Miss Clay." The former ambassador to the Porte briefly set a hand on her shoulder. "We made good time and met with no robbers."

Mrs. Thomas looped her arm through Edith's. "You've done wonders with this room."

She welcomed the distraction of the remark, no more because it was a heartfelt compliment. She was determined to surround herself with colors that she loved. "I was so worried the color would not be what I hoped, but it is precisely the shade of orange I wanted to have in this room."

"Perfection, if you ask me."

"Thank you." Mrs. Thomas had dressed in a reminder of her husband's former occupation, for she wore a turban and a gown of gold-and-blue silk brocade. A sash wound around her waist, and her slippers matched that band of silk. Her husband stood by his wife and beamed at her. "May I say what a lovely ensemble this is?" Edith said. "Wherever did you find such a fabric?"

"Anatolia. The souk in Aleppo. Mr. Thomas thought I'd gone mad, as much as I bought."

"No, no, not in the least." She gave the former diplomat a sideways smile. "No one would be mad to buy such gorgeous cloth as this. Why, to do so defines good sense and a rational mind."

"There, you see?" Mrs. Thomas sent her husband an arch and fond look. "*She* understands."

"Since you are divine in that gown, beloved wife, I cannot now disagree that you were correct when we were at the souk."

She blew him a kiss. "There was never a woman luckier in her husband than I."

"Nor I in my wife."

Edith wanted to sweep them both into a hug. They loved each other, and it brought both joy and tears to her heart to see that fondness.

The others arrived in short order. Distinguished and silver-haired Mr. Jacobs who, weather permitting, would lead their stargazing, Mrs. Bolingbase; Mr. Amblewise. Mr. Greene, a gifted artist, and his wife, and the Worthys. Mrs. Worthy, Edith had discovered, was pure inspiration at the piano-forte. No Oxthorpe as of yet, but since her receipt of his acceptance, she had decided that he would not, in fact, arrive. She'd given him the invitation too informally. His acceptance to her must have been sent in the same less-than-serious manner.

There was no reason for her to delay dinner. All the guests she'd expected to attend were present. Quite wisely, she'd not mentioned the possibility that the duke might attend. Their numbers for what she hoped would be a semiregular gathering were complete. She summoned a footman and gave instructions that dinner was to be served in twenty minutes.

Much sooner than she expected her butler appeared in the doorway.

"Ah," she said to the others, turning away from the door. "Dinner is served."

Behind her, Walker cleared his throat. "His Grace, the Duke of Oxthorpe."

The astonishment that paralyzed her was reflected in the faces of her guests. Mr. Thomas stood at the sideboard with the wine he intended for his wife. Those guests who were seated, rose. Edith turned and indeed, the duke was moving toward her. She blinked several times. He was here.

The duke took her hand. "Miss Clay."

"Duke." He was resplendent in a coat of midnight blue, a pewter waistcoat, and tan breeches. His much-traveled top boots were a divine complement to his attire. A sapphire gleamed from a ring on his index finger.

With a smile that was nearly friendly, he greeted those guests whom he already knew. She introduced him to the guests to whom he had not yet been introduced. After a brief, awkward silence as they adjusted to his unexpected arrival and the impact of his considerable presence, Mrs. Thomas filled in the conversation. Yes. Yes, indeed, she was the wife of a diplomat. Mrs. Worthy was of great assistance, too, in overcoming the difficulties. She was a delightful and attractive woman, who did not quail when the duke turned his pale eyes on her.

Imagined difficulties never emerged. Oxthorpe was not a man of many words, but neither was he the silent figure she'd feared he might be. His erudition shone through, and he listened attentively to the others when they spoke. He was charming in his quiet way, both interested and interesting. She did not think she was the only one to notice that he and Mrs. Worthy got on well, and it was a rare woman who managed that feat.

After dinner, they gathered again in the drawing room. Mr. Greene, who lived on the other side of the Lyft, picked up pencil and paper and sketched likenesses with his usual uncanny deftness, much to everyone's delight and appreciation.

"Tell me, Mr. Greene," Mr. Thomas said, "will you be at the assembly to dance with our Miss Clay?"

Still sketching, he glanced up from his sheet of paper long enough to wink at Edith. "Wouldn't miss it for the world."

"Did they not just have an assembly?" the duke asked. At the moment, he was sitting by the fire, holding a glass of French Burgundy that had come very dear. She had her own glass, as she refused to restrict the ladies to sherry. The vintage was worth every penny she'd paid to stock her cellar.

"You are thinking of last quarter, Your Grace." Mrs. Thomas peeked at Mr. Greene's work. "That's quite good."

"Thank you." Greene used a finger to smudge a line.

"The first Monday of every quarter, Duke."

Oxthorpe tilted his head. "Not this quarter, though. Is not the Christmas assembly to take place on the twenty-second?"

"Yes. Our holiday assembly is rightly famous, and the closer it is to the holiday, why, the better, Your Grace." Mrs. Thomas curtsied to the duke. "Thanks to generous gifts of benefactors such as Miss Clay and yourself. This year's Christmas assembly will be especially grand."

"Have no fear," Mr. Greene said, "I shall be there. Indeed, I cannot imagine a pleasanter way to spend an evening than dancing with Miss Clay and the other young ladies of Hopewell-on-Lyft and environs."

Oxthorpe nodded as if he were responsible for organizing the entire event. "I hope the young ladies and gentlemen of the town enjoy the gathering."

"We would be so pleased if you attended." Mrs. Thomas moved away from Mr. Greene and walked along the short side of the wall.

"I have a great many obligations."

"Yes, yes. You are traveling to Northumberland. You did tell me that. I'd forgotten."

Edith noted he did not correct Mrs. Thomas's supposition. Was he going after all, then?

And so the evening went. Moving from one subject to another, and each of them contributing. They were not, alas, able to stargaze, as the clear sky of earlier in the day had given way to clouds. There was not a star to be seen.

Oxthorpe made his good-byes at a quarter past eleven, and by half 'til midnight she was bidding good night to the last of her guests. Soon after, she told her staff to retire, for they'd made quick work of clearing the parlor and the dining room. The rest could be seen to in the morning.

She walked through the house and experienced one of those moments of still, quiet joy. She, Miss Edith Clay, once penniless and with a future of nothing but dependence, had given a dinner party all on her own. With her friends and acquaintances. The Duke of Oxthorpe had been in attendance, in her home. Hers. She headed for the stairs, but when she reached them, she did not go up. Instead, she drew her shawl about her shoulders and walked into her garden, never mind the incipient chill of winter.

As times like this, she was so grateful for the change in her circumstances she could scarcely contain her emotions. She tipped her head back to see the sky. The night had been too cloudy for stargazing, though now a few stars sparkled through the areas where the clouds had thinned. There was no moon to speak of, covered as it was by clouds, but there was light from the house.

"Miss Clay?"

She turned in the direction of the gate that led to the stable. "I thought you'd gone home."

"I misplaced Mr. Greene's sketch of me." The duke reached over to unfasten the gate. He crossed the lawn and joined her on her flagstone terrace.

"You needn't have gone to the trouble of returning when you might have sent a servant."

"I hadn't got far."

"Manifestly." He unsettled her, but not, now, because he was an object of magnificent terror. "But you make that complaint of me so often. I cannot pass by the chance to address your favorite admonition to you."

"Fair enough."

"In addition, Duke, it is cold."

He chuckled. "Then why, one wonders, are you outside, Miss Clay? You ought to be inside sitting before the fire."

"I shall be. Soon." She faced the house.

"What?"

She glanced at him, and there was enough light for her to make out his face, but not the details of his expression. "This is my house."

"It is indeed."

"I own it, free and clear, and I have money enough that I need not worry about the yearly taxes."

He took off his hat. "Not your cousin's."

"Not a single brick. It's miraculous."

"A good Nottinghamshire house often is."

She could not help a smile. "The very best county in which to own a house."

"I am glad to have had the chance to dine here. On dishes that match my eyes."

"Your Grace, one of these days, someone is going to realize you have a piquant sense of humor."

"You've kept my secret so far."

He'd come close, a head taller than she, and though it was too dark to make out any details of his expression, she knew what he looked like. He put his hands on either side of her face, gently pressing his palms to her cheeks.

She put a hand over one of his. The side of her finger brushed over the ring he wore. "Such warm hands."

His silence was comfortable now. She understood him better, knew this was simply his way. He moved closer, and that was a barrier crossed that made her breath catch.

"Edith."

Inside the house, the case clock in the rear parlor began its midnight chime. "This is not wise."

At the last chime of the clock, soft and distant, the duke bent his head to hers. "I don't care."

Her stomach took flight. He was going to kiss her. He was. He might.

The silence stretched out.

Please. Please, please.

"Go inside, Miss Clay. I would be devastated if you took a chill."

Chapter Thirteen

OXTHORPE SET HIS mare away from his hunting box on the vale side of Killhope Castle. He'd had good hunting yesterday, two stags sent back with his gamekeeper earlier this morning. He emerged from the woods into a gap that overlooked the Vale of West. To his right, the Lyft glittered with the morning sun. The canal and locks that would take a boater into Hopewell-on-Lyft were well behind him, on the complete other side of the castle. Ahead lay the stream that fed the pond between his property and Hope Springs, not yet frozen, though there would surely be a layer of ice.

The snow on the ridge was melting. Only the ground still in shadow remained white. The vale below glittered with frost. Before long, the vale, too, would be white with snow.

The three days of respite he'd promised himself were at an end, but he'd been tempted to extend his stay. Alas, he was due in Nottingham tomorrow afternoon. He had made an appointment with Mr. Madison some days ago so as to have an excuse to be away for that damned assembly. He urged his horse forward. A part of him was infernally aware of how close he was to the boundary with Hope Springs. Not a quarter mile distant. Less.

When, tomorrow morning, it became known he'd left Killhope, she'd think he was on his way to Holmrook to propose to Louisa. And she'd be pleased. Not devastated. No, she'd be devastated when he returned unencumbered by an engagement.

His horse continued along the path that led to the uppermost boundary line. For some fifty yards, this path demarked the two properties. Had it been his great-grandfather who had married the woman who'd brought that property into the Fletcher family holdings?

In the distance, he could see the pond and the hill that obscured a straight view to Hope Springs. More distant yet, the forest between Hopewell-on-Lyft and Hope Springs, traversed by the Great Northern Road. As he approached a curve in the path, he heard someone on the path ahead of him.

His gamekeeper? Not possible, since the man was on his way to Killhope with the venison and birds he'd taken. Mr. Amblewise, perhaps, if he was traveling between parishioners. Or the New Sheriff of Nottingham.

No sense taking chances. Before he rode around the corner, he checked the pistol in his pocket and kept it at the ready.

Not a servant, nor the vicar, nor a robber, but Edith. She stood at the edge of the path, the reins to a tall bay mare clenched in one hand, her whip in the other. Edith was not, as he had previously observed, an accomplished horsewoman. The horse was perhaps not the most suitable mount for a woman who was not confident in her abilities.

No wonder she'd been so worried about the purchase of another when she had bought, or more accurately, been sold a headstrong animal that did not suit her. Her groom was nowhere to be seen.

With a cheerful grin, she lifted her whip hand in greeting. "Good morning, Duke."

"Miss Clay." Not one word exchanged between them since he'd come so perilously close to kissing her. Not a word. He'd not dared take the liberty. His emotions rode too near to the surface with her.

"Lovely morning." She wore a green habit and a matching hat with black feathers. Her boots, too, were green.

"Where is your groom?"

"On his way back to Hope Springs. His horse threw a shoe."

"You did not accompany him?"

"I meant to. But she"—she nodded at her horse—"preferred otherwise. I don't know what's got into her. She's not usually this much trouble. Then I dismounted, and, well, you see the predicament I am in."

Indeed, he did. Unless she found a stump or a rock to stand on, she would not be able to remount that mare on her own. "Shall I assist you?"

Her relief touched him. "Thank you, yes. I was resigned to walking home."

"No need for that." He dismounted and joined her. He bent, hands cupped. She put her foot on his hands, he boosted her up, and she swung into her saddle, and that was that.

He remounted. "I will ride with you." With some effort, he gentled his voice. "If that would be agreeable to you."

"How kind of you, Duke. Thank you."

He did not move. Neither did she. She adjusted her skirts, an endeavor that included, deliberately, or by coincidence, her averting her gaze from him. He could not think what to say to her. The silence killed him. Crushed him. Desperation sent words from his brain to his mouth with no stop in between for reflection. "Did your bouquets of mistletoe pass muster with the assembly committee?"

"They did. We have been madly tying ribbons and lace ever since."

That night he thought he'd saved himself from a mistake, and now, he saw, he hadn't. Not at all. He could not bear the thought of having lost what little progress he'd made with her, yet he had. He had. "I regret I shan't be there to see them."

As he'd known, this brought a smile to her face. "Oh?"

"I have business to attend to."

"In Northumberland?"

He crushed her hopes, too. "In Nottingham." Another silence descended. Defeated, he nodded in the other direction. Away from Hope Springs. Toward Killhope. "This way, then."

"Hope Springs is that way." She pointed.

"There is a view," he said. "You will admire it." A command. All wrong. He meant for her to hear that he wanted her to see the view, but no. By habit, he demanded that she accompany him. "I should like for you to see it. Please."

She nodded. Whatever she thought privately of his peremptory manner, they rode in companionable quiet to the top of the ridge with its view of the Vale of West and the towers of Killhope Castle.

She leaned forward, and he saw the view with new eyes, hers. "This, sir, is why I chose to live in Nottinghamshire. Surely there is nowhere else in England so lovely as this."

"None."

Her gaze stayed on him. "Thank you, Your Grace, for sending William to me."

"I hope he gives satisfaction."

"I shall do my best to deserve your trust in me." She looked out over the vale again. "The gig is everything I wished. Thank you. I hope you received my cheque for the amount."

"Promptly." He let as many minutes pass as he could stand before he directed his horse along the path that would, as it happened, take them past his hunting box. She followed, and that he must take as a positive sign. If she could but forgive him that awkwardness at Hope Springs, he would be grateful.

"This is one of the prettier rides on Killhope lands." In deference to her lack of skill in the saddle, he kept his horse to a walk.

"It is lovely here."

They rode side by side on a path that wound through trees and past a meadow still covered in a dusting of snow. He would have passed by his hunting box, but she stopped at the top of the tree-lined drive, gazing curiously toward the building.

"I'd no idea this was here. Who lives here?"

"I do. When I am hunting." This time, he filled the quiet before it was unendurable. "Would you care for a tour?" He braced himself for a polite no.

"Yes, thank you."

At the end of the driveway, he dismounted and held out a hand to assist her down. "None of the staff is here. I closed up the house this morning."

"Is this where you've been?" At his inquiring look, her cheeks turned pink. She was still on her horse, her hand reaching for his. "It was remarked you were not at home these past days. We thought you'd gone to London."

He knew what she would say next.

"Or Northumberland."

"I was here. Hunting." He moved in, close enough to set a hand on her waist if need be, but she slid off without incident. She put her wrist through the loop that held up the long skirt of her habit, and they walked to the stable. She waited by the doorway while he settled their horses.

On their way to the house by way of the back garden and the path to the front door, she looked avidly at the grounds. He said, "If it were spring, there would be more to admire here."

"I like this well enough." He put a hand to the back of her arm. Edith ignored her reaction to that. "Did your hunting go well?"

"Two bucks. A doe. When they are dressed, I will send you a haunch. A pheasant as well, if you like."

"You are too kind. Thank you. What a Christmas dinner we shall have at Hope Springs with a goose, a pheasant, and venison."

He opened the front door for her and again had the odd experience of seeing the house as if it were new to him instead of familiar. As if he'd not spent the last three days here. He was not surprised that she walked first to what, at Killhope, would be the great hall. Here, a series of arched windows overlooked the woods only he had the right to hunt.

She went straight to the bow windows. There was a window seat, but she stood to the side, inches from the glass, one hand on the carved stone that separated the window casings. When he joined her, not too close, she turned. At ease because she did not see him with intimate eyes. Nothing at all like the way he saw her. "You think you don't notice, but you're wrong."

"About?"

"This. This lovely little house, and the panorama before us. Beauty like this becomes a part of one's heart and soul."

"It does."

"I've felt it happening to me since I came to Hope Springs."

"It is a pretty property."

"It is. You've shown me Killhope and your conservatory. That view. And now this." She whirled to the window again and spread her arms wide. "This, too, is a part of me."

He came to where she stood and sat on the window seat, arms crossed, legs stretched out. "I would say come here when you like, but this is no fit place for a lady."

She laughed, and the sound pierced his heart. "Can you imagine? You'd come here to hunt with all your gentlemen friends and acquaintances—"

"More likely only me."

"Even worse." She stared out the windows again, smiling. "You would say, 'Who has been sitting in my chair?'" She looked at the ceiling, laughing now.

He did not see how he could live without her. How could he bring himself to marry another woman when she owned his heart? Yet he must. He must. He could not remain unmarried, with no heirs. No sons. No children at all.

"You'd say, 'Who has been eating in my dining room and sleeping in my bed?' Then you would find a snoring lump on your chaise—"

"A chaise-longue, here? I think not."

She glanced around. There was little furniture, but chairs for servants or people asked to wait on his pleasure. A table or two against the wall. A carpet from India covered most of the floor here. "Very well, your favorite armchair, my shoes on the floor, my shawl fallen to the ground, and me, insensible from the beauty of the view."

She showed no awareness that she had said something one might take as meaning more than the mere words. Something salacious. Because she had not intended any such thing. Yet. Yet, he could not dismiss the idea. Of her in his bed.

She cocked her head. The ribbon tied beneath her chin glinted dully in the light. "Have I said something wrong?"

"No."

"I have." She stepped closer. "You are the most inscrutable man I have ever met."

He laughed. No mirth at all.

"I'm quite serious." She studied him. "No." Her quiet voice lanced through him. "Don't look away. Not when I am about to understand you."

"Are you certain you wish to?" He held her gaze, and the silence of his hunting box became unendurable. He fixed in his head an image of her in his bed. Nude. And of him, there to touch, and taste, experiencing that moment when his prick slid into her body. Her. Not any woman, but her. Specifically. The woman who made him see beauty where he'd once seen only duty.

She blinked, and her cheeks turned pink. She did not look away from him. Nor did he look away from her. Then she did glance away, but her attention came back immediately. He was too much aware of the difference in their ranks. She was a lady, one could not deny her that, but though she'd lived with relatives who had rank and property, she was herself without distinction, born to no fortune, in the care of a relative whose neglect of her told the world the value he placed on her.

She had no pretensions. None at all. In London, she had never put herself forward. She did nothing to anger her cousin, yet she'd been unfailingly a friend to Miss Louisa Clay. Her champion in all things. She struck to his center, to his heart. Found him out. Assessed.

"Do you think no one could love you?" she asked.

"I do not think that."

She tilted her head again, then again, eyes narrowed while she stared into his soul. "You do. But why? Why would you think such a thing?"

"I've no illusions I am well liked."

"One does not simply *like* a duke." She stripped off her gloves and set them on the portion of the window seat that he did not occupy, and his heart raced away. "Dukes are terrifying personages."

He took one of her hands in his. "I terrify you."

"Naturally."

"How easily you say that." What would happen to him if this did not end where he hoped?

"I would be a most unusual woman if you did not." With her free hand, she traced three fingers along the line of his cheek, the underside of his mouth.

"Are you this moment?"

"I have never been more terrified of anyone than I am of you this moment."

He released her, spread his arms wide, and leaned back. "Go then, if you are in terror."

She stepped toward him, and for him the world disappeared, but for her. She freed her wrist from the loop of her habit and ran her fingers lightly through his hair, brushing it back, and smoothing it down. Both hands. "Does your hair never lie flat?"

"Never." He set a hand on the back of her waist. He took and then let out a breath. "Edith." She left her hands on his head. He drew her closer and whispered, "I have never, ever forgotten you."

Her eyes fluttered. "You said that before."

"I did."

"What am I to make of that?"

"That it is true." He brought her toward him, and there was no denying at all that they had crossed another barrier. "I met you and never could think of any woman but you afterward."

"That can't be so."

"It is. I can't forget you. I never shall." The air trembled with awareness. "Another truth, Edith. I have never made love to a woman."

"No." Her eyes opened wide. "No, I don't believe that. I won't."

"I have fornicated." He removed her hat and stretched to set it on a nearby table. Having done that, he brought her back into his embrace. "Nothing but that."

She ran a hand over his head again, and then she leaned in and brushed her mouth over his.

Chapter Fourteen

Curiosity had separated her from good sense. Curiosity and a powerful longing to touch him. If they hadn't been so close, him with an arm around her and her with her hands in his thick, soft hair—not at all coarse, as she'd wondered—she wouldn't have dared. Plainly, quite plainly, he'd thought about this, too, or they'd not have ended up with her near enough to him to have touched his mouth with hers.

And?

And nothing.

He did nothing.

She put a hand to his chest and tipped her head back, waiting for the humiliation to pass, settling in herself the fact that she had misjudged their situation and his words. She tilted her head down, staring at the green fabric of her bodice, then at her fingertips on his breast. She would have to look at him. Not yet. Not yet.

His palm pressed against the small of her back. Deliberate, since she felt the flex of his biceps. She looked at him, and his eyes locked with hers, and she could not breathe for the need she saw there. A thousand thoughts flashed through his eyes, and he kept them all to himself. She had never known such a self-contained man, so few words and now none when she desperately needed them from him. His arms remained around her still.

She said, "Tell me if you want me to kiss you again, or if we must agree it did not happen. Tell me that much."

"Again, Edith."

She did. She leaned in again and kissed him, another light touch of her lips to his, before she drew away. "Like that?"

He shook his head. That was almost a smile. Almost.

"What could you mean, I wonder." She wound her hand around the back of his neck, above the collar of his coat. The world changed. Everything different. Everything new. Magical. She kissed him again. She smelled the outdoors. Him.

His arms were around her, his mouth under hers. More than a slide across his lips this time. At the last minute, his lower lip caught hers, and her life changed forever. Again.

Her body tingled, her chest tightened, she could not feel her knees. This was no game. No harmless flirtation. She went taut with need. She melted against him, tipped her head to his, and pressed her mouth against his. She kissed him, and he kissed her back, and she could not get enough of this ascension of her body into longing.

Had she really thought he would be as controlled in kissing as he was in everything else? How could she have? He cupped the back of her head, and she opened her mouth. She'd only ever kissed one other man. One lover. One devastation of her heart, and then Oxthorpe kissed her back. Not a game. Not something to be indulged and forgotten.

There was no mistaking his physical state, and they froze, the two of them, when she brushed a hand across the middle of the buttons on the left side of his breeches. He drew breath, and she saw His Grace, the Duke of Oxthorpe, who kept his silence, whom almost no one spoke of in terms of the qualities she knew he possessed. He was Oxthorpe, and the ability to say one knew him was the same as laying claim to power and influence.

He knew this. He knew and did not offer himself easily to anyone. He knew if he made his interest in a woman known that she might agree to anything. This, to a man like him, must be a fell power. How could anyone say no to Oxthorpe? The miracle, the miracle was that he'd not become a man who took every part of that power as his due.

Again, she brushed a finger along the fall of his breeches and decided against words. No words for now. She unfastened one of those left-most buttons, then another, then her fingers were sliding inside, between fabric, linen. No games. Just her growing need and the leap of tension between them.

He brought her toward him, his body shifting, pulled up handfuls of her habit, and she moved with him, and the only thought in her mind was that he was going to put his cock inside her, fill her, and that was the miracle, that they could find each other like this.

His hands slid underneath her clothes, then up to grip her bottom, and her life depended on balancing like this, on the spread of his thighs, him lifting her up and positioning himself. She did the same, made the necessary adjustments, and when he pushed inside her, she met that motion with a shiver of her entire being toward bliss.

A moan left her, unadulterated bliss, because his sex in her was beyond perfect, the way her body accepted him, took him greedily. Already she was slipping away. She bit her lower lip and concentrated on what she was feeling. The pressure of him inside her, the strength of his arms around her, the scent of him, the way his expression changed with each push inside her, each answering roll and thrust from him.

His hands on her bottom brought her forward then relaxed, and she could feel the tension in his arms and legs, and she forgot she'd meant to be silent, for she gripped his shoulders, and put her mouth by his ear and said, "I wish I was naked. I wish you could touch me everywhere."

He thrust up. "Yes?"

"Yes, please, like that." She licked the outside of his ear. "I wish you were naked, too. I wish I could touch you and see all of you."

"You've seen me naked."

With a slow rock of her hips timed with his and restricted by the fact they were sitting, balanced indelicately and mostly by dint of his strength and willingness to be uncomfortable, rather than in a bed, she said, "I did not see enough."

He held her still, lips twitching. "If I'd walked out of the pond, you'd not have been appalled?"

"I would have been, but if I'd known this—"

"Edith—"

"If I'd known this about you, I would have walked to the shore and pulled you from the water."

He held her tight, fingers pressing her toward him. "You drive me mad."

"I wish I could see your parts." She kissed the side of his jaw, and his skin felt smooth, and she found a place where his pulse beat, and she kissed him there, too. "I wish I could see right now, this moment."

He tipped his shoulders back, pushed farther back into the window seat, setting one shoulder against the side of the window to brace himself. "I always oblige a lady."

"No, no." She shifted and found an angle that sent him deeper. Her arousal, the angle of his penetration made words an inconvenience, and yet, the feelings in her were too big to keep to herself. She concentrated to find the words. "No, Oxthorpe. No." She grabbed either side of his face. "Stay or I'll never forgive you."

"I'll not disappoint, then." His words ended in a low growl, and she watched his eyes close, the shift of his focus to the physical, to the contact between them, more, more than that, to his contact with her body, and she was fiercely glad of the sight. They were wordless now, reduced to inarticulate sounds.

The moment came when she was nothing but a reach for her approaching pleasure, and Oxthorpe, he wrapped an arm around her hips and pulled her close, while his other hand worked beneath her skirts. His fingers stroked her, and she slipped away from everything but sensation.

Oxthorpe whispered, "Yes, my love. Yes."

She registered the sound, the satisfaction in those words, and then there were tears welling up along with her climax because such intense physical pleasure was not endurable. His fingers, the strokes of his fingers, and his cock moving in her, the reaction that caused annihilated her.

Chapter Fifteen

WITH A SINKING heart, Oxthorpe stood in front of the dark and empty parish hall. He must have mistaken the date of the assembly. It must have been Saturday, while he was still in Nottingham, cursing himself for wanting to send his regrets to Madison, at whose home he'd been invited to dine. Or perhaps Friday. It couldn't have been Sunday when he'd gone to church with Madison and then stayed at his hotel, telling himself he would not leave before his business was concluded Tuesday.

And then he had. He'd suffered through every appointment he'd made, interminable reviews of documents, and then dined with the actual Sheriff of Nottingham and left early. He'd left his valet at the hotel to arrange their return. He'd sent his regrets to Madison and left for Hopewell-on-Lyft. For nothing. All his hurrying and driving like a madman for nothing. His distraction and rudeness to Madison, with a steadily diminishing portion of his mind on business, and the bloody building hadn't a soul in it.

"Your Grace?"

He said nothing in response to his coachman's inquiry. He'd gone home first to change from traveling clothes to evening clothes, and now either he was too late, or he was here on the wrong day. All this commotion and disruption of his schedule, his heart entirely overtaken, and he'd come here on the wrong day?

"The roof is leaking again, Your Grace. They've moved the assembly to Carrington Close."

Slowly, he turned. "How do you know?"

The moon came out from behind the clouds, and he had a silvered view of his servant, bundled in scarfs, a thick coat, and gloves. With one heavy boot propped up, his coachman shrugged. He felt a pang of regret for keeping the man from the festivities. He must have wanted to attend. He'd given most of his staff at Killhope leave to attend. "That's what they did last year."

"Very well then." He kept his expression sober. Killhope had been quiet, not because it was late, but because all but a skeleton staff had been there. All the rest were at the assembly. "To Carrington Close."

"Aye, Your Grace."

He strode back to the carriage and closed the door more loudly than was necessary. It would be thirty minutes, longer given it was cold and dark and icy, before he arrived anywhere near Edith. At this rate, he'd get there only to find everyone on their way home. Nothing but servants cleaning up the detritus of a party hastily relocated. If he'd known, if he'd been home when the parish hall roof sprang a leak, he could have offered up Killhope as a location.

Carrington Close was not dark. The windows blazed with lights, and a groom promptly came out to meet his carriage. His heart settled. Outside, he gave the groom a coin and called up to the coachman, "You'll come in for food and dancing, then?"

"Your Grace."

Oxthorpe took the front stairs two at a time. A wreath of pine and holly hung on the front door, festooned with a bow of blue ribbon and gold lace—Edith's work, he was certain. Inside, handed over his hat, scarf and greatcoat and paid no attention to the glass of cider Mrs. Carrington's butler had hidden behind an urn.

At the door to the ballroom, he straightened the lay of his coat over his shoulders, tugged on his collar, smoothed his neckcloth. Another enormous wreath hung above the door, and there were blue ribbons and lace, and sprigs of holly all around the doorframe.

Inside, the music ended. The noise of the assembly reduced. Now, then. With a nod and a coin pressed into the waiting footman's hand, he walked into the ballroom as he should have every year the citizens of Hopewell-on-Lyft gave the party that brought them together in good cheer and spirits.

The footman rapped his staff on the floor loudly enough to cut through the noise. "His Grace, the Duke of Oxthorpe."

The lull in conversation died away to silence.

Wreaths and ribbons festooned the room. The mistletoe Edith had worked so hard to gather and decorate hung from every chandelier, sconce, or convenient beam.

Mrs. Carrington approached him with a pretty young woman at his side. Two of the ladies of the assembly committee followed her. Edith was not among them.

He would do this. Whether she was here or not, he would. The point was that he would not close himself off in solitude. Mrs. Carrington reached him first and sank into a curtsy. The young woman beside her curtsied as well. "Your Grace. You honor us with your presence."

"Not at all."

"Robina, may I introduce the duke?"

"I should be delighted."

"Miss Weston, the Duke of Oxthorpe. If you recall, I pointed out to you his home of Killhope Castle."

"Your Grace."

He smiled at Miss Weston, aware that he'd startled Mrs. Carrington. "You are the young lady who has been visiting Mrs. Herbert."

"Yes, Your Grace."

He was determined to make himself agreeable, and if that meant he astonished the good people of Hopewell-on-Lyft, so be it. "I hope you have been enjoying your stay in our village."

"Very much so."

"You must come to Killhope Castle for a tour."

"Thank you. I would like that very much, sir."

The other ladies of the committee reached him, and he greeted them in turn and accepted their exclamations of delight at his appearance. Alas, amid the decorations and tables laden with food and drink, the faces that gazed at him were not smiling because he was here. His arrival had made everyone tense. Did they think he would demand that they cease their merriment immediately? He wanted to do something that would astound everyone, something that would prove to Edith there was hope for him.

"Miss Weston." He sketched a bow to her. "You'll dance with me."

She managed to cover her astonishment. "I should love that, thank you."

He gave her a brilliant smile. Incandescent, he felt, and since, just then, the orchestra began the opening strains of another set, he held out his hand and waited for the very pretty Miss Weston to put her hand on his.

They danced, and she was a charming partner. Delightful. He ignored the stares and concentrated on amusing Miss Weston, and thank God, thank the Lord in heaven, that he had asked her to dance and not some other young lady with less self-possession than Miss Weston.

Presently, though, their dance was over. It was, he discovered, the last set before the orchestra broke to have something to eat and drink and for the others to do the same. He walked Miss Weston to the side of the room. They passed Mr. and Mrs. Wattles, and he stopped to bid them good evening. His mood lightened. He was often at The Duke's Arms, doing custom with the Wattleses, and who would not admire the industry of a man who brewed an excellent beer in his cellar?

He and Miss Weston spent some minutes in conversation while they were in queue for cider, quite welcome on a cold winter evening. Everyone stood aside for him, though, and there he and Miss Weston were at the head of the line. Someone called out, "The mistletoe!"

He glanced up and indeed Miss Weston was standing directly beneath the mistletoe. They exchanged a look and, thank God, she was no more dazzled than Edith had ever been. Not in the least. He stepped toward her, took a berry from the bunch and kissed her. A short kiss. A kiss that was nothing but the good cheer of a Christmas assembly where people gathered to enjoy each other's company and exchange wishes for the holidays.

When he stepped back, amid much clapping, she gave him a curtsy and a warm smile, and there. Everyone would see he was not an ogre come to spoil their fete. "Your Grace."

"Miss Weston." He stepped past her and accepted a cup of cider from the footman to give to her, and then another for himself. By the time he turned around, Miss Weston had gone.

But there was Mr. Thomas with Goodman, too. He hurried to join them when he saw Miss Amanda Houston, a buxom brunette with a fine opinion of herself, heading toward him. Purple plumes in her hat bobbed as she walked. He found Miss Houston difficult to endure for long, for she had no appreciation for brevity and more than half a mind to one day be a duchess.

Goodman and Mr. Thomas greeted him heartily and closed ranks. He did not see Edith anywhere. It did not matter. She was right. He was too much alone, he shared too little, he accepted too little of the goodwill of the denizens of Hopewell-on-Lyft.

Mr. Amblewise and the blacksmith joined them. He listened while he ate two excellent pasties. Mr. Thomas told an amusing tale from his time in Anatolia, of the monkey that had escaped into his house in the section of Pera where foreign diplomats to the High Porte lived.

Across the room, he caught a glimpse of his coachman with a cup of punch. He and Edith's butler broke into an impromptu carol. One a tenor, one basso. Others joined in the song and someone tapped out the beat and as he dealt with the unwelcome emotion of the moment, Edith came in one of the side doors.

Edith.

To the background of the song, he walked across the ballroom floor, empty of dancers at the moment. "Edith."

She curtsied, and he took both her hands in his, and she broke into a grin that would have won his heart if she had not already had it. Her fingers tightened around his. She squeezed her eyes shut and then opened them again. "Your Grace. I thought you'd gone to Holmrook after all."

"I told you more than once I would not go. That I would be in Nottingham."

"But you left, and my cousin Clay invited you, and who would go to Nottingham for so many days at Christmas?"

"A fool."

"You're no fool." Her eyes were bright with tears, and she used the side of a gloved finger to wick away the damp. "Don't say that you are."

"No, I am not."

"I thought you'd gone."

He drew her close to him, and if those nearby saw them, he did not care. "Never. I never would." He brought her far too close for good manners. "Edith."

"What is it?"

"Edith, you are standing under mistletoe."

"I am?"

He pointed up.

She looked, and she smiled slowly. "So I am."

He kept his arms around her waist. There was a time for words, and this was one. "Marry me, Edith. Marry me, and I will be the happiest man there ever was. Marry me, and I will spend my life making you happy. Marry me because I love you, and I do not want to imagine a life where I am not with you."

She blinked several times. "You love me?"

"Yes."

"I thought you did not care for me. You made me love you, and I thought you did not care for me the way I do for you."

"You were wrong."

She threw herself at him, arms tight around his shoulders. "Do you mean it? Do you really?"

"Darling," he whispered. "Darling Edith."

She stepped back and touched his cheek. "While you were gone, I realized I love you. I fell in love with you, and I was never so miserable in all my life than while I thought you'd gone to offer for Louisa."

"Marry me, Edith. I'll never be whole if you don't."

"Nor will I," she whispered.

"That is no answer."

Her smile warmed his soul. "Yes," she said. "Yes, a thousand times yes."

He drew her into his arms, and he kissed her. Not the polite kiss he'd given Miss Weston. This kiss was passion, and joy, and desire, and when he drew back, he looked into her eyes and she rested her head on his chest, and only then did he realize everyone was clapping. The entire room.

With Edith at his side, he returned to Thomas and Goodman, and others whom he must make his friends. He lifted his cider to the room at large and raised his voice. "My deepest, most sincere wishes for a holiday where we are surrounded by those we love, by the remembrance of those whom we have loved, and that we resolve we shall be men and women worthy of love. Merry Christmas to all."

Licensed to Wed

By
Miranda Neville

Chapter One

Lord Carbury's memoranda for August 1817

1. See Brougham re. suspension of habeas corpus.
2. Westfield farm tenancy.
3. Confer with counsel re. Smithson dispute.
4. Drainage etc. at Bourton Park.
5. Candidates for Bourton Abbas living.
6. The earl's valet no longer capable of controlling his master?
7. Inquire about commission in __th Regiment for Cousin Reginald Rogers.
8. Coutts bank re. Mansfield settlement.
9. Refuse appointment as Ernest Herbert trustee.
10. Propose to Robina Weston.

WYATT HERBERT, VISCOUNT Carbury, Member of Parliament for Bourton, grandson and heir to the Earl of Hillforth, leading light of the Whig party, and pillar of his extensive family, liked to be organized. He had a secretary to assist him, an employee who sorted his correspondence, took dictation, answered invitations, and reminded him which ones he'd accepted. But Carbury had never forgotten the occasion when Trumble failed to pass along word that an important vote in the House of Commons had been moved up, and he missed the division.

For this reason, and because his natural preference was to exert complete control over events, Carbury maintained the habit of making a monthly list of the most important goals and tasks ahead of him.

Before making his list for September, he trimmed his pen, dipped it in ink, and ticked off each item that had been completed. August had been a light month on the political front (item one) since he'd spent most of it in Yorkshire with his grandfather. Much of his time had been spent on estate business (items two through five) and managing the aging and increasingly cantankerous earl (item six), who was handing more of the important decisions to his heir but couldn't be relied upon not to argue about them. Carbury had answered every question with dispatch, avoided a lawsuit over a boundary, replaced an incompetent and crooked tenant with a man of stellar character, and even taken time to call on his more congenial neighbors.

This last matter, which should have been a source of nothing but satisfaction, caused him to frown. It was the cause of his only failure. Well, there were two if one counted item nine, but he'd never taken that one seriously. He never really expected to turn down a request to act on behalf of his cousin Ernest Herbert's widow and four sons; he never refused help to his relations, however distant and/or tiresome (items seven and eight).

But item ten was his Waterloo. Though he had visited Weston Hall three times, he hadn't managed to propose marriage to Miss Robina Weston.

Not because he'd never had a chance. The present owner and his wife had been eager to throw them together. They didn't want the daughter of the improvident former owner on their hands forever. Wyatt and Robina had found themselves seated together at dinner, partnered at whist, and even sent into the shrubbery on a spurious errand of retrieving a lost cricket ball. There was no cricket ball. As Robina had observed, her cousin Edwin abhorred any sports that didn't require a horse or a gun, and his sons were in the nursery. She'd been quite amusing on the subject, and Carbury had enjoyed the expedition. He liked Robina, whom he'd known most of their lives—or her life, since she was eight years his junior. He was perfectly comfortable with her, and she would make an admirable wife. Yet he hadn't been able to bring himself to utter the fateful words that would tie him to her for a lifetime.

He was in London now and so, shortly, would she be. The minute she reached her godmother Mrs. Madsen's house, he would call and make his offer. It was a priority for September. By George, when Wyatt Herbert was determined that nothing would sway him from his purpose, he remained unswayed. He never shirked his obligations, and if marriage was another duty, another responsibility, another call on his time, then he would have to find enough hours in his schedule to squeeze in the care and feeding of a wife. He took a fresh sheet of paper for a fresh list. Items one through four involved political matters that he needed to get out of the way.

Memoranda for September 1817...

5. Propose to Robina Weston...

WYATT SHUDDERED AT the recollection of sitting in Mrs. Madsen's drawing room, unable to summon the easy words that would have left him alone with Robina for a few minutes. Proposing shouldn't even take very long. Instead, he'd gazed at her, unable to reconcile the little girl whom he'd rescued from dozens of scrapes with the self-possessed young woman who regarded him so coolly.

Memoranda for October 1817...

2. Propose to Robina Weston.

Memoranda for November 1817...

1. Propose to Robina Weston.

December 1, 1817

CARBURY HAD A full day planned once he'd made his monthly list, the way he always did on the first of the month, to make sure he didn't miss anything important. But first he must see that November's tasks had been fulfilled. Lately, this moment of his monthly routine had been spoiled. Instead of anticipating satisfaction at the accomplishment of so much, the same vexing matter battered his conscience and threatened his self-esteem. His pen at the ready, he dreaded the moment when he must, for an unprecedented fourth month, ink a reproachful cross next to the first item on the list.

Propose to Robina Weston.

Carbury never did anything as unproductive as tear his hair out. Even running his fingers through his neat Caesar cut would require the attentions of his valet and waste precious moments he could ill afford. For the past three months, shortly after the first, he'd presented himself at Half Moon Street and asked if Miss Weston was at home. With a pit in his stomach, he was shown to Mrs. Madsen's drawing room, where he would sit for fifteen excruciating minutes, feeling the weight of expectations squeeze all wit or even sense from his conversation while Robina and her hostess looked at him in astonishment. Could this be the future Prime Minster speaking? More like the future village idiot. He would scurry off in disgust, resolved to make an effort to spend some time with Robina, so that he wouldn't be tongue-tied in her presence. A visit to the theater or an assembly would give them a chance to get back onto comfortable terms. The way they'd always been, before her father died. Before he had decided he must rescue the orphan from near poverty by marrying her.

He was always too busy. Look at today. Though Parliament wasn't in session, he had several meetings planned. Good Lord! If he didn't leave now, he'd never make it to the City in time for an appointment with Lord Hillforth's banker. He left the house with a sense of disquiet. Never had he set out on the first of the month without first making his list.

Desperate times called for desperate measures. As he left the bank, he remembered that Doctors Commons was just around the corner. If he acquired a special license for his marriage to Robina, he would have to propose to her. To do otherwise would be a waste of time and effort. Carbury never wasted either commodity. They were too valuable.

While waiting to speak to the archbishop's registrar, he formed an excellent plan. He would escort his betrothed home for Christmas, and they would be married in the village church in the presence of his grandfather, her cousins, and numerous mutual friends. They would leave for a quick honeymoon before returning to London in plenty of time for the opening of Parliament in January. The whole business could be concluded with minimum fuss and disruption of his schedule.

The next day, with the carefully folded parchment tucked into his pocket like a talisman, he knew he was in luck when the butler informed him that Mrs. Madsen was out and Miss Weston would receive him alone. If he had believed in omens, which he did not, he'd have said this chance was a guarantee of success.

His future wife rose to greet him. She was a graceful little thing and very pretty, with a neat figure, golden-blond hair braided and curled to frame her oval face.

"Lord Carbury," she said, and her hazel eyes flashed as she curtsied. Her complexion was creamy and flawless, and her mouth set in a pout that he noticed far more than a conventional smile. Was it possible she was peeved at him, or was it a flirtatious pout? He supposed he would be expected to kiss her after she said yes, and, though it wasn't something he'd thought about before, he quite looked forward to it.

Chapter Two

THREE MONTHS EARLIER, Robina would have greeted the news that Lord Carbury had called with pleasure. This morning, she didn't even bother to set aside her work and check her hair in the mirror over the mantelpiece. She was beginning to think Edwin Weston must have imagined that Carbury had said he would offer for her. Or, more likely, it was wishful thinking on his part, encouraged by his dreadful wife. Lucilla was even more anxious than her spouse to get her out from under their feet and their roof. Robina had been pleased too. She'd always liked Wyatt—as she'd called him as a child before his father died and he inherited the courtesy title of Carbury—and he was certainly eligible.

Since Carbury wasn't the sort of man given to whims, she blamed Edwin for her error and her humiliation. She'd come to London for the sole purpose of giving her and Carbury a chance to further their adult acquaintance. Far from taking advantage of the opportunity, he had virtually ignored her, except for a brief awkward call about once a month, when they didn't even manage to converse with the ease of long acquaintances.

After the last stilted fifteen minutes, she'd concluded that Edwin had made a hash of the matter, not for the first time. Her wretched cousin had probably managed to give Carbury the impression that Robina was setting her cap at him. He saw her as a desperate maiden and had been trying to brush off her advances by treating her with the minimum of politeness. As he followed the butler into the room, she cringed at the very idea that he had seen her efforts at sprightly conversation as amorous advances.

She rose from her seat at the morning room table and curtsied, tilting her chin and meeting him boldly in the eye, to assure herself—and him too, if he cared—that she had done nothing to be ashamed of.

"Robina," he said. He'd addressed her thus when they were younger, though lately they'd spoken formally. "My dear Robina…"

Then he stopped. As usual.

"Lord Carbury," she said coolly. "How good of you to call. Please sit down. I hope you don't mind if I continue with my work while we talk." *If we talk.* She resumed her seat and took up her paintbrush, filling it with the shade of light brown she'd carefully mixed before her visitor was announced.

"Please do." Instead of occupying the chair she'd indicated, he joined her at the table. "May I look at your painting?" With a shrug, she leaned back so he could see the square of vellum. Narrowing his eyes, he looked back and forth at her watercolor and the pinecone model. "It's very exact."

"Thank you," she said. Since he seemed to have finished his examination, she shaped the brush to a point on her palette and deftly applied highlights to the scales of the cone. "I like to make a study of plants and animals, but Mrs. Madsen's pug will not stay still, and in London in the winter, there isn't much choice of flora." Unless one was being courted by a man of wealth. Miss Cavendish next door received regular deliveries of hothouse flowers from her suitor. The absence of so much as a cheap posy should have alerted her to Carbury's lack of intentions.

"I didn't know you painted," he said.

"I learned in the schoolroom, as most young girls do, but only lately have I taken it up more seriously. One must have something to do." Trying to hold her father's erratic household together had left her no time for ladylike accomplishments.

"I thought young ladies preferred romantic scenes of blasted heaths and picturesque ruins."

"Not this one. But, then, I am not romantically minded." She wanted to make sure he didn't think she had any wrong ideas about them. Even though she had. She avoided looking at him and applied her brush with determined concentration.

"I know you are not," he said with some warmth. "That is why…" He stopped again.

For heaven's sake, how did the man ever manage to give a speech in Parliament? Suddenly, she was out of patience. She scraped her chair back and stood, causing him to back away clumsily, surprised at her force. "Lord Carbury," she said. "I may have been misinformed, but my cousin gave me to believe that you feel some obligation regarding my future. I would like to assure you that you owe me nothing and have aroused no expectations of any kind."

"You were not misinformed. Because of our fathers' close friendship, I feel responsible for your wellbeing."

Irritation warmed into something like anger. It was true that his father and hers, a pair of equally improvident charmers, had been neighbors and lifelong friends, until a hunting accident and a lung infection neglected during a marathon gaming session, respectively, had caused their early deaths. She recalled with annoyance what a dictatorial boy Wyatt had been. She barely remembered her childish worship of the splendid neighbor eight years her senior, or the schoolgirl *tendre* for the handsome young man on his occasional visits home.

"There isn't the slightest need. No one made you my guardian," she said.

"No, indeed, for you are of age and in control of your own fortune."

"Do you disapprove?" Trust him to know exactly how things stood. She was certain he knew to the penny how meager was the income left her from the portion of her mother's dowry that her father had not frittered away.

"As a general rule, I think it is wiser for a knowledgeable man to have government of a lady's money, but you have always been sensible, at least in practical matters." While not the compliment she would have chosen, at least he was talking to her and looked less like a dyspeptic bear. She'd been right to raise the subject and clear the air so they could go back to being on friendly terms. "I know how you protected your father's estate from complete disaster," he continued. "Edwin Weston has much to thank you for."

"Much gratitude I'll get from him," she said, rendered indiscreet by his praise.

"He's a paltry fellow, and his wife is worse. If he had any decency, he'd provide for you generously."

She could have warmed to the theme, but she despised people who complained about things outside their power to change. "He has children of his own, and Lucilla wouldn't let him. I shall manage with my sixty pounds a year." If she kept on saying that, it would be true. Two thousand pounds in the three percents was a respectable competence, if one was careful. Very careful.

"You know that you will not, and that is why you must marry me."

So Edwin had not been wrong after all. Robina collapsed weakly onto a sofa, letting her mind readjust its assumptions.

Carbury stood in the middle of the room, the very picture of a man approaching the height of his powers. At thirty-three, he had filled out from the reed-like slenderness of his youth. He was broad-chested beneath his perfectly cut dark blue coat and strong without an ounce of excess fat, from his firm chin down to his trim waist and muscular legs in fitted buff pantaloons and Hessian boots. His brown hair was short and neat. Neither fashionable excess in his coiffure nor a hint of bristle on his firm chin and jaw was allowed to mar the regularity of his features. He wasn't excessively handsome, merely a fine-looking English gentleman with all the arrogance of the breed.

Nothing in his expression spoke of the apprehension that should be felt by a man who had just offered marriage to the lady of his choice. He seemed to feel as much anxiety as he would about eating breakfast. And why not? Obviously, in his mind her acceptance was just as sure as his cook's preparation of the morning meal. He likely expected her to feel gratitude, and with the sensible side of her brain, she acknowledged the logic of his position. Another part of her head, one linked to her heart and other sentimental organs, protested.

"Was that a proposal of marriage?" she asked.

"You know it was."

"I thought it was more along the lines of a command."

"Come, my dear Robina. We have known each other too long, and we are both far too sensible to indulge in romantic postures. I know we shall deal very well together, and I cannot believe you do not think the same."

"Do you wish to marry me? Why?"

"Of course I do. I wouldn't have asked if I did not."

"But why? And don't mention our fathers, please. Let us stipulate that there is no obligation. I am not your duty."

"I beg to disagree. I have thought about the subject, and it's clear to me that the best way to ensure your future is to make you my wife. Only thus can I look after you as my conscience demands."

"And what if your conscience and my wishes lead us on different paths?"

"I find that hard to believe. I am sorry if you are piqued at my silence in the months you've been in London. I am a very busy man. Nevertheless, you deserve an apology for the inadequacies of my courtship. Pray forgive me and trust that I will not be as inattentive a husband." He didn't sound even remotely sorry.

When Robina was seven years old, she had escaped her governess and climbed an apple tree. She had amused herself attempting to toss unripe fruit into the gardener's water trough and made great strides in accuracy when Wyatt strolled through the orchard on his way to a neighborly call on the Westons. Without a by-your-leave, he'd lifted her down from her perfectly secure perch on the widest branch and gravely scolded her, not for wasting fruit, which would have been reasonable, but for endangering herself. He completely ignored her protests that she was an expert tree climber. Wyatt Herbert had been an insufferably interfering fifteen-year-old, and the tendency had only grown as he aged.

She pursed her lips, sealing in words unbecoming of a lady. Carbury seemed to take her silence for encouragement.

"I respect you too much to doubt you see the advantages of my offer. For my part, I know my duty, and I trust I will never shirk it."

Shirk was an ugly word. "If you think you need it, I give you my permission to *shirk* your duty to me. I never asked for charity, and that is what your proposal is." The reins on her temper slipped away. "You, Wyatt, are a pompous ass. It has never been my ambition to share my life and my bed with a man who treats me with such supreme condescension."

The reference to conjugal intimacies startled him. Good. She wasn't seven years old, but a twenty-five-year-old woman who knew what marriage meant. She'd rather remain a spinster than submit to life with a cold fish. Yet, a vision of Wyatt unbuttoned from his impeccable garments, his hair rumpled, his face unguarded, flashed through her head and kindled a spark in her chest. She blinked hard to dispel the impossible vision and regarded his patent displeasure with fierce satisfaction. Then his eyes cleared, and he nodded sharply.

"You are upset," he said soothingly.

"I. Am. Not. Upset." She stood and curtsied. "I must thank you, Lord Carbury, for the honor you do me with your offer of marriage, but I regret that I must decline. Now, if you don't mind, I have a pinecone to finish painting." She returned to the table with studied calm, marred only by the energy with which she stabbed her paintbrush into the water jar and swirled it in the block of dark brown watercolor.

His hand on her shoulder was a statement of possession, his deep voice an arrogant command in her ear. "You don't mean that, Robina. Let us discuss the matter rationally."

"There is nothing to discuss."

"What will you do if you do not marry me? How will you manage?"

"I shall manage very well. Most people pass their entire lives in tolerable ease without your interference, and I shall too."

"I don't care about most people."

"Do you care about me?"

"Of course I do. I have known you all your life. I daresay I held you as a babe in arms, though I confess I do not recall the occasion."

She wasn't sure which was less enticing: a husband who didn't recall your first meeting or one who remembered you as a squalling infant. That was the trouble, she realized. Carbury made her feel like a child because that was how he regarded her.

Shaking him off, she spun around. Paint flew off her brush and spattered his pristine starched white neckcloth. He jumped back, looking down at the speckled linen with comical dismay.

"I am so sorry, Carbury. Now you will have to hurry home to change before your next appointment. Don't let me keep you another minute. I know you have many important things to do. You can cross this proposal off your list with a clear conscience." She'd heard about his memoranda for years, and ignored his recommendation that she adopt the habit. That's all she was to him: an item on a long list of responsibilities.

Raising her chin proudly, she glared at him, her breath emerging in brief huffs from parted lips. He glared back, and she saw the discomposed man she'd imagined earlier. His perturbed gaze dropped to her lips, as though he might kiss her, and in a fraction of a second, she wondered what it would be like. Then he stepped back, the mask of perfect control settling back.

"I had set aside the whole morning for you, ma'am," he said with a stiff bow. "But since I am not to achieve satisfaction in the matter at hand, I will take my leave and apply my efforts in quarters where they are welcome. Let me assure you, Miss Weston, that I will always have your interests at heart, and you must feel free to call on me for assistance at any time."

Once he had left, Robina sank into her chair and stared at the painted pinecone through a veil of shock. Her right hand, still clutching the fatal paintbrush, shook a little. So that was that. She'd turned down the best, and possibly the only, proposal she'd ever receive.

Was she mad? She could have been a future countess, rich and secure with an interesting life involved in the political life of the country. Carbury was a decent man who would likely indulge her in every way as long as she obeyed him. And that was the rub. Obedience, a duty of the wife written into the marriage service, was never a virtue she had possessed. Assuming responsibility for the household and estate in the years after her mother's death had taught her to enjoy making her own decisions and to resent it when another, in that case her father, countermanded them. She had loved Richard Weston dearly, but he had also driven her mad with his mercurial improvidence. Too often she'd instituted economies, and used the savings to invest in estate improvements, only to have her efforts ruined by Papa announcing an unnecessary and wildly extravagant purchase or, worse, a ridiculous gaming debt. She now realized her mother had felt the same way, in her case untempered by affection. Robina didn't know why her parents married or if they had ever loved. All she could remember was scorn on her mother's side, answered by resentment on her father's. The lesson she'd drawn from observing the ill-matched pair was that a marriage without mutual respect and affection was worse than no marriage at all. Her father, though no more responsible, had been a good deal happier in his widowhood.

She stared at the pinecone and thought of herself growing old and dull and dry. Washing away the brown, she mixed up a deep, rich green and carefully brushed in a branch thick with needles. On a whim, she added a curly red ribbon as though decorating a Christmas wreath. She'd always loved an old-fashioned country Christmas, but there wouldn't be one for her this year, or perhaps ever again, now that she'd made a decision about her future.

Her godmother bustled in a while later and found her still at work. "My dear, I thought you were determined to paint only from the life."

"I decided the pinecone alone was a little drab and needed some color."

"Quite right. We all need color. Speaking of which, Bow's Warehouse has a marvelous new selection of silks. I bought a lavender sarsenet, and there is a light cherry that would suit you perfectly. I am determined to take you back tomorrow." Since Mrs. Madsen enjoyed shopping above everything else, it was fortunate her husband had left her comfortable.

"I have all the gowns I need and can afford," Robina responded lightly. "And pray do not let us revisit the old argument. You have been generous enough with my new evening gown, besides housing me all this time."

"I would gladly house you forever, my love," Mrs. Madsen said with the exaggerated enthusiasm that Robina had often seen her regret later. "But perhaps it won't be necessary. I hear," she said archly, "that Lord Carbury called. Was my absence enough to loosen his tongue?"

"Unfortunately, yes."

"My dear child! Whatever did he say to upset you? I suppose horrid Edwin was wrong as usual."

"No. For once, horrid Edwin was correct. Lord Carbury condescended to make me an offer."

Mrs. Madsen affected a sort of fluttering vagueness that had apparently endeared her to men in her youth, including the admirably rich Mr. Madsen, but she wasn't at all stupid. "Oh, dear," she said. "I hope you didn't do anything rash. You have so much common sense. Mr. Madsen used to remark on it often with surprise, considering what your parents were like. Not that I wasn't very fond of your mother. And Richard was a charming man, but not steady. I trust that I can wish you happy and begin to plan the wedding."

There was no way to put this tactfully. "I declined his offer."

Mrs. Madsen's elegant hands covered her mouth to cut off a shriek of horror. "Why?"

"I do not believe that we are compatible."

"What does..." Her godmother began to speak, then thought better of it. She regarded Robina with native shrewdness. "Lord Carbury is nothing like your father."

"No, indeed. I cannot think of anyone less like Papa. Carbury lives for duty and obligations. As he so kindly informed me, I am one of the latter."

"To be sure, it's more agreeable if a man shows a semblance of feeling when he proposes, but one can't have everything."

"I fear he is more like Mama." The thought, barely conceived, burst out. "I would displease him, and he would despise me."

"Carbury is far too correct in his manners to treat a wife unkindly."

Rather than reassuring, the statement sent a chill through Robina's blood. "His very consideration would lay such a weight of obligation on me that I would resent him. If I believed he had even a slight affection for me, beyond that of a childhood acquaintance, we might have a foundation for a good marriage. But I honestly feel that, for all he cares, Carbury might as well marry a statue."

She was sorry to disappoint her godmother, who worried about her. Mrs. Madsen hated to worry. Her, forehead, smooth and soft from the regular application of Olympian Dew, creased for a moment, then returned to serenity. "We shall find you a different match once people come to town for the Season."

"My darling Godmama, let us be practical. I am twenty-five years old, not more than passably pretty, with a fortune that is even less than passable." She schooled her features to hide her lack of enthusiasm for her plan. "I shall return to Yorkshire. Lady Halston has offered me a position in her house. And who knows? Perhaps I shall be lucky enough to attract a curate or a half-pay officer who will love me."

Mrs. Madsen groaned. "To think you could have had an earl. Yet you'd prefer to become a companion to that old dragon. I cannot bear to think of it."

"I shall manage her, never fear. And if we cannot abide each other, I know I can return to you." *For a brief visit*, she added silently. Her pride would not let her be a burden, and she had made up her mind that she would make her own way in life.

"Are you quite sure you won't change your mind and accept Carbury after all?"

"I doubt I will be given the chance. He would likely be rejoicing in his escape, if that wasn't a waste of time that could be better spent thinking of important matters. I was never more to him than an item on one of his wretched lists."

Chapter Three

Robina would have been surprised to know that Wyatt dwelt on his rejection all the way home. Having steeled himself to propose, he was mildly miffed that he remained unbetrothed. Failure was always abhorrent, but in politics, particularly in opposition, one became inured to it. On the other hand, in politics failure was only temporary. One merely came up with a different means to the same goal. In this case, he couldn't see an alternative, unless he abducted Robina and compromised her so that she had to accept him. Such a dishonorable method was quite out of the question. Moreover, being a thoroughly reasonable man, he could understand that she didn't wish to live with him for the rest of her life. He didn't want her, either.

He didn't want a wife, and now he need not have one. The special license and the half-written letter to his grandfather announcing his engagement would go to waste, but in terms of the efficiency of his life, Robina's refusal was a net benefit. Also, he had the rest of the morning free.

"I didn't expect you back so soon, my lord," his secretary said from his desk in the corner of the book room. Thank goodness he hadn't shared his intentions with Trumble. "You have a letter from the Bishop of Salisbury about the Church Buildings Act and asking if you could meet the committee on December the eighteenth. You didn't tell me when you intend to leave for Christmas at Bourton."

"The seventeenth," he replied firmly. There were bounds to everyone's sense of duty, and involving himself in the affairs of the Church and its most boring bishop was where he reached his. Then he thought about three weeks in the freezing corridors of Bourton Hall in December, catering to his increasingly irascible grandfather, without a bride to keep him company or to warm his bed at night.

Robina had looked very pretty this morning. Anger suited her, brightening her complexion and making her eyes glow.

But he wasn't going to marry. Ever. He didn't have time, and there were plenty of male cousins with male children to eventually inherit the earldom. Speaking of which...

"I'd better answer Sybilla Herbert's letter."

Trumble located the missive, likely aided by the scent of attar of violet that permeated the lady's person and correspondence. Wyatt held it gingerly by one corner, as far from his nose as would allow him to decipher Sybilla's curlicued script.

He'd always thought his second cousin Ernest's widow a very silly woman, and this letter did nothing to alter his opinion. Three months ago, he'd taken over the guardianship of her four sons, the eldest of whom would now be his heir, and so far he'd been called upon only to make routine decisions regarding the trusteeship of the children's funds. Now his presence was required to consult their mother about…something. Sybilla could wander around a point for days without ever hitting it.

He'd better do it, he supposed. Dinfield Park, Ernest's house, was in Nottinghamshire and on his route north. He'd stop there a day or two before proceeding on to Yorkshire for Christmas. He'd never been much interested in seasonal celebrations, regarding holidays as something to be enjoyed by those who had nothing better to do. Nonetheless, the thought of a cheerless Yuletide at Bourton, sharing Christmas dinner with no one but his grandfather, made him feel depressed.

Which was ridiculous and unnecessary.

TRAVELING IN WINTER was never agreeable, even on the Great North Road. Wyatt preferred to go post, for speed and convenience, and by the time he reached Stamford, he elected to spend the night at an inn and conclude his journey to Nottinghamshire by daylight. Thoroughly jounced on wet, rutted roads, he entered the elegant confines of Dinfield Park with a good deal more pleasure and less trepidation than he would normally feel.

Sybilla Herbert looked at least ten years younger than her thirty-seven years, and she knew it. Always well-dressed, her light gray gown trimmed with pinkish-purplish things flattered her excellent figure. Widowed just under a year, she had taken an expansive approach to the confines of mourning. As far as Wyatt was concerned—and he wasn't a man to pay much attention to the details of the feminine toilette—she could have been any fashionable London matron. Which was exactly what she had been before her husband's demise sent her into retirement on the estate now owned by her eldest son, Ernest, known as Nolly.

"Dear Carbury." She greeted him in her parlor with outstretched hands. "I am so glad to see you. You shall tell me what to do, and I can stop worrying." It was such a pleasant change from Miss Robina Weston's lack of respect for his advice that he kissed her hand and got a mouthful of lace. Her fingers were covered with the most idiotic mittens he'd ever seen. "Come and sit down and let me ring for wine. You must be tired and cold. Winter always has a dreadful effect on my spirits. I am quite downcast."

She didn't seem downcast now, and Wyatt warmed at her flattery, her attention, the blazing fire that dispelled the December damp, and her excellent Madeira. They sat for a while, speaking of London news. He disappointed her by knowing fewer details of the latest *ton* scandals than she did, but she listened with almost convincing interest and very little comprehension to the political gossip.

"What can I do for you, Sybilla?" he asked finally. "The change in guardianship has been completed, and I saw your banker before I left. There's nothing amiss there."

"It's Nolly!" she exclaimed tragically. "He has fallen into low company, and you must save him."

"The boy should be at Oxford," he replied. "At seventeen, he must be bored to death at home and bound to get into mischief." He did not add that there was plenty of mischief and low company to be had at university, which was the main point of attending if you were entirely without academic pretensions. The boy needed the freedom to explore such delights free from his clinging mama.

"I can't do without him. I am accustomed to having a man about the house, and I could not manage his brothers without him."

Wyatt frowned. "You can't keep him here forever. A young man needs to see something of the world."

Sybilla's eyes glistened, and she blinked bravely. Wyatt recalled that his late cousin Ernest had been helpless before that look. "I cannot let him go now. Next year perhaps, if I am no longer alone." She tilted her head coyly. *She's got a new suitor*, he thought. *Good. Let's hope the man is sensible.*

Never in the mood to hear sentimental tales of courtship, he ignored the opening. "What seems to be the problem now? Has he taken up gaming? If so, I'll nip that in the bud by cutting off his allowance."

"Worse!"

"What can be worse?"

"He's in love with a scheming hussy, a low creature."

"I daresay that'll happen a few times before he grows up. Do the boy some good. It's not as though he can marry her. Who is the girl?"

"Peg Wattles, the daughter of the innkeeper at The Duke's Arms."

"My dear Sybilla. No one could possibly fall in love with a girl with a name like that." He stopped and thought about one of the (very few) indiscretions of his youth. "Not unless she is especially pretty. Does the girl have designs on him? I shall speak to her father, and that'll be the end of it."

"Thank you." She leaned over and took one of his hands between both hers. "The boys need a father."

"Indeed, they do. In the meantime, you may rely on me to take care of things." He was a little disappointed. Such a simple problem could be solved in an hour or two, and he was committed to remain at least a couple of days before going on to

Yorkshire. He'd caught up on all his correspondence before he left and felt very strange not to be busy. "How are the other boys?"

Johnnie, Toby, and George apparently were giving no trouble at all, excellent boys except for an excess of energy that sometimes fatigued their mama, with the twins home for the holiday and George's tutor gone to spend Christmas with his family. Their rude health and buoyant spirits were admirably displayed during dinner, a meal notable for the absence of the eldest son of the house. After the meal, to forestall any hysteria on Sybilla's part, Wyatt announced that he would go to the inn now and see what Nolly was doing.

In need of exercise after days on the road, he elected to take a lantern and walk the mile into the village of Hopewell-on-Lyft. Picking his way briskly through patches of snow, Wyatt skirted the woods at the edge of the Dinfield estate and was greeted by the lights of the village.

The Duke's Arms was a typical country inn, situated on the main road a little way past the bridge over the River Lyft. Inside, he was greeted by the obviously respectable landlord—not a man likely to risk his livelihood by encouraging his daughter to seduce members of the local gentry.

"Wattles, at your service, sir. Are you wishing for a room?"

"Thank you, no. I am Lord Carbury, staying over at Dinfield Park. I had heard young Mr. Herbert might be here."

Wattles shook his head. "I haven't seen him tonight, my lord, but he often stops in of an evening for a mug of my home-brewed. Will you take a seat by the fire and take off the chill while you wait for him? Our Peg'll bring your ale, unless you prefer brandy."

Carbury ensconced himself on a wooden settle in the taproom and awaited developments. In short order, a girl brought him a foaming tankard, curtsied, and asked him if he needed anything else. "That's all," he said. "Busy night?"

"A bit less than usual, sir," she said. "I reckon the highwayman is keeping them home." Her eyes shone in her pleasant, pink face. Peg was no beauty, but she had a friendly manner and a pretty smile. He could imagine a bored boy finding her a suitable object for his first infatuation.

"Highwayman?"

"Oh, yes, sir. The New Sheriff of Nottingham, they do call him. He's robbed ever so many carriages this last week or so."

After such a sensational revelation, it was going to take some tact to bring the subject around to Nolly. Though a measly challenge to his political skills, Wyatt was willing to undertake it when a hullabaloo of voices drifted in from the entrance. "The Sheriff has struck again!"

Chapter Four

IF ANYTHING WOULD make a young woman regret turning down an offer from a rich man, it was three days on the stagecoach with another to go. It was almost a relief when, at some distance past Grantham, the coach lurched sideways, its wheel stuck in a frozen rut. Although still early afternoon, the coachman expressed his gloomy opinion that it was likely to be dark before help came and the vehicle was back on the road. Though chilly and damp, the kind of weather when drizzle or sleet might commence at any moment, Robina accepted an offer from a farmer to take the two female passengers in his cart as far as the inn at Hopewell-on-Lyft, where they could wait in warmth until the coach caught up with them.

Huddling on a pile of hay in her warm cloak, she tucked her chin into the swan's-down tippet that was her godmother's parting gift and enjoyed the clean air free from the odors of sweat and onions exuded by her fellow passengers on the stage. Lulled by the clip-clop of the cart horse's hooves, she dwelt on visions of tea and soup and a fire. She could have traveled in a comfortable private chaise if she'd accepted Carbury. But he would have ordered her life to his convenience. That her querulous employer would do the same, without providing the benefit of luxurious transportation, she tried not to dwell on. As she counted her blessings that she wasn't on foot, a cry interrupted her thoughts.

"Stand and deliver." A bad day just got worse.

It didn't take much for the horse to stand. The beast's driver lowered his reins, and the cart jolted to a halt. "That'll be the New Sheriff of Nottingham," he said without any show of panic. "Give him your money, and he won't harm you."

Robina examined their assailant through the gloom. His face was hidden beneath a tricorn hat and a turned-up collar, but the metal of a small pistol gleamed in the fading daylight, trained on the farmer.

"I ain't got nothing," the latter said laconically. "Naught but a load of hay. No coin."

The robber turned his pistol on a thin, nervous woman whose complaints had irritated Robina since she'd boarded the coach at Stamford. "Deliver your valuables, or I'll shoot this old mort."

"Give him everything. He'll kill me," the woman shrieked, and delivered. She tossed her purse over.

With regret, Robina abandoned a half-formed notion of distracting the fellow, who wasn't very large. She couldn't trust the driver to take advantage of the moment to take his whip to the thief. And the woman might be a ninny, but she didn't deserve to be shot. Robina's reticule joined the woman's purse on the ground, and the highwayman, his pistol steady, scooped them up and stuffed them into the capacious pocket of his long coat. "Drive on now, and don't look back. If you stop, I'll shoot."

The cart lumbered on, the woman wept, and the farmer said nothing. After a minute or two, Robina dared to turn her head and glimpsed the robber slipping off into the woods. Her heart sank. She was a day's journey from her destination without a penny to her name to pay for food and lodgings. It had seemed wise to keep all her valuables—her money and the few pieces of jewelry inherited from her mother—in her reticule instead of her valise. Her bag was safely in the stagecoach, defended by an armed coachman, and she was now penniless. Stiffening her back, she refused to mourn the loss of her pearl brooch and coral necklace. She would not think about the way she'd whistled away a brilliant marriage, or her drab future. She needed to solve the immediate problem of how to quiet a stomach that hadn't been fed since breakfast and was rumbling ominously.

According to the farmer, who became quite chatty, the picturesquely named New Sheriff of Nottingham had robbed a number of vehicles and was being sought, fruitlessly, by the authorities. Robina thought the man wouldn't be relishing the tale if the thief had run off with his hay. By the time he pulled into the yard of The Duke's Arms, she'd had enough of his tales and could barely summon the civility to thank him for the ride. Her apology for being unable to pay him bordered on the waspish.

The landlord rushed out to greet them, and Robina's fellow passenger relapsed into even louder hysterics and described a massive brute of a man who had all but ravished them.

"Come, madam," Robina said, putting an arm around her. "Calm yourself." She urged her into the inn and managed to request tea over the shrieks, wondering how on earth they were to pay for it. Suddenly, she felt chilled to the bone and on the verge of joining her unwanted companion in a bout of tears. She'd set out bravely to make a life for herself without the charity of friends and relations, but her bid for independence had started poorly. Tantalizing smells wafted into the hall, spicy and delicious and reminding Robina that Christmas was almost upon them. It was possible that she would spend the holiday working off her debt in this inn in the middle of nowhere.

Plucking up courage to explain her plight to the landlord, she was scarcely aware of a door opening to her side.

"Robina?" Her first reaction to the familiar voice was disbelief, followed by heart-stopping joy and an urge to hurl herself into Carbury's arms. "What on earth are you doing here?" He strode out looking handsome and disapproving.

"My cart was held up by a highwayman."

"Your *cart?*"

"The stagecoach was stuck, so I accepted a ride in this farmer's cart as far as the inn."

If he'd expressed any concern for her ordeal, she might indeed have flung herself at him, an action he would doubtless regard as childish. He saved her from making a fool of herself. "You are going to Yorkshire for Christmas, I presume. I cannot believe that you were foolish enough to go alone on the stage, or that Mrs. Madsen permitted it. You should be traveling post, or Edwin Weston should have sent his carriage. Really, Robina. I had more confidence in your common sense."

Gathering tears of self-pity turned to rage. "My arrangements are none of your affair. I told you that you aren't responsible for me. Neither do you have any right to criticize my conduct. Please go about your business. I must speak to the landlord about accommodation for the night."

Even as she spoke, she knew she was a fool. Refusing to marry him was one thing. Brushing him off in her present plight was sheer pigheadedness. But his self-righteous arrogance made her want to scream.

He rolled right over her dismissal. Taking her arm with his usual deliberation, he attracted the attention of the landlord merely by looking Carburyish. "I need a vehicle, Wattles," he said. "Anything will do, just as long as it will carry Miss Weston and me to Dinfield Park."

"It would be most improper," she said, trying to shake off his grip.

"Don't be ridiculous. I am staying with my cousin Mrs. Herbert."

Her resistance weakened. "I can't impose on her."

"Sybilla will do as she is told." Perhaps he realized this was high-handed, even for him. "She has a large house and will be delighted to welcome another guest. Where are your bags?"

"On the stagecoach. I can't go without them."

Not deigning to answer this objection, in a few efficient sentences he had commandeered the inn's gig, arranged for her luggage to be retrieved and delivered to Dinfield, and ordered tea. The innkeeper bowed and scraped, agreed to every demand, and carried it out immediately. Carbury gave her two minutes to swallow her drink, then bundled her into the gig and giddy-upped the horse down the road.

"I'm sorry it's an open vehicle, but I had to take what I could get. It's barely a mile, which is why I walked over earlier. Are you cold?"

Softened, slightly, by his concern for her comfort, she couldn't bring herself to speak. The awkwardness of being rescued by the man she'd turned down choked her. She was both grateful and humiliated, a noxious combination. He didn't seem to notice her silence as he described his host's family and assured her of her welcome.

"It's lucky for you I came up to visit my wards on the way to Yorkshire. If you had any sense, you would have asked me to escort you since we are going to the same place. You, my dear girl, need a keeper."

This was too much. "If that is true, which I dispute, I made it clear in London that you would not be mine. And, for your information, I am not going to spend Christmas with Edwin and Lucilla—as though I would! I am on my way to Lady Halston's."

Carbury grasped her meaning at once. "The only way that old beldam would house you is as paid companion, and precious little pay at that."

"There's nothing wrong with honest employment. I told you I could look after myself, and I can. I wish you would take me back to the inn."

She knew she was being absurd. If he obeyed her request—and there was as much chance of that as sunshine at midnight—she would have to ask him to lend her a guinea or two, and she could just imagine his supercilious response. He'd given her the lantern to hold while he drove. In the pool of light, his face was impassive, his attention on the task of steering the horse along a dark road. But Carbury rarely displayed much emotion. He was cold as ice.

Yet a distant memory crossed her mind: Wyatt at the gathering after her mother's funeral in all his nineteen-year-old magnificence, taking a sad little girl by the hand, feeding her cake, and telling her he would always be her friend. And again a few months ago, when he brought her the news of her father's death in London, he had seemed a rock to cling to in a sea of misery.

If only a rock had feelings for the drowning sailors it saved.

"You would prefer to live as a poor relation?" He didn't need to add that he meant she'd prefer it to marrying him. "You will be little better than a servant."

"There are different kinds of servitude, and at least with this one, I will have the choice of leaving."

Carbury's fine mouth hardened, and she wondered if her implied insult had hurt him. Perhaps a little, but only his pride. He said nothing more until they arrived at Dinfield Park.

Mrs. Herbert, a slender dark woman, received Robina politely as a country neighbor of Carbury's who had been stranded by a coach accident. Clearly bursting with curiosity, she insisted on showing her unexpected guest upstairs herself. Robina had the impression her languid hostess would normally have left the task to a servant and expected an interrogation.

"I suppose your abigail will arrive with your bags," Mrs. Herbert said, lingering while Robina washed the dirt of the journey from her hands and face.

"My bag is on the stagecoach. I traveled alone."

"How very singular." Her hostess's fine eyebrows arched, suggesting that such a lowly creature was unworthy of one of the best bedchambers. It was a charming room, draped in chintz patterned with floppy pink and yellow roses. "How precisely are you connected to Carbury?"

"Our fathers were friends and neighbors."

"Let me see. Oh, yes. Sir Richard Weston. I believe I remember hearing of his death. My condolences." Clearly she knew of Sir Richard's sensational collapse onto the table of a London gaming hell, scattering a terrifying pile of his IOUs all over the crowded room.

"Thank you, ma'am. I didn't wish to impose, but Lord Carbury insisted."

"Of course, I will always welcome any acquaintance of Carbury's. Do you see much of him?"

"In recent years, very little."

Robina had the impression the lady was relieved by the answer. Beneath her die-away look she subjected Robina to a very beady examination and liked what she saw: her oldest and shabbiest carriage dress suitable for a lady's companion traveling on the stage.

"Wyatt—Carbury, I mean—has such a strong sense of duty, even toward the merest connection." *Very mere* was her message. "He is guardian to my boys, you know, and I rely on him completely. He is excessively fond of them, almost like a father. He insisted on coming to Nottinghamshire in person to see us since I am settled in the country until my year's mourning has passed. After that, I expect we shall join him in town."

So Mrs. Herbert had designs on Carbury, did she? Robina wondered if the gentleman was aware of the fact. "I understand that your eldest son is almost eighteen."

"Not for many months. I was almost a child bride, you know."

"I would never guess that you had a son almost grown," Robina said. She meant it too. She wasn't much taken with Sybilla Herbert, but she could admit the lady was very handsome and looked little more than thirty. There was no reason why Carbury shouldn't marry a woman a few years older than he. From this lady he would doubtless receive the degree of gratitude and obedience his domineering character demanded. She hoped they would be very happy.

A maid entered to light the fire and apply a warming pan to the sheets. Robina expressed every polite appreciation of the comfort while Mrs. Herbert waited until they were alone. She hadn't finished her questions.

"Why were you on the stagecoach?" she asked. "Such an uncomfortable vehicle, at least that is what I have heard. I do not believe any of my acquaintance is accustomed to travel thus."

"I am on my way to take up a position as companion to Lady Halston in Yorkshire." She briefly described the drama of the last part of the journey.

Her hostess shrieked with horror that the local highwayman had struck again, but otherwise seemed pleased, all fear of Robina as a rival for Carbury's hand put to rest. Her china-blue eyes took on a calculating look. "Since you may have to stay a day or two, I would like you to mind the younger boys. Their tutor is away, and they are sorely in need of supervision." She lowered her voice to an attractive purr with a little confidential lilt. "I shall be busy with Carbury and would be much obliged."

It appeared that Robina's life of servitude was to begin sooner than expected. On the whole, she was pleased. Entertaining three young boys would get her out of the house, and she wouldn't have to watch Sybilla Herbert's gratitude and obedience or Carbury's arrogant delight in the face of female fawning. The pair of them were well-suited, and there was no reason for Robina to be upset about it. None at all.

But she'd rather not have to witness such a revolting sight.

Chapter Five

Robina's job as makeshift tutor began the next morning after breakfast when the younger Herbert boys announced their intention of gathering greenery to decorate the house for Christmas.

"I am told it is unlucky to bring it into the house before Christmas Eve," their mother objected.

"We'll keep it outside until then," George said. "Please, Mama. We could look for a Yule log too."

"I don't want a dirty, wet thing dragged across my carpets."

"I've seen them burned in old houses," Robina said. "But the fireplaces here are too small. Not," she added tactfully, "that they don't put out splendid heat. I would be happy to go out with the boys, ma'am." She was dying for fresh air, and she loved snow.

The eldest, Nolly, who had consumed cold beef and bread in sulky silence, announced in lordly tones that he might as well come too. Mrs. Herbert's objections to herbaceous decoration melted away when she realized she would be left alone with Carbury.

"We've never been at Dinfield Park for Christmas," Johnnie said. Or perhaps Toby. They were twins and not only very alike, they also tended to speak in a duet of just-broken voices. "When Papa was alive, we only came to Dinfield for the summer." "Our housekeeper has been telling us about all the country customs for Christmas." "It's going to be ripping fun."

Ten-year-old George had charged ahead with the forceful energy peculiar to small boys. "I'll beat you to the holly," he yelled over his shoulder, and that was the end of the twins' attention to her. Not to be outdone by their junior, they raced off over the snowy fields, and the three of them were soon attacking a bush with little finesse, undeterred by the prickles.

"They are very young," Nolly remarked from his elevated stance of seventeen years. "They will tear their clothes, and Mama will fret."

Robina supposed she should prevent the rending of garments, but since her position of tutor was both unpaid and temporary she decided not to spoil their fun.

Nolly was a slender young man with his mother's good looks, as yet unmarred by bristles. Unlike Carbury, who had gravely carried the weight of the world on his shoulders for as long as she could remember, the eldest Herbert boy evinced a veneer of ennui.

"Are you up at university, Mr. Herbert?" she asked. "If so, I daresay you find country life less exciting than your brothers do."

"Mama says she can't do without me and I must remain on the estate and learn how to manage it now that Papa is gone. But," he burst out, "there's not much to do but listen to the steward bore on about crops and drainage. I wish I was going to Oxford with the other men from school."

"It's a beautiful park and house. Did your father build it?"

"M'grandfather," Nolly said with an air of pride. They stood for a minute looking over rolling meadows toward a substantial wood.

"Part of those woods are mine. The rest belong to the Duke of Oxthorpe, who lives at Killhope Castle on the other side of the village. The Great North Road marks our boundary. I say, Miss Weston, would you tell me about the highwayman? Cousin Wyatt says I should not ask because it might distress you, but I should like to hear about it, if you don't mind."

Robina rolled her eyes. "I'm not such a weakling that a little matter of being robbed at gunpoint would overset me."

"I should think not! I wish I could have an adventure like that."

They discussed the activities of the New Sheriff of Nottingham for a while. Nolly had made quite a study of the crimes of the local thief who had evaded all attempts at capture. Nolly was keenly interested in Robina's description of the man. They ambled along, happily chatting, until the younger boys rejoined them.

"We've cut piles and piles of holly," Toby said, "but how shall we get it home? Do you have any idea, Nolly?"

"You should have thought of that, you idiots. I have other things to do." Nolly bowed to Robina, his courtesy intact when not addressing his brothers. "I enjoyed our conversation, Miss Weston, but I must take my leave. I have a matter to attend to." He took off at a brisk walk in the direction of the road to the village, the route she had driven with Carbury the night before. She turned her attention to the boys' problem. Before they found a solution, help was to hand. Lord Carbury came across the field, followed by a gardener pushing a large wheelbarrow.

"I thought you'd need help bringing home the branches," he said. Within a couple of minutes, he had the boys collecting greenery in a methodical way and piling their bounty in the cart.

The gardener directed them to an oak tree in the woods with a supply of mistletoe, and the three of them tore off. Carbury offered Robina his arm. "Shall we follow at a more sedate pace?" he asked.

She accepted his invitation with trepidation. The sight of him striding toward them, his greatcoat hanging from his broad shoulders, buttoned tight so the breeze didn't disturb the folds of cloth, his tall hat perfectly straight on his perfect head, had given her strange quivers in her stomach. She wanted to drink in the sight of his splendid masculine figure. And she had the oddest urge to unbutton him and knock him over so that he was as dirty and torn and rumpled as his young cousins.

"Did Nolly say where he was going?" he asked.

"He said he had a matter to attend to. Do you need him?"

"Perhaps Sybilla is right. She thinks he's entangled with the innkeeper's daughter. The boy needs to be unloosed from his mother's apron strings. While he remains at home with no independence, he is bound to get into trouble." He hesitated. "Do you think it possible he is in love?"

"I am surprised you wish for my opinion." *On any subject*, she added silently.

"As a lady, you know more about these things than I."

"I see. Love is a matter of no importance and thus can be left to females."

"That is not what I said," he replied calmly.

Instead of stamping her foot at being put in the wrong, as usual, she made herself answer his original question. "Nolly is not likely to confide in me, but I think there's something on his mind. We spoke mainly of the highwayman."

"I told him not to," he said with a frown.

"I'm not made of glass, and I survived the encounter. I thought about tackling the man, but I decided I couldn't do it alone." She knew that would get up his dander.

"How could you be so foolish?"

"I wasn't. I considered the matter, as any person of spirit must, and rejected it as unwise. I am just as capable of rational behavior as you are."

"I'm not going to answer that," he said with odious serenity, "because I don't want to quarrel with you."

Robina gave him marks for recognizing her provocation. It occurred to her that she would enjoy a good quarrel, and it might be good for Carbury. He was far too used to getting his own way. "Does anyone ever defy you, Carbury?" she asked.

He actually smiled, a look that suited him all the more for not being often seen. "I wish they did not. I am a member of the party in opposition. Even if my opinion prevails among my Whig colleagues, by no means a certainty, I am usually defeated by the government."

"Why do you do it, then? Politics sounds very disagreeable."

"It is the most hateful business in the world and the most absorbing. There are so many important issues before us, so much that needs to be done for the improvement of the nation and its people. Yet the practice of politics is hard and often unpleasant. Do not ever tell a politician that he always gets his own way."

"I assume the world would be a better place if you always carried your argument."

"*I* think so." He laughed. "You are teasing me. You always were a pestilential little girl."

"How can I resist? Perhaps the frustrations of your work in Parliament make you a dictator in other parts of your life. Or perhaps you are naturally tyrannical." She put a gloved finger to her lips and pretended to consider the matter. "I believe it is the latter."

"You are unfair. I wish to look after my dependents, not to dominate them."

"I'm not sure you know the difference, and that is why I do not wish to be your dependent."

The air felt thick with the knowledge of her refusal.

"I do not like to see you alone in the world, Robina," he said.

"I don't understand why you can see that Nolly needs to be free, but I do not."

"The answer is obvious. You are a woman."

"I am twenty-five years old and far more capable of making sensible decisions than a seventeen-year-old boy."

"That's not saying much, I fear. I respect your intelligence, but you are a member of the sex with less strength and power than men. It is the way of the world."

"Sometimes I wish it were not," she said, pleased at the implication that her impotence was dictated by society rather than by natural inferiority. "It seems unfair. Do you know that if I had accepted your proposal, my paltry two thousand pounds would become yours?"

"I assure you I did not offer for you for your money. As my wife I would have given you far more. I would have taken care of you."

"You want to take care of everyone." It came out as an accusation, yet wasn't that unjust? Care for others was an admirable trait, and Carbury was very good at it. But Robina didn't want to be another on his long list of responsibilities.

He didn't seem embarrassed about speaking of his offer. She would grant that he possessed the virtue of not being easily offended. Still, raising the subject had been gauche, and she'd sooner die than have him think she was hinting for a repetition. She removed her arm from his and increased her pace to get ahead of him. "I wonder if the boys have found the mistletoe."

WYATT HAD JOINED the greenery party because a little of Sybilla's company went a long way. He'd fended off questions that were none of his affair. He might be guardian to her sons, but he was not required to have an opinion about what she should wear to the Christmas assembly, even if the Duke of Oxthorpe was rumored to be attending. Why the devil should she think he was qualified to judge the merits of deep flounces and bias tucks, whatever they were, or even remotely interested in the topic? Pleading genuine and heartfelt ignorance, he escaped the overheated parlor into the pleasantly cool outside.

Intending to spend time with his wards, instead he'd got into conversation with Robina and started to feel mildly regretful that she'd turned him down. Perhaps it was only the contrast with Sybilla, but he enjoyed their talk and even found her disagreements stimulating. He didn't understand her decision about her future—he often found women incomprehensible—but she intrigued him. And because they were walking in a muddy field covered with half-melted snow, and he didn't have a dozen appointments crowding in on him, he had time to explore her mysteries.

Possessed of wealth and influence, time was the one thing he could not create. Leisure was an unaccustomed luxury. He breathed deeply and filled his lungs with clean air. Light-headed as he hadn't been in years, he grinned at Robina striding on ahead of him, taking a moment to appreciate that she had a neat figure and her hips swayed prettily. He caught up with her at the wheelbarrow, parked near the edge of the woods and piled high beyond capacity with holly, pine, and laurel boughs.

"I don't think Sybilla is keen to welcome half a forest into her house." They stood together, contemplating the bounty. "When I left her, she was complaining about pine needles on the carpets."

"She's a very fashionable lady and doesn't like the country ways of celebrating Christmas."

"I don't know much about them. My grandfather is too much of a curmudgeon to go in for celebrations of any kind. Though my father never met an event he couldn't celebrate, wholesome ancient customs were not his preferred form of amusement."

"Hard to believe such a different pair were father and son. You are more like your grandfather, I think."

"Lord, I hope not. I may not have my father's charm of person, but I trust I am always rational. Hillforth has become...difficult in his old age."

"Did you ever find yourself in the middle of their quarrels?"

He didn't want to sully her mind with tales of the ferocious rows that he'd tried to referee from an early age and that made him dread their annual visits to Yorkshire. Visits during which calling on their neighbors the Westons and their daughter had been a welcome respite. "Let's say it was good training for the practice of politics. I look forward to some quaint country Christmas customs, if Sybilla allows them."

"I do hope she will, for the boys are excited about snapdragon and wassail and hobby-horses. Like you, the poor things have spent most of their lives in London."

"Do you dislike London?" he asked.

"How could I? I saw so much when staying with Mrs. Madsen. The theaters, the shops, the sites of so many critical events in our history. It's like being in the center of the world."

It was how he felt too, and yet he detected a tension in her voice. Her fists clenched against her skirt, not the kind of thing he usually noticed. "Are you remembering your father's death?" he asked gently.

"Not just that," she said quietly. "London held Papa in thrall and was the source of his downfall. I used to dread him leaving home for town." He knew how hard she'd worked to keep the estate going, only to have the improvident Sir Richard fritter away the fruits of her efforts. He'd made it his business to know just how things stood.

Lightly he touched one of her gloved hands, and for a moment she leaned toward him, as though she would accept his physical condolence, just as she had wept on his shoulder when he brought her news of Weston's death. At the time, he'd been offering comfort as he had when she was a child, whether mourning her mother's loss or crying at a scraped knee. There and then he'd decided to marry her, but it was only now that he truly comprehended that she was a grown woman and not his neighbor's sweet and sometimes aggravating little daughter. If he embraced her now it would not be a child in his arms.

She tossed her head, sniffed, and stepped away. "Let us not dwell on the past. The sight of holly berries and the scent of pine make me happy. I loved Christmas in Yorkshire. My mama used to adorn the house, and I continued to do so."

"I have a faint memory of playing at snapdragon before my mother died. After that I was always in London with my father. I don't know anything about Christmas decorations."

"I'm quite talented at forming branches into garlands. I could teach you how."

"Better teach Sybilla. If I know her, she'll take shameless advantage of you unless you stand up to her."

Robina pursed her lips in the same naughty way she always had, but with an adult quality that warmed his blood. "Didn't you hear that I am the boys' new tutor? Not for long. I hope I can catch the stage tonight or tomorrow."

"Absolutely not." Now that he had her in his care, she could not be permitted to expose herself to bad roads, uncertain weather, and highway robbery. "If you persist in this madness of taking employment, I shall escort you to Lady Halston's myself. I promised Sybilla I would stay for the village assembly tomorrow night, but after that I am at your service. Pray do not fight me on this." Her mouth hardened into a stubborn look. "And do not even think about running off to the inn without my knowledge."

"Very well. I accept." She smiled faintly. "How did you know what I was contemplating?"

"Don't you know that I am omniscient?"

"It's odd to hear you joke. If that was a joke." Now she gave him a grin that was infectious and made him feel young and carefree. They stood for a moment, smiling into each other's eyes, and something shifted in his chest.

A long moment of harmony was interrupted by his youngest ward. "Cousin Wyatt," George cried, tugging on his sleeve. "I've found a huge ball of mistletoe, bigger than the one Johnnie and Toby found, but it's too high for me to reach."

"Show me!" Robina said. She took the boy by the hand, and they tripped off into the woods.

Wyatt shook off his trance, said a few words to the gardener about getting the wheelbarrow back to the house, and followed them, guided by the sound of laughter and crackling bracken. He wondered how Robina would react if he put a sprig of mistletoe to its traditional use. The pleasant musing turned to apprehension when he discovered her climbing the giant oak, aiming for a mass of green leaves and white berries at a dangerous height.

"Stop at once, Robina. You'll fall."

"Never!" she cried. "You're not getting me down from the tree this time." He had no idea what she was talking about.

His heart in his mouth, he watched her scramble up the broad trunk, out of his reach. A vision of Robina broken, even dead, on the woodland floor seared his brain. Suddenly, he couldn't imagine life without her. She'd always been there, almost as long as he could remember.

Even hampered by skirts and petticoats and a heavy cloak, she managed to reach her quest and started breaking off sprigs of mistletoe, tossing them to George on the ground, while holding on to the tree with her left hand in the most careless fashion. All he could do was plant himself at the foot of the tree, ready to catch her when she inevitably fell.

"Is that enough?" she called.

"Plenty," Wyatt ground out. "Now come down. Very, very carefully. Better yet, wait, and I will come and fetch you."

"That's a terrible idea. I've been climbing trees almost since I could walk, and I'll wager I do it better than you. You've been wasting time in London while I practiced useful skills." She leaned over and actually stuck her tongue out at him.

"Don't look down!"

But she insisted on looking at him as she descended in admittedly tidy steps from branch to branch until she reached the smooth part of the trunk where there were no footholds. "I'm going to jump now," she said, and she did.

Her skirts betrayed her, catching a jagged stump where a low horizontal branch had broken away. She lurched to the ground, facing the tree, retaining her balance, and exposing an endless expanse of legs. The display of shapely stockinged calves, gartered just below the knee, sent a roar to his brain and blood to his breeches. He stared in a manner unbecoming of a gentleman at the wondrous sight. If he hadn't already realized that Robina was a woman, he knew it now.

She rearranged her skirts, veiling the glorious sight in layers of wool, and turned with a rueful twist of her mouth. He'd thought before he wouldn't mind kissing her and wondered how he'd been such a fool not to notice then that she had luscious pink lips, easily the most kissable he'd ever laid eyes on in his life. Stepping forward without conscious thought, he would have acted on his impulse had blasted George not intruded again.

"Well done, Miss Weston! What a splendid climber you are. Will you give me lessons?"

"Of course I will, if you don't mind taking instruction from a girl."

George bit his lip. "Let's wait until the twins have gone up to the house, and they'll never know."

What were they talking about? Was she mad? Of course she was.

"You must never, ever do that again," he blurted out.

"Don't be tedious, Wyatt. I shall climb the tallest tree on the estate, the tallest tree on the duke's estate even, and you can't stop me."

She called him Wyatt. She'd done so as a child, before he inherited his father's courtesy title, but now the name on her lips—her lips!—seemed delightfully intimate.

He wanted to shake her until she saw sense then wrap her in his arms and kiss her senseless. For Robina Weston wasn't just a beautiful woman, she was the woman he loved. The woman he wanted to marry so that he could possess her forever and make sure she never imperiled herself again.

Given the stupendous nature of his discovery, he couldn't believe she was unaware that she had just changed his life. She ought to know that they belonged together. Unfortunately, judging by the way she scowled at him, she didn't share either his feelings or his rock-solid certainty that their destinies were entwined.

When he tried to speak, his brain froze, and his mouth was full of chalk. He was back in Mrs. Madsen's house without a thing to say. If he couldn't speak, how the devil was he going to change her mind?

Chapter Six

ON THEIR RETURN from the greenery session, the family gathered for a nuncheon of cold meats, cakes, and hot chocolate, during which Wyatt confirmed that love had rendered him mute. He didn't mind. It wasn't as though he wanted to talk to Sybilla. He spent the meal staring at Robina, who carried on an animated discussion with the three younger boys about Christmas customs.

Robina laughed heartily at jests that drew a raised eyebrow from their mama. She had a deft hand with youngsters, but then he had a feeling she could manage anyone. No wonder she was fearless about taking on the well-known Tartar Lady Halston. He'd even back her against the political intriguantes of Devonshire and Melbourne Houses.

Wyatt caught himself mooning about celebrations at Bourton with their children and, better yet, dwelling on the conception of these offspring. He plotted how to get her to himself that afternoon. After such a strenuous morning, she would surely wish to rest. He certainly didn't want her going out again and risking her health in the cold wind. Her eyes glowed almost green in a face flushed from healthy exercise. What he'd like was to get her alone in a room with a comfortable sofa and find out what it was like to kiss her. No conversation needed.

"Wyatt!" Sybilla, rather sharply, demanded his attention.

"I beg your pardon, Sybilla. Did you say something?"

"I should like you to accompany me in the carriage this afternoon when I deliver baskets of food and wine to the estate workers and tenants."

"Surely Nolly should do that." Then he'd dispose of the other boys, with bribery if necessary, leaving him in sole possession of the house and Robina.

"Nolly isn't here." She cast him a reproachful look, and he realized he'd scarcely given a thought to the eldest Herbert, who was, after all, the reason for his presence. "It doesn't matter. The tenants always have questions and complaints, and who better than Nolly's trustee to answer them?"

"Your land steward?"

"I must insist, Wyatt." She dropped her voice and placed her hand—mittened in pink lace this time—on his wrist. "I need you, and I would enjoy your company. I've hardly seen you today. There are so many matters on which I need your advice." Her blue eyes were innocent, but he detected steel determination behind the apparent meekness.

Sybilla, he realized, might claim to bow to his every wish, but she had a habit of getting her own way. He surrendered to his fate and climbed into the carriage beside her, casting a despairing glance at Robina and the boys, who were commencing a strenuous snowball fight. "Don't climb any trees," he yelled, but if she heard him, she didn't acknowledge it by turning his way. She was too busy shaking snow out of her bonnet. He felt old and stuffy, one of the adults going off to do their duty, leaving the young people at play.

"I do hope Miss Weston doesn't let the boys get into trouble," Sybilla said as they drove away.

"I'm sure she'll keep an eye on them, but it isn't her responsibility."

"Since she is here, I asked her to stand in for the boys' tutor."

"Good Lord, Sybilla. Robina isn't a servant."

Her eyes widened. "I'm sorry if I misunderstood. She is on her way to become a lady's companion, is she not? I thought she'd feel more comfortable if she had something to do."

"You are quite wrong." He was about to scold her for treating his future bride so shabbily, but refrained. He'd been overconfident when he proposed before.

"Later, we will call at the inn and see if the stagecoach is running tomorrow. Miss Weston must be anxious to be on her way."

"No need. I shall escort her to Yorkshire on Tuesday, after the assembly."

Sybilla tucked her hand into his arm. "Will you stand up with me? It will save me from melancholy thoughts of my poor dear Ernest, who was with me for last year's ball. I know it's less than a year, but I feel ready to dance again. It will raise my spirits, and I know Ernest would have wanted it."

Wyatt couldn't argue with that. He'd never understood how Ernest, a cheerful and sensible fellow, had tied himself to such a clinging vine. Seduced by beauty, he supposed. Not like him, he thought smugly. Robina was lovely, but she was also bright, and he couldn't imagine her clinging. Though under the right circumstances, clinging would be delectable. And rational too, when she wasn't climbing trees and dashing off in stagecoaches. When they were married, he'd be able to curb those dangerous tendencies. "I will be honored to dance with you," he said. "And with Miss Weston."

"Will Miss Weston come to the assembly?"

"Why would she not?"

"I wouldn't think she'd have a suitable evening gown, and it is rumored that the duke is to attend. I mean it kindly, because I wouldn't wish her to be uncomfortable."

Wyatt turned to look out at the snowy fields, shocked at Sibylla's ill-nature. Her excuse was pure nonsense: A public country assembly was open to people of every station in life. Whatever did she have against Robina? A groom from The Duke's Arms had delivered her bag that morning and collected the gig. Little used to paying attention to feminine garments, he worried that Robina wouldn't be as finely gowned as she deserved. He noted Sibylla's smart carriage dress, her sable tippet and matching muff, and thought of Robina in such an ensemble. He would enjoy lavishing such gifts on her. Jewels too. Those were calls on his precious time he wouldn't begrudge. He made a mental list.

1. Discover identity of best modiste in London.
2. Buy betrothal ring.
3. Inquire where women buy silk stockings…

"Have I annoyed you?" Sybilla's irritating little-girl voice broke into his vision of Robina's legs.

"I am sure that the daughter of Sir Richard Weston has a dress good enough for a country assembly, even if the Prince Regent himself was present."

And if she turned up in rags, it wouldn't matter to him. For the first time in his life, he looked forward to a ball for the sheer pleasure of dancing.

Chapter Seven

A FRESH FALL of wet snow overnight had the boys itching to go out. Robina wondered if Carbury would join them again. Their conversation yesterday had intrigued her. She'd never seen him so open. She'd teased him, and he hadn't pokered up. Even the incident at the tree, infuriating because it epitomized his imperious pomposity, had pleased her a little, because he'd shown a care for her wellbeing. On the other hand, it had been over a silly matter, and she'd wanted to knock him over and make him roll in the snow until all his arrogance was washed away.

"Why don't you come with us, Lord Carbury?" she asked on impulse, when she and the three boys gathered in the hall, cloaked, gloved, and muffled to the tips of their ears.

"Yesterday you called me Wyatt," he said.

"I beg your pardon. I reverted to childhood under the stress of the moment. The danger of being up a sturdy tree with an angry man yelling at me, you know."

"You're not a child now." He gave her a look she couldn't read. Was he telling her she should continue to address him formally? Was this a snub at her impertinence, another scold? He glanced at Mrs. Herbert, who was having a word with her butler at the foot of the stairs. "I'll fetch my coat."

The clouds had blown away, and cold sunlight glistened on the expanse of pristine snow covering a broad lawn that lay to the south of the house and the undulating valley beyond. Robina filled her lungs with clean air that seemed to sweep away a weight of care: grief for her father and anxiety about her future. Though nothing had changed, her spirits lightened with what felt like pure happiness. From the corner of her eye, she took in Wyatt, standing beside her, handsome and grave, surveying the same view. "It's beautiful, isn't it?" she said. "What could go wrong on a day like this?"

Their eyes locked, and she felt something shimmer in the air between them, something frightening and wonderful.

"It'll be a clear night," he said. "The almost full moon will make easy traveling for the assembly." And she was left wondering if she had imagined the moment when the two of them were an island of warmth in a frozen landscape.

The boys, with little regard for the majesty of untrodden snow, charged across the lawn, shouting and stumbling as they gathered snowballs and hurled them with varying degrees of accuracy. "Come on," she said and ran after them, joining the fray. If Carbury wanted to be a stuffy old man, let him. She didn't care a rap halfpenny if he thought her childish.

A pitched battle formed, she and Johnnie side by side against Toby and George. The wet snow easily cohered into big missiles, and in short order all of them were thoroughly soaked. Leaning over to gather fresh ammunition, a fat one caught her in the back of the neck, seeping beneath her scarf. Her opponents were ahead of her, and her ally kept up his offensive barrage. She spun round to find Carbury, not six feet away, with a grin that made him look like a boy himself.

"Who's a child now?" she cried. Leaving nothing to chance, she ran at him and smashed her handful of snow right in his face. He lost his footing, fell backward, and she went with him, both laughing themselves into stitches.

The warmth of their earlier shared moment was nothing to the blazing heat that rushed through her as she lay sprawled over his big body. Through layers of wool, she sensed his strength. He was all hard physicality in contrast to her own softness. She was intensely aware that he was a man and wouldn't have been astonished if steam rose from her damp clothing.

"I told you before, Robina. You are most surely not a child." The timbre of his voice made her shiver, but not with cold. She had a mad urge to kiss him on the lips and see what he would do. Though very likely they wouldn't notice, the presence of three noisy boys deterred her.

And Sybilla Herbert. "Wyatt!" The woman had quite a strong voice when she wanted to make herself heard, as she did now, from the terrace next to the house. "I need you, Wyatt. What happened?"

Carbury swore mildly, and before he could push her off, Robina scrambled away and staggered to her feet.

"An accident, Sybilla," he said, standing up and brushing the snow from his front. How could he remain calm while her heart threatened to burst? "Don't come down. It's slippery."

"I have no intention of stepping out another foot," she said. "I wanted to let you know that Nolly is waiting to speak to you in the library."

"I'll be in immediately." He turned to Robina. "You should come in too and get out of those wet clothes."

"Please do, Miss Weston," Mrs. Herbert said. "I want to ask your opinion about my gown for the ball."

That was a surprise. Robina was sure her hostess had seen her from the window and rushed out to break up anything developing between her and Carbury. Since she could have left Robina out with the boys, she must have something to say, and the odds were it had nothing to do with assembly finery.

Carbury looked pleased. "I'm sure Robina will give you excellent advice." They went in together, and he made a little fuss about removing her cloak and bonnet. Sometimes it was nice to be fussed over.

"She's quite dry underneath," Mrs. Herbert said. "Come with me now." She almost pushed Robina toward the stairs while gifting Carbury with an enticing smile. "I look forward to displaying the results of our consultations."

It was a lovely gown, lavishly trimmed with embroidery, seed pearls, and lace, the muted colors of lavender and dove gray the sole concession to the lady's widowhood. But then it was clear to Robina that Sybilla's mourning was no more than conventional at this point. She was after fresh game, and the only question was whether she would bag it. Robina's advice was not required, only her admiration.

"What shall you wear, Miss Weston? I fear you may not have anything suitable. I'd lend you one of mine, but they would all be too small for you. My figure hasn't altered by an inch since I was a girl, so I am able to order all my clothes from London without any fittings. I expect you are used to Yorkshire dressmakers."

"Thank you for your kind offer," Robina said, "but though we are of similar height, I am larger in the bosom." She rather envied Mrs. Herbert's slender grace, but wild horses wouldn't make her admit it.

"Wyatt called me a sylph when we drove out together yesterday."

"How unlike Lord Carbury."

Sybilla simpered. "He's not a man who is free with compliments but when we are alone together, he is quite affectionate."

Though tending to doubt the lady's word, which she suspected was an invention inspired by hope, Robina couldn't help feeling a little pique. He certainly never complimented her, even when proposing marriage.

"This is very awkward, dear Miss Weston, and I don't quite know how to say it." Alarms rang in Robina's head at the utterly insincere endearment. "It would be perfectly acceptable for you to excuse yourself on the grounds that you do not possess a ball dress."

"But I do," Robina said, indignation fighting amusement at such tactics.

"That is not my meaning. The assembly has been moved to Mrs. Carrington's house, and she is a very proper and elegant woman, and her house is very fine. Not only that, the Duke of Oxthorpe will be present, and it may be embarrassing to you, given your status, to mix in exalted company."

"Thank you, but I think I would like to go." She affected some of Sybilla's sham drama. "I shall sit in a corner and observe my betters. For such a low creature as I, it will be a sufficient treat to be present."

The sharp look this flight garnered told her she might have gone too far. "If you insist. I don't suppose you will dance, unless Carbury asks you out of duty. He has engaged me for the first set, of course."

"As is his duty to his hostess."

But he hadn't asked Robina to dance, even though he'd had a perfect opportunity when making remarks about moonlight. Not romantic walks by moonlight but safe travel. How could a man manage to make moonlight dull?

And yet they'd had a moment this morning. Two, if she counted lying on top of his supine body, and she was inclined to do so. She resolved to be the belle of the ball and dance every dance to spite Sybilla. And if it had the effect of making Wyatt take notice, so much the better.

Chapter Eight

Robina had never been anything approaching a belle at the local balls in Yorkshire. Not that she was a wallflower, because she knew everyone and never lacked for partners. But the young men were those she'd known all her life—like Wyatt—and they tended to look on her as a dashed good sort of girl, almost as good as a fellow. She lacked the delicate beauty of the young ladies that received offers. And of course everyone knew that her profligate father's estate was entailed and there'd be precious little left for her.

When she had arrived in London and confided to her godmother that Carbury intended to offer for her, Mrs. Madsen had been thrilled at the match. She'd spent the best part of three months planning a grand betrothal ball, and that meant Robina must have a new gown for the occasion. Although the occasion never arose, the gown was made, and Robina knew she looked her best in the sage green silk. It was every bit as fashionable as Sybilla Herbert's ensemble and, in her humble opinion, far more tasteful. Her hostess was showing a lot of bosom. Or as much as she was able, Robina thought unkindly.

Sybilla's face when Robina joined the assembly party in the hall made up for a sea of aggravations. Carbury's was even better. He was struck dumb, judging by the way his mouth fell open and a faint croaking noise emerged from his throat but not a single word.

"I say, Miss Weston, you look splendid." Fairly stunned by Wyatt's black coat and satin knee breeches molded to his figure, she hadn't even noticed that Nolly was there too, boyishly attractive though less perfect in evening dress.

"Very nice," Sybilla said, scanning her from silk slippers upward and obviously searching for flaws. "I'm so glad I sent my maid to help you dress." Strictly speaking, that was true, in that the inexperienced housemaid who had laced her stays and buttoned her gown was a household employee. Sybilla's trained dresser hadn't set foot in Robina's room, and it was fortunate that she was accustomed to arranging her own hair.

Carbury nodded approvingly. "Very good of you, Sybilla. Robina looks lovely."

A compliment! But was it for her or Sybilla?

Sybilla held out her hand to him with a graceful flourish and smiled coyly. Even a man as little given to pretty gestures as Carbury couldn't miss the message. "You are always elegant," he said and kissed her hand. Robina wished it were proper for gentlemen to kiss the hands of unmarried ladies.

"Let me help you into your wrap." He was looking at Robina, but Sybilla quickly thanked him, and he could do nothing but take the velvet and fur cloak from the waiting butler. Robina distinctly saw her lean back into Carbury's chest as he placed it around her shoulders.

Robina put on her own cloak, the sturdy all-purpose garment she traveled and walked in. Sybilla talked without cease during the drive to Carrington Close, describing in exhaustive detail the activities of the Christmas assembly committee. She moved on to a list of everyone who would be there, reminding Carbury of every local worthy of his acquaintance and cutting out Robina, who naturally knew nobody. Nolly leaned back in the corner, looking bored.

The dancing was about to start when they arrived, and Sybilla demanded Carbury's hand, leaving Robina forlorn. She raised her chin and admired the decorations with their plentiful use of mistletoe. Nolly, showing a glimpse of social tact, aroused himself to ask Robina to stand up with him.

"Why, thank you, Mr. Herbert." She could hardly keep from smiling at his lack of enthusiasm. "Are you very fond of dancing?"

"Mama made me come. And I wish you would call me Nolly. I'm not much one for females, but you're quite decent for a girl."

They took their places in line, and she noticed a number of the male dancers were on the young side. "There are a good many men of your age or thereabouts here."

"Our mothers make us. They're on the committee."

"Oh?"

"There are always too many females at these affairs and not enough fellows to dance with them."

"You're in good company, then."

"Many of my friends are here, and we'd have a splendid time if we didn't have to dance."

"That is the point of a ball, after all."

"I know, and it's a rotten shame. Now I'd better pay attention, or I'll step on your toes."

As they went through the movements of the country dance, Robina was treated to a sotto voce commentary on the general awfulness of the occasion. She supposed that she was flattered to be excluded from the wholesale condemnation of the Ladies' Assembly Committee and all its works. Confirming that she had been appointed an honorary youth, he offered to lead her to the punch bowl at the end of the set and introduce her to some of the fellows. "They all want to hear about the New Sheriff of Nottingham."

Carbury, with Sybilla on his arm, was at the other end of the ballroom. Perhaps he'd follow her to the refreshment table and request the next dance. Surrounded by youths who pelted her with questions about the highwayman, she kept an eye on the couple. Instead of separating and moving on to new partners, they occupied a settee partly shielded by a large orange tree, absorbed in conversation.

"No, I didn't see his face," she said as she watched them. They made a striking couple, their heads close, Sybilla's gloved hand white against Carbury's dark sleeve. "He was of average height, and I'm afraid there was nothing distinguished about him at all."

"How splendid if we could catch him," one of the young men said. She listened with only half an ear. The fact that Sybilla Herbert might catch Wyatt suddenly seemed a real and intolerable possibility. Why else was he sitting out the second set with her instead of dancing with someone else? Why wasn't he dancing with *her*?

"What was that, Nolly?" she said. "Thank you, I will take another glass of punch." She downed it in a single draught, and whatever was in it lifted her into a state of desperate gaiety. She had neither right nor reason to expect Wyatt would pay her special attention. She might feel they'd become closer in the last couple of days but on slender evidence. When she turned down Wyatt, she'd left him free to wed anyone else. If Sybilla Herbert was his choice, she wished him to be very happy with her.

Truly.

As for her, she'd catch the stagecoach tomorrow and celebrate Christmas by beginning her life as companion to Lady Halston, a kind and charming person beneath her somewhat gruff exterior.

Truly.

And now she would dance the night away with every man who asked her. She hoped some of them would be older than eighteen so she could demonstrate to Carbury that other men found her attractive.

AFTER HIS FIRST duty dance with Sybilla, Wyatt intended to stand up with Robina, as often as was proper and even more. In truth, he had it in mind to be her partner for most of the evening. First, he had to find Sybilla a drink, but when he returned with two glasses of punch, snatched from the tray of a convenient footman, she patted the settee beside her.

"I need a word with you," she said.

"Can't it wait?" When she responded with an injured moue, he repressed a sigh and resolved to escape as soon as good manners permitted. For the first time in his life, duty and courtesy seemed an intolerable burden.

"You haven't told me about your talk with Nolly."

He didn't see why this couldn't wait till morning, but at least he could reassure her. "Nolly isn't even remotely interested in Miss Wattles. He laughed when I suggested it. You may set your mind at rest."

"But where does he go? He's always disappearing."

"He wouldn't tell me, but I'm sure it's some harmless boyish mischief with his friends." He looked across the room where Nolly stood in the middle of chattering youths. Robina looked beautiful and animated. The boys were listening to what she had to say with every evidence of fascination. He envied them and felt old and staid again.

"Wyatt!"

"I'm sorry. Did you say something?"

"I'm worried about him."

"I told you before, the lad is bored."

"The younger boys need him."

"Nonsense. They'll be back at school in a few weeks."

"*I* need him. I cannot be all alone here without a man's company."

"That's easily solved. You will go to London for the Season. Have you thought of marrying again? You're an attractive woman."

"Oh Wyatt!"

What? To his amazement, she laid her hand on his sleeve and stroked him.

"I knew I couldn't be mistaken in your intentions, in all your kindnesses since dear Ernest died."

The back of his neck prickled with acute discomfort. "I'm only doing my duty to my cousin's family," he said stiffly.

"It's more than that. A woman can always tell."

This woman was severely mistaken. He'd always thought Sybilla a fool, but he hadn't realized she was weak in the head. "I'm sorry if I've done anything to give you the wrong idea, but I am nothing more than the boys' guardian. After all, Nolly will eventually inherit the earldom if I don't have a son." His plans definitely included the possibility of progeny, and Nolly was likely to be out of luck.

The wide blue eyes spelled determination and trouble. "If Nolly had a father, naturally I would defer to him. To my husband, I mean. I was always an obedient wife."

He didn't want an obedient wife. He wanted a wife who argued with him without artifice, who challenged him and teased him and made him laugh. A wife he wanted so much he'd hurry home from a late session in the House rather than waste the night plotting and scheming with his fellow members. A wife with an independent spirit and the courage of a lion who would wed him because she loved him and for no other reason. He wanted a wife he loved back. And that woman was dancing with another man (all right, boy), while he was stuck in a corner listening to utter drivel from a female who would drive him to distraction within a week. Or an hour.

"We would be perfect together. Ernest always said you didn't mean to marry, but your position *requires* a wife. A lady of birth and connections who can act as hostess and assist you in your career. There are many calls on your time, and I could help you."

She had a point. He'd been blind all these years to believe he was better off alone. Now that he welcomed a particular marriage, he could see the advantages of the institution.

"Say something, Wyatt. I have opened my heart to you, and you are silent."

Though he doubted her heart was at risk, he saw that she had exposed herself to embarrassment by virtually proposing marriage to him. He had to find a tactful way of refusing her. Her eyes shone ominously, and he felt all the dread of a man about to be involved in a public scene. The idea of explaining away an attack of the vapors made him shudder with horror. Robina would never have put him in such an invidious position. Sybilla had no compunction about invoking the tyranny of the weak.

He patted her hand in what he hoped was a cousinly fashion. "This is neither the time nor place for this conversation. Let us talk about it in the morning. Since you are dancing this evening, I'm sure all your friends and admirers will want to stand up with you. I see Squire Hungerford looking at you. Let me take you to him."

By the time he'd settled her with the red-faced local magistrate, Robina had found another partner and was passing down the line of a country dance with a good deal of esprit. Corralled into standing up with a wallflower, he was placed in a different group of eight and couldn't even have the pleasure of touching her hand in passing. Before he could reach her for the next, she was partnered by another fellow, slightly older than most of Nolly's friends. The callow young man flirted with her outrageously, and she encouraged him.

A STERN MATRON, doubtless a member of the infamous committee, had broken up the youthful group, commanding them all to mind their manners and find partners *at once*. Several of them competed for Robina's hand, a twenty-five-year-old almost old maid who had actually seen the New Sheriff of Nottingham being a far more desirable partner than a dewy maiden in white muslin whom they'd known all their lives. The next few dances passed in an energetic whirl of heys, poussettes, and promenades fortified by sips of punch.

Carbury's tête-à-tête with Sybilla was over, for now, though he stood up with her once more, as well as with two or three young ladies who appeared gratified by his attention and a Miss Houston, a very forward young woman whom Robina wouldn't trust alone with a lame grandfather. Of course he was a graceful dancer. Ballroom prowess was a skill possessed by every gentleman, and he did everything properly. She wondered what it would be like to waltz with him.

A country dance brought them together, and they joined hands for an all-too-brief moment. "Are you quite well, Robina? You are flushed."

"I'm having the most marvelous time!" she said defiantly. "This is the best ball I've ever attended."

"I've been trying to speak to you—"

"I haven't been anywhere," she said and hiccupped.

"Be careful of the punch. It's strong."

"It's the best punch I've ever tasted," she called over her shoulder as she turned, and the bright tune swept her away. What a tyrant he was!

Then she saw a rabbit. A fluffy brown rabbit peeping out from behind a large urn. She blinked, twice, and it disappeared. Maybe she had drunk a bit too much. She looked for Carbury again, but the dance had taken him far away.

Later, when another dance had ended and she was speaking to Mrs. Carrington, her hostess for the night, she saw Wyatt across the room, and he seemed to be heading in her direction. She tossed her head, trying to look both indifferent and enticing, a feat she wouldn't have attempted without the false courage of the punch, when all conversation ceased with the announcement of His Grace, the Duke of Oxthorpe.

She'd heard the duke described variously: as excessively proud by a couple of ladies; with awe by Nolly's friends as the man who'd single-handedly fought off a couple of local ne'er-do-wells pretending to be the New Sheriff of Nottingham; and by Sybilla as a very handsome man with a proper appreciation for his rank. For once, Sybilla was correct, at least as far as his appearance was concerned. Not as handsome as Carbury but with dark good looks, not at all the stiff-backed middle-aged man she'd imagined a duke to be. To her astonishment, he asked her to dance and led her onto the floor with a brilliant smile.

WYATT HAD COME to the ball with every intention of being charming, not easy when he felt ever more irritable and churlish as the evening progressed. Finally given the chance to speak to Robina, he'd accused her of being drunk. Not the most charming behavior, but she *was* tipsy. He wouldn't put it past Nolly and his irresponsible friends to have spiked the punch.

Wyatt regarded Oxthorpe's presence with indifference. He'd encountered the duke in London from time to time, but Oxthorpe didn't travel in Whig circles and held himself aloof from society. He'd hardly given the man a second glance until he astonished the company by condescending to dance. With Robina. With growing disgust, Wyatt watched the pair trip through a set in animated conversation. It was one thing to flirt with boys, but Oxthorpe was another matter entirely.

Damn rake. Wyatt was sure he'd heard stories about Oxthorpe's perverse proclivities.

Five minutes later, after the dance ended, while Wyatt was vainly attempting to fight his way through the crowd to Robina's side, Oxthorpe caught her under the mistletoe and kissed her. She curtsied and smiled, and Wyatt wanted to commit murder.

Just as he reached her side, a brouhaha arose about a rabbit loose in the house. The ball degenerated into a hunting party with Nolly's coterie leading the charge, and finally, at long bloody last, he was able to get her to himself.

"Carbury!" she cried. "Mrs. Carrington's bunny is lost, and we must help find him. I saw him earlier and thought I must be suffering from visions."

"I wouldn't be surprised if you suffered an hallucination from too much punch. Come." He grabbed her hand and dragged her toward the nearest door.

"I'm sure he went that way," she said, resisting his pull.

"I saw him leave by this door." A useful lie because, having visited Carrington Close on a previous occasion, he remembered a handy little sitting room.

"All right! I can't wait to see him again. His name is Franklin, and he's adorable. I hope we are the ones to find him." She tripped along beside him quite happily, chattering on about nonsense as though she hadn't been driving him to Bedlam all evening.

A WALTZ WOULD have been ideal, but a rabbit hunt with Wyatt came a close second-best. He seemed to be in one of his impossible moods, but surely even he wouldn't be immune to the charms of furry pets. And truth to tell, her head was a tiny bit fuzzy. The main thing was that she had his attention at last. He wasn't stalking bunnies with Sybilla Herbert. The thought of their indolent hostess in such a pursuit made her giggle.

"What?" he barked, tugging her down a narrow passage.

"You're going too fast. We should be searching."

"Let someone else do it." He opened the door to a small parlor, warm from a fire but dimly lit. She didn't know why he'd brought her here, but they were entirely alone.

"I want to talk to you about Oxthorpe," he said. "How dare you kiss him."

He sounded jealous, and the hopes that had been dashed by his neglect reawakened. She fluttered her eyelids. "I've never met a duke before, and I was ever so flattered that he asked me to dance. Everyone was so surprised." And envious, in the case of the ladies. She'd enjoyed a glimpse of Sybilla looking sour as she'd swung by in the duke's arms. "He's a charming man. We talked about Conisbrough Castle and other places in Yorkshire."

A little frisson of anticipation was dampened by the way Wyatt stood with his back to the fireplace, one thumb tucked into the fob pocket of his white silk waistcoat, the other slapping his white gloves against his thigh. He wore a frown like a bishop in an alehouse. Thus he must look when making a speech in the House of Commons, except that his hair was disarranged and her fingers itched to sweep it back from his forehead.

"As for the kiss, it was only the mistletoe. The place is infested with the stuff." She looked around, but sadly the decorating committee hadn't penetrated this obscure corner of the house.

"You're a fool if you think Oxthorpe means anything by his attentions to you. He's the proudest man in England, and you can be sure he isn't serious about someone like you."

Robina suddenly felt quite sober.

"I was dancing with him, Carbury, that's all. I'm at a ball, and when one is at a ball, one dances. And one is pleasant to people, because it is supposed to be an enjoyable occasion. You don't seem to understand this simple fact. Don't think I didn't notice you scowling at your partners. So enjoyable for them, I don't think."

"Better than flirting with bloody Oxthorpe and every grubby-minded boy in the county as well, and giving them ideas too, like the veriest hussy. Don't you think that *I* didn't notice them staring at your bosom and enjoying it far too much. That gown is indecent." His nostrils flared as his eyes descended to her bosom.

"It doesn't display nearly as much as your dear Sybilla's dress."

"She doesn't have as much to display."

Instead of pleasure that he had noticed her charms, she felt cheap and soiled. He was supposed to be jealous, not berate her as a drunken trollop. She put her hands on her hips and glared back at him, refusing to yield an inch. "I'm going back to the ballroom," she said. "I promised the next dance to Mr. Amblewise, and there is nothing you can do to stop me. He's a delightful man and quite handsome, and I daresay I shall enjoy a delightful flirtation." Never mind that the gentleman in question was a very proper clergyman with a doting mama.

She turned her back on him with a defiant sway of her hips. She'd show the pompous ass what a trollop was like. Not that she had any experience of the breed, but wiggling her behind at a man seemed the kind of thing one would do. She reveled in her vulgarity.

"Come back." Two hands grasped her shoulders. Before she had a moment to object, he'd turned her round, manacled her wrists behind her back with one powerful hand, and used the other to hold her head still while he sealed her gaping mouth with his own.

Shock and anger turned to searing pleasure she had never imagined. Wyatt wanted her! Trapped by his strength, she had never felt more free, free to relish the rough kiss of cloth pressed against her chest and his lips working magic on hers. If he'd done this the day he'd proposed to her, she would have said yes. How could she resist such bliss?

Releasing his hold on her head, his finger caressed her cheek and then her neck, sending extraordinary thrills straight down her body and making her ache in places she shouldn't mention. Her theoretical knowledge of relations between a man and a woman became practical as every inch of her flesh, every drop of blood, sent the same message to her brain: want, need.

Her throat croaked a protest when he withdrew from her, but it was only to murmur her name before he took her mouth again, deeper and harder, claiming her for himself and filling her with a fierce joy. No longer a duty, no longer a child, she was a woman who could drive a man to madness.

He let go her hands so that his could cup her derriere, pulling her against the evidence of his desire. His plunder of her mouth grew wilder, and there seemed a desperate quality to his kiss. Then he released her mouth and dragged his down the column of her throat and buried his face in the valley of her bosom.

His tugging at the neck of her gown awoke her from the sensual haze.

He'd called her a hussy.

And now he was treating her like one, and her acquiescence, her very delight, proved him right.

With all the force she could muster in her weakened state, she shoved him away. "No," she croaked. "No."

He leaped back as though stuck with pins. His eyes were crazed and his hair truly disheveled. She'd never seen him less contained. "Robina..."

"I am not a trollop," she cried, and ran out, eyes tight with gathering tears. He was saying something, but she couldn't hear and wouldn't wait. The joy of the evening had turned to heartbroken misery.

A room had been set aside for the ladies to fix their toilettes, pin up torn hems and lace, and take care of private business. In the rabbit-seeking chaos, it was easy for Robina to reach it without drawing attention to a disordered coiffure teetering on the edge of total collapse. Thankfully, the room was empty, and she was able to repair the damage to her hair. With hands no longer trembling, she stood before the cheval glass and smoothed the creases from her beautiful silk gown. She couldn't see that she looked different, but she felt it. In the course of her life, she had suffered grief for two parents, loneliness, and anxiety. But she couldn't ever recall the sensation of self-loathing that filled her now. Fueled by an excess of liquor, her behavior had forfeited Wyatt's good opinion. Inexperienced as a flirt, she'd made a hash of trying to arouse his jealousy and managed only to disgust him. The things he'd said, the way he'd mauled her, showed he thought her nothing but a wanton jade.

Throughout the years they'd known each other, she had resisted his dominance and resented his occasional disapproval. But never once had he scorned or despised her. His care and affection, sometimes taking a form that chafed her patience, had been unstinted and utterly reliable. Her reasons for rejecting his proposal had seemed rational at the time, but she'd been blind to how much he meant to her. She had lost his respect, and the loss made her heart sore. She didn't know how she could live without it.

Pinching her lips till they hurt, she relived their encounter this evening. He'd treated her as no gentleman should ever treat a lady. Such a punctilious man would behave thus only under severe provocation. The terrible thing was that she had reveled in his kisses and every shocking touch. Clearly, she was no lady, for underlying her shame and misery was an overwhelming wish that he would do it again.

Chapter Nine

WYATT COULDN'T BLAME the punch for his behavior. He'd scarcely swallowed a cup of the stuff. Deeply ashamed of himself, he didn't attempt to approach Robina for the remainder of the assembly. What he had to say to her—and how he would word the apology, he had no idea—needed quiet and privacy. To make matters worse, Sybilla continued her pursuit. On the way home the widow addressed all her comments on the ball to him with a kind of possessive intimacy that set his teeth on edge. How had he failed to notice her designs on him? Meanwhile Robina huddled in a corner, silent and never looking his way, her resentment palpable.

Clearly, when it came to women, he was a complete idiot. To complete his misery, Oxthorpe had become engaged to Miss Edith Clay later in the evening. His overreaction to a mistletoe kiss might have destroyed his hopes.

He fully expected Robina to insist on catching the stagecoach the next day. Luck was on his side when they learned a heavy snowfall ten miles to the north had put a halt to all travel in that direction. She wasn't going anywhere, by public coach or in his hired post chaise. They were very likely stuck until at least St. Stephen's Day.

Despite the size of Dinfield, he found it impossible to find a moment to speak with Robina privately. Sybilla kept them all running around, a martinet beneath a veneer of languor. There was a hopeful moment when she ordered Robina into the village shop for red ribbon to festoon the garlands that her guest's deft fingers had woven. When Wyatt offered to walk with her, Sybilla insisted he needed to speak to a tenant on the far side of the estate and sent Nolly with him.

If he should wed Sybilla, heaven forbid, he'd certainly be under the cat's paw. The experience made him understand how Robina had felt when he issued orders and resolved that when—if—she married him, he would curb his domineering tendencies.

On Christmas Eve, when the house rang with the excited cries of boys hauling in ever larger barrow loads of greenery, he decided he must again be master of his own fate. So he sat down and made a list.

Memoranda for December 24th, 1817.

1. Tell Sybilla no.

2. Propose to Robina.

3. Make her say yes.

4. Kiss Robina. (Contingent on success of item 3.)

He looked out over the snowy lawn and drifted off into a trance in which items five, six, seven, etc. ad infinitum, became progressively less decent and more delightful. But first, Sybilla.

As an experienced politician, he knew the best thing to do when telling someone they couldn't have what they wanted was to offer him or her something else.

"I am deeply honored by your regard, my dear Sybilla," he said. "As Ernest's widow, you will always be a valued member of my family. But I know I am not the right man for you." His lips twitched. "I have it on good authority that I am a pompous ass."

"Good Lord, Wyatt. Who dared say that to you?" Her eyes narrowed. "Miss Weston, I suppose."

"Your perspicacity amazes me. Now let us speak of your future…not together," he said, before she started arguing. Or insulting Robina, in which case he might say something that would lead to an irrevocable breakdown in relations. "If you wish to marry again, we must find you someone who will make you much happier than I could."

"I don't see how that can happen. There's no one eligible in the area except the duke, and he's to marry Miss Clay." She sniffed scornfully. "I don't know what he sees in that nobody."

He played his ace. "You will come to London for the Season, and since you often complain that your house on Brook Street is too small, I will arrange for you—and the boys when they aren't at school and Nolly isn't at Oxford—to have the use of my grandfather's house in Grosvenor Square."

"Hillforth House." Her eyes gleamed with avarice, as he'd known they would. He loathed the oversize, overfurnished mansion, preferring a cozy billet closer to Westminster, but he knew she would love lording over such grandeur. "If I give a ball, will you act as host?"

"I'll have to see if my time allows it." Every negotiation left a few minor details to be settled later. He hoped Robina wouldn't have her heart set on Hillforth House, because he was pretty sure she wouldn't want to share it with Sybilla. That was another bridge to cross later. After she'd said yes. If she said yes.

Each time they'd met since the ball, Robina had looked away. It reminded him of the stiff morning calls he'd made to her in London, and finally he understood why he'd been unable to speak for so many months. It wasn't reluctance to marry her, but uncertainty about the change in their relationship from friends to lovers. He'd better have devoted some of his time over the year to studying women and how to woo them, because he still didn't know what to say. He watched her hungrily as she conjured beauty out of bits of greenery and red ribbons, and he remembered the exquisite pinecone he'd seen her paint. While devoted to the quotidian business of her father's estate, Robina hadn't neglected the finer things that made life a little brighter. When—if—they married, he decided that they would celebrate Christmas with every frivolous extravagance.

He pilfered a sprig of mistletoe from the mantelpiece and slipped it into his pocket. When he got her alone, he would be prepared.

AVOIDING BEING ALONE with Carbury, Robina managed to have a youth or two on hand at all times. She counted the hours until the road north was clear and she could catch the stagecoach. Sharing a carriage with him was out of the question. Thank goodness she wasn't given to blushing, or she would have been scarlet whenever she caught his glance. She blushed inside imagining his thoughts about her behavior at the ball.

Sybilla assisted her, she suspected deliberately. Mrs. Herbert had got over her aversion to Yuletide decorations and was quite tireless in finding more places for Robina to ply her skills. Guessing that much of her dislike was rooted in rivalry for Wyatt's affection—sadly unwarranted—her new geniality suggested that she was sure of winning.

"That's quite lovely," she said, tweaking the bow on a ball of holly. "You're very clever, Miss Weston. I was just remarking on it to Wyatt. Did I tell you we have it all settled between us? Nolly is to go up to Oxford, and I will go to London to spend the Season at Hillforth House..." She drifted off, leaving Robina plunged in gloom.

Unable to contemplate the horror of sitting down to dinner with the happy couple, she told the butler that she was feeling unwell and would stay in her room. Claiming herself too fatigued to eat, she asked not to be disturbed.

Chewing her fist, she found herself making a list.

1. Nobly refrain from murdering Sybilla Herbert.
2. Go into a decline.

Never again would she feature in one of Wyatt's, except possibly...

1. Attend Robina's funeral.

Her sense of the ridiculous saved her from decline and death. As the midwinter light faded and everyone else was changing for dinner, she wrapped up warmly and slipped out of the house to enjoy fresh air, solitude, and despair. By the time she reached the end of the drive, it was almost dark and snowing lightly. She ought to go back, but Dinfield Park had become a place of horror, the glorious decorations she'd worked on so hard a mockery of the spirit of Christmas. Her cheeks were cold and damp, whether from snow or tears she neither knew nor cared.

What she wanted to do was continue down the lane that would take her straight to The Duke's Arms, but with the fresh snowfall there was no question of the coach running tonight. She was about to turn around when a male voice called her name. Her heart beat a tattoo as she thought it was Wyatt come to find her. Except he'd only berate her for foolishness at being out so late, with reason.

But the figure that emerged from the gloaming was Nolly's slender one. "I say, Robina, what are you doing out in the dark?"

"Just taking a walk. I've been busy indoors all day. And you, Nolly?"

"The same." But he was a poor liar and couldn't disguise a note of excitement.

"Really? I didn't see you helping with the decorating." He muttered something about it not being in his line. "So what are you doing? I'd like to hear a good story."

"Since you're a good fellow with a spirit of adventure, and because you saw the New Sheriff of Nottingham, I think you deserve to know. A couple of the fellows and I have a plan to catch him. We're going to borrow Cobby's father's carriage and drive along the road where the Sheriff usually appears. When he does, we'll be ready."

"Does Cobby's father know about this scheme?"

"Robina! You wouldn't be a spoil-sport."

"No, I wouldn't, not least because I have no idea of Cobby's father's name or where he lives. How can you be sure the highwayman will hold you up? He doesn't strike every night, does he?"

"We can't, of course, but some think he has an accomplice at the inn. We're going to boast about our plans in the taproom and mention that Cobby is carrying a large sum of money he won at cards."

"That's clever. Are you armed?"

"All three of us. I have Papa's pistols with me." He dug into his pocket, and a weapon glittered in his hand.

"I'm impressed. And I want to come with you." A wild idea, but it would keep her out of the house and her mind off her troubles for a few hours.

"You can't! You're a girl."

"A minute ago, I was a fellow with a spirit of adventure. But go on without me." Wyatt had always been impossibly stubborn, but other very young men were easily managed. "I'll walk back to the house and tell your mother."

Nolly's face fell. "You will not."

"No, I won't, because I'm coming with you. I'm in an adventurous mood. Besides, he stole my money and jewelry, and I have a right to revenge." And she wanted to see Wyatt's face when he heard of the escapade. She'd give him safe.

"Very well. Don't get in the way when things get hot."

"On the contrary. I intend to help. Give me one of those guns."

"WHERE'S NOLLY?" SYBILLA asked when they sat down to dinner. "I despair of the boy."

"Where's Miss Weston?" Wyatt asked, tired of his eldest ward and his moods.

"She is feeling unwell and doesn't wish to be disturbed. I fear we worked her too hard today." Sybilla was behaving well, not wanting to jeopardize the loan of Hillforth House.

He didn't believe it. Robina didn't want to see him. Hell and damnation! When was he going to have the chance to speak? He brooded through the meal, hardly hearing Sybilla's chatter. When the latter withdrew at the end of the meal and the three boys went about their boyish business, he asked the butler to inquire how Miss Weston was doing. "I know she said she didn't wish to be disturbed, but she may need something. Has she eaten? No? Send someone up with some soup and a glass of wine with my compliments."

Foolish girl to go without dinner. Or else she was truly ill. He paced the hall, waiting for the man's return.

"Not in her room?" he yelled a quarter of an hour later. "Didn't you see her go out?"

"No, my lord. The only person I've seen leave the house this evening is Mr. Nolly, but I cannot be everywhere."

"Fetch my coat. And a lantern." She'd gone to the inn, he was sure, looking for a coach because she couldn't bear to share a carriage with him. Who could blame her? She must be terrified that he would maul her again. Or worse.

Anxiety turned to terror when he discovered that a few flakes of snow had turned into a white maelstrom. He could have ordered a mount, but he didn't want to waste the time. Supposing Robina had fallen by the wayside, he might miss her from horseback.

It was the worst mile-long walk of his life as he battled through the thick flakes, trying to hear and see through the wind and the white swirls, his lantern barely lighting the way a yard ahead. Clinging to the hope that she'd left before the snowfall began in earnest, he arrived at the inn, praying as he never had in his life that he'd find her safely by the fire, alive and drinking tea so that he could wring her neck.

No. He wouldn't do that. Merely hold her tight and never let her go.

The first person he saw as he burst through the door was Nolly.

"Where's Robina?" he asked, stamping his boots. "Tell me she's here."

"I had Wattles put her in a room for the night," the boy said.

Wyatt exhaled a sigh of relief, and for a moment he couldn't speak. Nolly regarded him in nervous silence.

"What the devil were the pair of you doing out on a night like this?" Wyatt asked.

"It was barely snowing when we left, and she *would* come with me. She's a damned fine female."

Wyatt found himself grinning. "That she is. Maybe it's time you told me why you keep vanishing." He nodded at Peg Wattles as she passed through into the taproom. "Not that."

"I couldn't tell Mama because she'd have made a fuss—you know what's she's like. We've been trying to catch the New Sheriff of Nottingham. And do you know, Cousin Wyatt, I believe we'd have managed it tonight if it hadn't started snowing so hard. Not even a thief is out in weather like this." He described the plan he and his friends had conceived. "It's the shabbiest thing. We drove five miles and back and almost got stuck in the snow, and not a sign of the Sheriff."

"A very poor kind of villain to be deterred by the weather," Wyatt commented wryly.

"That's what I think. The four of us had our pistols primed and never got a chance to use them. Robina was dying to get a shot at the man who robbed her."

Wyatt's relief evaporated. "Damn it, Nolly," he yelled, barely restraining himself from strangling the lad. "You took Robina on a dangerous wild-goose chase and let her carry a gun? What were you thinking?" He paused. If he'd never been able to keep Robina from putting herself in danger, why would Nolly? "Never mind. Where are you off to?"

"I'm going to Cobby's for the night. His house is in the village."

"Take my lantern and go home. Your mother will be worried."

"What about you?"

"I need to speak to Miss Weston. Tell them not to wait up for me."

Miss Wattles came into the hall again and asked if he wanted anything. "There's a good fire in the taproom, my lord. Can I take your coat?" He was covered with an inch of snow, like a monstrous snowman.

He didn't want to talk to Robina in a public place. He fished in his pocket for a coin and found a guinea. "Which room is Miss Weston in? And keep it to yourself, if you don't mind."

She looked a bit doubtful but wasn't proof against the glint of gold.

"I don't mean her any harm." Visiting a young lady in her bedchamber was the most shocking thing he'd ever done, but frankly, he didn't care if word leaked out. His intentions were entirely honorable, and if Robina's hand was forced by scandal, too bad. A good politician seized every advantage, fair or foul.

Chapter Ten

ROBINA ENJOYED HER adventure, even though its only achievement was getting chilled to the bone as the carriage limped the five miles back through thickening snow, the young men taking the reins in turn. She wondered if an outlaw foolish enough to be out in such weather would hesitate to attack a vehicle emitting waves of raucous laughter. Mostly high spirits, though a flask of brandy was circulated. After her experience with the punch, she'd limited herself to a sip against the cold. Once they reached the inn, the disappointed but cheerful party enjoyed a bit of hot supper and a warm fire. Then she borrowed a nightgown from Peg Wattles and got into bed.

The last person Robina expected to see in her room at The Duke's Arms was Wyatt. But why should she be surprised? He'd hunt her down to the ends of the earth for the sole purpose of telling her she was a fool.

"Good evening, Robina," he said. "May I come in?" He stepped through the door and closed it behind him.

"You're covered in snow." Wet hair clinging to his scalp suited him. Despite everything—his scorn and subsequent engagement to Sybilla—she felt a quiver of excitement at the piquancy of having him alone in a small bedchamber.

"That tends to happen when you walk a mile through a storm in search of a lady who is supposed to be in bed."

She shrugged. "I am in bed." Wyatt seemed very calm. Not that agitation was his common state, but he didn't even appear disapproving.

"I saw Nolly downstairs. He told me what you had been doing."

"I suppose you've come up to scold me for imprudence and self-endangerment."

Wyatt opened his mouth to speak, then thought better of it. "I just remembered," he said after a moment. "The apple tree in your orchard. You were about seven."

"Yes. You made me get down, and then you tried it again the other day. I was perfectly fine both times."

"You may be right," he said. "And at this point, you are old enough to decide for yourself, although I'd prefer it if you refrained from climbing trees without someone, preferably me, being there to catch you. I'm not so sanguine about you driving around chasing armed villains."

"We had fun and we were armed too. But go ahead and scold me. You may as well get it over," she added defiantly.

"Had you asked my opinion of the venture, I would have advised against it, but I am glad to see you survived without injury."

Thoroughly unnerved by such unwonted tranquility, she tugged up the blankets to hide the coarse linen nightgown. "Uh, well. Thank you for your concern. I won't keep you."

He stood there, dripping water onto the wooden floor, and gazed at her. Staring back at his dear face—how she ever thought him merely good-looking baffled her, for he was surely the handsomest man in the world—it appeared, incredibly, that he was nervous. Yet she was the one most at fault. After a moment's uncomfortable silence, she pulled herself together. They couldn't go on like this, and she must attempt to repair their friendship. Much as it would pain her to see him married to another, she couldn't manage without Wyatt in her life. He had always been there, a reliable and reassuring presence, even when she rarely saw him.

"Wyatt—"

"Robina—"

They interrupted each other.

"Let me speak," he said. "I owe you an apology."

"Do you?" she said faintly. That, she hadn't expected. Wyatt rarely apologized, since he never thought himself wrong.

"Of course I do. At the assembly, I behaved in a way that was a disgrace to the very name of a gentleman. I forced myself on you." He closed his eyes for a second.

"It doesn't matter. I suppose a hussy asks for such treatment."

"No one deserves it. What I did must have appalled you." Which meant that she must indeed be a hussy, because she'd loved every second of it. His actions hadn't hurt her, only the motives behind them.

"Please, Wyatt. Let us forget that evening and never mention the subject again."

"I cannot. I must assure you that if my hopes are realized, I will never again treat you so brutally. You have, and will always have, my most profound respect."

"I'm glad. And when you wed Sybilla, you would certainly not be kissing another woman." She looked at him doubtfully. She knew that men sometimes strayed, but she couldn't conceive that he would dally with *her*.

"Marry Sybilla? Don't be ridiculous."

So Sybilla had been causing mischief, and she felt like cheering.

"Naturally, I must marry you. How could you think otherwise?"

"Must? How many times do I have to tell you that you owe me nothing? Don't tell me it was because you kissed me. And if it's only because we're alone in a bedchamber at an inn together, that's easily solved. You can leave at once."

"Why can't I find the right words to persuade you? I always seem to say the wrong thing when I propose to you." He shook his head, and she thought she detected hunger in his eyes, not merely annoyance. Clearly the man needed a hint.

"It doesn't matter what you say," she said softly. "It's what you feel that's important."

His shoulders drooped, and Wyatt never slouched. "I never have the least difficulty saying what I mean to most people, but proposing to you is the hardest thing I've ever done."

"Is that why we suffered those excruciating morning calls in London? Because you couldn't bring yourself to make the offer and felt obliged because of what you said to Edwin?"

"Yes...no. I wanted to marry you."

"You didn't give me that impression."

"But not for the right reasons. Then. It's different now."

"How?" Her chest fluttered in desperate hope.

His eyes were wild, his lips pinched. He seemed unable to speak, and then he took a deep breath. "I love you." The words came out so fast they ran together. She had no problem understanding them, but her incredulous brain lagged in grasping their significance. It was her turn to be struck dumb while Wyatt rediscovered his eloquence. "I love you, Robina. I love your beauty and your wit and your kindness. I love your intelligence and the way you create enjoyment around you even when things are difficult. I love the way you challenge me and refuse to accept second-best. I love that you refused me because I proposed for the wrong reasons, even though the sensible thing was to say yes. My greatest wish is to change your mind, and I will never stop trying." The flood of words ceased but only for a second. "I love you, and I always have. It took me too long to see you as more than a family friend."

When Wyatt found the right words, they were marvelous ones. She needed to speak, but her heart was caught in her throat. He cast about him and started to rifle through the pockets of his coat, tossing things onto the carpet until he found a folded sheet of paper.

"You'll laugh at this"—his smile contained a final plea—"but I made a list."

"Only one?" The impertinent words popped out as the lump in her throat dissolved into glee.

"I love it when you tease me," he said. "Of course more than one. Every month this autumn, I put it on my list. 'Propose to Robina.' I never did, and finally I understand my reluctance. I didn't know why I should offer for you and now I do. This is the list I made this morning."

He handed her the paper, and she read it in wonder.

1. *Tell Sybilla no.*
2. *Propose to Robina.*
3. *Make her say yes.*

4. Kiss Robina. *(Contingent on success of item 3.)*

"'*Make* her say yes?' Really?"

"Will it help if I beg?"

"Begging is good. But what really settles it is the contingency. Yes."

"What was that?"

"Yes, I will marry you, and now could we move on to item four? Immediately." She held out her arms, but he didn't move.

"Are you sure, Robina? You must feel nothing but fear after the way I attacked you last time. I'll try to be gentle in future."

"Don't you dare, Wyatt. I enjoyed every moment."

"Why did you push me away, then?"

"Because you had called me a hussy, and I was behaving like one. I hated how you despised me."

"It was myself I despised, never you."

She couldn't wait another second to have his arms around her, his lips on her. "What are we waiting for, then, Wyatt? After all the orders you've given me in my life, it's my turn to issue a command. Kiss me. Now."

Wyatt took to obedience like a duck to water. And though he started out tenderly, sipping sweetly at her lips, when he sensed her response gentleness gave way to a passion that burned. A respectful embrace devolved into a tangle of blankets and limbs as he lay on top of her, causing the bed to creak. Instinctively she parted her legs so that his length rested between them and lit a fire in her depths. Her body arched, begging to be touched and taken. "Please," she implored. "More." She pushed against him, grasping handfuls of his wet coat to urge him on.

"I shouldn't," he said roughly.

"You should," she replied and pulled his head down, adoring his damp hair threaded by her fingers, the slight roughness of his chin and jaw, and the hot taste of his mouth. He was Wyatt and this was only the beginning of how she wanted to know him.

His hands pulling down the neck of her gown and caressing her breast caused her no panic, only a lovely yearning that intensified the sensations below her belly. "More," she repeated and gave a mewl of protest when he rolled off her, breathing heavily.

"I have to stop. We have to stop." He stood beside the bed with his hands behind his back. "If I touch you again, I'll end up doing what should wait until we are married."

Regretfully, she agreed. Sitting up, she arranged the nightgown over her breasts and sat up with her legs folded beside her. "Your coat melted on me." No longer heated by his proximity, she tugged at patches of wet linen, cold against her skin. "I may have to take this off."

"Not while I'm in the room, please."

"I wish you didn't have to go." Having become betrothed—for the right reasons—she should have the chance to savor the experience. "When you proposed to me in London you set aside the whole morning. We've only been engaged for fifteen minutes and you're leaving already."

"We can talk tomorrow. The walk back to Dinfield will cool me off, and I need it." They smiled at each other for a minute, reluctant to part. "You make me happy, Robina."

"I love you." She hadn't said it before.

"I love you too." He dropped a quick kiss on her lips and gathered up his purse and other odds and ends he'd tossed onto the floor earlier. Besotted, she thought how lovely it would be to have a tidy husband. An unromantic quality, but she didn't want Wyatt to change. The burden of responsibility she'd carried so long became feather-light now that she shared it with a man who would never let her down.

She pointed at a thick folded parchment that had fallen under the washstand. "Don't forget that. I wouldn't want you to lose any important documents." He scooped it up. "What is it?" she asked, only to prolong his departure by a minute or two.

"I completely forgot that I left it in this coat." His astonishment that he could have forgotten *anything* made her laugh. "It's a special license from the Archbishop of Canterbury for the marriage of Lord Carbury and Miss Robina Weston."

"That's pretty presumptuous of you, Carbury. How long have you had it?"

"Since the day before I offered for you. In London."

"Very presumptuous." She blew him a kiss to soften the blow.

"I'm ashamed to say I was entirely confident that you'd accept me. I had a plan. Don't laugh at me, you wretched girl. There's nothing wrong with being organized. I was going to take you to Yorkshire, where we would be wed during Christmastide in front of our families and friends."

"Was it on your list?"

"Actually, no. I obtained it on an impulse."

"Wyatt, how splendid! Your first?"

"Perhaps, but not my last."

"I thought you wrote everything down."

His look made her toes curl. He picked up the paper that still lay on the bed, unscathed by their recent romp. "I had a few more items on *this* list I didn't write down."

"Tell me."

"After we are married."

She looked at the list and then at the parchment, and back again. "We have a special license. We're virtually married. We could be married tomorrow."

"Tonight even, in the unlikely event I could persuade a parson to come out in this storm."

"Let's pretend we did." In case he didn't understand her, she pulled her nightgown over her head and tossed it aside. Instead of embarrassment at kneeling naked before a man, she felt a surge of delight at the way his dark eyes bored into her. In her bones she knew she never needed to be shy in front of Wyatt.

He looked serious and determined, and she expected him to resist her. "You have two minutes to change your mind," he said, and his top coat dropped to the floor.

"Never."

He pulled off his boots.

"Keep doing what you're doing," she said.

He unbuttoned his waistcoat. "Last warning."

"I'm enjoying the spectacle."

"You've completely undermined my morals."

"You're not the only one capable of executing a plan."

He undid the last button on his breeches. "Very last warning." The garment hit the ground, and she gasped. The naked male in reality was larger than she'd expected.

"Wyatt," she said faintly.

"Yes, my darling? Are you sending me away after all?" He sounded agonized.

"Lord, no. Come up here immediately."

"You're warm," he said, pulling her against him so they were touching everywhere they could.

His skin was cool—he'd been out in the snow not so long ago—and she rubbed against him. Lying in his arms was indescribably lovely, both cozy and thrilling. The prospect of a lifetime of sharing a bed with Wyatt choked her with joy. She pressed her lips to his chest and squeezed back happy tears.

For a while they kissed and stroked each other with no great urgency, but she felt his male part pressing against her stomach. "Wyatt," she whispered. "What's next on the list? I don't know what I'm doing, and you do. Tell me what to do. I know you love to give orders, and I promise to obey without question."

"I don't want to hurt you."

"Would you?" she asked.

"I hope not, but I'm not precisely an expert myself."

"You mean you've never…?"

"I've been with women over the years, and I won't go into details, but I've been too busy to…study the subject."

It was such an odd way of putting it, she wanted to laugh, but she sensed a tension in the muscles of his back. She wouldn't hurt him for the world, and she guessed this wasn't a place where he would enjoy her teasing. "I trust you completely."

"Let's go about this methodically," he said, making her want to laugh more, because it was so adorably like Wyatt to apply logical thought to lovemaking. She settled for a tender kiss, which he seemed to appreciate. "I will try things," he said after an interval, "and you can tell me if you like them. Anything disagreeable, say so at once, and I shall stop. Promise?"

"I promise."

He stretched her out on the bed where he could see her. She missed his embrace, but his intense gaze traveling the length of her body was exciting in a different way. He started to stroke her breasts, fingering the nipples. "Do you like that?"

"Yes."

He pinched them lightly, one by one. "That?"

Strangely, she did. The tiny pain sent a line of sensation streaking through her, right to her hidden place. "Don't stop."

He touched her in different places, using both hands and mouth: her neck, her stomach, the backs of her knees, even her feet. She learned that her rib cage, just beneath her bosom, was especially sensitive. With each new move, he asked her if she liked it, and she kept assuring him that she did, with her voice and the blissful writhing of her body. "I like everything," she said finally. "I like everything about you and everything you do. Why don't we assume it unless I say otherwise?"

"I like to hear your voice."

She *loved* to hear *his* voice, yet having his mouth busy in other ways was utterly delightful. While he sucked on one nipple, which was pure bliss, she ventured to stroke the hard plane of his stomach, whence a narrow line of hair led down to his sex. When she brushed against his male organ, he groaned. "Did I hurt you?"

"God, no. It's perfect. You're perfect. Do you mind if I touch you down there?"

The nerves in the area in question told her yes. "I'm wet," she said, feeling timid for the first time. It was one thing when she'd occasionally, shamefully, experimented with herself and quite another thing for a man to do so.

"That's as it should be. It makes it easier and more pleasurable for both of us when I enter you. Do you know what that means?"

"Yes, and I want it." She wanted it badly and immediately, but first he stroked her down there, all the time kissing her, in the ear, which drove her almost mad with delight, and all over her face, and whispering that she was beautiful and he loved her.

His caresses created a delicious tension until she almost wept with need. "Please," she cried. "Like that. More. Now. Please." She squeezed her eyes tight, the world reduced to his hand and one little spot in her body.

"Easy, my darling." And with a fiendishly clever flick of a finger, he sent her shooting off into rapture and she saw stars. Waves of bliss consumed her, and she hardly noticed him mount her until she felt his hard member demand entrance to the shaking passage. "Easy," he said. "Tell me if it hurts."

It was tight and a little awkward at first, but she was slick inside. He slid in, and she felt nothing but a pressure that relaxed once he was fully lodged and turned to pleasure. She opened her eyes and found him resting on his elbows, gazing anxiously into her face. "That was the best thing ever," she assured him, bobbing her head up to peck at his lips. "Now carry on, Lord Carbury."

And he did, working long and hard, while she met his thrusts until they were wet with perspiration, hot bodies sliding together. After she had another burst of rapture, less intense than the first but all the sweeter for coming when they were joined, his head reared back, his muscles snapped taut, and with a muted shout of triumph, he spent. As she felt the gush of his seed within her, he rolled onto his side, taking her with him in protective arms, and fell into a doze.

She watched him for a while. He looked years younger and less burdened by care than he had ever been, even in his youth. When she kissed his forehead, he opened his eyes. "You are mine," he said with a delicious self-satisfied smile. "You can't change your mind now." And fell asleep again before she could assure him that as far as she was concerned, they were already married, and he could expect to take orders from her for the rest of his life.

WYATT WOKE UP wondering why he felt so happy, considering that he was in a small lumpy bed of the kind found in inns that didn't cater to the quality. He could see his breath, and his foot was hanging over the side in the chill air. He pulled it back under the covers and remembered the reason. His future wife was curled up at his side, sleeping. He succumbed to temptation.

"Oh!' she said, opening her eyes and jerking her leg out of his way. "Your foot is cold."

"It's one of the duties of a wife to warm her husband's cold feet."

"You just made that up," she said, but she moved her leg back so that he could rub his foot against it.

"Good morning, Lady Carbury," he said and gave her a kiss. Their first good-morning kiss.

"Not yet."

"As soon as we can get out of here and travel to Yorkshire. I'm not staying with Sybilla a day longer than I can help it." He gathered her into his arms and thanked God, and every angel and saint, that he had Robina in bed and hadn't, in some horrible nightmare, ended up with his cousin's widow.

"What will we say about being out all night?" She smiled saucily. "I never thought to sleep in The Duke's Arms. May I say that I found it thoroughly agreeable?"

"Has anyone ever told you that you are a hussy?"

"Why, yes. Someone did recently, but I have forgotten who. Shall I tell your cousin Sybilla that I was with Oxthorpe?"

"All she needs to know is that we were caught in the snow and stayed at the inn. We will not mention that we shared a room."

"The Wattleses must know. Word will get out."

He felt amazingly unconcerned about the prospect of a scandal. "By the time it spreads, we'll be far away and married. It was on my list."

"No, it wasn't. Getting the license was an impulse, remember?"

Silly arguments with Robina were so enjoyable he had to kiss her again. He didn't want to do anything or go anywhere else.

"You are right," he said after a while. "It wasn't on the list, but it was a plan. After our wedding, we were to have a short honeymoon."

"Short? Now I am insulted. That part of the plan is in sore need of adjustment."

"I am confident our honeymoon will last forever, but I need to be back in London for Parliament. I confess, I've never in my life felt less like doing my duty."

"The fact that you say that makes me determined to make sure you do. We can't have any shirking. How otherwise are you to become Prime Minister and solve the problems of the nation?"

"As a married man, it is my duty to spend a great deal of time with my wife. And if it means I don't end up Prime Minister, so be it. The minute I can get free, we're going somewhere alone. How do you feel about Italy?"

"Very warmly." She shivered and snuggled into his side. "I wish we were there now. Goodness, I forgot it was Christmas Day. Where are you going?"

He dashed naked across the room and fumbled in the pocket of his coat—not the topcoat, but the green riding jacket he'd changed into before setting forth in the snow, the same one he'd worn that afternoon.

Returning to bed in triumph, he held up a sprig of mistletoe. "Happy Christmas, Lady Carbury. Here's to many more."

The Spy Beneath the Mistletoe

By
Shana Galen

Chapter One

❦

THE INN WOULD be a difficult building to explode. The thatched roof would burn easily enough, but the whitewashed fieldstone exterior looked to Eliza to have weathered a good many years and a good many winters. Colder winters than this one.

Although snow poured from the leaden sky and the windows of The Duke's Arms glowed with the promise of a roaring fire in the hearth, she tarried in the yard. Her legs were cramped from days on the road, and she was happy to stretch them.

Her fellow passengers hobbled and stumbled past her into the cozy inn. Their cold, damp boots would soon be dry and warm. Beyond the inn, the coach road curved like a white ribbon, past hedges dotted with white and oak and maple trees, whose naked branches reached for the sky like sharp icy fingers. In the spring, the prospect would be far more pleasing. Flowers would dot the rolling green hills with spots of color, the oaks and maples would offer leafy shade, and verdant ivy would lend a swath of color to the pale walls of the inn.

The prospect today was not quite so charming. The gray sky matched her mood. Christmas was only a few days past, and a provincial inn on the Great North Road was the last place she wanted to be. Scratch that. The Barbican group's Piccadilly office was the last place she wanted to be. Still, this inn, with its ragged holiday wreath on the door and a few browning sprigs of mistletoe hung near the window, depressed her. Not that she didn't enjoy the Yuletide holiday. She'd spent it with her sister in London. The two of them, spinsters both, always managed to have a lovely, if quiet, Christmas and New Year.

Eliza hefted her valise and started for the inn. She could have refused the assignment. Baron's brows had risen when she'd accepted. She'd surprised him, but was she to remain a weaponry engineer forever? She rather liked her work, and at one time she might have been content to pursue it forever. Now she wanted time away from her little workshop.

And a world away from Pierce Moneypence.

The Duke's Arms hardly qualified as traveling the world, but it was a start. She would complete this mission quickly, return victorious to the Barbican, and Baron would recognize her talent and assign her more missions. Exciting missions in Paris or Milan or Budapest—wherever that was. Eliza stamped her numb, booted feet free of snow and pushed the door of the inn open.

The warmth from so many bodies and the blazing hearth rushed at her with a vengeance. She staggered back, momentarily overwhelmed by the scents of wet wool, tallow, and the cloved oranges left over from the holiday. Her gaze swept the room efficiently, looking for exits, threats, and allies. She was a spy and a woman traveling alone—though a plain, uninteresting woman—so she kept her head down.

A pair of tattered boots paused before her, and Eliza looked up into the face of a harried serving girl, who pushed a tangle of dark, sweaty hair from her forehead. "Welcome, missus. There's a table there, if ye like."

A small wooden table with two empty seats nestled in a nook. Now that her feet had begun to thaw, they itched, and she longed for the warmth of the fire. But spies weren't interested in comfort. The back table offered a view of the entrances and exits and kept her out of the way. She squeezed past the throng of fellow travelers, eyes downcast, until she reached it. She dropped the heavy valise so it obstructed the path to the table and took a seat with her back to the wall.

No one paid her any heed. With her drab brown hair in a knot, her spectacles sliding down her nose, and rumpled but modest clothing, there was nothing much to see.

The inn was very much like any other she'd visited. This was the public room, and there would be a private area nearby for those who wished to pay for it. Simple wooden stairs led to the upper floors and the rooms for rent. The kitchen was in the back or downstairs, and her mouth watered at the smell of some sort of meaty stew.

The serving girl set down a tray with six tankards of ale one table over, which was crowded with men who spoke with the local accent.

"Do you care for refreshment, missus?"

The girl's use of *missus* made Eliza feel old. She was too old to be a *miss* any longer, and the world seemed intent upon reminding her at every turn. Eliza's age wasn't this maid's fault. She was still in the blush of youth, with her ample curves, long, dark hair pulled away from her face, and lively dark eyes. The maid's life was far from flirtation and frolic, though. The hands on the swell of her hips were red and raw from work.

"Tea, please," Eliza said. "And would you tell the innkeeper I need to rent a room?"

The girl nodded. "I'll fetch my father, straightaway."

"Might I have the tea—"

The serving girl had already whirled away, and Eliza resigned herself to waiting. The stifling heat took its toll, and she loosened her scarf and tugged at her gloves. Above her, a sprig of the ubiquitous mistletoe drew her attention. She had the urge to cut it down.

A shadow fell over the table. "What are you doing here?"

Eliza caught her breath and schooled her features, sliding her hand under the table to reach unobtrusively for the dagger in her boot. Slowly, she lowered her gaze from the mistletoe.

"What are *you* doing here?" she sputtered.

She barely recognized the skittish clerk he'd been when she'd last seen him in London. He had the same lean form, the same rigid posture, the same stiff neckcloth, but his usually soft brown eyes were hard.

Moneypence folded his arms. He probably thought it made him look gruff and foreboding. He probably thought it made him look intimidating. And he would have been right. That and the day's worth of stubble added a touch of the ruffian.

What would that stubble feel like under her fingertips…or against her lips?

Banish that thought. She'd never touch Pierce Moneypence again.

Moneypence used the toe of a scuffed boot to push her valise aside. "We can't talk here. Would you step outside with me for a moment, Miss Qwillen?" He held out a hand sporting more calluses than any clerk's should and beckoned her impatiently.

Miss Qwillen. All that had happened between them, and he still called her *Miss Qwillen.*

"I most certainly will not," she said, annoyed at him for no reason she could put a finger on. She had the urge to pull down the mistletoe and throw it at him. "I have just come in from the cold." She gestured to the window, which framed an ominous-looking sky. "It's snowing."

"But you agree we must speak privately?"

Moneypence would be here only because of the mission. But why would Baron send both of them? And why not tell her he'd already sent Moneypence? "I agree. Perhaps—" She was prevented from suggesting an alternate meeting place when a large, red-faced man in his middle years approached.

"Welcome to The Duke's Arms, missus. I'm Wattles. Mrs. Wattles and I own this fine establishment. Mrs. Wattles does all the cooking, and she is the finest cook in the county." He caressed his expansive girth. "Pretty as the day we married too and doesn't look a day older. My daughter Peg tells me you want a room."

"A pleasure to meet you, Mr. Wattles," Eliza said, rising and giving a perfunctory curtsey. "I am Miss Qwillen." With a glance at Moneypence, she dredged up the story she'd invented. "My sister is traveling to London from Scotland. She's never been to Town before, and I promised to meet her here and travel the last leg of the trip with her. I am not certain when she will arrive. She might be another day or two, depending on the weather north of here."

Wattles squeezed a towel, wringing it this way and that. "I'm afraid, Miss Qwillen, that I've let the last room."

Eliza hadn't considered this possibility. With the holidays upon them, many travelers were on the roads. In any other case, she might have simply inquired at another inn, but she'd studied a road guide before leaving home. This was the only inn for miles. Above her, the mistletoe swung merrily. She needed a pistol. "I see."

"If only you'd arrived a little earlier," Wattles said, darting a look at Moneypence. "This man took possession of my last available room."

Moneypence grinned. If she'd had that pistol she could have rid herself of the mistletoe and Moneypence's smirk.

"That is unfortunate," she said. "What's more, I have no option but to stay here and wait for my sister. If you will pardon the reference to Mary and Joseph, is there a stable where I might spend the night?"

Wattles's hands ceased torturing the towel, and he pulled his stained apron over a prodigious belly. "I can't allow you to sleep in the stable, missus!"

"I assure you, Mr. Wattles, I will be fine."

She was slim and small, but she was no milksop miss. Mr. Wattles began to wring the towel between his hands again. "Begging your pardon, Miss Qwillen, but I can't allow it. The grooms bed there. I'm sure they're good fellows, but it wouldn't be appropriate."

Of course he was correct. She couldn't sleep in the stable with a half-dozen men. Just then the driver of the mail coach pulled the inn door open, and a burst of cold air fanned her overheated face. "Last call for the mail coach. Last call!" He announced the next stop, but Eliza didn't listen. She wasn't going to the next village.

She was looking at Moneypence.

And then Mr. Wattles looked at him too. Wattles took a bit longer than Eliza would have liked, but he finally released the twisted towel and said, "Of course, if this gentleman were willing to give up his room, that would solve your problem."

It would indeed. The mail coach passengers were filing out, and the inn felt suddenly empty. A half-dozen men still occupied the seats around the room, but a hush had descended. Or perhaps Eliza simply imagined it because Moneypence was looking at her with daggers in his deep-brown eyes. "It would be my pleasure to give up my room to this lady," Moneypence said. He did not sound as though he were filled with pleasure.

"Of course, there's no charge to sleep in the stable," the innkeeper assured him. He wrung his towel again. "For a small fee, I can provide blankets and other essentials."

Moneypence's expression turned even more poisonous, if that were possible. "A small fee. Of course. I'll collect my things, and Miss Qwillen may have possession of the room in order to refresh herself."

"Thank you, kind sir," she said with a smile.

"Please do not mention it, Miss Qwillen."

Oh, she wouldn't. Easier that way to ignore the fact that a traitorous part of herself was glad he was here.

ONE MOMENT, PIERCE had been perfectly situated at a cozy table in the common, where he might overhear any information relevant to the mission. The next, he was sneezing and treated to the fragrance of horse manure. How the devil had this happened?

Pierce had no fondness for horses. They bit, and they'd bitten him enough times that he must look like a ripe apple to them. Wattles had shown him an empty loose box and given him a cot on which to place the blanket for which Pierce had paid. One blanket. And a cot. He'd requested a brazier, but the innkeeper had muttered something about hay and fire and that had been that.

He set his valise on the cot and then seated himself there, testing it. It sank in the middle, almost swallowing him. He flailed about until he was sucked in, arms and legs sticking out as his backside all but touched the ground.

"Mr. Moneypence!" a female voice called. He struggled to extricate himself, but the cot refused to release its prey. "Mr. Moneypence?"

Perhaps if he didn't answer, she would go away. Forever. But he knew she wouldn't. She would find him in this undignified state, and he'd be mortified for the rest of his life.

"Oh, Mr. Moneypence!" She'd found him, of course.

"I do not require assistance," he said, but his words were incoherent due to the fact that his face was buried in his knees. She tugged at his wrists, and he waved about to dislodge her grip. He moved this way and that in a gross parody of what he imagined resembled the mating dance of an ugly fish and finally managed to fall out of the cot and onto his knees on the hard stable floor.

He looked up at her, all fresh and pretty and unscathed by man-eating cots. "What do you want?" he asked, rising without grace and brushing his trousers off. They were covered with straw. For the next fortnight, he'd probably be finding straw in parts of him he didn't want to think about even after his work here was done.

"I had hoped we might discuss this...situation."

She sounded as though she were laughing. She'd clapped a hand over her mouth. To conceal a smile? He would throttle her. She lowered her hand and straightened. "You must leave immediately."

Pierce brushed at the straw tickling his nose. "I was here first."

She clasped her hands behind her back, either because she thought it would intimidate him or distract him with the way the material pulled taut over her breasts. He raised his gaze to her eyes.

"I was asked by Baron to come here. Considering he is the head of the"—she lowered her voice—"Barbican, *you* should be the one to leave."

He had assumed she had come of her own accord. He'd assumed she had heard rumor of the mission and decided to investigate on her own. With the holidays nigh, agents were scarce at the moment.

He'd also hoped she had come to see him, to make amends. He was an idiot, as usual.

He surrendered to the straw itching his nose and bent to reassemble the cot. "I am also here on official business," he said, not naming the Barbican. Really, did the woman have no sense? Even a whisper might be overheard. "Bonde ordered me to come."

She huffed out a breath and lifted his blanket from the dusty floor. "That explains everything then." She turned as though to leave.

"What does that mean?" he asked, blocking her retreat from the box. "Bonde has more authority than Baron."

"So says *you*." She gave the wreck of the cot a meaningful glance. "Baron is the head of the...of our organization. Not Bonde. He issues the orders."

"Bonde is the best agent we have and the natural successor to M." She was Lord Melbourne's niece, after all. "Baron is in charge only temporarily."

"Aha!" She snapped his blanket, releasing more dust into the air and making his eyes water. "You admit he is in charge. That means my mission is valid, and you should take your leave."

"I'm not leaving," he said. "Even if I have to sleep in the stable, I'm not leaving."

"Well, you're not sleeping with me!"

"Perish the thought!" He hadn't perished the thought. He entertained the thought all too often, and now that she was in his presence, he was having difficulty forming any other thought. "If you are intent upon staying, perhaps we might work together."

"Absolutely not," she said, brandishing the blanket. He snatched it from her before she set another dust storm in motion. "I would rather stick my hand in acid than work with you."

He gaped at her, glad he had resisted the urge to straighten her bonnet. It sat crookedly on the dark curls coming loose from her knot. The angle made her look like a ship listing to port. "What did I ever do to you to deserve that response?"

She jabbed a finger painfully into his chest. "You asked me to marry you!"

He wanted to grasp the hand poking into him, perhaps break the finger or perhaps kiss it. Instead, he tried to ignore the heat flowing into him from it. "You say that as though a proposal of marriage is a bad thing."

"It is, and you know why."

He did not begin to comprehend her objections, but he was not foolish enough to admit as much. "I merely thought it would be a mutually beneficial arrangement."

"An arrangement. Yes, that is what I want. An arrangement."

"I could call it something else—"

"But it wouldn't be any different! You want a wife to further your career. You want some sort of political hostess who looks pretty and says the right things and spends her days making certain your needs are seen to."

"I never said that."

"So you aren't applying for a position in the Swiss offices?"

"I am, but—"

"And you didn't assume I would give up everything here—my work, my family, my life—to follow you?"

"Not everything."

She pinned him with large brown eyes. "Then they need a weaponry designer in Switzerland?"

He realized he was gripping the blanket and loosed his grip. "I don't know."

"Exactly." She poked him again, and this time he caught her finger and held it.

"Eliza—"

"Miss Qwillen."

"I tried to explain. If you'd only listen."

"No, because no matter how often you explain, you will never understand what *I* am trying to explain."

He waved the blanket, a green flag of surrender. "You don't want to give up your work. I don't want you to. If that is all—"

"No, that's not all. That's not even the beginning."

She yanked her hand, and he released it. The woman was a ridiculous amount of trouble and confusing as the devil. He really should put her out of his mind. He had a mission, and her presence here need not interfere. He'd find the highwaymen terrorizing this area of Nottinghamshire and return to London with the capture of the man or men who'd adopted the sobriquet of the New Sheriff of Nottingham to his credit. Then he would begin the Switzerland appointment with not only experience as a clerk but also agent credentials.

"Very well then," he said, stepping back into his cold, dark stall. "You go your way, and I'll go mine."

"That suits me." She stalked out of the box and then, perhaps thinking better of her behavior, stepped back into sight. "Good luck."

"Good luck to you," he said.

"Thank you for the room."

He was reminded of the sad state of his cot and made another futile attempt to right it. "It was nothing, seeing as I had no choice."

"Yes, well, thank you anyway."

Why was she postponing her leave-taking? Did she feel some sense of guilt for relegating him to sleeping in the stable? Why did she not go so he could pull out his files and decide where best to begin his search for the highwayman?

She started away, and he kicked the cot in frustration. Now where was that file? He'd opened his satchel to search for the documents when hoofbeats thundered.

"The coach! The coach!"

Pierce ran, almost knocking Eliza over when he dashed from the stable. Cursing, he paused to steady her. She shrugged off his assistance, and without speaking, they walked quickly toward the rider. The innkeeper and several men had exited the inn.

"What's wrong?" called Mr. Wattles.

"It's the New Sheriff of Nottingham," the rider said, his breath coming out in great puffs. "He just held up the mail coach!"

Chapter Two

E LIZA'S PULSE JUMPED. The highwayman was nearby and growing braver. He'd attacked the coach in daylight, fleeting as it was with the gray sky and the fat snowflakes falling from the heavy clouds. Still, this was her chance to intercept the man. If she'd had a horse, her task would have been made easier.

She hadn't thought she would need a horse here. From all accounts, the Sheriff was always on foot. The speculation was that he lived in or near Hopewell-on-Lyft and did not want to risk his mount being recognized. She could walk and investigate the site of the robbery. By the time she reached the scene of the crime, the thief would be well away. Nightfall approached, and any sort of investigation of the scene would have to wait until morning.

That evening she'd gather a different sort of information.

The inn's patrons streamed out of the common to hear the news.

"Was anyone hurt, Mr. Dowell?" Wattles called.

"All are well, Mr. Wattles. A bit lighter in the purse."

Peg, the serving girl and Wattles's daughter, whispered something to her father. Their whereabouts during the robbery were accounted for. Eliza could not vouch for Dowell. He might have acted the highwayman and then come to report the theft to deflect suspicion. Other men stood about in the yard. She did not yet know their names, but when she did, she could take them off the list of suspects.

"I know that look," Moneypence said. He watched her, his expression speculative.

"I'm merely making note of those men. They have been here since I arrived, which means they cannot be the Sheriff. However—" She'd grown accustomed to confiding in him, to sharing her thoughts. That was necessarily at an end.

"However?"

She drew away from him and the feel of his warm breath on her ear. "However, you must make your own deductions. Good evening, Mr. Moneypence."

She started for the inn, making her way to her small but clean room, and freshening herself before dinner. Under normal circumstances she would have dined alone in her room, having no coin for the private rooms below. Tonight she would linger in the common to learn the names and faces of the regular patrons. If she'd been able to gather that information earlier, she might have been able to note who had been at The Duke's Arms when the coach had arrived and who had been suspiciously absent during the time of the robbery. The quicker she learned the names of the locals, the quicker she could make such observations.

Eliza entered the dining room and took the seat Peg offered her, close to the warmth of the hearth. She turned so she might face the room and found herself staring at Moneypence, seated across the room and facing her. He inclined his head, but she ignored him. Eliza busied her restless hands, plucking at the wrinkles in her skirt. The only other woman in the room was an elderly lady who appeared to be in frail health. She was seated close to the hearth as well, and Eliza nodded at her and the two exchanged pleasantries.

The vaunted agents of the Barbican group had to blend in everywhere, from London's underworld to Paris high society. How did they manage it? She was so much more at home in her little laboratory, designing new weapons. If she was frustrated, a large explosion always made her feel better. She couldn't very well explode anything here.

Her one consolation was that Moneypence looked as out of place as she. He probably wished he were back at his desk in the offices on Piccadilly. Neither of them was going home until the Sheriff was caught, so she might as well make a start. When Peg returned, Eliza ordered the roasted mutton, and then conversed with the lady near her.

Mrs. Penter was accompanied by her nephew Mr. Wilson. Mr. Wilson lived in the little village nearby, and his aunt had come from London to visit him a few months ago after the death of Mr. Penter. She was staying at the inn and near her dear nephew until a suitable ladies' companion might be engaged to live with her in her flat in Cheapside.

"Cheapside?" A tingle of pleasure raced through Eliza. "My sister and I also live in Cheapside. On what street do you reside? Perhaps we are neighbors."

Mrs. Penter was overcome by a coughing fit that rendered her unable to speak for the next few minutes. In the meantime, Eliza's dinner arrived. She had cut into her mutton when the gentleman on her left leaned closer.

"I overheard you say you're from London, Miss Qwillen."

Eliza paused in her carving. "Why, yes."

"I'm George Langrick." He nodded to his companion. "This is Henry Barber."

She inclined her head. "Mr. Langrick. Mr. Barber." The two men were both stout and low-browed with dark hair and eyes. She would have put them at the top of her list as the highwayman, but they'd been loitering in the yard when Dowell had given the report. She could not, however, recall Mr. Wilson having been in the yard.

"I know it's not my business, but I wanted to make sure you knew that the village and the inn are safe, Miss Qwillen," Langrick said. "With all the talk of highwaymen, poor Wattles is afraid the mail coach will no longer stop at The Duke's Arms."

"I am sure that would be a hardship for him."

"It would indeed," Barber said, his voice low and rough. "For all of us. Wattles serves the best mutton pies in these parts. You'll see." He nodded to her dinner, which she had quite forgotten.

"I hope I'm not presuming," Langrick added, "but has word of our troubles reached London?"

Eliza could hardly say what the ordinary Londoner was or was not discussing from day to day, but she had not taken note of the highwayman until Baron had brought him to her attention. "No, Mr. Langrick. The crime in London is such that one highwayman in Nottinghamshire is not of paramount concern. Indeed, there was only a little talk of your Sheriff on the coach I occupied here."

"Thank you, miss. That is good to know," Langrick said, returning his attention to his mutton.

Eliza cut another slice of meat then risked a peek at Moneypence. Their gazes met, and he quickly resumed a conversation he had been engaged in with a fellow seated beside him. That man was not one she recognized from the yard earlier.

Moneypence had been watching her. Why? Jealousy? Because of the mission? Because he still cared for her? No, she could not harbor those sorts of thoughts. He had made himself clear that night in his bedroom. Her face heated when she remembered how they'd spent that night and how he'd made his offer of marriage while they were both in a state of dishabille. He hadn't asked her to be his wife because he loved her. He'd asked her out of obligation. He felt it was his duty to marry her after he had ruined her.

Eliza had not wasted time telling him that one could not ruin something no one wanted. She was thirty-five and past the debutante years when men cared about chastity and such. She'd thought she might go to the grave never knowing the touch of a man. When the opportunity to share a night with Moneypence—Pierce—had arisen, she had known what she was doing.

She did not regret it, except perhaps that it had ended so badly with that ridiculous proposal. But even without the proposal, Eliza had been disappointed. Her experience with Moneypence had been awkward, uncomfortable, and the pleasure short and one-sided.

Eliza had checked that item off her list and was ready to move on to other, more edifying, experiences. Why then, did she still think about kissing Moneypence? About touching him? Why did she still feel warm when his gaze rested on her?

She placed a forkful of mutton in her mouth. Perhaps she had been wrong to insist they not work together. That suggestion had been due to her need to stay away from him, to avoid those still-simmering feelings. But by working together they could discover more information and generate suspects more quickly. She would have to arrange to speak to him in private.

She wasn't going to go back out into the cold. It was dark now and snowing harder. She felt a twinge of guilt for making Moneypence sleep in those conditions but quickly put it aside. He would have to come to her room.

The Barbican group had developed several universal symbols. They were secret, known only to those employed by the elite spy group. Moneypence and Eliza knew them as well as all of the field agents. She hadn't ever used one, but that was beside the point.

What was the symbol for *meet me*? She thought for a moment then rose, turned around, and sat back down.

The numbskull wasn't even looking at her. Annoying man! Eliza waited until he had ceased speaking to the man near him, rose, turned in a circle, and sat.

Thank heavens! He'd seen her this time, but he was looking at her as though he thought her daft. She probably was daft to be considering working with him. He nodded to the serving girl, who served him a pear tart, and cut into it.

One last time, and if he didn't understand this time then he was beyond hope. Eliza rose and turned, but as she was sitting, Mr. Langrick said, "Are you well, Miss Qwillen?"

Truth be told, she was a bit dizzy. "Yes, perfectly. Why?"

"No reason."

Moneypence was finally paying attention. He raised his brows, and she looked at the ceiling. *My room*. He looked at the ceiling, and then his eyebrows came down in a look that said he was confused. She looked again—more pointedly—at the ceiling.

"Is something in your eye, missus?" Peg asked, stopping at her table.

Eliza almost jumped. "No. No, I was admiring your ceiling. The beam work is splendid. Tudor?"

Peg looked up and then down again. "I couldn't say, missus."

She could feel the tingle of Moneypence's gaze on her. It started at the nape of her neck and slid languidly down her spine, heating her flesh as it spread. She risked a glance at him. Moneypence gave a short nod and looked back at his tart.

TWO HOURS LATER, the inn was silent as the winter night, and Eliza was warm by the fire in her small room. She hadn't undressed, but she'd rung for the maid to bring the water for washing so the servants would not be waiting on her. She'd have to find a way to undress herself or sleep in her stays.

She had been sitting and waiting for him too long, that was all. He was on her mind. It wasn't as though she desired him. Very much.

In truth, she missed him. She missed their discussions of everything from flowers to politics. She missed hearing about all of the clerical sorts of things he'd done each day and telling him about her latest success with a new pistol that looked like a lady's fan. She missed having him in her life.

And, oh very well, she missed having a man hold her, having him kiss her, feeling the weight of his body beside hers. On top of hers.

Of course, Moneypence chose that moment to tap softly on her door. Pulling it open, she yanked him inside and shut it again.

"Did anyone see you?" she asked.

"No. I was discreet. Are you well? Your face is flushed."

She touched her cheeks. They were indeed warm, probably because of the direction of her thoughts just a few moments ago. "I've been sitting too close to the fire."

"Am I correct in assuming you wished to speak to me?"

"Yes."

His eyes were dark and his light brown hair flecked with snow. She'd forgotten what it was like to be this close to him. His scent, bergamot mingled with the clean fragrances of hay and fresh snow, made her heart beat a little faster. Her gaze dipped to his lips. Would his mouth be warm or deliciously cool against her hot skin?

"About?"

He sounded impatient for her to continue and brushed snow off his sleeve to punctuate his annoyance. "About this mission. I've changed my mind."

"You're going home?" he said with a hopeful tone.

"No." She flicked a piece of straw from his hair. "We should work together."

But he didn't speak.

"I was making a list of our suspects," she said, "and between the two of us, we would generate such a list more quickly. You spoke to people I did not at dinner."

"I see. And what if I don't want your help?"

"You wanted it earlier."

Slowly, he unwound his scarf from his neck. "You can't keep changing your mind."

"I haven't changed my mind. I have only reconsidered this one point."

"How do I know you won't change it again?"

Frustrating man. Why did she feel as though he was speaking about more than this mission? "I won't, but if you don't want to work with me—"

She'd waved her arm at him, and he caught her hand in his. His skin was cool, giving her a little shock. "I didn't say that. I merely wanted to make certain I understood where we stand."

"We're colleagues working together on a mission for the Barbican group," she said. "Nothing more."

He looked down at her hand.

Heaven help her. She was making little circles with her thumb on his palm.

"I beg your pardon." She tried to pull her hand away, but he didn't release her. She didn't try very hard to free herself either.

"There's nothing to apologize for. I've missed your touch."

"I've missed yours." She regretted the words as soon as she'd spoken them. Why hadn't she simply suggested they work together and ordered him out? She would never rid herself of him now, and the worst of it was that she didn't want to.

"Have you?" He moved closer, and his scent washed over her. She almost closed her eyes to bask in it. "What else have you missed?"

Nothing. That was what she should say. That was the answer that would make him go.

"Your kisses." She was very bad, indeed. He would kiss her now, and that had been what she'd wanted all along.

But he didn't take her mouth with his. He squeezed her hand lightly. "Shall I kiss you now?"

No. But she didn't say it. To her credit, she didn't say yes, either. She did tilt her head back, giving him clear access to her lips. Oh, but she was wanton! He put an arm about her waist and pulled her close. Her eyelids closed, and she waited for the feel of his strong mouth on hers.

"Did you know," he said, "the Dungeon has volumes on topics other than intelligence matters?"

Her eyes snapped open. "What?"

"The Dungeon," he repeated.

"I know what it is." Every agent for the Barbican group knew the Records Room, where all of the research and confidential files were kept. The place was a veritable maze where, it was rumored, an agent could become lost. "What does the Dungeon have to do with anything?"

Now his finger traced a light path up her back, tickled the bare skin at the nape of her neck. "There are books there, Eliza."

Of course there were books there. It was a library of sorts. "What books?" Had he heard the catch in her throat?

His wicked smiled grew even more wicked, if that was possible, so she knew he had. "Books about kissing."

Her pulse raced, and the blood thrummed in her ears. "Kissing?"

He held her close, their bodies pressed together intimately, his touch on her skin light but possessive. "Among other...activities."

"I see." She could barely draw a breath.

"I read the books, Eliza."

She was dizzy from the warmth in the room, from his scent, from the feel of his body against hers. "Books? More than one?"

"Most definitely. Wicked, wicked books about wicked, wicked acts. Nothing you would want to know about."

"No. I'm not wicked."

"If you change your mind," he said, releasing her, "you will tell me, won't you?"

She nodded, words escaping her as she focused on not grabbing him back and pushing her aching breasts against him. The need for him to touch her, kiss her, do all manner of wicked things to her was overpowering.

"Shall we go for a walk in the morning and discuss suspects?" he asked.

"Yes," she said, surprised her voice sounded even.

He bowed, and she realized he was leaving. She wanted to shout, *No*. She wanted to keep him there. She clasped her hands tightly to restrain herself as he silently opened her door, peeked out, and then disappeared without a word.

Eliza slumped into her chair by the fire, heaving in a great breath and still unable to fill her lungs. This was the drawback to working with Pierce Moneypence. Everything had been perfectly fine—lovely, in fact—until he'd proposed marriage. She hadn't minded a proposal of marriage. She'd never had one before, and as a spinster, she'd rather thought she never would.

But a woman wanted a marriage proposal for the right reasons. She wanted a man to propose because he couldn't live without her. Because he was desperately, madly, and unreasonably in love with her. Pierce had proposed because, after bedding her, he thought it was the right thing to do, not to mention a wife might further his career. There was nothing romantic about a proposal of that sort. A proposal of that sort was the antithesis of romance.

Still...books describing wicked acts. What sorts of wicked acts? And heaven forgive her, but she wanted Pierce to demonstrate.

Chapter Three

He waited in front of The Duke's Arms for Eliza to fetch her pelisse and muff so they might stroll. Thankfully, the snow had stopped. The ground beyond the inn was pristine white and sparkling in the morning sunshine. It was a perfect day for a walk. In fact, he nodded cordially to a woman walking past the inn, a pretty dun rabbit in her arms. The woman and her bunny seemed to be enjoying the sunshine.

He'd almost forgotten what sunshine looked and felt like. The winter, especially in London, had been so dreary. The door to the inn opened, and there stood Eliza. He forgot all about the beauty of the sun on the new-fallen snow. *She* was breathtaking.

Her pelisse was cranberry in color, and the vibrant shade did wonders for her complexion. Her cheeks were pink and her lips ruby. He was not used to seeing her out of the dim lamplight available in the bowels of the Barbican headquarters. In those gloomy corridors, everyone took on a sallow, sickly pallor. But here Eliza looked young and fresh and pretty. Her mass of brown hair had been pulled back by a ribbon that matched her hair and flowed down her back in a riot of curls. He hadn't realized her hair was quite so long or how young she would look without it pinned up. He couldn't remember ever having seen it unpinned, not even when he'd shared her bed.

She was a small woman, petite and slender. He knew her body—not as well as he might have liked—but well enough to be able to trace its curves even within the covering of the pelisse. She had shapely legs, small, pert breasts, and a tiny waist.

She pushed her spectacles onto her nose, a gesture he recognized as a nervous habit. The spectacles were necessary because she could not see long distances. When she was reading or at home, she often removed them. He liked her better with them on, though. They gave her face definition and enlarged her light brown eyes so he could see the flecks of hazel in them.

"Have you been waiting long?"

"Just a few moments. The weather is perfect. Shall we walk, Miss Qwillen?" He used her surname in the event anyone was listening.

"Certainly."

"Did you sleep well?" He nodded to one of the locals tending to a horse in the yard.

"I did. And you?"

He cut her a look. "Very well," he lied. The stable had been cold and drafty, just as Pierce had expected. The cold had cooled his ardor. The noises the horses made had woven themselves into his dreams—nightmares of stallions chasing him down in order to chomp on his fingers. He shuddered.

They walked in silence for several moments, until they were well away from the inn and then, as though of one mind, turned toward the road away from the little village of Hopewell-on-Lyft. The road traveled through a wooded area cut in half by the River Lyft. The woods worked to the advantage of the New Sheriff of Nottingham. They would not walk as far as the woods, but the relative isolation of the path was preferable.

"I took the liberty of inquiring as to the arrival of the next coach," Eliza said.

"And?"

"Just before noon," she answered. "That will give us time to make a list of suspects and to observe who is and is not present should the highwayman make another attempt."

"I can hardly think the man would be so foolish as to strike again so soon. The coachman will certainly be ready for him with a blunderbuss, if not a more deadly weapon."

"Be that as it may," she said, stiffening, "it does no harm to be prepared."

He could not argue. He really had very little to say to this woman who seemed so cold and efficient. He'd liked her much better last night, when he'd met her in her room. She'd been warm and more like the Eliza he'd known before. He'd easily been able to picture taking her to bed. Last night he had been certain his revelations about the books in the Dungeon had aroused her. Now he was not so confident.

"Shall we discuss suspects?" he asked.

"By all means. I have Mr. Langrick and Mr. Barber in the clear column. I saw them in front of the inn when Mr. Dowell announced the highwayman's attack last night. Likewise, Mr. Wilson is a local, and his aunt, the widow Mrs. Penter, seems far too invalid to be a suspect."

"I agree about Langrick and Barber, but I am not willing to clear Wilson quite yet. Did you see him yesterday when Dowell arrived?"

Her pace slowed. "I cannot remember."

"Neither can I. Dowell is a suspect."

"Of course. He might be attempting to deflect suspicion by acting as the messenger. Who else have you met?" she asked.

This sort of conversation was familiar, the sort of dialogue spies conducted all the time. They fell into it easily, and he told her his list of suspects included a Mr. Freeland, who was a local, a Mr. Cardy whom he had not yet spoken to, and a Mr. Goodman, who was a guest at the inn and rarely left his rooms.

"Wattles and Peg were also present when the last attack occurred," Eliza said.

"The serving girl?" He dismissed her with a flick of his wrist. "Do you really think a woman could be the highwayman?"

She gave him a look that shot daggers. "Have you met Bonde, Butterfly, Saint?"

Female spies, all of them. "You are, as usual, correct. Put Peg on the list for form's sake. While we are discussing women, add the perpetually young and pretty Mrs. Wattles. I haven't yet seen her about."

"She's probably confined to the kitchen, but we will add her just the same."

"Mrs. Penter must be added."

Eliza paused to shake her head at him. "As I said, she's old and invalid."

"It could be a disguise. How long has she been in the county?"

"A few months." She paused under a barren oak tree, whose large branches all but swept the ground. "Interesting timing as that is when the highwayman began his attacks. But, in all honesty, I am much more interested in Cardy, Goodman, and Freeland. Goodman, in particular, concerns me. Why is he such a recluse? We should attempt to find a way to converse with him."

"Perhaps we divide and conquer," Pierce suggested. "You seek out Mrs. Wattles, attend to Mrs. Penter, and keep an eye on Peg. I will investigate Goodman and the other men."

"Yes, sir." She tossed him a mock salute. "Shall we convene in my room to discuss our findings tonight after dinner?"

The branches on the oak tree must have been exceptionally interesting, because she kept her gaze locked on them.

"Excellent plan," Pierce agreed. "I will see you tonight." He offered his arm. When Eliza took it, her breast brushed against his bicep. He would have known the feel of those soft mounds anywhere, so he knew it was not his imagination. But was he wrong in thinking that she'd touched him on purpose? Was it possible she *wanted* to be seduced?

PIERCE STALKED ACROSS the dark coach yard, cursing the Sheriff for taking a holiday. If only the man—or woman—had acted, Pierce would certainly have caught the highwayman. He'd studied his targets assiduously all day and would have known if any of them had disappeared without good reason.

He'd gathered information about recent attacks, including that of a Miss Weston. He'd also questioned a Mr. Thomas, a Mr. Quinn, and a Mr. Pembleton, area locals, as to what they knew of the Sherriff.

Pierce had even gained access to Mr. Goodman. He'd asked Mr. Wattles if the man might like company for tea. Wattles had inquired, and Pierce had been obliged to take tea with the gentleman. He claimed to be a solicitor for the Duke of Oxthorpe, and he was staying at the inn until he finished his business at Killhope Castle.

It seemed a reasonable excuse and easy enough to verify. Being in the duke's employ also gave Goodman a reason to leave the inn whenever he pleased. He might claim an appointment with the duke or arrange to be summoned in order to hide clandestine activities.

Goodman wasn't the only one possibly engaged in clandestine activities. Pierce slipped into the darkened inn, pausing to be certain all was quiet. It was after eleven, which was later than he'd wanted to visit Eliza, but he'd had to wait until the grooms grew quiet, and they had been playing vingt-et-un for several hours.

He'd taken the servants' stairs the night before, and he found them again, ascending quietly and carefully, as he didn't have a lamp. The door opened into the hallway a few steps from Eliza's room—his former room. The light under her door still glowed, and he tapped quietly.

She opened immediately, and he stepped inside. He almost stepped directly out again. She wore her nightgown. He'd seen it before, seen the muslin wrapper she wore over it as well. It was perfectly proper, not scandalous in the least, but he could remember ruching it up to reveal those shapely thighs and the dark curls at their junction.

He forced his gaze to rest on her face, not that thin wrapper.

"I didn't want to risk you being seen by the maidservant who might be about, waiting for me to call, so I already rang for her."

That explained her state of dress—or rather, undress. He'd been hoping she'd dressed thus to seduce him. She stepped aside, revealing the fire. He was an idiot, as usual.

"You must be cold. Please warm yourself. I'm afraid I don't have anything to offer you—"

"Eliza." The use of her name was enough to quell her rambling. She was nervous. Because they were alone together, and she feared passion might flare between them? Or perhaps she *hoped* passion might flare between them?

He took his time warming himself by the fire, lifting the poker to stoke it for her. "I don't have much to report. Goodman is a solicitor for the Duke of Oxthorpe. He has not been here long and will not stay after he completes his business with the duke. Freeland and Cardy have lived in the village for years. Neither man is married, and they take their meals at the inn. One of them might be the highwayman, but it seems unlikely."

She sat in the chair beside the fire. "I see what you mean. It would have been helpful had the Sheriff attacked today."

"Not a very obliging criminal." He poked the fire again. Anything to avoid looking directly at her in the nightgown. "What did you learn?"

She straightened her shoulders as though giving a report. "Mrs. Wattles was indeed in the kitchen and quite busy there. I fail to see how she could step away and not be missed. However unlikely, such a feat is possible. I suggest she remain on the list. Peg was likewise too busy to speak with me. Her mother and father keep her occupied, but she flirted with your Mr. Cardy. Her father made certain the two of them didn't converse for long."

"Cardy must have spoken to her when I was with Goodman." Pierce replaced the poker and wiped his brow. "And what of Mrs. Penter?"

"You should remove your hat and scarf," she remarked.

He didn't need to be asked twice to remove one of the heavy layers.

"Mrs. Penter remained in her rooms all day. I couldn't verify that, as the maidservant said she hadn't called for her, but the girl also said she hadn't seen her leave. The nephew is presumably at his home in the village."

Pierce laid his coat and scarf over one arm and leaned on the mantel. "This is a less-than-promising beginning."

"I agree, but the Sheriff will not rest long. Surely, he will strike again soon."

"We can only hope."

The fire crackled and hissed in the silence.

"Are you eager to return to London?" she asked.

"Not particularly." Except for attending a church service, he'd spent Christmas Day alone. "Are you? I'm sure you want to spend the rest of the holiday with your sister."

"I do. I...I never asked if you have any family in Town."

"I don't." He should take his leave now. The conversation had turned strained and awkward, and the matters related to their mission had been discussed. He wanted to stay with her, prolong this encounter, fill his eyes with the sight of her with her hair down and her prim nightgown and its little bow tied at her neck. He wanted to loose that bow. "My father and mother died several years ago. I have brothers and sisters, but we aren't close, and none of them live in London."

"Friends?"

"Difficult."

"Because of the work." She pushed up from the chair, but her gaze was everywhere but on him. She took the poker and prodded the fire, though he'd already seen to it.

"I would have to say other than my sister June, Bonde has been my only real friend. We do tend to make friends with those we see daily."

"Yes." His friends tended to be the other clerks at the Barbican. "Even our lovers are among the Barbican elite. Look at Wolf and Saint, Baron and Butterfly. I had thought you and I..."

She dropped the poker with a clatter. "Pierce, I don't wish to discuss this again. We shared one night together, and then you felt obligated to ask for my hand in marriage."

"What?"

She gave him a hard stare. "Do not deny it. You didn't ask me because you loved me."

He lifted the poker and handed it to her. Stupid, that. She didn't need it, didn't want it. "I asked because I enjoyed your company and I desired you. I thought love might come in time. Did you love—I mean, do you—"

"I think you should go."

As a child, he'd always run from bullies and conflict. He never faced the problems head-on. Would he run now? "Give me another chance," he said, standing his ground.

"Pardon me?"

"Another chance."

He dropped his coat and scarf, and because she hadn't said no, pulled at the bow closing the nightgown at her neck. "Let me show you what marriage to me might be like. That first time—"

Too late, she swatted his hand away. "I don't think that's wise."

"Fiend seize *wise*," he said, trailing a finger down the soft, exposed skin just below her neck. "Why can't you and I, for once, be spontaneous, passionate, *reckless*?"

"Reckless?" Her voice was breathy, and the color had risen in her cheeks. "Reckless was taking those *books* from the Dungeon."

"So you haven't forgotten those. Would you like me to show you what I learned?"

"That wouldn't be wise."

"Oh, no. Definitely not." He loosened the tie on her robe and pushed the garment off her shoulders.

"What are you doing?" she asked.

"Undressing you."

"Is that necessary?"

"Yes." He tugged at another ribbon on her nightgown.

"*All* of my clothing must go?" She sounded appalled.

He felt the pulse of lust beating in his veins. He'd never seen a woman completely naked before him.

"All of it."

"I don't—"

The ribbon parted, exposing more of her soft skin. "You're going to like this." Dear God, he hoped she would. He hoped he could remember what he'd had in mind when he finally had her stripped naked. Her gaze never left his as he slid his finger down her lips, her chin, her neck, and into her cleavage. Another tug, and the ribbon revealed a glorious sliver of pale flesh.

Her gown was open to mid-chest now, and he'd run out of ribbons. He'd have to pull it over her head. She hadn't objected yet, so he smoothed his hands slowly down her belly, feeling the barest hint of the swell of her breast. The books had said he should go very, very slowly, but it was a trial because he was so eager to touch her.

When his hands spanned her small waist, he clutched the linen in one hand and tugged upward. Her small white feet were revealed, followed by her shapely calves.

He waited for her to protest, but her eyes only darkened and stayed locked on his. He saw in those brown depths a trust he hardly thought he'd earned.

He'd earn it now.

He tugged again, and the fabric slid over her thighs then higher to reveal the apex of those thighs, her rounded hips, the indention of her waist, and then he could not go slowly any longer, and he pulled the gown over her head. She raised her hands to cover her nakedness and then stopped herself and forced them back to her sides. He needed to reassure her, but his throat was too dry for speech.

She was magnificent. Not magnificent in the way the courtesans he sometimes glimpsed at the theater, when he could afford to attend, were magnificent with their sparkling gowns, large bosoms, and dazzling jewels. Eliza was magnificent because she had no pretenses—no face paint, no beauty marks, no corseted breasts. Petite and exquisitely formed, her legs were long for her height and perfectly shaped. Her hips flared out slightly from her waist, and her breasts were small and pert, the aureoles dark pink and the nipples red as wine. Her shoulders were pale and bony, and he could see some of her ribs. She didn't eat enough, didn't take good enough care of herself.

He could take care of her. He would.

He'd been clutching the nightgown, and now he dropped it on the floor with a swish. "You are so beautiful," he murmured. "I have to kiss you." *Slowly*, he reminded himself.

He stepped closer, and it was as though her naked flesh was a lodestone to his body. He wanted so desperately to press himself against her. Instead, he touched her lips with his, kissing her softly and sweetly. When she returned the kiss, he cupped her head and slid his hand into her thick hair. His fingers tangled in the curls, and he gripped them to keep himself firmly rooted on the ground.

The book had mentioned open-mouthed kisses and the use of tongues. He'd heard of this but had never thought to try it. Now he would, and if he shocked her, if she demanded he leave, then so be it. He'd come this far, and he had much further to go.

Gently, he opened his mouth and used the tip of his tongue to trace the seam of her lips. Her lips were soft, and she tasted of brandy. She stiffened slightly, and then she opened her lips to him, and he entered. When their tongues met, hers tentative and shy, he felt a jolt of heat that rushed straight to his groin. He was instantly hard as the poker he'd used to tend the fire and just as hot. He had to ignore that now. He had to ignore his own needs and focus on her. He nipped at her lips, teased her tongue, and as the kiss deepened, drew her closer and closer until her body was flush against his.

His hand dipped from her hair down her smooth, bare back. He hadn't known women could have such soft skin, like warm satin under his fingers. He learned her curves and her planes, tracing them over and over again. Finally, his hands cupped her buttocks.

"Pierce—"

The word ended in a moan, the sound low and deep in her throat. The groan of pleasure caused him a strange thrill. He was the cause of that pleasure. Her hands tightened around his neck as he walked her back toward the small bed on the other side of the room.

Her legs bumped against the bed, and he gently lowered her to the coverlet, kissing her until she arched against him. She'd always been a passionate woman. What did one expect from a woman who enjoyed finding new and inventive ways to create explosives? The temptation when she responded so enthusiastically was to drink his fill of her and slake his lust.

But he would not do that tonight. He wanted to show her he hadn't asked for her hand out of obligation. She wanted love. Did he love her? He didn't know, wasn't sure what love felt like, but surely they could discover what it meant to love and be in love together. He was using her passionate nature against her, making certain she was not quite so eager to push him away, but he was practicing self-denial. Surely that was punishment enough.

She dragged her mouth from his. "What are you doing to me?"

"Chapter three," he murmured.

"Sweet Jesus. How many chapters are there?"

"Thirty-two."

"I'll never survive."

He lowered his mouth, trailing kisses from her neck to her shoulder and back again. He would seduce her slowly, though the way she moved against him made the blood pound through his body and his heart beat like the horses that had kicked the damn walls of the stall half the night. He dipped lower, teasing the slope of her breast and then resting his mouth on the hard peak of her nipple.

The books had been explicit on this matter, and they had not been wrong yet. He darted his tongue out and licked the hard point. She smelled faintly of apples, a fragrance she probably used in her toilette. She'd stilled when he licked her, but she hadn't complained, and now he bent and took her nipple in his mouth, sucking gently.

"*Oh*." She offered her breast to him, pushing it into his mouth. "Still chapter three?" she panted.

"I believe I might have skipped to chapter five now."

He repeated the action on the other breast. He liked kissing her breasts, but he wanted to feel them, and while he lapped and teased, he cupped one and fondled it. How many times had he wanted to touch her breast? Wanted to put his hands on her? Now he held that soft flesh, and it was all he could do not to take her then and there.

He had more pleasures to show her, more chapters from his books. His hand slid lower to the warm juncture of her thighs. With one knee, he edged her thighs apart and slid his hand between them. She was hot there, and when he cupped her, he felt dampness.

Dampness was good. Gently, he stroked her until he found her center, and then he slid a finger into that warm wetness. She inhaled sharply when he withdrew and went absolutely still when he returned with two fingers.

The books had mentioned a small, sensitive nub, and he moved his thumb about, seeking it. When he couldn't locate it, he pulled back and peered down at her.

"Pierce!" She sounded scandalized.

He didn't look away. "Can I not look at you? You're all pink and lovely." It was true of her body in general. She was flushed, her skin every color, from sweet, pale rose to wanton scarlet. "Open your legs," he said, surprising himself with the order. He half-expected her to refuse, but when he nudged her thigh with his knee, she complied.

Ah. There was the nub he sought. Lightly, he brushed his thumb over it, and her hips rose off the bed.

"You like that."

"I *love* that. Do it again."

He slid his fingers into her and swirled his thumb about her center. In and out he moved, pausing at one point to lick his thumb to wet it. She tasted sweet and a bit salty. Another time he would put his mouth there and taste her directly. He hadn't thought he would want to, but now he knew he must.

Eliza was beyond noting what he did. She might have been appalled or aroused by seeing him lick her wetness from his fingers. But her eyes were closed, her head thrown back, her breasts arched upward. He bent and closed his lips on a taut peak, sucking hard as he slid his fingers into her. This time, he pressed on the nub, then flicked it gently until she shuddered.

"Please, please."

He thrust again, deeper this time, and when he filled her to the hilt, he moved his thumb rapidly until her entire body began to tremble. Her muscles contracted around his fingers, and though he was in awe of the feeling, he remembered to suckle her again, taking her swollen nipple into his mouth and teasing her with tongue and fingers, until she let out a muffled scream and dissolved, panting on the bed.

Chapter Four

"That was..."

Her lips fumbled the words. She lay in a sated stupor on the bed, all pleasantly heavy and full. Days or even weeks would have to pass before she'd be able to open her eyes, much less move. She knew what an orgasm was. She'd pleasured herself on the odd winter evening, alone in her cold bed, thoughts of Pierce making her restless. That was before he'd even known she was alive, much less looked at her as a woman.

"This was..."

What he'd done to her was so much more than she'd ever felt before. The pleasure had been violent and consuming, draining all of her strength. Her body thrummed with life and warmth, separate from that of Pierce's body.

The satin of his waistcoat brushed against her sensitive breast, and she forced her eyes open. He watched her. He was fully dressed, right to his knotted cravat—and wasn't there something wicked about that?—and he made no move to take his own pleasure. She did not know what to say, did not know if her mouth would even work. Finally, she managed, "That was..."

He propped his head on his hand.

"Lovely."

"Lovely?" He straightened.

"Wonderful?"

His hand thumped the bed. "Perhaps I didn't do it right. Let me try again."

She laughed and caught his hand. "I couldn't possibly survive another climax like that one so soon. Perhaps I should have said it was explosive."

He curled his fingers around hers.

"And that was in the books you read?"

"That and more. Shall I show you?"

Oh, yes. But she could feel sense beginning to creep back into her mind, and that always overcame passion. "Are you trying to kill me?"

"Exactly the opposite," he said, moving away. She immediately missed the feel of his body pressed against hers. "It is late and you need to sleep. Shall we meet again tomorrow?" He eyed her through lowered lashes. "To discuss the mission?"

"Of course."

Barbican matters required she drag the coverlet over her body. "Surely the highwayman will strike tomorrow. It didn't snow today, and the roads will be clear. If the weather holds into tomorrow, I think he will act."

"Too risky to wait long," Pierce agreed, straightening his neckcloth. "The weather might take a turn any day."

"Then if we do not catch him tomorrow, shall we meet here again tomorrow night? To discuss the mission, of course."

"Of course." He moved to the door, and still wrapped in the coverlet, she followed him. He peered out, looked left and right, then slipped into the darkness of the corridor. Eliza closed the door quietly then leaned against it, hands pressed to her cheeks.

What was she going to do now?

GIVE ME ANOTHER *chance*.

The request had surprised her. He wanted another chance. He'd *asked* for another chance. She would have had too much pride to do such a thing. Pierce had pride too. If he was willing to forgo it, wasn't that an indication of love?

Foolish girl. He wasn't in love with her. He wanted to marry her because it suited his political aspirations. He was leaving the country, and there was nothing for her in Switzerland. Although, she supposed if she were going to design weapons, she could do it just as well in Switzerland as in London. The Barbican group wasn't in Switzerland, but Pierce wouldn't stay in Switzerland forever. He'd return to London in a few years, and with foreign diplomatic experience, be able to find a better job than as a clerk for the Foreign Office.

The Barbican group was the most elite branch of the Foreign Office, and the most secret, but the fact remained that Pierce was still a clerk, no matter how elite the branch he served.

What choice besides going abroad did he have if he wanted to advance his career?

Eliza understood all of that. Was she was willing to sacrifice her own work? She *did* care for Pierce.

She pulled the pillow over her head.

Dare she say it?

She had loved him. She loved him still.

She wanted him to love her too. She wanted him to value the sacrifice she was willing to make. Last night had proved one thing to her—he cared about her. He cared enough to read books about lovemaking and to give her pleasure and not take any of his own. But was that love?

Pierce thought love might come in time.

What if it didn't?

She would not waste time dwelling on tonight and what might happen when he came to her rooms again. Perhaps they would catch the highwayman today. Then there would be no need for a midnight rendezvous.

The thought made her unaccountably sad. She should have been eager to return to London, basking in the mission's success. She shouldn't want it to drag on another night. But she did...

Eliza rang for the maid to help her to dress and breakfasted in her room, although that was not conducive to her purpose, which was spying on the patrons in an effort to discover the highwayman's identity. After breakfast she spent an hour staring out her window and turning pages in her tattered copy of *Animadversions of Warre*. Finally, she had to admit she was avoiding Pierce, and she tucked her ancient book back in her valise and started for the common room.

She arrived just as the coach did, which was truly fortuitous timing. She had a moment to observe which patrons were in the common room right before the coach passengers bustled inside to crowd the inn. Eliza felt warmth tingling on the back of her neck. Pierce watched her from a table in the corner. Situated in the back and well away from the hearth, what it lacked in warmth it made up for in location. He had a perfect view of the room.

"Care to join me, Miss Qwillen?"

"Thank you, Mr. Moneypence. The room does appear a bit crowded," she added, in case anyone should be listening. She sat with him, ordered tea from Peg before the poor girl was besieged by travelers.

"Peg and Mrs. Penter are accounted for." The elderly woman was sitting hunched by the fire. "Although I do not see her nephew, Mr. Wilson."

Pierce lowered his tea cup. "Mrs. Wattles will likewise be difficult to locate, although we might ask Peg if she is in the kitchen. As to our other suspects, I noted Cardy and Langrick. No sign of Freeland or Barber. Mr. Goodman left earlier, supposedly in answer to a summons from the duke."

"Barber is not a suspect," she reminded him. "He was present when Mr. Dowell brought news of the last attack. Speaking of whom, where is Dowell?"

Pierce nodded to a table on the other side of the room. "He came in with the passengers from the coach. Regaling them with tales of the New Sheriff of Nottingham, no doubt."

Eliza crossed off suspects and added others to the list she kept in her mind. "Very well. If there is an attack on this coach, and if no one mysteriously disappears between now and then, our suspects remain Mrs. Wattles, Mr. Wilson, Mr. Freeland, and Mr. Goodman."

She reached for the tea cup and bumped his hand. Mortified, she pulled her own back. "Your tea. Pardon."

Where was *her* damn tea? And why were her cheeks heating? She was a woman of five and thirty. She should not be embarrassed to think those same brown eyes that studied her now had studied a far more intimate part of her last night.

"I concur," he said. "It's a simple matter to ascertain whether or not Mrs. Wattles is truly in the kitchen." He paused when Peg returned to their table with Eliza's tea. "Give my regards to your mother for the delicious breakfast," he said. "She is the one who cooked it?"

Peg bobbed her head. "She does most of the cooking, although we have an undercook who helps a bit. Anything else, sir?"

"No. I—"

But she was already away, weaving between tables and taking orders.

Eliza rose. "I will wander into the back, pretending I became lost. I want to be certain Mrs. Wattles is there before we remove her from the list."

Peg was busy enough serving tea to the coach's passengers that Eliza was relatively certain she had a few minutes before the girl would return to the kitchen. The coach would not stop long, and the girl had to hurry in order to serve all of the passengers before they were off again. Mr. Wattles was in the front room, assisting where he could, so Eliza followed the noise of clinking spoons and pots until she reached a small room behind the dining room.

The door was closed, but she eased it open and peered inside. The room was hot, although cool air blew in from the door opposite, which opened into the yard. Plenty of windows allowed light to penetrate, and the two women inside moved almost in tandem from hearth to stove and chopping block. One woman was quite young, probably not yet twenty. The other was older and stouter. That must be Mrs. Wattles. The innkeeper must have loved his wife dearly to think she was still pretty as the day they wed. Her arms were red and chafed and thick as the trunk of an oak. Sweat poured from her temples and pooled at her armpits.

She pointed a sausage-like finger at a large black pot. "Stir that now. Don't let it burn."

"Yes, missus." The young woman was respectful to Mrs. Wattles, though she had already moved to stir the contents of the pot before being told.

Eliza was about to ease the door closed again when a figure moved through the yard, where the grooms were busy changing the horses on the coach. Eliza removed her spectacles, wiping the moist air fogging them, and replaced them. It was Mr. Wilson. Why would he be in the stable yard? Was he perhaps observing the coach and planning his attack?

Closing the door again, Eliza stepped back and made her way back to the common room. She returned to the table she shared with Pierce. His plate was clean now. "Did you see her? Is she as pretty as Wattles seems to think?"

"She...cooks well enough." Eliza lifted her tea and sipped. It had grown cold but it was sweet. Had she added sugar before she'd stepped away? She didn't remember doing so. "She and an undercook were hard at work."

"Then what is it?"

"How do you know anything is amiss?"

"I know you better than that, Eliza," he murmured so no one else would hear him use her Christian name. The admission and the truth of it warmed her through.

"It may be nothing," she began, "but Mrs. Wattles had the outer door open."

"Not surprising," Pierce said. "I imagine it grows rather warm with the oven."

"Yes." She studied her tea. "Did you add sugar?"

"Of course. That's how you take it."

"Of course."

He remembered how she took her tea. She couldn't have said how he took his.

"Through that outer door, I spotted Mr. Wilson."

Pierce raised his tea cup in the direction of the elderly lady, coughing quietly near the hearth. "Mrs. Penter's nephew?"

"The same. I couldn't think what he would be doing in the yard. Perhaps it is the fastest way to reach the inn, and he is coming to visit his aunt."

He looked pointedly at the elderly woman, who still sat alone. "Or perhaps not. Well done, Eliza."

She felt that infusion of warmth again. She couldn't have said why his praise would matter so much to her, but it did. She was saved from a reply when the coachman called for his passengers to return, and the small group bustled back out into the cold.

"Now we wait," she said.

He sat back, settling in.

She looked up. The sad mistletoe was still above them. Was it her imagination or did it look less droopy? She studied the pattern on her tea cup and the scars on the table. She lifted her tea and ended up knocking the spoon onto the floor with a loud clatter. She retrieved it, bumping her shoulder on the table, almost upsetting it. Pierce righted the table and then grasped her shoulder. "Before you do any further damage, perhaps we might go for a walk."

"Excellent idea." She'd thought she would have to dump tea in his lap before he fastened on that idea. She fetched her pelisse and met him outside. He offered his arm, and they walked along the road, newly marked by the coach's wheels. "How I wish we had a horse," she mused aloud.

"So we could follow the coach more closely?" Pierce dropped his scarf about her shoulders. It smelled of bergamot and straw.

"We'd scare off any possible attempt. Better to lie in wait for the man."

"But where?" She tried not to inhale the scent of him on the scarf, tried not to bask in the warmth it still held from his body.

"I'm certain were we to walk the roads, we would find any number of sites conducive to ambush. The real test would be waiting out in the cold and hoping the man showed himself."

Eliza shivered at the thought. How did the agents for the Barbican do this sort of thing day in and day out? They endured worse conditions than the Nottinghamshire countryside in winter to conduct surveillance on targets. And here she was balking at a little cold air; although, truth be told, the wind had a bite to it this morning. It stung her cheeks and made her ears ring.

The brisk country air made her feel invigorated. It smelled cleaner here than in London. There, she had to become used to the scent of unwashed bodies, coal fires, and refuse in the streets. Here there was the scent of snow on the air, pine trees, and sweet wood smoke curling from chimneys.

"Do you want to talk about it?" Pierce asked.

Was it cowardly to bury her face in his scarf again?

"You're not blushing, are you?"

That comment brought her head up quickly. "Not at all. I'm not ashamed."

"Then what do you feel?" His breath curled out and hung in the cold air between them. "Did you like it?"

"You know I did." She glanced down at her sturdy brown boots, dark against the white snow. Bending, she scooped up a handful, packed it tightly, arranging a piece of ice on the outer rim.

"Good."

She could hear the smile in his voice, and she loosed her missile on a hapless tree.

"I do have a question."

He eyed her warily, looking from the tree back to her.

She scooped another ball of snow into her hands and packed it tightly. It would hurt more on impact that way.

"Why?" She squeezed the cold snow.

"I don't follow."

"Why did you...do what you did? You didn't even take any pleasure for yourself."

"Of course not. It was for you."

She flung the snowball like a catapult might and smiled to herself when he jumped. "Why?"

"I told you," he said, eyeing the tree she'd hit twice. "I want another chance."

"So you're...you're wooing me?" She gathered more snow in her hand, but he caught her wrist.

"Yes. In a manner of speaking. I told you. I want you for my wife."

"And I told you—"

A shot rang out in the distance. Pierce grabbed her arm. "The Sheriff!" she said, shaking him off and breaking into a run.

"Eliza, be careful!" He was right behind her.

She ran in the direction the coach had taken, the same direction as the sound of the shot. They couldn't possibly reach the coach before the highwayman was away, but she would try.

Slowly, Pierce overtook her. That was the advantage of long legs and the absence of cumbersome skirts. She would have hated him for making allowances for her, so she merely pushed herself harder. She would never match him stride for stride, but she managed to keep up with him for a half-mile or more. Finally, she could not catch her breath, and she had to slow and bend at the waist. Pierce glanced at her over his shoulder, but she motioned him to go on without her.

Of course, the man stopped and walked back.

"Keep going," she panted. "I am fine."

He put a hand to his heaving chest. "I don't like leaving you."

She patted her reticule. "I'm not without protection. I have a pistol inside as well as a fan with a hidden dagger."

"Are you certain?"

"Yes! Go!" she urged. Finally, he went on without her. When he had disappeared around a bend and she'd caught her breath, she continued on, walking rapidly. About a quarter hour later, she caught up to Pierce and the mail coach.

Pierce was quizzing the coachman, who looked pale and shaken. The passengers were all clustered around a man who leaned on the door of the coach. He was gesturing with both hands, and his fellow passengers drank in his every word. Because Pierce was speaking with the coachman, she approached the group of passengers.

"Is everyone well?" she asked. "Is anyone hurt? We were out walking and heard the shot."

"It was that blo—blasted highwayman," the man leaning against the door said. He'd removed his hat and waved it with every word. His face was red and perspiration sheened his bald pate.

"He fired at you?" All reports had indicated the New Sheriff of Nottingham was not violent.

"He did," a young woman said, tears streaming down her cheeks. "He took my reticule, and that was all the money I had in the world."

"And he took my ear-bobs." The woman, who clutched the arm of a man Eliza assumed was her husband, spoke in a shaky voice. "They were my grandmother's. I don't care about the guineas, but my ear-bobs!"

Her husband patted her shoulder as she burst into tears. For the first time, Eliza was struck by the fact that the acts of this criminal were more than a nuisance for the locals and a chance for her to prove her worth as an agent. There was a human cost as well.

She did what she could to comfort the small group and asked questions as casually as possible. What, exactly, had the highwayman said? Did the man have a regional accent? Where had he stood? Were those his boot prints? Finally, the coachman determined they would go on and had best not allow the horses to stand any longer.

Pierce moved beside her as Mr. Langrick approached on horseback. "What is amiss?"

Pierce gave him the details, and then asked if he would take Eliza back to the inn. "Miss Qwillen is quite overwrought."

"No, I'm—"

He dropped his hand heavily on her shoulder, and she closed her lips.

"Of course," Langrick said, removing his hat. "Miss Qwillen is welcome. I'll have her back before the fire in no time."

Eliza shot Pierce a look that she hoped would boil his insides, and he leaned close and murmured, "The coachman said he saw no sign the highwayman had a horse. In which case, you should make it back to the inn before he has any chance of doing so. Take note of who is present and who is absent."

Eliza could see the logic in this request. Mr. Langrick was a perfect gentleman, and he conveyed her quickly back to the inn, where Peg fussed over her and brought her tea with brandy.

Eliza sipped it and noted the patrons present.

Freeland was absent.

A careful inquiry told her Goodman had been back in his rooms for a half hour before the highwayman struck. He might have sneaked out again, but she thought it unlikely.

Mr. Wilson was unaccounted for at present and during the attack. His poor aunt sat beside her at the hearth, coughing quietly.

Dowell had been at the inn during the attack, as had Cardy. That removed the two of them from the list of suspects.

That left Freeland and Wilson.

Of course, Freeland might be at his home. There was no reason to assume that the highwayman, whoever he was, would attack and then come to the inn. He probably had a secret place where he stashed his—what did the thieves in the rooks call it? Cargo? Even if Freeland or Wilson walked in now, it did not prove either was the highwayman.

The door opened, and Eliza wondered if her thoughts had conjured one of the suspects, but it was only Pierce. The poor man had ice on his muffler, and the parts of his face not covered were also covered in icy white. Before she could rise and coo over him—which would not have been wise, considering the speculation already stirring about them after their walk—the maid brought him over to the fire and Wattles produced a glass of fine brandy.

How typical. She received tea with a spoonful of brandy, while he was given it straight. She spent the afternoon trying to speak to him alone, but it was quite impossible. Everyone who came into the inn wanted to know what they'd seen or heard, and the coaches that subsequently passed by were filled with passengers whose eyes grew wide at the story. Fortunately, the Sheriff didn't attack again. Eliza was trapped in the inn and would have never caught him. From that conversation, she did learn Pierce had been able to obtain a reasonably good description of the criminal. It was most definitely a man, although he hid his face under a tricorn hat and a turned-up collar. He didn't appear to be on horseback, but he did carry two small pistols, one of which he shot into the air when the guard had been slow to discard his weapon.

He was neither fat nor too slim, of average height, and witnesses reported he had brown hair. It could have easily been Freeland or Wilson. Both men matched that description, though for her part, Eliza suspected Wilson.

She retired early, giving Pierce a look before she started for the stairs. He didn't respond, but she knew he'd seen. He would come to her later. Tonight she would make sure their interaction dealt only with the mission. There would be none of the…other. She was resolved to capture the highwayman quickly now that she'd seen the toll his antics had taken. At least her mind was resolved. Her body, traitor though it was, already anticipated Pierce's touch.

Chapter Five

PIERCE STOOD OUTSIDE her door and took a shaky breath. He was glad to leave the stables for the warmth of Eliza's rooms. Of course, the heat of the fire was not the only reason he wanted to see her or the only warmth he craved. He'd lain on his cot in the cold stall, the sound of those dreadful horses all around him, and thought about what he would do to her when he was with her. Those naughty books had given him so many delicious ideas, but he knew the one he wanted to try most of all.

He raised his hand and paused. What if she didn't want him any longer? She'd been about to argue something when they'd heard that shot. Were his efforts to seduce her into agreeing to marry him all for naught? He couldn't stand the thought of that. He couldn't stand the thought of living the rest of his life without her.

Was that love? Was fear at the prospect of losing her the same thing as love? Perhaps it was, but he felt there should be something more. Some sort of deep, accompanying emotion. He wasn't an emotional man. Perhaps he couldn't feel love. Did Eliza feel love? She said she wanted him to marry her for love, but she'd never said whether or not she loved him. The thought of Eliza loving him, being in love with him, made him feel as though he could take on anything—a band of pirates, a horde of thieves.

No one loved him.

Surely his parents had, but they were dead now. Who loved him now?

He was still standing outside her door—careless that—when it opened suddenly. Eliza stood in the frame, hands on her hips. "Will you ever knock?" she hissed.

"I was just about—"

"Then come in before you're seen." She grabbed him and yanked him inside.

"How did you know I was out there?"

She closed the door quietly and locked it. "I've worked with spies for years. I have ways."

That was intriguing. What was also intriguing was that she'd changed into her nightgown and wrapper again. Did that mean she wanted him to ravish her?

"I think we should discuss our mission and nothing else."

"Very well." He caught a glimmer of disappointment on her face, but then she offered him one of the two chairs by the fire, taking the other. Her feet were bare when she curled her legs under her. Trying not to think about how much he wanted to see those bare toes again, Pierce reiterated the coachman's description of the highwayman. "That description fits any number of men."

"Yes." She tucked a loose strand of hair behind her ear. "Only two of our original suspects were not accounted for at the time of the attack—Wilson and Freeland."

"I agree. I would suggest we focus our efforts on those two, but I worry we might be ignoring other suspects. What if it's not someone who frequents The Duke's Arms at all? It might be one of the men who lives in Hopewell-on-Lyft."

"I've thought of that," she admitted. "The coach does travel directly through the village."

"All mail coaches travel on regular schedules. Everyone has access to that information and might lie in wait."

"True."

They sat in silence for a few moments. Pierce could not stop his gaze from traveling to her legs, where those pink toes were safely tucked out of sight. It appeared they would need to investigate the townspeople and make a list of possible suspects there as well. They might be here days or weeks more. That thought cheered him. He had plenty of wicked pleasures to show her to fill up the nights of those days and weeks, if she'd allow it.

"He took that older woman's ear-bobs," Eliza said quietly.

"What do you mean?"

She lowered her leg, and Pierce followed the movement. When her toes peeked out from the hem of her nightgown, he pulled at his cravat. The damn fire was too hot.

"That older woman and...was he her husband?"

"Mr. and Mrs. Howard? Passengers on the coach today?"

"Was that their name? She told me the highwayman took her ear-bobs. She was quite distraught because they had once belonged to her grandmother."

"That is too bad." Pierce admired Eliza's tender heart, but what did she expect a thief to do? Of course he would take a woman's ear-bobs.

"No, don't you see?" she said, her hands fluttering with animation. "The Howards had to have been traveling inside the coach, and when the highway man ordered the coachman to *stand and deliver*, Mrs. Howard would have clutched at her husband and sought his protection. She was doing so when I spoke with her."

"And so the ear-bobs would have been difficult to see."

"If not all but impossible inside the dark coach." Her voice had risen in volume and pitch, and she bounced in her chair. "Our man had to have been at the inn at some point when the passengers either arrived or withdrew in order to know to demand the ear-bobs."

She was clever, very clever. He'd always known that. She had to be to design the weapons she crafted. Now, watching her mind at work fascinated and aroused him.

"And that brings us back to Wilson and Freeland," he said.

She sat forward. She was so far forward in her chair now, he half-worried she would topple out of it. Or perhaps he hoped. She would fall directly into his arms.

"I would wager all on Wilson." She cut her hand across the air. "Remember I saw him in the yard before the coach departed. He had no reason to be out there unless it was to take a look at the passengers. He never came in to visit with his aunt. The poor woman sat coughing by the fire for most of the morning."

"Then we have our man."

She rose. "Shall we bring him in for questioning? Perhaps we could use one of the inn's outbuildings? I could develop several devices that would be beneficial in an interrogation."

Damn fire was definitely too hot. "Torture?"

"I wouldn't call it that."

"No, you wouldn't. Stop crafting medieval devices that belong in a dungeon for a moment and consider we might be better served simply by catching the man in the act. We follow him."

She slumped. "That isn't very exciting."

"Field work rarely is. Or so I hear." He stood and moved back from the hearth. The conversation was almost at an end, and now was the time for him to take his leave. Except he didn't want to leave. How would he find a way to take her in his arms and then to bed?

"No, it's not," she agreed. "The excitement comes with the capture and the mission's success." Suddenly, she embraced him. "We almost have him, Pierce!"

"OH! I BEG your pardon."

Embracing him had been a mistake. One moment, Eliza's mind was on the highwayman and the accolades they would receive when they completed the mission. The next moment, all thoughts of the mission had fled, and she could think of nothing but the way Pierce's body felt pressed against hers.

"Anything but my pardon." His arms came around her, slid up her back, and enveloped her in his warmth. She was already surrounded by his scent. In London, he had a sophisticated scent—bergamot mixed with the aromas of ink, fine paper, and antique books. She could still detect those scents.

"You smell all wrong," she said. "Like...horses and leather."

"Is that why your breathing is so fast?"

Was she breathing fast? That scent... It made her think of danger and intrigue and forbidden passion.

His hand slid to the nape of her neck, his fingers caressing the sensitive, almost ticklish, flesh there. She hadn't taken her hair down, and now his hand dove into those upswept tresses, loosening them, and relieving the ache.

"You are so proper," she whispered. "So correct except...when you're not."

"You have that effect on me. I love how you"—he lowered his lips to hers—"taste."

The first touch of his flesh to hers always excited her. When he kissed her, he lost all formality. She knew the real man, and that man burned with need and desire to rival any man.

He teased her lips open with his tongue—when had he learned that little trick?—and at the same time pulled pins from her hair, catching them before they could fall to the floor. Her hair tumbled down, and that first feeling of release was wonderful. And then his tongue mated with hers. She didn't know how else to think of it. The way he stroked and teased mimicked lovemaking perfectly. She must have made some small sound of approval, because he nipped at her lower lip.

"You like that?"

Her ears rang like they did after a particularly violent explosion. She opened her eyes, dismayed to find the room seemed to tilt. "Have you always kissed me like that?"

"I'll always kiss you like that from now on." His hand cupped her jaw, and his thumb slid along her cheek, the friction warming her skin.

"From now on? Is there more?"

"Much more. In fact, there's something I want to show you."

The books again. She did not know if she could survive more of his book learning. She did not know if she could survive without him showing her. He bent, and before she realized what he was about, he had his hands behind her knees. She almost toppled over but clutched him just in time. "What are you doing?"

"Sweeping you off your feet," he said, sounding annoyed. He tried it again and all but sent her sprawling on her arse.

"Wait!" she called before he injured her or the noise from her fall woke the entire inn. "Try it this way." She put her arms about his neck and stepped up onto one of the chairs by the fire. "Now."

He took a moment to figure out the logistics, and then he cradled her in his arms. He staggered a little, which did nothing to boost her confidence, but then he gained his feet and carried her to the bed.

"Am I heavy?" she asked.

"Light as a feather," he said, sounding strained.

Poor Pierce. He really was trying. Perhaps he'd always wished to be a strapping sportsman, whereas she had always dreamed of being a diamond of the first water. But here they were—Eliza and Pierce—two very ordinary people...well, except for the espionage bit.

He tried to set her on the bed, but stumbled at the last moment, and she went toppling down. His face went white, but she laughed. He colored, and she feared it was from embarrassment, but then he moved over her, kissing her, and she knew he wanted her far too much to be embarrassed. The kiss was unskilled, all passion and longing, and she couldn't stop herself from wrapping her arms around him and kissing him back.

This was folly. Involving herself further with him would only make it more difficult when they had to part. But she wanted him so much. How could she not want him when he was so sweet and clumsy and—how could she forget—so newly skilled in the arts of pleasure? Just for tonight, she wanted to ignore the fact that she was Eliza Qwillen and he was Pierce Moneypence. She wanted to be just a woman who needed the comfort of a man.

He drew back and tugged at her wrapper, and she felt bold. She rose to her knees and stripped it off, then discarded the nightgown too. "I love how you look at me. Your eyes turn so dark and lovely."

"I love to look at you. I can't drink my fill." His gaze roved over her, taking her in slowly, and the reverence with which he reached out to stroke her left her breathless.

She was no great beauty. Her hair was too curly and wild. Her arms were too skinny, her breasts not full, her hands scarred and red from her work. She had decent legs, but one couldn't exactly show them off. But Pierce looked at her as though she were the highest-paid courtesan. He looked at her as though he wanted her. He did want her, and that made it all the sweeter.

"Take your coat off," she said. He obliged. He didn't wear his coats cut as close to his figure as many men did, and he easily shed it. "Now your neckcloth."

He loosened it and tossed it aside.

She unfastened the buttons at his throat. Pressing her lips to his skin, she kissed and then licked, tasting him. The flavor was uniquely Pierce, masculine and refined and with that hint of foreignness that was horse and leather and which she found so erotic tonight.

Her hands slid over his chest. His body was slim and elegant but also firm and strong. She loved his long, lean lines. She dipped lower, feeling his erection and grasping the length in her hand. She stroked him, but he pulled her hand away.

"Not yet," he murmured, kissing her again. She thought of protesting, but why should she when he was lowering her to the bed again, settling his weight pleasantly over her? She abandoned herself to the sensation of his linen shirt against her sensitive breasts and the wool of his trousers sliding over her bare legs. She wrapped her arms around him and tightened her legs about his waist.

He inhaled sharply and seemed to struggle for control. His kisses grew more insistent, more passionate, and then he retreated from her lips and tended to other parts of her. He kissed the line of her jaw, the tender skin just beneath it, the ticklish part of her earlobe, and the hollow at the base of her throat.

He worshipped her, kissing and tasting her. She thought he might linger on her breasts, but he surprised her by moving lower and sliding his tongue over her abdomen.

Hot and insistent need flared in her as his tongue dipped lower. "What are you about?" she gasped.

He looked up at her, his head almost at the juncture of her thighs. "More wicked suggestions from my naughty books. Do you mind?"

"I..." Did she mind? She had never dreamed a man, much less Pierce Moneypence, would even consider doing what he was about to do—or at least what she thought he was about to do. As if reading the uncertainty in her eyes, he moved lower and used one hand to part her legs. Oh, she had little doubt what he had in mind, especially when he leaned down and his warm breath tantalized that most intimate part of her. She shuddered and squirmed, but his weight held her in place.

"I want to taste you," he said. "I've read it can be extremely pleasurable when a man applies his lips and tongue to this part of the female anatomy."

His words were so scientific, and yet, they aroused her more powerfully than anything else he'd said.

"I don't mind," she squeaked.

"Good," he said, his words vibrating against her inner thighs. "Because I've been thinking a lot about this."

"You have?" He thought about doing things like this to her? How often? When? And then she could not think at all, because he pressed his mouth to her and the feeling was so delicious, she couldn't form a coherent thought for several long, long moments. He had an aptitude for this, or had studied his books diligently, because he quickly brought her to a fierce climax. She cried out, and then covered her mouth in embarrassment.

Pierce slid beside her and nuzzled her neck. "You enjoyed that."

"I've probably woken the entire inn." She rose on her elbows to ensure the door was locked. "I do hope the maid doesn't come to check on me."

"Just tell her it was a nightmare." He was still nuzzling her neck, which was distracting, especially when his hands wandered to her breasts. She pulled at the tails of his shirt.

"Why don't you take this off? Take everything off while you're at it and show me what else you've learned from that naughty book."

"Oh, no." He captured her hands in his. "There are far too many other pleasures I'd rather show you."

"But what about your pleasure?"

"Time for that when we marry."

She sat up abruptly, and he lost his balance and toppled over into the indention she'd left in the bed. "So this is all some ploy to convince me to agree to marry you, and then once we're married, you'll have no use for seduction."

He sat, looking bewildered. "No, not at all—"

"So you don't want me to marry you."

"Of course I do, but I'll still seduce you after we're wed."

She rose on her knees, hugging the sheet to her. "Why?"

"Why?" He looked close to panicking, but she was not going to give him the correct answer. "Because you like it? Because I enjoy it?"

"Get out."

"What? Eliza, no, let's talk about this."

She was already up and out of bed. She stomped to the door then paused, looking back at him. He was climbing slowly off her bed, looking as though he'd lost his puppy. "Very well, let's talk. Do you love me?"

There was the shocked-deer look she remembered so well. That was answer enough, but the foolish man stammered and stuttered and attempted a reply anyway. She was patient. This might at least be entertaining.

"I feel—that is to say—I care very much about you. In my heart—the warmth—truly I do esteem you, I am very fond—"

"Fond? You are fond of me? How romantic. A man who is *fond* of me. Do you do"—she gestured to the bed—"*that* with all the women you are fond of?"

"No! Eliza, you know there is only you."

"But I don't know that, Pierce. I am certain you could find any number of other women you are fond of who would be happy to go with you to Switzerland."

His chin notched up. "Is that what this is about? You think I want you to abandon your work for the Barbican group. I don't. You can design weapons in Switzerland."

"What if I enjoy my life here? What if I don't want to go to Switzerland?" A pregnant silence filled the room, and she knew, quite suddenly, that this was the moment she had been waiting for. She held her breath with anticipation, willing him to say the words she wanted. If he couldn't say *I love you* perhaps he could show her.

"It's only for a few years. We would return..."

He was still speaking, but she wasn't listening any longer. He wouldn't even offer to forgo his plans for her. She wouldn't have made him give up his ambitions, but she would have known that he was willing to make the sacrifice. If he only cared for her that much, then she thought he might fall in love with her, given time. But he was like every other man, thinking himself better and more important than any woman.

Better to remain a spinster, a bluestocking with a shocking expertise in weaponry, than trade her soul for a warm body beside her night after night.

"Out," she said, pointing to the door. "Take your coat and go."

He lifted his coat as though it was laden with bricks. "Eliza, please."

"We'll have to meet elsewhere to discuss the mission from now on. Don't come here again." She opened the door.

She thought he might bow his head and scurry away. Instead, he stepped into the corridor and looked her directly in the eye. "This isn't the end."

She closed the door on him and locked it. "Oh, yes, it is." She was done behaving as a foolish girl would, hoping he would come to love her, hoping he might change. She had to stop being swayed by her baser instincts. He'd certainly learned new bedsport, but marriage was more than a romp in bed. She had to remember that. Most important, she had to forget the promise of all the other tantalizing talents he'd learned.

Chapter Six

PIERCE HOBBLED TOWARD the inn, shivering as he cut through the icy yard. The sky was gray and heavy with low-hanging clouds. It would snow again before the day was through. He was annoyed after spending another night in the stable. The annoyance stemmed, in part, from the ache in his back and shoulders and neck and…well, every part of him ached after spending two nights on that cot.

Pierce also suspected that a reasonable amount of his frustration stemmed from not slaking his needs with Eliza. Why hadn't he just taken her when she'd offered? Why did he have to be noble, forsaking himself for her pleasure? Why had he tried to speak? He had never been a skilled orator. More often than not, he stumbled over words rather than used them. He'd thought Eliza was different. He'd thought he'd finally found a woman with whom he could be himself, with whom he could share his thoughts and hopes and dreams. But she seemed to want something he couldn't give.

Perhaps he should simply lie to her and say he loved her, but even though he was a spy (oh, very well, a clerk to spies), he didn't like to lie. And he didn't do it very convincingly. That was no way to begin a marriage. If he could just fall in love with her! As he entered the warm inn and removed several tedious layers, he thought that task might be easier were she to allow him to share her bed. Relegating a man to the stables did not engender warm feelings.

He spotted her almost as soon as he took a seat at an empty table. He should have been cheered to find she was up early, looking a bit tired around the eyes. But the evidence that she had not slept well failed to cheer him. He knew her. Her mind was set, and she would not change it. Her only weakness had been pleasure. She was a passionate woman. He'd taken advantage of that part of her nature, hoped to use it to sway her, but now that avenue was closed to him as well.

He should focus on the mission. He'd thought of nothing but Eliza all night, when he should have been planning how to trap Mr. Wilson.

Wilson and his aunt sat together this morning close to the hearth. Mrs. Penter coughed quietly, keeping her handkerchief close to her nose, where she perpetually held it. Did she know her nephew might be the New Sheriff of Nottingham? Pierce glanced at his pocket watch. He had time to break his fast before the first coach arrived, assuming coaches were still traveling this way, considering the number of times the highwayman had struck recently.

When Peg appeared, he ordered tea, toast, and jam and focused on every corner of the room except Eliza's. But every corner had a sprig of mistletoe in it. Would it draw attention if he ripped them all down and tossed them into the fire?

Best to leave the trappings of Christmas in place. He would ignore them. Langrick and Barber sat at a table with Mr. Dowell. Freeland and Cardy were absent, and Goodman was also not accounted for, although Pierce assumed he was either dining in his room or at the duke's estate.

Freeland's absence was suspicious. Wilson seemed the more likely suspect, but Freeland was still a candidate. If the highwayman struck, and Freeland was absent, Pierce would not hesitate to have the man arrested.

As it was, Pierce spent two uneventful days observing Wilson and Freeland as often as possible. The Sheriff did not strike, and Pierce feared not only his relationship with Eliza but the mission as well was lost.

He attempted to speak to Eliza. He even tried to walk with her, but when she saw him coming, she walked the other way. For a short woman, she could walk quickly. When he endeavored to have a conversation with her, she answered briefly and politely and managed to strike up conversations with another guest or one of the coach's passengers.

In the meantime, he slept alone in the cold stable on the uncomfortable cot. The evening of the second night with no sign of the Sheriff, a storm blew in, and at dinner, Pierce could hear the wind battering the walls of the inn and see the swirl of snow through the windows. Most of the locals had stayed at home, not wanting to brave the weather, and it was only Eliza, Langrick, and himself at dinner. Mrs. Penter and Mr. Goodman had taken dinner in their rooms.

When Eliza retired to her room and Langrick braved the storm to return to his home, Pierce stayed in his seat, turning his mug of Wattles famous ale this way and that. He had no desire to return to the stable. Fiend seize the perpetually full inn. Pierce was weary of spending every night shivering. Better to stay at the inn for as long as Wattles would allow it. Not because he was closer to Eliza here. Not because he could imagine her tucked snugly into her small bed, her pink toes curled under her. Not that he wished, more than anything, he was tucked around her.

Wattles had been wiping the table beside his for about five minutes. Now the innkeeper was watching him. Pierce drank from his ale.

"I fear I'm keeping you from your bed. I'll retire."

"No rush," Wattles said good-naturedly. He righted a beeswax candle and retied the green velvet ribbon. "You look as though you have a weight on your shoulders." He gave the table one last swipe with the rag then sat opposite Pierce. Pierce clutched the mug, but unless he was willing to subject himself to the cold, he would have to tolerate the man's presence. It wasn't such a hardship. He hadn't spoken to anyone, other than to find out information relating to the Sheriff, in days.

"Oh, this and that," Pierce said non-committally.

"Is Miss Qwillen *this* or *that*?"

Pierce's chin jerked up, but Wattles merely spread his hands and smiled. "When you are an innkeeper as long as I've been, you become an observer of sorts. That's the way to anticipate guests' needs. I can see you and the lady are friendly." He waggled his brows. "More than friendly, perhaps."

"I assure you nothing untoward—"

Wattles waved a hand. "I'm not suggesting or accusing, I'm just saying you look like a man whose heart has been broken. Does she love another?"

Pierce thought about protesting that he had no idea what the innkeeper spoke of, but why not tell the man? It wasn't as though Pierce had anything to lose. "Actually," he said, staring at his ale, "I think she loves me."

Wattles clapped him on the shoulder, and Pierce almost fell off his bench. "That's good news!" Wattles exclaimed.

"One would think so, but when I asked her to marry me, she said no."

"Ah."

Ah? What did *ah* mean? "Is that all you're going to say?"

Wattles lifted the towel again, gave it a friendly twist. "The problem seems obvious enough to me."

"Oh, does it? Then please enlighten me."

Wattles pointed the rag at him. "You're the problem. You've done something to put her off."

"I haven't! I've done all I could to woo her."

Wattles gave him a dubious look. "Not everything, I wager. What is it she wants?"

Pierce slumped. He shouldn't slump. It was bad posture, but it was better than the alternative, which was sliding under the table and hiding. "She wants me to love her," he muttered. He rather hoped Wattles hadn't heard him.

The man nodded and said, "Ah" again. If he said it a third time, Pierce would strangle him. The innkeeper must have seen Pierce's annoyance, because he sat forward.

"The solution seems simple enough to me. Tell her you love her."

Pierce swallowed the remainder of his ale, the brew bitter as it went down. "Don't you think I would if I could?"

Wattles crossed his arms over his expansive girth, the towel dangling at his side. "What's holding you back?"

"I don't know that I do love her, obviously," Pierce said. "I don't want to prevaricate."

Wattles shook the towel. "You London types are all the same. You think too much. It's obvious you love the girl. Tell her and marry her."

"How?" Pierce demanded. "How is it obvious?"

"Look at you." Wattles slapped the rag on the table.

Pierce flinched and looked down at himself. His coat and cravat were still neat and straight. He wasn't foxed, and he didn't think his hair was tousled.

Wattles caressed his towel and chuckled. "I mean, your face is so long, you might be a hound. You're sitting here all alone, dreading going to your bed."

"That might be because I have no bed—"

"You're the very picture of a heartsick man." Wattles ignored his mention of the lack of a bed. "All alone under the mistletoe." He glanced at the decaying foliage hanging above them.

It occurred to Pierce that Wattles was married. "Do you love your wife?" he asked.

"Of course. Loved her when we married six and twenty years ago, and I love her now." The towel received another caress. "How could a man not fall in love with a woman as pretty as my Mrs. Wattles?"

"How did you know you loved her?"

"Ah."

Pierce was about to reach across the table and grab Wattles's neck, but the innkeeper continued, "That's an easy one. But you're not asking because you care about my romance with Mrs. Wattles. You want to know the signs for yourself."

"I suppose."

"Very well, then ask yourself this. Do you think about her all the time?"

Pierce thought about her quite a lot.

"Are you willing to sacrifice for her? By that I mean, is her happiness more important than yours?"

He thought of the nights he'd seduced her, forgoing his own pleasure for hers. On the other hand, she was against him going to Switzerland. Could he give that up for her? He looked around the empty room and saw the rest of his life. Yes, to have Eliza at his side, he could give up Switzerland. He could find ways to advance his career here. If he asked, Baron would help.

"Lastly, would you do anything for her? Would you give up your life for hers?"

Pierce wasn't certain of the answer to that one.

"I remember when Mrs. Wattles was delivering Peg. Poor woman had so much trouble with that birth."

Pierce reached for his ale and drank the last three drops. If he had to hear a tale involving childbirth, he needed a drink.

"She screamed and screamed, and the midwife thought the baby would never come. We thought they'd both die. I tell you what, my boy, I went down on my knees in this very room and begged God to spare her. I pleaded with the Almighty to take me and not her. And I meant it too. I would have done anything, even traded my life, so she could live. But all's well that ends well, as the poet says. My Peg was born, and Mrs. Wattles recovered, though she was abed for a good long time. I supposed it was all the blood she lost. I never seen so much blood—"

The room spun, and Pierce held up a hand. "No talk of b-blood, sir, I beg you."

Wattles squinted at him. "Are you ill, sir? You look a bit peaked."

"Thank you for your insights," Pierce answered. "I'll give it some thought." He rose. His legs were a bit wobbly, because he still had the image of blood in his mind, but he thought the cold air might revive him. He started for the door, but Wattles called out.

"Don't think, Mr. Moneypence. That's your problem. You love the girl. That's as plain as day. Tell her and be done with it."

Pierce stepped into the wind and the snow. Later, when he lay on his cot shivering, the sound of the horses and the wind whistling through the stable's cracks keeping him awake, he thought of what Wattles had said. He wanted to love Eliza, but he wasn't certain he did.

***

ELIZA SIPPED HER morning tea in the common, her gaze on Freeland and Wilson over the rim. For a change, Goodman was also seated in the room. He had his paper open and did not look receptive to conversation, but after the long, cold night, even he wanted to stretch his limbs a bit.

For three days the Sheriff had not struck, and she had high hopes for today. The first coach would arrive in less than an hour, and the weather was perfect for an attack. The sun shone on the new-fallen snow. That new snow would slow the coach and the horses who had to tromp through it. That slowing might work to the highwayman's advantage.

Eliza decided to ride with the next coach, hoping the highwayman attacked when she was a passenger. She had the money to pay for passage to the next village, if it came to that. But if the coach was attacked, and she managed to capture the highwayman, she would be a hero and have completed the mission successfully.

She wasn't certain where Pierce was. She'd seen him this morning, and they'd exchanged curt but polite greetings. That was unfortunate. She wished they might have parted on amicable terms. She wished they hadn't had to part at all. The last two nights she'd lain awake for hours, wishing he'd come to her room, though if he had, she would have sent him away. Contrary woman! So frustrating to want him and to know he didn't want her in the same way.

He obviously cared for her. He was willing to make an effort to seduce her, but how long would that last once he won her? Not long. She had made a promise to herself not to compromise. She would marry a man who loved her or not marry at all.

Eliza heard the clatter of the coach arriving and checked her reticule for the small pistol she always carried. Although designing weapons was her profession, there was nothing special about this pistol, except she'd modified it to ensure it shot straight and true. That was all a situation like this required.

She set down her tea cup, glancing at the table where Mr. Wilson sat alone. Mrs. Penter had come down earlier and then retired again, saying she felt a little tired. Since Wilson was sipping his tea and studying the paper, it did not look as though he planned to depart any time soon. Eliza almost decided against soliciting passage on the coach. But she approached the driver anyway. If nothing else, the journey would be beneficial because she could study the road. Perhaps she might see a clue about the Sheriff.

As she climbed aboard the coach, she did wonder for a fleeting instant how she would return to The Duke's Arms, but she decided to follow her instincts. Agent Saint was always going on about listening to instincts. Maybe there was something to that approach. If not, Eliza would certainly give Saint a piece of her mind when she finally made it back to London.

Eliza seated herself next to another woman, pleased she was beside a window and could peer out. After the passengers exchanged pleasantries, an uneasy silence descended. This was the stretch of the journey where so many other coaches had been waylaid. The woman who shared Eliza's seat clutched her valise tighter, and Eliza held her own reticule close. She wasn't concerned about losing her valuables—she didn't carry any—she wanted easy access to her pistol.

The snow-covered landscape tumbled by as the coach moved forward at a brisk pace. Several points along the snow-covered landscape would make good ambush spots. The foliage was thick and provided good cover. She wished it had not snowed so recently. Then she might have been able to study the tracks the highwayman had left during previous attacks. As it was, everything was covered with an obscuring blanket. That worked in the Sheriff's favor, but—

A blur of movement caught her attention, and she all but pressed her nose against the glass. Fiend seize it—as Pierce would say—the highwayman was attacking! The Sheriff wasn't Wilson, after all. Eliza deftly lifted her pistol from her reticule, lowered the window, and heard the man shout, "Stand and deliver!" To accent his words, he fired a shot in the air.

The horses shied, and the carriage veered to the right, sending the groom tumbling into a ditch without, it seemed, his blunderbuss. The driver finally managed to take control again. By that time, the highwayman had primed his pistol again, making him dangerous.

Ignoring the rocking coach, the screams of her fellow passengers, and the shouts of the highwayman, Eliza leaned out of the open window and aimed her pistol. She didn't want to kill the criminal, but she wanted to wound him so he would no longer be a threat. She aimed and cocked the hammer just as the coach slammed to a stop. The jolt moved her arm, and her shot went wild, the pistol ball hitting the snow a few feet to the right of the Sheriff.

She'd attracted his attention, and he turned his gaze and then his pistol on her. "Down!" she yelled to her fellow passengers. She tried to duck herself, but she had to pull her arms in from the window. The highwayman aimed, and Eliza yanked one arm inside. He cocked the hammer, and if his aim was true, she was in trouble. She couldn't possibly pull her arm in and duck in time. She should have felt some sense of horror, but instead she felt completely detached, as if it was someone else being fired upon.

A familiar figure rushed at the Sheriff, and all sense of detachment fled. "No!" she screamed, but it was too late. The Sheriff's pistol fired, and Pierce blocked the shot with his body.

"No!" Eliza screamed again as Pierce crumpled to the ground.

Nothing and no one moved for a long, long time. No more than a second or two had passed, but in that brief period, she went over every moment she and Pierce had spent together. She recalled every sweet word, every tender look, every time he had made her smile.

Eliza reached for the door and all but fell out of the coach. She could prime a weapon in her sleep, and she readied her pistol while kneeling on the ground by the coach. Raising it, she saw the Sheriff had not moved to prepare his weapon. He was staring at Pierce's body with open-mouthed shock.

Eliza raised her pistol, and with what she considered admirable restraint, moved the barrel slightly to the left, then fired. She hit the Sheriff in the thigh, and he went to his knees with a yelp. Ignoring him, she ran to Pierce and knelt by his side.

The cold, wet snow immediately seeped through her pelisse and her dress, but she didn't care. Pierce was lying on his side, his back to her, and she reached for his shoulder. Her gloved hand hovered in the air above him. What would she do if he was dead? What would become of her? How would she live without him?

She loved him.

All the rest didn't matter. Where they lived, whether he told her in so many words he loved her, whether she ever designed another weapon. Pierce *was* her life. Hand trembling, she clutched his shoulder and rolled him onto his back. The scarlet stain on the snow where Pierce had lain caught her eye. "No," she whispered, her gaze flicking to his face. His eyes were closed, his complexion pale and lifeless. "No," she sobbed, lowering her head to his chest. She needed to listen for his heartbeat, but she was sobbing too much to hear. God was cruel to allow her to hold him, feel his warmth, this last time before he grew cold as the snow she knelt upon.

"Pierce!" she cried. "No. You can't die. I forbid it. Fight, damn you!" She sat and shook him, eliciting no response from him. "Please fight. You have to live. I-I love you. You know that, don't you? I *love* you, foolish man. I'll go to Switzerland with you. I-I'll go anywhere with you—even somewhere awful like India or the United States. Please live. Please."

Her head fell into her hands, and grief overwhelmed her.

Chapter Seven

Pierce didn't know what that awful sound was, but he pushed through the blackness to make it stop. He waved his hand, brushing against something solid but pliable. With his gloves on, and his fingers so numb they were probably frostbitten, he couldn't feel a thing. He pried his eyes open and stared at Eliza's bent head. She was on her knees beside him, her shoulders shaking as though she wept.

He waved his arm again, brushing it over her arm. Her head snapped up, and she stared at him as though she were seeing a ghost. "Pierce!" she screamed. "You're alive."

Ah. That explained the crying. But there had been more. She'd been talking. Telling him…she loved him? "You love me?" he said, his voice raspy.

She gathered him into her arms, causing a slice of pain in his shoulder. "Of course I love you. I've always loved you. How dare you jump in front of that highwayman? You might have been killed!"

"I couldn't let him shoot you." And that was when he realized he loved her too. He couldn't believe he hadn't always known it, but perhaps that was why he hadn't known. It was so much a part of him. He'd sacrificed himself for her because it was second nature to do so. And he'd been wounded by the pistol ball for his pains.

He remembered the blood. His head began to spin, and he forced his thoughts away. This was no time to faint at the sight of blood. Eliza needed him. They had a mission to complete.

"The Sheriff?" he asked, sitting. The world tilted, but he tried to pretend that was normal—and thank the Maker he had not eaten much for breakfast.

At the mention of the highwayman, Eliza opened her mouth like a hooked fish. She lost her balance, then scrambled up. Pierce tried to follow, but it was a moment before he could climb to his feet. By then she was standing over a man lying on the ground not far from where Pierce had been lying. He recognized the gray coat. He'd seen the man set out from the inn and followed, thinking he would turn out to be simply going home. But when the man had started for the road, Pierce thought he might have his Sheriff of Nottingham—except it couldn't have been Wilson. He'd been sitting in the public room when Pierce had stepped outside.

"Be careful, miss!" the driver called. He'd stayed with the coach, and all of the passengers were peering out of the windows with trepidation.

"You shot me," the man groaned. He was doubled over and clutching his leg. Pierce made certain not to look anywhere near the wound. Instead, he focused on the man's face, what he could see of it. He'd had a view of the criminal's back all morning but hadn't caught sight of the face. He didn't recognize the fellow at all.

"You should be thanking me," Eliza said, leaning over and confiscating his pistol. "I could have easily shot you through the heart."

"Why didn't you? I'm dead anyway."

"Who are you?" Pierce asked. "I don't recognize you."

The man looked up at him, a slight smile creasing his grimace of pain. "It was a good disguise. No one would have ever suspected us."

Eliza shot Pierce a look, and he nodded. The highwayman had used the pronoun *us*. Clearly, he was not working alone. But fiend seize it if Pierce knew who he was or who he worked with. What had his disguise been? One of the maids? A groom?

And then the man coughed quietly, and Pierce knew. Eliza spoke first. "It's Mrs. Penter!"

The highwayman coughed again, and Eliza shook her head. "We never even considered Mrs. Penter. No, wait." She looked at Pierce, admiration shining in her eyes. "You said you were not willing to clear her name initially. You did suspect her."

"I didn't seriously consider her. If Wilson is part of this, the two of them had the perfect game. He could rob some coaches, and *she* could do others. If suspicion fell on him, he only need be in the presence of witnesses the next time the Sheriff struck. No one would ever suspect her."

"If Wilson is part of this," Eliza said, "one of us must return and take him into custody before he flees. You are injured. I'll go, and you return with Penter—or whatever his name is—and the coach to The Duke's Arms."

Before he could even agree, she was away. It took some time to move the man whose name was actually Penter into the coach. Several of the passengers elected to walk back to the inn, rather than ride in the coach with a criminal, but Pierce sat beside him. His shoulder hurt like the very devil, but a quick investigation with his fingers told him the ball had only nicked him. He'd have someone clean and bandage the wound when he returned.

After a brandy or twelve, he'd be fine.

Of course, the afternoon was more complicated. When Pierce returned, Eliza did have Wilson in custody, and everyone from the village seemed to be crowded into the inn to hear the tale and gawk at the highwaymen. The magistrate arrived, and the men spilled their tale. Wilson had needed money, and he'd applied to his uncle in London, Penter, to help him. Penter was a thief from Whitechapel, and he'd come prepared to do what he did best. The two had been successful criminals for several months. A search of Wilson's home uncovered a room full of valuables the two planned to take to Nottingham to fence.

Eliza and Pierce were commended for capturing the thieves, but instead of accepting the ale and free meal Mr. Wattles tried to give him, Pierce asked to be allowed to lie down. Eliza had been swept away by the crowd, and for once Pierce was content in the stable, where at least it was quiet. Peg cleaned and bandaged his wound, which she called little more than a scratch. Pierce glimpsed the blood, but fainted only once, and then he drank three fingers of brandy and fell asleep.

When he awoke, it was dark outside. He had no idea how long he'd slept or what had transpired since he'd left. Surely Eliza hadn't needed him. Had she even missed him? Perhaps he'd been somewhat delusional after he'd been shot and only imagined that she'd told him she loved him, that she'd go anywhere with him. What happened now? Should he propose again? He still hadn't told her he loved her. Perhaps he should rectify that.

"Oh, good," a voice said from the door of the stall. "You're awake."

"Eliza?" He sat, causing the blankets to slide down. His hair felt as though it were stuck to his head in the frightful manner it did every morning.

"You were expecting someone else?" she asked, moving inside. The light of a brazier illuminated her sweet form.

Pierce squinted. "Wattles allowed me a brazier?"

"I promised to keep watch over it." Her gaze fell to his chest, which was bare, but she was looking at the bandage, which ran over his shoulder and under his arm. "I should have done that. I'm sorry."

He waved her words away. "Someone had to play hero and receive the accolades. I didn't have the strength."

"And how are you feeling now?" she asked, sitting beside him on the cot. The poor thing almost collapsed. "Better?"

"Much."

"I brought you bread and cheese. Are you well enough to eat?"

Pierce devoured the bread and cheese as Eliza looked on with a small smile. With a full belly, including two mugs of ale, he was feeling much more like himself.

As he ate, they'd been talking about the mission, and Eliza had told him how the magistrate had taken the highwaymen away. But now an awkward silence descended.

"About what I said earlier...when you were lying in the snow," Eliza began.

Pierce looked down at his feet. He wished he had pulled his shirt on before this moment had come. He felt strangely vulnerable and naked without it. "You don't have to say anything," he said. "You were distressed. You spoke in the heat of the moment. I won't hold you to it."

"What are you talking about?"

The cot jerked as she jumped to her feet. Her hands were on her hips, and she was obviously annoyed. "I—ah, nothing."

"I was not distressed nor did I speak in the heat of the moment." She moved closer so he could feel the heat of her body on his naked flesh and smell the scent of apple. "I do love you, Pierce. I should have said it before."

"*I* should have said it before," he interrupted.

"*You?*"

He took her hand, pulling her close. "I think about my feelings so much I forget to…feel them, I suppose. I do love you, Eliza. I didn't realize how much until the moment I saw Penter—or whatever his name is—point his weapon at you."

"You dove in front of a man firing a pistol." She sounded almost angry, although her eyes were wet with tears.

"Love makes a man do foolish things. I knew in that moment, without thinking, that I couldn't live without you. I would have rather died than lived without you."

She squeezed his hand almost painfully and pulled him to his feet. "Pierce, you realize that is the most romantic thing anyone has ever said to me."

"It may be the last romantic words from my lips. I'm no poet, Eliza."

She released his hand and stepped into his embrace, wrapping her arms around his neck. "I know exactly who you are, Pierce. And I love you."

She kissed him then, her mouth hungry and full of unleashed passion. She'd not kissed him like this before, without any hint of reserve. It fired his blood, and he knew this night would be a true test of his willpower. Her soft body pressed against his bare chest, and her hand slid over his skin until she cupped his hard length. He broke the kiss. "Eliza, let me—"

"Oh, no. None of your naughty books tonight. Tonight there is just you and me and this." She kissed him again. He would have laid her on the cot, but the pathetic excuse for a bed might very well collapse if the two of them tested it. Instead, he pushed her up against the wall of the stall, his eyes meeting that of the horse occupying the stall beside his.

"Perhaps we should go inside," he suggested. She slid her mouth over his neck, scraping her teeth along his flesh. His hands clenched on her hips. "There is no privacy here."

"Everyone is inside," she murmured. "Besides, we're spies." She smiled up at him. "We like adventure and risk."

"I keep forgetting." And then he did forget everything but the feel of her in his arms, the shape of her body as it molded to him, and the sounds she made as he joined with her.

Later, when they were both spent and exhausted, they lay on a blanket in a cozy bed of clean straw and looked up at the roof. The brazier had expended almost all of its coal, and Pierce would send Eliza to her warm room before the hour was up. He turned to look at her, so beautiful with her hair spread on the blanket and her eyes half-closed.

"I'm not going to Switzerland."

She opened her eyes. "What do you mean?"

"I can't leave you, and your place is in London, at the Barbican." Amazing how easy it was to make sacrifices for her now that he knew he loved her. They weren't really sacrifices at all.

She pushed up on one elbow. "But Switzerland is a wonderful opportunity for you. You can't stay a clerk forever, even a clerk in the Barbican group."

"I'll be close to you, and that is what I want." He stroked her cheek, happy in the knowledge he could freely touch her now. She was his.

"You will be close to me in Switzerland. I'm going with you."

He stared at her. "No. Your work is here—"

She put a finger over his lips. "My life is where you are, and I'm not going without stipulation."

He raised a brow.

"You must promise to return to England."

"Of course. The appointment is for a year or two at most."

She kissed him. "Good. If I can work for the Foreign Office abroad, I will. If not, the Barbican group will go on without us for a little while."

"Then you want to return to work for the Barbican group at some point?" he asked.

"Of course. One day, I plan to be the director."

"You plan…" But why not? This was Miss Qwillen—Q. She could do anything.

Twelfth Night, London

THE NOISE FROM the revelers on Piccadilly was muted within the secure stone walls of the Barbican headquarters. But it said something of the spirit of the celebration that Q and Moneypence could hear it at all in the bowels of the building, deep in the Dungeon.

As this was the night of feasting and balls, the offices of the Barbican were largely empty. The agents were either out reveling or home with family exchanging the traditional gifts. It was the perfect night for Eliza and Pierce to peruse some of the lesser-known volumes of the Dungeon. They sat side by side at one of the stone tables in an alcove hidden behind rows and rows of files.

Moneypence pushed a book toward her. "What do you think of this?"

She turned the book upside down, and then right side up. "I do not believe my body will contort into that position."

He laughed. He laughed much more these days. "It will be excessively diverting to try it."

"Perhaps for you!"

"For both of us," he said, and his expression grew serious.

She drew back slightly. "What is it? You did not buy me a gift, did you? I thought we agreed."

"If I have a gift for you, it's not the sort one might buy." He winked, his eyes full of promise. "I shall give it to you later."

"You are very naughty." And she loved him for it.

"I want to ask you for a gift."

"Of course. Anything."

He pushed back from the table, and she realized he was falling to one knee. "Pierce!"

"We've spoken of it, Eliza, but I must do this properly." He took her hand in his and looked into her eyes. Ever since she'd been a small girl, plain and mousy, she'd dreamed of the day a man asked for her hand in marriage. She had not thought any man would ever see her, much less want her for his bride. And now Pierce was asking her, his words as sweet to her ears as honey was on her tongue.

"Eliza, will you do me the honor of becoming my wife? I love you. I cannot live without you. Please say I will never have to. Please give me the gift of your love."

She kissed him tenderly. "Yes. Oh, Pierce. With my whole heart, yes."

He had impeccable timing. On this night of traditional present-giving, when all the world celebrated the gifts given to celebrate God's greatest offering to humanity, how could she not say yes? Pierce was correct. This love between them was the perfect gift, the most wonderful gift of all.

About The Authors

GRACE BURROWES

Grace Burrowes started writing romances as an antidote to empty nest and soon found it an antidote to life in general. She is the sixth out of seven children, and grew up reading voraciously when she wasn't enjoying the company of her horse. Grace is a practicing child welfare attorney in western Maryland, and loves to hear from her readers.

For more excerpts, special give aways and news, sign up for Grace's newsletter.

Visit her on the web at http://www.GraceBurrowes.com.

ABOUT CAROLYN JEWEL

Carolyn Jewel was born on a moonless night. That darkness was seared into her soul and she became an award-winning author of historical and paranormal romance. She has a very dusty car and a Master's degree in English that proves useful at the oddest times. An avid fan of fine chocolate, finer heroines, Bollywood films, and heroism in all forms, she has two cats and two dogs. Also a son. One of the cats is his.

Sign up for Carolyn's newsletter so you never miss a new book!

Visit Carolyn on the web at carolynjewel.com

ABOUT MIRANDA NEVILLE

Miranda Neville grew up in England, loving the books of Georgette Heyer and other Regency romances. Her historical romances include the Burgundy Club series, about Regency book collectors, and The Wild Quartet. She lives in Vermont with her daughter, her cat, and a ridiculously large collection of Christmas tree ornaments. She is thrilled to finally write a Christmas story in collaboration with three amazingly talented ladies.

Sign up for Miranda's newsletter for notification of new books

Visit Miranda on the web at: http://www.mirandaneville.com

ABOUT SHANA GALEN

Shana Galen is the bestselling author of passionate Regency romps, including the RT Reviewers' Choice The Making of a Gentleman. Kirkus says of her books, "The road to happily-ever-after is intense, conflicted, suspenseful and fun," and RT Bookreviews calls her books "lighthearted yet poignant, humorous yet touching." She taught English at the middle and high school level off and on for eleven years. Most of those years were spent working in Houston's inner city. Now she writes full time. She's happily married and has a daughter who is most definitely a romance heroine in the making.

Wonder what Shana has coming next? Join Shana's mailing list [http://-shanagalen.com/contact.php#mailinglist], and be the first to receive information on sales and new releases. Shana never spams or sells readers' information.

Made in the USA
San Bernardino, CA
17 December 2014